THEIR
Marriage
PACT

USA TODAY BESTSELLING AUTHOR
CAITLIN CREWS

MILLS & BOON

MIX
Paper | Supporting responsible forestry
FSC® C001695
www.fsc.org

CONTENTS

Untamed Billionaire's Innocent Bride

Books by Caitlin Crews

Harlequin Modern

Undone by the Billionaire Duke

Conveniently Wed!

Imprisoned by the Greek's Ring
My Bought Virgin Wife

One Night With Consequences

A Baby to Bind His Bride

Bound to the Desert King

Sheikh's Secret Love-Child

Stolen Brides

The Bride's Baby of Shame

The Combe Family Scandals

The Italian's Twin Consequences
Untamed Billionaire's Innocent Bride

Visit the Author Profile page
at millsandboon.com.au for more titles.

USA TODAY bestselling and RITA® Award–nominated author **Caitlin Crews** loves writing romance. She teaches her favorite romance novels in creative-writing classes at places like UCLA Extension's prestigious Writers' Program, where she finally gets to utilize the MA and PhD in English literature she received from the University of York in England. She currently lives in the Pacific Northwest with her very own hero and too many pets. Visit her at caitlincrews.com.

CHAPTER ONE

LAUREN ISADORA CLARKE was a Londoner, born and bred.

She did not care for the bucolic British countryside, all that monotonous green with hedges this way and that, making it impossible to *get* anywhere. She preferred the city, with all its transportation options endlessly available—and if all else failed, the ability to walk briskly from one point to the next. Lauren prized punctuality. And she could do without stiff, uncomfortable footwear with soles outfitted to look like tire tread.

She was not a hiker or a rambler or whatever those alarmingly red-cheeked, jolly hockey-sticks sorts called themselves as they brayed about in fleece and clunky, sensible shoes. She found nothing at all entertaining in huffing up inclines only to slide right back down them, usually covered in the mud that accompanied all the rain that made England's greenest hills that color in the first place. Miles and miles of tramping about for the dubious pleasure of "taking in air" did not appeal to her and never had.

Lauren liked concrete, bricks, the glorious Tube and abundant takeaways on every corner, thank you. The very notion of *the deep, dark woods* made her break out in hives.

Yet, here she was, marching along what the local innkeeper had optimistically called a road—it was little better than a footpath, if that—in the middle of the resolutely thick forests of Hungary.

Hive-free thus far, should she wish to count her blessings.

But Lauren was rather more focused on her grievances today.

First and foremost, her shoes were not now and never had been sensible. Lauren did not believe in the cult of *sensible shoes.* Her life was eminently sensible. She kept her finances in order, paid her bills on time, if not early, and dedicated herself to performing her duties as personal assistant to the very wealthy and powerful president and CEO of Combe Industries at a level of consistent excellence she liked to think made her indispensable.

Her shoes were impractical, fanciful creations that reminded her that she was a woman—which came in handy on the days her boss treated her as rather more of an uppity appliance. One that he liked to have function all on its own, apparently, and without any oversight or aid.

"My mother gave away a child before she married my father," Matteo Combe, her boss, had told her one fine day several weeks back in his usual grave tone.

Lauren, like everyone else who had been in the vicinity of a tabloid in a checkout line over the past forty years, knew all about her boss's parents. And she knew more than most, having spent the bulk of her career working for Matteo. Beautiful, beloved Alexandrina San Giacomo, aristocratic and indulged, had defied reason and her snooty Venetian heritage when she'd married rich but decidedly unpolished Eddie Combe, whose ancestors had carved their way out of the mills of Northern England—often with their fists. Their love story had caused scandals, their turbulent marriage had been the subject of endless speculation and their deaths within weeks of each other had caused even more commotion.

But there had never been the faintest whisper of an illegitimate son.

Lauren had not needed to be told that once this came out—

and it would, because things like this always came out eventually—it wouldn't be whispers they'd have to be worried about. It would be the all-out baying of the tabloid wolves.

"I want you to find him," Matteo had told her, as if he was asking her to fetch him a coffee. "I cannot begin to imagine what his situation is, but I need him media-ready and, if at all possible, compliant."

"Your long-lost brother. Whom you have never met. Who may, for all you know, loathe you and your mother and all other things San Giacomo on principle alone. This is who you think might decide to comply with your wishes."

"I have faith in you," Matteo had replied.

And Lauren had excused that insanity almost in that same instant, because the man had so much on his plate. His parents had died, one after the next. His fluffy-headed younger sister had gone and gotten herself pregnant, a state of affairs that had caused Matteo to take a swing at the father of her baby. A perfectly reasonable reaction, to Lauren's mind—but unfortunately, Matteo had taken said swing at his father's funeral.

The punch he'd landed on Prince Ares of Atilia had been endlessly photographed and videoed by the assorted paparazzi and not a few of the guests, and the company's board of directors had taken it as an opportunity to move against him. Matteo had been forced to subject himself to an anger management specialist who was no ally, and it was entirely possible the board would succeed in removing him should the specialist's report be unflattering.

Of course, Lauren excused him.

"Do you ever *not* excuse him?" her flatmate Mary had asked idly without looking up from her mobile while Lauren had dashed about on her way out the morning she'd left London.

"He's an important and very busy man, Mary."

"As you are always on hand to remind us."

The only reason Lauren hadn't leaped into *that* fray, she told herself now as she stormed along the dirt path toward God knew where, was because good flatmates were hard to find, and Mary's obsession with keeping in touch with her thirty thousand best friends in all corners of the globe on all forms of social media at all times meant she spent most of her time locked in her room obsessing over photo filters and silly voices. Which left the flat to Lauren on the odd occasions she was actually there to enjoy it.

Besides, a small voice inside her that she would have listed as a grievance if she allowed herself to acknowledge it, *she wasn't wrong, was she?*

But Lauren was here to carry out Matteo's wishes, not question her allegiance to him.

Today her pair of typically frothy heels—with studs and spikes and a dash of whimsy because she didn't own a pair of sensible shoes appropriate for mud and woods and never would—were making this unplanned trek through the Hungarian woods even more unpleasant than she'd imagined it would be, and Lauren's imagination was quite vivid. She glared down at her feet, pulled her red wrap tighter around her, thought a few unkind thoughts about her boss she would never utter out loud and kept to the path.

The correct Dominik James had not been easy to find.

There had been almost no information to go on aside from what few details Matteo's mother had provided in her will. Lauren had started with the solicitor who had put Alexandrina's last will and testament together, a canny old man better used to handling the affairs of aristocrats than entertaining the questions of staff. He had peered at her over glasses she wasn't entirely convinced he needed, straight down his nose as he'd assured her that had there been any more pertinent information, he would have included it.

Lauren somehow doubted it.

While Matteo was off tending to his anger management sessions with the future of Combe Industries hanging in the balance, Lauren had launched herself into a research frenzy. The facts were distressingly simple. Alexandrina, heiress to the great San Giacomo fortune, known throughout the world as yet another poor little rich girl, had become pregnant when she was barely fifteen, thanks to a decidedly unsuitable older boy she shouldn't have met in the first place. The family had discovered her pregnancy when she'd been unable to keep hiding it and had transferred her from the convent school she had been attending to one significantly more draconian.

The baby had been born in the summer when Alexandrina was sixteen, spirited away by the church, and Alexandrina had returned to her society life come fall as if nothing had happened. As far as Lauren could tell, she had never mentioned her first son again until she'd made provisions for him in her will.

To my firstborn son, Dominik James, taken from me when I was little more than a child myself, I leave one third of my fortune and worldly goods.

The name itself was a clue. James, it turned out, was an Anglicized version of Giacomo. Lauren tracked all the Dominik Jameses of a certain age she could find, eventually settling on two possibilities. The first she'd dismissed after she found his notably non–San Giacomo DNA profile on one of those ancestry websites. Which left only the other.

The remaining Dominik James had been raised in a series of Catholic orphanages in Italy before running off to Spain. There he'd spent his adolescence, moving from village to village in a manner Lauren could only describe as itinerant. He had joined the Italian Army in his twenties, then disappeared after his discharge. He'd emerged recently to do a stint at university, but had thereafter receded from public view once more.

It had taken some doing, but Lauren had laboriously tracked him down into this gnarled, remote stretch of Hungarian forest—which Matteo had informed her, after all her work, was the single notation made in the paper version of Alexandrina's will found among Matteo's father's possessions.

"That was what my father wrote on his copy of my mother's will," Matteo had said cheerfully. *Cheerfully*, as if it didn't occur to him that knowing the correct Dominik James was in Hungary might have been information Lauren could have used earlier.

She didn't say that, of course. She'd thanked him.

Matteo's father might have made notes on Alexandrina's will, but he'd clearly had no intention of finding the illegitimate child his wife had given away long before he'd met her. Which meant it was left to Lauren to not only make this trek to locate Dominik James in the first place, but also potentially to break the news of his parentage to him. Here.

In these woods that loomed all about her, foreign and imposing, and more properly belonged in a fairy tale.

Good thing Lauren didn't believe in fairy tales.

She adjusted her red wrap again, pulling it tighter around her to ward off the chill.

It was spring, though there was no way of telling down here on the forest floor. The trees were thick and tall and blocked out the daylight. The shadows were intense, creeping this way and that and making her feel...restless.

Or possibly it wasn't shadows cast by tree branches that were making her feel one way or another, she told herself tartly as she willed her ankles not to roll or her sharp heels to snap off. Perhaps it was the fact that she was here in the first place. Or the fact that when she'd told the innkeeper in this remote mountain town that she was looking for Dominik James, he'd laughed.

"Good luck with that," he had told her, which she had found remarkably unhelpful. "Some men do not want to be found, miss, and nothing good comes of ignoring their issues."

Out here in these woods, where there were nothing but trees all around and the uneasy sensation that she was both entirely alone and not alone at all, that unhelpful statement felt significantly more ominous.

On and on she walked. She had left the village behind a solid thirty minutes ago, and that was the last she'd seen of anything resembling civilization. She tried to tell herself it was lucky this path didn't go directly up the side of the brooding mountains, but it was hard to think in terms of luck when there was nothing around but dirt. Thick trees. Birds causing commotions in the branches over her head. And the kind of crackling sounds that assured her that just because she couldn't see any wildlife, it didn't mean it wasn't there.

Watching. Waiting.

Lauren shuddered. Then told herself she was being ridiculous as she rounded another curve in her path, and that was when she saw it.

At first, she wasn't sure if this was the wooded, leafy version of a desert mirage—not that she'd experienced such a thing, as there were no deserts in London. But the closer she got, the more she could see that her eyes were not deceiving her, after all. There was a rustic sort of structure peeking through the trees, tucked away in a clearing.

Lauren drew closer, slowing her steps as the path led her directly toward the edge of the clearing. All she'd wanted this whole walk was a break from the encroaching forest, but now that there was a clearing, she found it made her nervous.

But Lauren didn't believe in nerves, so she ignored the sensation and frowned at the structure before her. It was a cottage. Hewn from wood, logs interlocking and tidy. There was smoke curling up from its chimney, and there was absolutely no reason that a dedicated city dweller like Lauren should feel something clutch inside her at the sight. As if she'd spent her entire life wandering around without knowing it, half-lost in forests of wood and concrete alike, looking for a cozy little home exactly like this one.

That was ridiculous, of course. Lauren rubbed at her chest without entirely meaning to, as if she could do something about the ache there. She didn't believe in fairy tales, but she'd read them. And if any good had ever come from seemingly perfect cottages slapped down in the middle of dangerous forests, well. She couldn't remember that story. Usually, an enchanted cottage led straight to witches and curses and wolves baring their teeth—

But that was when she noticed that the porch in front of the cottage wasn't empty as she'd thought at first glance. That one of the shadows there was a man.

And he was staring straight at her.

Her heart did something acrobatic and astonishing inside her chest, and she had the strangest notion that if she surrendered to it, it could topple her straight to the ground. Right there on that edge where the forest fought to take back the clearing.

But Lauren had no intention of crumpling.

No matter who was lurking about, staring at her.

"Mr. Dominik James?" she asked briskly, making her voice as crisp and clear as possible and projecting it across the clearing as if she wasn't the slightest bit unnerved, because she shouldn't have been.

Though she was standing stock-still, she couldn't help but notice. As if her legs were not necessarily as convinced as she was that she could continue to remain upright. Especially while her heart kept up its racket and ache.

The man moved, stepping out from the shadow of the porch into the sunlight that filled the clearing but somehow did nothing to push back the inky darkness of the forest.

It only made her heart carry on even worse.

He was tall. Much too tall, with the kind of broad shoulders that made her palms itch to…do things she refused to let herself imagine. His hair was dark and thick, worn carelessly and much too long for her tastes, but it seemed to make his strong, bold jaw more prominent somehow. His mouth was flat and unsmiling, yet was lush enough to make her stomach flip around inside her. He was dressed simply, in a long-sleeved shirt that clung to the hard planes of his chest, dark trousers that made her far too aware of his powerful thighs, and boots that looked as if they'd been chosen for their utility rather than their aesthetics.

But it was his eyes that made everything inside Lauren ring with alarm. Or maybe it was awareness.

Because they were gray. Gray like storms, just like Matteo's. *San Giacomo gray*, Lauren thought, just like Alexandrina's had been. Famously.

She didn't need him to identify himself. She had no doubt whatsoever that she was looking at the lost San Giacomo heir. And she couldn't have said why all the tiny hairs on the back of her neck stood up straight as if in foreboding.

She willed herself to forge on.

"My name is Lauren Clarke," she informed him, trying to remember that she was meant to be efficient. Not...whatever she was right now, with all these strange sensations swishing around inside her. "I work for Matteo Combe, president and CEO of Combe Industries. If you are somehow unfamiliar with Mr. Combe, he is, among other things, the eldest son of the late Alexandrina San Giacomo Combe. I have reason to believe that Alexandrina was also your mother."

She had practiced that. She had turned the words over and over in her head, then gone so far as to practice them in the mirror this morning in her little room at the inn. Because there was no point hemming and hawing and beating around the bush. Best to rip the plaster off and dive straight in, so they could get to the point as quickly as possible.

She'd expected any number of responses to her little speech. Maybe he would deny the claim. Maybe he would launch into bluster, or order her away. She'd worked out contingency plans for all possible scenarios—

But the man in front of her didn't say a word.

He roamed toward her, forcing her to notice the way he moved. It was more liquid than it ought to have been. A kind of lethal grace, given how big he was, and she found herself holding her breath.

The closer he came, the more she could see the expression on his face, in his eyes, that struck her as a kind of sardonic amusement.

She hadn't made any contingency plan for that.

"When Mrs. Combe passed recently, she made provisions for you in her will," Lauren forced herself to continue. "My employer intends to honor his mother's wishes, Mr. James. He has sent me here to start that process."

The man still didn't speak. He slowed when he was face-to-face with Lauren, but all he did was study her. His gaze moved all over her in a way that struck her as almost unbearably intimate, and she could feel the flush that overtook her in reaction.

As if he had his hands all over her body. As if he was testing the smoothness of the hair she'd swept back into a low ponytail. Or the thickness of the bright red wool wrap she wore to ward off the chill of flights and Hungarian forests alike. Down her legs to her pretty, impractical shoes, then back up again.

"Mr. Combe is a man of wealth and consequence." Lauren found it was difficult to maintain her preferred crisp, authoritative tone when this man was so…close. And when he was looking at her as if she were a meal, not a messenger. "I mention this not to suggest that he doesn't wish to honor his commitments to you, because he does. But his stature requires that we proceed with a certain sensitivity. You understand."

She was aware of too many things, all at once. The man—Dominik, she snapped at herself, because it had to be him—had recently showered. She could see the suggestion of dampness in his hair as it went this way and that, indicating it had a mind of its own. Worse still, she could smell him. The combination of soap and warm, clean, decidedly healthy male.

It made her feel the slightest bit dizzy, and she was sure that was why her heart was careening about inside her chest like a manic drum.

All around them, the forest waited. Not precisely silent, but there was no comforting noise of city life—conversations and traffic and the inevitable sounds of so many humans going about their lives, pretending they were alone—to distract her from this man's curious, penetrating, unequivocally gray glare.

If she believed in nerves, she'd have said hers were going haywire.

"I beg your pardon," Lauren said when it was that or leap away from him and run for it, so unsettled and unsteady did she feel. "Do you speak English? I didn't think to ask."

His stern mouth curled the faintest bit in one corner. As Lauren watched, stricken and frozen for reasons she couldn't begin to explain to herself, he reached across the scant few inches between them.

She thought he was going to put his hand on her—touch her face, or smooth it over her hair, or run one of those bluntly elegant fingers along the length of her neck the way she'd seen in a fanciful romantic movie she refused to admit she'd watched— but he didn't. And she felt the sharpest sense of disappointment in that same instant he found one edge of her wrap, and held it between his fingers.

As if he was testing the wool.

"What are you doing?" Lauren asked, and any hope she'd had of maintaining her businesslike demeanor fled. Her knees were traitorously weak. And her voice didn't sound like her at all. It was much too breathy. Embarrassingly insubstantial.

He was closer than he ought to have been, because she was sure there was no possible way *she* had moved. And there was something about the way he angled his head that made everything inside her shift.

Then go dangerously still.

"A beautiful blonde girl walks into the woods, dressed in little more than a bright, red cloak." His voice was an insinuation. A spell. It made her think of fairy tales again, giving no quarter to her disbelief. It was too smoky, too deep and much too rich, and faintly accented in ways that kicked up terrible wildfires in her blood. And everywhere else. "What did you think would happen?"

Then he dropped his shockingly masculine head to hers, and kissed her.

CHAPTER TWO

HE WAS KISSING HER.

Kissing her, for the love of all that was holy.

Lauren understood it on an intellectual level, but it didn't make sense.

Mostly because what he did with his mouth bore no resemblance to any kiss she had ever heard of or let herself imagine.

He licked his way along her lips, a temptation and a seduction in one, encouraging her to open. To him.

Which of course she wasn't going to do.

Until she did, with a small sound in the back of her throat that made her shudder everywhere else.

And then that wicked temptation of a tongue was inside her mouth—*inside* her—and everything went a little mad.

It was the angle, maybe. His taste, rich and wild. It was the impossible, lazy mastery of the way he kissed her, deepening it, changing it.

When he pulled away, his mouth was still curved.

And Lauren was the one who was shaking.

She assured herself it was temper. Outrage. "You can't just… go about *kissing* people!"

That curve in his mouth deepened. "I will keep that in mind, should any more storybook creatures emerge from my woods."

Lauren was flustered. Her cheeks were too hot and that same heat seemed to slide and melt its way all over her body, making her nipples pinch while between her legs, a kind of slippery need bloomed.

And shamed her. Deeply.

"I am not a storybook creature." The moment she said it, she regretted it. Why was she participating in whatever bizarre delusion this was? But she couldn't seem to stop herself. "Fairy tales aren't real, and even if they were, I would want nothing to do with them."

"That is a terrible shame. What are fairy tales if not a shorthand for all of mankind's temptations? Fantasies. Dark imaginings."

There was no reason that her throat should feel so tight. She didn't need to swallow like that, and she certainly didn't need to be so *aware* of it.

"I'm sure that some people's jobs—or lack thereof—allow them to spend time considering the merit of children's stories," she said in a tone she was well aware was a touch too prissy. But that was the least of her concerns just then, with the brand of his mouth on hers. "But I'm afraid my job is rather more adult."

"Because nothing is more grown-up than doing the bidding of another, of course."

Lauren felt off-kilter, when she never did. Her lips felt swollen, but she refused to lift her fingers to test them. She was afraid it would give him far too much advantage. It would show him her vulnerability, and that was unconscionable.

The fact she had any vulnerability to show in the first place was an outrage.

"Not everyone can live by their wits in a forest hut," she said. Perhaps a bit acerbically.

But if she expected him to glower at that, she was disappointed. Because all he did was stare back at her, that curve in the corner of his mouth, and his eyes gleaming a shade of silver that she felt in all those melting places inside her.

"Your innkeeper told me you were coming." He shifted back only slightly, and she was hyperaware of him in ways that humiliated her further. There was something about the way his body moved. There was something about him. He made her want to lean in closer. He made her want to reach out her hands and—

But of course she didn't do that. She folded her arms across her chest, to hold him off and hold herself together at the same time, and trained her fiercest glare upon him as if that could make all the uncomfortable feelings go away.

"You could have saved yourself the trouble and the walk," he was saying. "I don't want your rich boss and yes, I know who he is. You can rest easy. I'm not interested in him. Or his mother. Or whatever 'provisions' appeared in the wills of overly wealthy people I would likely hate if I'd known them personally."

That felt like a betrayal when it shouldn't have felt like anything. It wasn't personal. She had nothing to do with the Combe and San Giacomo families. She had never been anything but staff, for which she often felt grateful, as there was nothing like exposure to the very wealthy and known to make a person grateful for the things she had—all of which came without the scrutiny and weight of all those legacies.

But the fact this man didn't want his own birthright...rankled. Lauren's lips tingled. They felt burned, almost, and she could remember the way his mouth had moved on hers so vividly that she could taste him all over again. Bold and unapologetic. Ruthlessly male.

And somehow that all wrapped around itself, became a knot and pulled tight inside her.

"My rich boss is your brother," she pointed out, her voice sharper than it should have been. "This isn't about money. It's about family."

"A very rich family," Dominik agreed. And his gaze was more steel than silver then. "Who didn't want me in the first place. I will pass, I think, on a tender reunion brought about by the caprice of a dead woman."

Her heart lurched when he reached out and took her chin in his hand. She should have slapped him away. She meant to, surely.

But everything was syrupy, thick and slow. And all she could feel was the way he gripped her. The way he held her chin with a kind of certainty that made everything inside her quiver in direct contrast to that firm hold. She'd gone soft straight through. Melting hot. Impossibly…changed.

"I appreciate the taste," he rumbled at her, sardonic and lethal and more than she could bear—but she still didn't pull away from him. "I had no idea such a sharp blonde could taste so sweet."

And he had already turned and started back toward his cabin by the time those words fully penetrated all that odd, internal shaking.

Lauren thought she would hate herself forever for the moisture she could feel in her own eyes, when she hadn't permitted herself furious tears in as long as she could remember.

"Let me make certain I'm getting this straight," she threw at his back, and she certainly *did not* notice how muscled he was, everywhere, or how easy it was to imagine her own hands running down the length of his spine, purely to marvel in the way he was put together. *Certainly not.* "The innkeeper called ahead, which means you knew I was coming. Did he tell you what I was wearing, too? So you could prepare this Red Riding Hood story to tell yourself?"

"If the cloak fits," he said over his shoulder.

"That would make you the Big Bad Wolf, would it not?"

She found herself following him, which couldn't possibly be wise. Marching across that clearing as if he hadn't made her feel so adrift. So shaky.

As if he hadn't kissed her within an inch of her life, but she wasn't thinking about that.

Because she couldn't think about that, or she would think of nothing else.

"There are all kinds of wolves in the forests of Europe." And his voice seemed darker then. Especially when he turned, training that gray gaze of his on her all over again. It had the same effect as before. Looking at him was like staring into a storm. "Big and bad is as good a description as any."

She noticed he didn't answer the question.

"Why?"

Lauren stopped a foot or so in front of him. She found her hands on her hips, the wrap falling open. And she hated the part of her that thrilled at the way his gaze tracked over the delicate gold chain at her throat. The silk blouse beneath.

Her breasts that felt heavy and achy, and the nipples that were surely responding to the sudden exposure to colder air. Not him.

She had spent years wearing gloriously girly shoes to remind herself she was a woman, desperately hoping that each day was the day that Matteo would see her as one for a change. He never had. He never would.

And this man made her feel outrageously feminine without even trying.

She told herself what she felt about that was sheer, undiluted outrage, but it was a little too giddy, skidding around and around inside her, for her to believe it.

"Why did I kiss you?" She saw the flash of his teeth, like a smile he thought better of at the last moment, and that didn't make anything happening inside her better. "Because I wanted to, little red. What other reason could there be?"

"Perhaps you kissed me because you're a pig," she replied coolly. "A common affliction in men who feel out of control, I think you'll find."

A kind of dark delight moved over his face.

"I believe you have your fairy tales confused. And in any case, where there are pigs, there is usually also huffing and puffing and, if I am not mistaken, blowing." He tilted that head of his to one side, reminding her in an instant how untamed he was. How outside her experience. "Are you propositioning me?"

She felt a kind of red bonfire ignite inside her, all over her, but she didn't give in to it. She didn't distract herself with images of exactly what he might mean by *blowing*. And how best she could accommodate him like the fairy tale of his choice, right here in this clearing, sinking down on her knees and—

"Very droll," she said instead, before she shamed herself even further. "I'm not at all surprised that a man who lives in a shack in the woods has ample time to sit around, perverting fairy tales to his own ends. But I'm not here for you, Mr. James."

"Call me Dominik." He smiled at her then, but she didn't make the mistake of believing him the least bit affable. Not when that smile made her think of a knife, sharp and deadly. "I would say that Mr. James was my father, but I've never met the man."

"I appreciate this power play of yours," Lauren said, trying a new tactic before she could get off track again, thinking of *knives* and *blowing* and *that kiss*. "I feel very much put in my place, thank you. I would love nothing more than to turn tail and run back to my employer, with tales of the uncivilized hermit in the woods that he'd be better off never recognizing as his long-lost brother. But I'm afraid I can't do that."

"Why not?"

"Because it doesn't matter why you're here in the woods. Whether you're a hermit, a barbarian, an uncivilized lout unfit for human company." She waved one hand, airily, as if she couldn't possibly choose among those things. "If I could track you down, that means others will, as well, and they won't be nearly as pleasant as I am. They will be reporters. Paparazzi. And once they start coming, they will always come. They will surround this cabin and make your life a living hell. That's what they do." She smiled. Sunnily. "It's only a matter of time."

"I spent my entire childhood waiting for people to come," he said softly, after a moment that stretched out between them and made her...edgy. "They never did. You will forgive me if I somehow find it difficult to believe that now, suddenly, I will become of interest to anyone."

"When you were a child you were an illegitimate mistake," Lauren said, making her voice cold to hide that odd yearning inside her that made her wish she could go back in time and save the little boy he'd been from his fate. "That's what Alexandrina San Giacomo's father wrote about you. That's not my description." She hurried to say that last part, something in the still way he watched her making her stomach clench. "Now you are the San Giacomo heir you always should have been. You are a very wealthy man, Mr. James. More than that, you are part of a long and illustrious family line, stretching back generations."

"You could not be more mistaken," he said in the same soft way that Lauren didn't dare mistake for any kind of weakness. Not when she could see that expression on his face, ruthless and lethal in turn. "I am an orphan. An ex-soldier. And a man who prefers his own company. If I were you, I would hurry back to the man who keeps you on his leash and tell him so." There was a dangerous gleam in his eyes then. "Now, like a good pet. Before I forget how you taste and indulge my temper instead."

Lauren wanted nothing more. If being a pet on Matteo's leash could keep her safe from this man, she wanted it. But that wasn't the task that had been set before her. "I'm afraid I can't do that."

"There is no alternative, little red. I have given you my answer."

Lauren could see he meant that. He had every intention of walking back into this ridiculous cottage in the middle of nowhere, washing his hands of his birthright and pretending no one had found him. She felt a surge of a different kind of emotion at that, and it wasn't one that spoke well of her.

Because *she* wouldn't turn up her nose at the San Giacomo fortune and everything that went along with it. She wouldn't scoff at the notion that maybe she'd been a long-lost heiress all this time. Far better that than the boring reality, which was that both her mother and father had remarried and had sparkly new families they'd always seemed to like a whole lot more than her, the emblem of the bad decisions they'd made together.

They'd tossed her back and forth between them with bad grace and precious little affection, until she'd finally come of age and announced it could stop. The sad truth was that Lauren had expected one of them to argue. Or at least pretend to argue. But neither one of them had bothered.

And she doubted she would mind that *quite* so much if she had aristocratic blood and a sudden fortune to ease the blow.

"Most people would be overjoyed to this news," she managed to say without tripping over her own emotions. "It's a bit like winning the lottery, isn't it? You go along living your life only to discover that all of a sudden, you're a completely different person than the one you thought you were."

"I am exactly who I think I am." And there was something infinitely dangerous beneath his light tone. She could see it in his gaze. "I worked hard to become him. I have no intention of casting him aside because of some dead woman's guilt."

"But I don't—"

"I know who the San Giacomos are," Dominik said shortly. "How could I not? I grew up in Italy in their shadow and I want no part of it. Or them. You can tell your boss that."

"He will only send me back here. Eventually, if you keep refusing me, he will come himself. Is that what you want? The opportunity to tell him to his face how little you want the gift he is giving you?"

Dominik studied her. "Is it a gift? Or is it what I was owed from my birth, yet prevented from claiming?"

"Either way, it's nothing if you lock yourself up in your wood cabin and pretend it isn't happening."

He laughed at that. He didn't fling back his head and let out a belly laugh. He only smiled. A quick sort of smile on an exhale, which only seemed to whet Lauren's appetite for real laughter.

What on earth was happening to her?

"What I don't understand is your zeal," he said, his voice like a dark lick down the length of her spine. And it did her no favors to imagine him doing exactly that, that tongue of his against her

flesh, following the flare of her hips with his hands while he…
She had to shake herself slightly, hopefully imperceptibly, and
frown to focus on him. "I know you have been searching for
me. It has taken you weeks, but you have been dogged in your
pursuit. If it occurred to you at any point that I did not wish to
be found, you did not let that give you the slightest bit of pause.
And now you have come here. Uninvited."

"If you knew I was searching for you—" and she would have
to think about what that meant, because that suggested a level
of sophistication the wood cabin far out in these trees did not
"—why didn't you reach out yourself?"

"Nobody sets himself apart from the world in a tiny cottage
in a forest in Hungary if they wish to have visitors. Much less
unannounced visitors." His smile was that knife again, a sharp,
dangerous blade. "But here you are."

"I'm very good at my job." Lauren lifted her chin. "Remarkably good, in fact. When I'm given a task to complete, I complete it."

"He says jump and you aim for the moon," Dominik said
softly. And she could hear the insult in it. It sent another flush
of something like shame, splashing all over her, and she didn't
understand it. She didn't understand any of this.

"I'm a personal assistant, Mr. James. That means I assist my
employer in whatever it is he needs. It is the nature of the position. Not a character flaw."

"Let me tell you what I know of your employer," Dominik
said, and his voice went lazy as if he was playing. But she
couldn't quite believe he was. Or that he ever did, come to that.
"He is a disgrace, is he not? A man so enamored of this family
you have come all this way to make me a part of that he punched
his sister's lover in the face at their father's funeral. What a paragon! I cannot imagine why I have no interest involving myself
with such people."

Lauren really was good at her job. She had to remind herself
of that at the moment, but it didn't make it any less true. She

pulled in a breath, then let it out slowly, trying to understand what was actually happening here.

That this man had a grudge against the people who had given him to an orphanage was clear. Understandable, even. She supposed it was possible that he wasn't turning his nose up at what Matteo was offering so much as the very idea that an offer was being made at all, all these years too late to matter. She could understand that, too, having spent far more hours than she cared to admit imagining scenarios in which her parents begged for her time—so she could refuse them and sweep off somewhere.

And if she had been a man sent to find him, she supposed Dominik would have found a different way to get under her skin the same way he would any emissary sent from those who had abandoned him. All his talk of kissing and fairy tales was just more misdirection. Game-playing. Like all the scenarios she'd played out in her head about her parents.

She had to assume that his refusal to involve himself with the San Giacomos was motivated by hurt feelings. But if she knew one thing about men—no matter how powerful, wealthy or seemingly impervious—it was that all of them responded to hurt feelings as if the feelings themselves were an attack. And anyone in the vicinity was a collaborator.

"I appreciate your position, Dominik," she said, trying to sound conciliatory. Sweet, even, since he was the first person alive who'd ever called her that. "I really do. But I still want to restore you to your family. What do I have to do to make that happen?"

"First, you go wandering around the forbidding woods in a red cloak." Dominik shook his head, making a faint *tsk*-ing sound. "Then you let the Big Bad Wolf find out how you taste. Now an open-ended offer? My, my. What big eyes you have, little red."

There was no reason she should shiver at that, as if he was making predictions instead of taking part in this same extended game that she had already given too much of her time and attention.

But the woods were all around them. The breeze whispered through the trees, and the village with all its people was far, far away from here.

And he'd already kissed her.

What, exactly, are you offering him? she asked herself.

But she had no answer.

Looking at Dominik James made Lauren feel as if she didn't know herself at all. It made her feel like her body belonged to someone else, shivery and nervous. It made her tongue feel as if it no longer worked the way it should. She didn't like it at all. She didn't like *him*, she told herself.

But she didn't turn on her heel and leave, either.

"There must be something that could convince you to come back to London and take your rightful place as a member of the San Giacomo family," she said, trying to sound reasonable. Calmly rational. "It's clearly not money, or you would have jumped at the chance to access your own fortune."

He shrugged. "You cannot tempt me with that kind of power."

"Because, of course, you prefer to play power games like this. Where you pretend you have no interest in power, all the while using what power you do have to do the exact opposite of anything asked of you."

It was possible she shouldn't have said that, she reflected in some panic as his gaze narrowed on her in a way that made her...shake, deep inside.

But if she expected him to shout or issue threats, he didn't. He only studied her in that way for another moment, then grinned. Slowly.

A sharp blade of a grin that made her stop breathing, even as it boded ill.

For her. For the heart careening around and battering her ribs.

For all the things she wanted to pretend she didn't feel, like a thick, consuming heat inside her.

"By all means, little red," he said, his voice low. "Come inside. Sit by my fire. Convince me, if you can."

CHAPTER THREE

DOMINIK JAMES HAD spent his entire life looking for his place in the world.

They had told him his parents were dead. That he was an orphan in truth, and he had believed that. At first. It certainly explained his circumstances in life, and as a child, he'd liked explanations that made sense of the orphanage he called home.

But when he was ten, the meanest of the nuns had dropped a different truth on him when she'd caught him in some or other mischief.

Your mother didn't want you, she had told him. *And who could blame her with you such a dirty, nasty sneak of a boy. Who could want you?*

Who indeed? Dominik had spent the next ten years proving to everyone's satisfaction that his mother, whoever she was, had been perfectly justified in ridding herself of him. He had lived down to any and all expectations. He'd run away from the orphanage and found himself in Spain, roaming where he pleased and stealing what he needed to live. He'd considered that happiness compared to the nuns' version of corporal punishment mixed in with vicious piety.

He had eventually gone back to Italy and joined the army, more to punish himself than as any display of latent patriotism. He'd hoped that he would be sent off to some terrible war where he could die in service to Italy rather than from his own nihilistic urges. He certainly hadn't expected to find discipline instead. Respect. A place in the world, and the tools to make himself the kind of man who deserved that place.

He had given Italy his twenties. After he left the service, he'd spent years doing what the army had taught him on a private civilian level until he'd gotten restless. He'd then sold the security company he'd built for a tidy fortune.

Left to his own devices as a grown man with means, he had bettered himself significantly. He had gotten a degree to expand his thinking. His mind. And, not inconsiderably, to make sure he could manage his newfound fortune the way he wanted to do.

He didn't need his long-lost family's money. He had his own. The computer security company he had built up almost by accident had made him a very wealthy man. Selling it had made him a billionaire. And he'd enjoyed building on that foundation ever since, expanding his financial reach as he pleased.

He just happened to enjoy pretending he was a hermit in the Hungarian woods, because he could. And because, in truth, he liked to keep a wall or a forest between him and whatever else was out there. He liked to stay arm's length, at the very least, from the world that had always treated him with such indifference. The world that had made him nothing but bright with rage and sharp with fury, even when he was making it his.

Dominik preferred cool shadows and quiet trees these days. The comfort of his own company. Nothing brighter than the sun as it filtered down through the trees, and no fury at all.

Sharp-edged blondes with eyes like caramel who tasted like magic made him…greedy and hot. It made him feel like a long-lost version of himself that he had never meant to see resurrected.

He should have sent her away at once.

Instead, he'd invited her in.

She walked in front of him, those absurd and absurdly loud

shoes of hers making it clear that she was not the sort of woman who ever expected to sneak up on a person, especially when they hit the wood of his porch. And he regretted letting her precede him almost at once, because while the cloak she wore—so bright and red it was almost as if she was having a joke at his expense—hid most of that lush and lean body from his view, it couldn't conceal the way her hips swung back and forth like a metronome.

Dominik had never been so interested in keeping the beat before in his life. He couldn't look away. Then again, he didn't try that hard.

When she got to his front door, a heavy wood that he'd fashioned himself with iron accents because perhaps he really had always thought of himself as the Big Bad Wolf, he reached past her. He pushed the door open with the flat of one hand, inviting her in.

But that was a mistake, too.

Because he had already tasted her, and leaning in close made him...needy. He wanted his mouth right there on the nape of her neck. He wanted his hands on the full breasts he'd glimpsed beneath that sheer blouse she wore. He wanted to bury his face between her legs, then lose himself completely in all her sweet heat.

Instead, all he did was hold the door for her. Meekly, as if he was some other man. Someone tamed. Civilized.

A hermit in a hut, just as he pretended to be.

He watched her walk inside, noting how stiff and straight she held herself as if she was terrified that something might leap out at her. But this cabin had been made to Dominik's precise specifications. It existed to be cozy. Homey.

It was the retreat he had never had as a boy, and he had absolutely no idea why he had allowed this particular woman to come inside. When no one else ever had.

He wasn't sure he wanted to think about that too closely.

"This is a bit of a shock," she said into the silence that

stretched taut between them, her gaze moving from the thick rugs on the floor to the deep leather chairs before the fire. "I expected something more like a hovel, if I'm honest."

"A hovel."

"I mean no disrespect," she said, which he thought was a lie. She did that thing with her hand again, waving at him in a manner he could only call dismissive. It was...new, at least. "No one really expects a long-haired hermit to live in any kind of splendor, do they?"

"I am already regretting my hospitality," Dominik murmured.

He looked around at the cabin, trying to see it through the eyes of someone like Lauren, all urban chic and London snooti-ness. He knew the type, of course, though he'd gone to some lengths to distance himself from such people. The shoes were a dead giveaway. Expensive and pointless, because they were a statement. She wanted everyone who saw them to wonder how she walked in them, or wonder how much they cost, or drift away in a sea of their own jealousy.

Dominik merely wondered what it said about her that her primary form of expression was her shoes.

He also wondered what she was gleaning about him from this cabin that was his only real home. He didn't know what she saw, only what he'd intended. The soaring high ceilings, because he had long since grown tired of stooping and making himself fit into spaces not meant for him. The warm rugs, because he was tired of being cold and uncomfortable. The sense of airi-ness that made the cottage feel as if it was twice its actual size, because he had done his time in huts and hovels and he wasn't going back. The main room boasted a stone fireplace on one end and his efficient kitchen on the other, and he'd fashioned a bedchamber that matched it in size, outfitted with a bed that could fit two of him—because he never forgot those tiny cots he'd had to pretend to be grateful for in the orphanage.

"It's actually quite lovely," she said after a moment, a note of reluctant surprise in her voice. "Very...comfortable, yet male."

Dominik jerked his chin toward one of the heavy chairs that sat before his fire. Why there were two, he would never know, since he never had guests. But when he'd imagined the perfect cabin and the fireplace that would dominate it, he had always envisioned two cozy leather chairs, just like these. So here they were.

And he had the strangest sensation, as Lauren went and settled herself into one of them, that he had anticipated this moment. It was almost as if the chair had been waiting for her all this time.

He shook that off, not sure where such a fanciful notion had come from. But very sure that he didn't like it. At all.

He dropped into the chair opposite hers, and lounged there, doing absolutely nothing at all to accommodate her when he let his long legs take over the space between them. He watched her swallow, as if her throat was dry, and he could have offered her a drink.

But he didn't.

"I thought you intended to convince me to do your bidding," he said after a moment, when the air between them seemed to get thick. Fraught. Filled with premonition and meaning, when he wanted neither. "Perhaps things are different where you're from, but I would not begin an attempt at persuasion by insulting the very person I most wanted to come around to my way of thinking. Your mileage may vary, of course."

She blinked at him, and it was almost as if she'd forgotten why they were there. She shrugged out of that wrap at last, then folded her hands in her lap, and Dominik let his gaze fall all over her. Greedily. As if he'd never seen a woman before in all his days.

She was sweet and stacked, curvy in all the right places. Her hair gleamed like gold in the firelight, the sleek ponytail at her nape pulled forward over one shoulder. There was a hint of real gold at her throat, precisely where he wanted to use his teeth—gently, so gently, until she shuddered. Her breasts begged for a man's hands and his face between them, and it would take so little. He could shift forward, onto his knees, and take her in hand that easily.

He entertained a few delicious images of himself doing just that.

And she didn't exactly help matters when she pulled that plump lower lip of hers between her teeth, the way he'd like to do.

But Dominik merely sank deeper into his chair, propped his head up with his fist, and ignored the demands of the hardest, greediest part of him as he gazed at her.

"I would be delighted to persuade you," she said, and did he imagine a certain huskiness in her voice? He didn't think he did. "I expected to walk in here and find you living on a pallet on the floor. But you clearly like your creature comforts. That tells me that while you might like your solitude, you aren't exactly hiding from the world. Or not completely. So what would it take to convince you to step back into it?"

"You have yet to explain to me why that is something I should want, much less consider doing."

"You could buy a hundred cabins and litter them about all the forests of Europe, for a start."

He lifted one shoulder, then let it fall. "I already have a cabin."

And properties across the globe, but he didn't mention that.

"You could outfit this cabin in style," she suggested brightly. "Make it modern and accessible. Imagine the opportunities!"

"I never claimed to live off the grid, did I? I believe you are the one who seems to think this cabin belongs in the Stone Age. I assure you, I have as much access to the modern world as I require."

Not to mention his other little shack that wasn't a shack at all, set farther up the mountainside and outfitted with the very latest in satellite technology. But that was yet another thing that could remain his little secret.

"You could buy yourself anything you wanted."

"All you have to offer me is money," he said after a moment. "I already told you, I have my own. But the fact that you continue to focus on it tells me a great deal about you, I think. Does this brother of mine not pay you well?"

She stiffened at that, and a crease appeared between her brows. "Mr. Combe has always been remarkably generous to me."

He found the color on her cheeks…interesting. "I cannot tell if that means he does or does not pay you what you deserve. What's the going rate for the kind of loyalty that would lead a woman clearly uncomfortable with the outdoors to march off into the forest primeval, deep into the very lair of a dangerous stranger?"

Her chin tipped up at that, which he should not have found as fascinating as he did. "I fail to see how my salary is your business."

"You have made anything and everything my business by delivering yourself to my door." And if he was overly intrigued by her, to the point his fingers itched with the need to touch her all over that curvy body until she sounded significantly less cool, that was his burden to carry. "Why don't you tell me why you're really here?"

The color on her cheeks darkened. The crease between her brows deepened. And it shouldn't have been possible to sit any straighter in that chair, but she managed it.

"I have already told you why I'm here, Mr. James."

"I'm sure they told you in the village that I come in at least once a week for supplies. You could have waited for me there, surrounded by creature comforts and room service. There was no need at all to walk through the woods to find me, particularly not in those shoes."

She looked almost smug then. As if he'd failed some kind of test.

"You don't need to concern yourself with my shoes," she said, and crossed her legs, which had the immediate effect of drawing his attention to the shoes in question. Just as she'd intended, he assumed. "I find them remarkably comfortable, actually."

"That you find them comfortable, or want me to think you do, doesn't mean they are. And it certainly doesn't make them practical for a brisk hike on a dirt path."

That gaze of hers was the color of a sweet, sticky dessert, and he wanted to indulge. Oh, how he wanted to indulge. Especially when her eyes flashed at him, once again letting him know that she felt superior to him.

Little did she know, he found that entertaining.

Even as it made him harder.

"In my experience, anyone who is concerned with the practicality of my footwear is casting about in desperation for some way to discount what I have to say," she told him. "Focus on my shoes and we can make sweeping generalizations about what sort of person I am, correct? Here's a little secret. I like pretty shoes. They don't say anything about me except that."

Dominik grinned, taking his time with it and enjoying it when she swallowed. Hard.

"Let me hasten to assure you that I'm in no way desperate. And I would love nothing more than to discount what you say, but you have said very little." He held her gaze. "Make your case, if you can. Explain to me why I should leave the comfort of my home to embrace this family who have ignored me for a lifetime already. I'm assuming it would be convenient for them in some way. But you'll understand that's not a compelling argument for me."

"I already told you. The paparazzi—"

He shook his head. "I think we both know that it is not I who would dislike it if your reporters found me here. I am perfectly content to deal with trespassers in my own way." He could see by the way her lips pressed together that she was imagining exactly how he might handle trespassers, and grinned wider. "But this rich boss of yours would not care for the exposure, I imagine. Is that not why you have made your way here, after searching for me so diligently? To convince me that his sudden, surpassing concern for my privacy is a genuine display of heretofore unknown brotherly love rather than his own self-interest?"

"Mr. Combe was unaware that he had a brother until recently," she replied, but her voice had gone cool. Careful, perhaps. "If anything should convince you about his intentions, it should be the fact that he reached out to find you as soon as he knew you existed."

"I must remember to applaud."

She didn't sigh or roll her eyes at that, though the tightness of her smile suggested both nonetheless. "Mr. Combe—"

"Little red. Please. What did you imagine I meant when I asked you to convince me? I've already had my mouth on you. Do you really think I invited you in here for a lecture?"

He didn't know what he expected. Outrage, perhaps. Righteous indignation, then a huffy flounce out of the cabin and out of his life. That was what he wanted, he assured himself.

Because her being here was an intrusion. He'd invited her in to make certain she'd never come back.

Of course you did, a sardonic voice inside him chimed in.

But Lauren wasn't flouncing away in high dudgeon. Instead, she stared back at him with a dumbfounded expression on her face. Not as if she was offended by his suggestion. But more as if…such a thing had never occurred to her.

"I beg your pardon. Is this some kind of cultural divide I'm unfamiliar with? Or do you simply inject sex into conversations whenever you get bored?"

"Whenever possible."

She laughed, and what surprised him was that it sounded real. Not part of this game at all.

"You're wasting your time with me." Her smile was bland. But there was a challenge in her gaze, he thought. "I regret to tell you, as I have told every man before you who imagined they could get to my boss through me, that I have no sexual impulses."

If she had pulled a grenade out of her pocket and lobbed it onto the floor between them, Dominik could not have been more surprised.

He could not possibly have heard her correctly. "What did you just say?"

There before him, his very own Little Red Riding Hood… relaxed back against the leather of her armchair. Something he also would have thought impossible moments before. And when she smiled, she looked like nothing so much as an over-satisfied cat.

"I'm not a sexual person," she told him, and Dominik was sure he wasn't mistaking the relish in her voice. It was at odds with the sheen of something a whole lot like vulnerability in her gaze, reminding him of how she'd melted into his kiss. "It's a spectrum, isn't it? Some people's whole lives are completely taken over by the endless drive for sex, but not me. I've never understood all the fuss, to be honest."

He was half convinced he'd gone slack-jawed in astonishment, but he couldn't seem to snap out of it long enough to check. Not when she was sitting there talking such absolute nonsense with an expression that suggested to him that she, at least, believed every word she was saying.

Or, if he looked closer, *wanted* to believe it, anyway.

"You are aware that a kiss is a sexual act, are you not?"

"I've kissed before," Lauren said, and even shook her head at him, wrinkling up her nose as if he was…silly. Him. *Silly.* "I experimented with kissing when I was at university. As you do. That's how I know that it isn't for me."

"You experimented," he repeated as if that would make sense of what she was saying with such astonishing confidence—though, again, when he looked closer he was almost sure it was an act. Did he merely want it to be? "With kissing."

"As I said, there are all sorts. Not everyone is consumed with the urge to flail about naked. Not that there's anything wrong with that, but some of us have other things to think about." Her expression turned virtuous and Dominik was sure, then, that while she might believe what she was saying, he'd...rocked her foundations. She was overselling it. "More important things."

"And what, dare I ask, is it that consumes your thoughts if not...flailing?"

"You've made quite a few references to my being at Mr. Combe's bidding, but I take my job very seriously. It requires dedication. Focus and energy. I couldn't possibly siphon all of that off into all that trawling about from pub to pub every night, all to..."

"Flail. Naked."

"Exactly."

Dominik knew two things then as surely as he knew himself, his own capabilities and the fact she was lying about her own sexuality. One, if he wasn't misunderstanding what she was telling him, his sharp, majestically shoed and caramel-eyed blonde was a virgin. And two, that possibility made him hard.

Very nearly desperately so.

Because he already knew how she tasted. He'd heard the noises she'd made when he kissed her, and no matter what she told herself and was trying to tell him now, he did not believe that she had been unaffected.

He knew otherwise, in fact, as surely as he knew his own name.

"I can see how you're looking at me," Lauren said. She was still entirely too relaxed, to his way of thinking, leaning back in the leather chair as if she owned it. Clearly certain that she was in total control of this conversation. And him. "I don't understand why men take this as such a challenge."

Dominik's mouth curved. "Do you not?"

It was her turn to shrug. "I'm perfectly comfortable with who I am."

"Obviously." He settled back against his chair until he mirrored her. And for a long moment, every second of which he could feel in the place where he was hardest, he simply...studied her. Until her smile faded and she looked a whole lot less *certain*. "For reference, little red, people who are perfectly comfortable with themselves rarely mentioned their sexuality at all, much less bludgeon others over the head with it."

"Oh, I see." Her smile was bland again, and this time, distinctly pitying besides, though he could see the uncertainty she tried to hide. "You're upset because you think I'm saying this because I didn't like your kiss. Don't worry, Mr. James. I don't like any kissing. Not just yours."

"Of the two of us sitting here, Lauren," he said, enjoying the taste of her name in his mouth and the faint tremor in her sweet lower lip that told him the truths she couldn't, "I am the one who is actually comfortable with himself. Not to mention fully aware. I know exactly how much you liked my kiss without you needing to tell me all these stories."

"I'm glad to hear it." Her chin tipped up again, her eyes flashing as if that could hide the glint of doubt there. "I've seen this a thousand times before, you know. First, you will proposition me. Then you'll throw a temper tantrum when I decline your kind offer to see what I'm missing, with you as selfless guide. It's always the same old story."

"Is it? Why don't you tell it to me?"

She waved that hand of hers again. "You will want to kiss me, certain that a mere touch of your lips will awaken me to the joys of the flesh. It won't work, it's already failed to awaken me to anything, but you won't believe me. I can see you already don't believe me." She had the gall to try to look bored. "And if it's all the same to you, I'd rather fast-forward straight through that same old song and dance. It's tedious."

"If you insist." He found himself stroking his jaw with his fingers, because he knew that if he reached over to put them on her, she would take it as evidence of this theory of hers. This *song and dance*. No matter how much she liked it. "And what is on the other side? Once we're finished with all this fast-forwarding?"

"Why, business, of course. What else?"

"But in this case, little red, your business and mine are the same. Aren't you here to tempt me out of my humble cabin and into the great, wide world?"

"I am. All you need to do is name your price."

And Dominik was not an impulsive man. Not anymore. He had learned his lesson, time and again, in his misspent youth.

But there was something about this woman that got to him. She was still smiling at him in that pitying way when he'd already tasted her. When he knew better. He couldn't tell if she was lying to herself as well as him, but try as he might, he couldn't think of a single good reason to deny himself.

Not when Lauren Clarke was the most entertainment he'd had in ages.

And Dominik was no longer in the army. He no longer ran his security company. If he wanted to live his life in pursuit of his own amusement, he could now.

Even if it meant involving himself with the blood relations he had located when he was still in the army, but had never seen any reason to contact.

Because like hell would he go begging for scraps.

"You must let me kiss you whenever I wish," he said, keeping his voice mild so she wouldn't see that driving need for her inside him, greedy and focused. "That's it. That is my price. Agree and I will go wherever you wish for me to go and do whatever you wish me to do."

"Don't be ridiculous."

He could tell she thought he was kidding, because she didn't bother to sit up straight. Her cheeks didn't flush, and she was still smiling at him as if he was a fool. He felt like one. But that didn't make him want to take back what he'd said.

Especially when he could see the truth all over her, where she couldn't smile it away.

"This fairy tale obsession of yours has gone too far, I think. Let's return to the real world, which I understand is hard out here in an enchanted cottage in the deep, dark woods."

"The first thing you will learn about me is that I'm never ridiculous," Dominik told her, his voice low. "And when I make a promise, I keep it. Will you? You must let me kiss you whenever I like. However I like. This is a simple request, surely. Particularly for a person such as you who doesn't care one way or the other about kissing."

"I already told you, I know how this goes." She'd lost that smile, and was frowning at him then. "You say *kissing*, but that's not what you mean. It always goes further. There's always a hand."

"I do have a hand, yes. Two, in fact. You've caught me."

"One way or another it always leads back to the same discussion. When we can just have it now." She shook her head. "I'm just not sexual. That's the beginning and the end of it."

"Marvelous. Neither am I, by your definition." Dominik gazed at her, and hoped he didn't look as wolfish as he felt. "Let's be nonsexual together."

She blinked at him, then frowned all the more. "I don't think…"

"We can make rules, if you like." It was his turn to smile, and so he did, all the better to beguile her with. "Rule number one, as discussed, you must allow me to kiss you at my whim. Rule number two, when you no longer wish me to kiss you, you will tell me to stop. That's it. That's all I want."

"But…" Her voice was faint. He counted that as a victory.

"And in return for this, little red, I will trot back to England on your boss's leash and perform the role of long-lost brother to his satisfaction. What will that entail, do you think? Will it be acts of fealty in public view? Or will it simply be an appropriate haircut, the better to blend with the stodgy aristocracy?"

She looked bewildered for a moment, and if Dominik had ever had the slightest inkling to imagine himself a good man—which he hadn't—he knew better then. Because he liked it. He liked her off balance, those soft lips parting and her eyes dazed as if she hardly knew what to do with herself.

Oh, yes, he liked it a great deal.

"I don't understand why, when you could have anything in the world, you would ask for...a kiss."

He could feel the edge in his own smile then. "You cannot buy me, Lauren. But you can kiss me."

She looked dubious, but then, after a moment or two, she appeared to be considering it.

Which Dominik felt like her hands all over his body, skin to skin.

"How long do you imagine this arrangement will go on?" she asked.

He shrugged. "As long as your Mr. Combe requires I remain in his spotlight, I suppose."

"And you give me your word that you will stop when I tell you to."

"I would not be much of a man if I did not," he said, evenly. "There are words to describe those who disregard such clear instructions, but *man* is not among them."

"All you want from the news that you're one of the richest men alive is a kiss," she said after another moment, as if she was selecting each word with care. "And I suppose you can't get much kissing out here in the middle of nowhere, so fair enough, if that's what you like. But why would you choose me?"

Dominik restrained himself—barely—from allowing his very healthy male ego to tell her that he had no trouble finding women, thank you very much. That this cabin was a voluntary retreat, not an involuntary sentence handed down from on high. But he didn't say that.

"What can I say? I've always had a weakness for Little Red Riding Hood."

She sighed, and at the end, it turned into a little laugh. "Very well. If that's what you want, I'll kiss you. But we leave for England as soon as possible."

"As you wish," Dominik murmured, everything in him hot and ready, laced through with triumph and something far darker and more intense he didn't want to name. Not when he could indulge it instead. "But first, that kiss. As promised."

CHAPTER FOUR

LAUREN WAS BAFFLED.

Why would anyone want a kiss—or, she supposed, a number of kisses—when there were so many other things he could have asked for? When the world was at his feet with the combined Combe and San Giacomo fortunes at his service?

She had met a great many men in her time, most of them through work, so she considered herself something of an expert in the behavior of males who considered themselves powerful. But she'd never met anyone like Dominik James. He had no power at all that she could see, but acted like he was the king of the world. It didn't make sense.

But it didn't matter. She wasn't here to understand the man. All she had to do was bring him back to London, and no matter that she felt a good deal less steady than she was pretending.

"Now?" she asked. She looked around the cabin as if sense was another rug tossed over the wood floor that could rise up and assert itself if she could only locate it. "You want me to kiss you *now*?"

Dominik lounged there before her, something glittering in the depths of his gray eyes, though the rest of his face was perfectly serious. He patted his knee with his free hand while what she thought was a smile *almost* changed the stern line of his mouth.

She pushed herself to her feet, still feeling that odd, liquid sensation all throughout her body. It was the way she felt when she slipped on a new pair of the shoes she loved. It made her feel...dangerous, almost. She'd always loved the feeling, because surely that was what a woman was meant to feel.

She'd long thought that if Matteo ever looked at her the way she looked at her shoes, she'd feel it. But he never had.

Lauren didn't understand why she felt it now, in a cabin in the middle of the woods. Or why Dominik was so determined to ruin it with more kissing.

Because the way he'd kissed her out there in the clearing had been different from her halfhearted youthful experiments, true. But Lauren knew it wouldn't last, because it never did. She knew that sooner or later he would grow ever more keen while she became less and less interested.

That was how it had always gone. She had discovered, time and again, that *thinking* about kissing was far preferable to the unfortunate reality of kissing.

She preferred this moment, right now. The moment when a man looked at her and imagined she was a desirable woman. Feminine straight through and capable of feeling all those things that real women did.

Capable of wanting and being wanted in return, when the truth was, *want* wasn't something that Lauren was capable of.

But he had already kissed her, and she told herself that was a good thing. She already knew what she'd agreed to. And it wasn't as if kissing Dominik had been as unpleasant as it always had been in the past.

Quite the opposite, a sly voice deep inside her very nearly purred.

She brushed that aside. It was the unexpected hike, no doubt, that had made her feel so flushed. So undone. She was unaccustomed to feeling those sorts of sensations in her body—all over her body—that was all.

"Perhaps you do not realize this, since you dislike kissing

so much, but it is generally not done while standing across the room," Dominik said with that thread of dark amusement woven into his voice that she couldn't quite track. She could feel it, though. Deep inside all those places where the hike through the woods had made her sensitive.

She didn't understand that, either.

"Do you expect me to perch on your knee?" she asked without trying all that hard to keep the bafflement out of her voice.

"When and where I want," he said softly, gray eyes alight. "How I want."

And Lauren was nothing if not efficient. She had never been wanted, it was true, and was lacking whatever that thing was that could make her want someone else the way others did so readily. So she had learned how to be needed instead.

She had chosen to pursue a career as a personal assistant because there was no better way to be needed—constantly—than to take over the running of someone's life. She liked the high stakes of the corporate world, but what she loved was that Matteo truly *needed* her. If she didn't do her job he couldn't do his.

He needed her to do this, too, she assured herself. He wanted his brother in the fold, media-ready and compliant, and she could make it happen.

And if there was something inside her, some prickle of foreboding or something much sweeter and more dangerous, she ignored it.

The fire crackling beside them seemed hotter all of a sudden. It seemed to lick all over the side of her body, and wash across her face. She had never sat on a man's lap before, or had the slightest desire to do such a thing, and Dominik did nothing to help her along. He only watched her, no longer even the hint of a smile anywhere on his face, save the suggestion of one like silver in the endless gray of his gaze.

She stepped between his legs, thrust out before him in a way that encouraged her to marvel at both their length and strength, and then she eased herself down, putting out a hand to awkwardly prop herself against him as she sat.

"Do you plan to kiss me from this position?" She could swear he was laughing at her, though his face remained stern. "You are aware that kissing requires that lips meet, are you not?"

He had kissed her so smoothly out there at the edge of the woods. So easily. And now that Lauren thought about it, she had never been the one to initiate a kiss. She had always been a recipient. But there was something deep inside her that refused to tell him that.

It was the same something that bloomed with shame—because it had to be shame, surely—there between her legs.

She shouldn't have thought about that just then. Because she was sitting there on his hard, muscled thighs, so disastrously and intriguingly hot beneath her, and she couldn't seem to help herself from squirming against him.

And as she did she could feel something tense and electric hum to life in the space between them.

The fire was so hot. The air seemed to thicken with it as if there were flames dancing up and down the length of her arms, and the strangest part was that it didn't hurt. Burning should hurt, surely, but in this case it only seemed to make her breathless.

She eased closer to the wall of his chest, twisting herself so she was level with his face, and close enough to kiss him. Or she thought it was the correct distance, having never experimented with this position before.

He moved, but only a little, sliding his hands to grip her lightly at her waist.

Lauren couldn't think of a single reason why that should make her shudder.

Everywhere.

She gulped in a breath, aware of too many things at once. Those broad, blunt fingers of his like brands through the thin shell of her blouse. The iron forge of him beneath her, making her pulse and melt in places she'd never felt much of anything before.

This close, and knowing that a kiss was about to happen, she noticed things she hadn't before. The astonishing lines of his face, from his high cheekbones to the blade of his nose. The supremely male jut of his chin. And that thick, careless hair of his, that for some reason, she longed to sink her fingers into.

Her heartbeat slowed, but got louder. And harder, somehow, as if it was trying to escape from her chest.

She searched that implacable gray gaze of his, though she couldn't have said what she was looking for. She burned still, inside and out, and the fire seemed to come at her from all sides, not just from the fireplace.

Slowly, carefully, she lowered her mouth.

Then she pressed her lips against his.

For one long beat, there was only that. The trembling inside her, the feel of his firm lips beneath hers.

There, she thought, with a burst of satisfaction. *This is even easier than I expected—*

But that was when he angled his head.

And he didn't kiss the way she had, halting and unsure.

He smiled against her mouth, then licked his way inside, and Lauren…ignited.

It was as if the cabin caught fire and she was lost in the blaze.

She couldn't seem to get close enough. Dominik's big hands moved from her waist, snaking around her back to hold her even more fiercely. And she moved closer to him, letting her own hands go where they liked. His wide, hard shoulders. His deliciously scratchy jaw. And all that gloriously dark hair of his, thick and wild, like rough silk against her palms.

And still he kissed her, lazy and thorough at once, until she found herself meeting each thrust of his wicked tongue. Until she was the one angling her head, seeking that deliriously sweet fit.

As if they were interlocking parts, made of flame, intoxicating and dangerous at once.

Lauren was the one meant to be kissing him, and this was nothing but a bargain—but she forgot that. She forgot everything but the taste of him. His strength and all that fire, burning in her and around her until she thought she might have become her own blaze.

And she felt a different kind of need swell in her then, poignant and pointed all at once. It swept her from head to toe, then pooled in the place between her legs where she felt that fire most keenly and pulsed with a need too sharp to be shame—

She wrenched her lips from his, startled and shamed and something else that keened inside her, like grief.

For a moment there was nothing but that near-unbearable fire hanging in the air between them. His eyes were silver and bright, and locked to hers. That mouth of his was a temptation and a terror, and she didn't understand how any of this was happening.

She didn't understand much of anything, least of all herself.

"You promised," Lauren managed to say.

And would likely spend the rest of her life reliving how lost and small she sounded, and how little she thought she had it in her to fix it. Or fight her way back to her efficient and capable self.

"I did," he agreed.

His voice was a dark rasp that made her quiver all over again, deep inside.

"You promised and you've already broken that promise. It didn't even take you—"

Her voice cut off abruptly when he ran his palm down the length of her ponytail and tugged it. Gently enough, so there was no reason she felt…scalded straight through.

"What promise did I break?" he asked mildly. So mildly she found herself frowning at him, because she didn't believe it.

"One kiss," she said severely.

And the way his mouth curved then, there below the knowing silver of his gaze, made her shiver.

"You're the one who has to say stop, little red. I don't remember you saying anything of the kind. Do you?"

And for another beat she was...stupefied.

Unable to breathe, much less react. Unable to do anything but gape at him.

Because he was quite right. She hadn't said anything at all.

In the next second she launched herself off him, leaping back in a way that she might have found comical, had she not been so desperate to put space between her and this man she'd made a devil's bargain with.

"This was our agreement, was it not?" Dominik asked, in that same mild voice. He only watched her—looking amused, she couldn't help but notice—as she scrambled around to the back of the chair facing him. "I hope you do not plan to tell me that you are already regretting the deal we made."

And Lauren did not believe in fairy tales. But it occurred to her, as she stared back at this man who had taken her over, made her a stranger to herself, and made her imagine that she could control something she very much feared was far more likely to burn her alive—she realized that she'd been thinking about the wrong kind of fairy tale.

Because there were the pretty ones, sweeping gowns and singing mice. Everything was princesses and musical numbers, neat and sweet and happy-ever-afters all around.

But those weren't the original fairy tales. There were darker ones. Older versions of the same stories, rich with the undercurrent of blood and sacrifice and grim consequences.

There were woods that swallowed you whole. Thorn bushes that stole a hundred years from your life. There were steep prices paid to devious witches, locked rooms that should have stayed closed, and children sent off to pay their fathers' debts in a variety of upsetting ways.

And there were men like Dominik, whose eyes gleamed with

knowledge and certainty, and made her remember that there were some residents of hidden cottages who a wise girl never tried to find in the first place.

But Lauren hadn't heeded all the warnings. The man so difficult to find. The innkeeper's surprise that anyone would seek him out. That damned uninviting path through the woods.

She'd been so determined to prove her loyalty and capabilities to Matteo during this tough period in his life. If he wanted his long-lost older brother, she, by God, would deliver said older brother—once again making it clear that she alone could always, always give her boss what he needed.

Because she did so like to be needed.

She understood that then, with a lurch deep inside her, that once Matteo had mentioned Dominik this had always been where she would end up. This had always been her destination, which she had raced headlong toward with no sense of self-preservation at all.

This deal she'd made. And what it would do to her.

And she knew, with that same lurch and a kind of spinning sensation that threatened to take her knees out from under her, that it was already much too late to save herself from this thing she'd set in motion.

"I don't regret anything," she lied through lips that no longer felt like hers. And though it was hard to meet that too-bright, too-knowing gray gaze of his, she forced herself to do it. And to hold it. "But we need to head back to England now. As agreed."

His lips didn't move, but she could see that smile of his, anyway. All wolf. All fangs.

As if he'd already taken his first bite.

"But of course," he said quietly. "I keep my promises, Lauren. Always. You would do well to remember that."

CHAPTER FIVE

BY THE TIME they made it down out of the mountains in the hardy SUV Dominik kept back behind the cabin, then onto the private plane Lauren had waiting for them at the nearest airfield, she'd convinced herself that she'd simply…gotten carried away.

Once out of the woods, the idea that she'd let *trees* get into her head and so deep beneath her skin struck her as the very height of foolishness.

She was a practical person, after all. She wasn't excitable. It was simply the combination of hiking around in heels and a man who considered kissing currency.

It was the oddness that had gotten to her, she told herself stoutly. And repeatedly.

By the time they boarded the plane, she had regained her composure. She was comfortable on the Combe Industries jet. In her element. She bustled into her usual seat, responded to her email and informed Matteo that she had not only found his brother, but would also shortly be delivering him to England. As requested.

It was amazing how completing a few basic tasks made her feel like herself again.

As if that strange creature who had lost herself on a strange man's lap had never existed at all.

She threw herself into the work that waited for her, delighted that it gave her the opportunity to continue pretending she had no idea who that girl could have been, wild with abandon on Dominik's knee. The farther they got from those woods, the farther she felt from all those bizarre sensations that had been stirred up in her.

Fairy tales, for God's sake. What had she been thinking?

Lauren resolved that she would do whatever she could to make sure she never succumbed to that kind of nonsense again, no matter what bargains she might have made to get Dominik on this plane.

But all through the short flight, no matter how ferociously she tried to concentrate on her computer screen and all the piled-up emails that required her immediate attention, she was aware of Dominik. Of that considering gray gaze of his, following her every move.

And worse, the heat it kicked up in its wake, winding around and around inside her until she was terribly afraid it would make her burst wide open.

Fairy tale nonsense, she told herself sharply. People didn't *burst*, no matter what they felt.

That was what came of tramping about in the wilderness. Too much clean air obviously made her take leave of her senses.

Back in London she felt even more like herself. Calm. Competent. In control and happily surrounded by tarmac. Concrete. Brick buildings. All the solid reminders of the world she knew. And preferred to inhabit, thank you very much.

"England's greenest hills appeared to be rather more gray puddles and a procession of dingy, squat holdings," Dominik said from beside her in the backseat of the car that picked them up from the private airfield outside the city. "What a disappointment."

Lauren congratulated herself on her total lack of reaction to him. He was nothing more than a business associate, sharing a ride.

"Surely, you must know that it rains in England," she said, and even laughed. "A great deal, in fact."

She would have said nothing could possibly divert her attention from her mobile, but every cell in her body went on high alert when Dominik turned. And then faced her, making it impossible for her to pretend she didn't notice the way his big body took up more than his fair share of room in the car. His legs were too long, and those boots of his fascinated her. They seemed so utilitarian. So ruthlessly masculine.

And she couldn't even bring herself to think about the rest of him. All those long, smoothly muscled limbs. All that strength that simmered in him, that she was dimly surprised he managed to contain.

He didn't sit like a San Giacomo. He might look like one of them, or a feral version, anyway, but he was far more…elemental. Matteo and his sister, Pia, shared those same gray eyes, and they had both looked stormy at one time or another.

But Lauren couldn't help thinking that Dominik *was* a storm.

And her body reacted appropriately, prickling with unease—or maybe it was electricity.

Lightning, something in her whispered.

"What happens now?" Dominik asked, but his voice was lazy. Too lazy. She didn't believe he cared what happened now. Or ever. This was all a game to him.

Just as she was.

That thought flustered her, and she didn't make it any better by instantly berating herself for feeling anything at all. She tried to settle her nerves—the ones she didn't believe in—as she stared at him sternly.

"What would you like to happen?" she asked, and told herself she didn't know why she felt as if she were made of glass.

"I assume you are even now in the process of delivering me safely into the bosom of my warm, welcoming family." His smile was as sharp as she felt inside. Jagged. "Will there be a fatted calf?"

"I'm currently delivering you to the London headquarters of Combe Industries," Lauren replied as crisply as she could manage. Especially when all she could seem to concentrate on was his sardonic mouth. "Once there, you and I will wait for further instructions from Mr. Combe."

"Instructions." Dominik looked amused, if darkly. "I can hardly wait."

Lauren gripped her mobile in her hand and made herself stop when she realized she was making her palm ache.

"Mr. Combe is actually not in England at present," she said, and she didn't know why she was telling him this now. It could have waited until they were out of this car. Until they were safely in the office, the place where she felt most at home. Most capable. "He is currently in Perth, Australia. He's personally visiting each and every Combe Industries office."

If Lauren had expected Matteo to greet the news that she'd found his brother by leaping onto a plane and heading straight home to meet him, she kept that to herself. Because Matteo showed no sign of doing anything of the kind.

And it felt disloyal to find that frustrating, but she did.

"The great saint is not in England?" Dominik asked in mock outrage. "But however will we know how best to serve him if he isn't here to lay out his wishes?"

"He is perfectly able to communicate his wishes at all times," she assured him. "It's actually my job to make certain he can, no matter where he is. Don't worry. You'll know exactly what he expects of you."

That was the wrong thing to say, but she only realized that once the words were out there between them. And Dominik's eyes gleamed like silver as he gazed at her.

"Between you and me, little red, I have never done well with expectations." His voice was much too low for her peace of mind. It was too intimate. Too…insinuating. "I prefer to blaze my own trail."

"There is no blazing of trails in the San Giacomo family,"

she retorted with far more fervor than she'd intended. But she tried to keep her expression impassive when his dark brows rose. "The San Giacomos have existed in some form or another for centuries. They were once a major economic force in the Venetian Empire. While their economic force might have faded over time, their social capital has not."

"They sound marvelous," Dominik murmured. "And wholly without the blood of innocents on their hands, I am sure."

"I couldn't say what the San Giacomo family did in the eighth century, of course. But I think you'll find that Matteo Combe is a good and decent man."

"And you his greatest defender," Dominik said, and there was something less lazy about his voice then. "He must pay you very well indeed."

Her breath caught, but Lauren pushed on. "Whether you like expectations or do not, I'm afraid that the blood in your veins means you must meet them, anyway."

That dark amusement in Dominik's eyes made them bright against the rain outside. "Must I?"

"There are more eyes on the San Giacomos now than usual," Lauren said, and wasn't nervous. Why would she be nervous?

"It would seem to me that those eyes are more focused on the Combe side of the family," Dominik said after a moment. "Less Venetian economic might and more Yorkshire brawler, if I remember correctly."

Lauren didn't instantly bristle at that, which struck her as evidence of more disloyalty on her part.

"I'm not sure that there's any particular model of behavior for how a man is expected to act at his father's funeral," she said quietly. "Especially when his mother died only weeks before."

"I wouldn't know," Dominik replied, and that voice of his wasn't the least bit lazy any longer. "Having never met anyone who would claim me as a son in the first place."

Lauren felt as if he'd slapped her. Worse, she felt a flush of shame as if she deserved the slap he hadn't actually given her.

"Why don't we wait to have this argument—"

Dominik laughed. "Is this an argument? You have a thin skin indeed, little red. I would have called this a discussion. And a friendly one, at that."

"—until we are in the office, and can bring Mr. Combe in on a call. Then he can answer all these questions instead of me, which seems more appropriate all around."

"Wonderful," Dominik said, and then his mouth curved in a manner she could only call challenging. "Kiss me."

And she had truly convinced herself that the bargain they'd struck had been some kind of hiking-inspired dream. A Hungarian-woods-inspired nightmare, made of altitude and too much wildlife. She had been sure it had all been some kind of hallucination. She'd been *sure*.

You're such a liar, a voice deep inside her told her.

"You can't mean now. Here."

"Will you make me say it every time?" Dominik's voice was soft, but the look on his face was intense. Intent. "When, where and how I want. Come now, Lauren. Are you a woman of your word or not?"

And it was worse, here. In the back of a town car like so many other town cars she'd ridden in, on this very same stretch of motorway. Here in England, on the outskirts of London, where she had always prided herself on her professionalism. Her competence and efficiency. Where she had built a life made entirely of needs she could meet, and did.

She still hadn't figured out who the Lauren Isadora Clarke was who had kissed this man with such abandon and hunger. But the intrusion of the fairy tale story she refused to accept was real into her life—her real life—was a shock. A jolt.

Her stomach went into free fall.

And Dominik shook his head sadly, making that *tsk*-ing sound as if he could read her every thought right there on her face. "You agreed to this bargain, Lauren. There's no use pretending you suddenly find the notion disgusting." His eyes were much too bright. "It is almost as if kissing makes you feel things, after all."

That shook her out of the grip of her horror—because that was what she told herself it had to be, that wild, spinning sensation that made her feel drunk from the inside out. It spurred her into action, and she didn't stop to question why it was she was so determined that this man never know that his kiss was the only one that had ever gotten to her at all.

It was information he never, ever needed to know.

She hardly wanted to admit it to herself.

And she threw herself across the backseat, determined that whatever else happened, she would do what she'd promised she would. That way, he would never know that she didn't want to do it *because* she wasn't bored by him the way she wanted to be.

Dominik caught her as she catapulted herself against his chest, then shifted her around so that she was sitting draped over his lap, which didn't help anything at all.

He was much too hard. There was the thick, enticing steel of his thighs, and that hard ridge that rose between them. And Lauren felt...soft and silly, and molten straight through.

And she was sitting on him again, caught in the way he gazed at her, silver in his eyes and his hands at her waist again.

"I know you know how to do this, little red," he said, his voice a soft taunt. "Or are you trying to play games with me?"

"I don't play games," she said stiffly.

As if, should she maintain proper posture and a chilly tone, she might turn this impossible situation to her advantage. Or at least not drown in it.

"So many things you don't do," Dominik murmured, dark and sardonic. "Until you do."

She wanted him to stop talking. And she wanted to get this over with, as quickly as possible, and somehow those two things fused together and made it seem a terrific idea to lift her hands and use them to frame his face.

He stopped talking.

But the trouble with that was, her brain also stopped working.

She was entranced, suddenly and completely, with that strong jaw of his. She marveled at the feel of him, the rasp of his unshaven jaw beneath her palms.

A giant, hot fist she hadn't known lurked there inside her opened then. Slowly, surely, each finger of pure sensation unfurled, sending ribbons of heat to every last part of her.

She studied the sweep of his cheekbones, the lush shape of his mouth, and felt the shiver of it, so deep inside her it made parts she hadn't known she had bloom into life.

And she had the craziest urge to just…rub herself against him.

But instead, she kissed him.

She had some half-baked notion that she would deliver a peck, then retreat, but the moment she tasted him again she forgot about that. His mouth was a temptation and sin at once, and she was giddy with it. With his taste and heat.

With him, full stop.

So she angled her head and took the kiss deeper.

Just the way he'd taught her.

And for a little while, there was nothing at all but the slide of her tongue against his. The tangle of their breath, there in the close confines of the back of the car as it moved through the London streets.

Nothing but that humming thing that kicked up between them, encircling them both, then shuddering through Lauren until she worried, in some distant part of her head, that she would never be the same.

That she was already forever changed.

She kissed him and kissed him, and when she pulled her mouth away from his she fully expected him to follow her.

But he didn't.

She couldn't begin to describe the expression on his face then, or the steady sort of gleam in his gaze as he reached over and traced the shape of her mouth.

"Good girl," he said, and she knew without having to ask that he was deliberately trying to be provocative. "It's nice to know that you can keep your promise even after you get what you want."

"I am a woman of my word, Mr. James," she said crisply, remembering herself as she did.

And suddenly the fact that she was sitting on him, aware of all those parts of him pressed so intimately against her, was unbearable.

She scrambled off him and had the sinking suspicion that he let her go. And then watched her as if he could see straight through her.

And that was the thing. She believed he could.

It was unacceptable.

"The only thing you need to concern yourself about is the fact that you will soon be meeting your family for the first time," she said, frowning at him. "It wouldn't be surprising if you had some feelings around that."

"I have no feelings at all about that."

"I understand you may wish—"

"You do not understand." His voice was not harsh, but that somehow made the steel in it more apparent. "I was raised in an orphanage, Lauren. As an orphan. That means I was told my parents were dead. When I was older, I learned that they might very well be alive, but they didn't want me, which I believed, given no one ever came to find me. I don't know what tearful, emotional reunion you anticipate I'm about to have with these people."

Lauren was horrified by the part of her that wanted to reach over to him again. This time, just to touch him. It was one more thing that didn't make sense.

"You're right, I can't understand. But I do know that Mr. Combe will do everything in his power to make sure this transition is easy for you."

"You are remarkably sure of your Mr. Combe. And his every thought."

"I've worked for him for a long time."

"With such devotion. And what exactly has he done to deserve your undying support?"

She flexed her toes in her shoes, and she couldn't have said why that made her feel so obvious, suddenly. Silly straight through, because he was looking at her. As if he could see every last thing about her, laid out on a plate before him.

Lauren didn't want to be known like that. The very notion was something like terrifying.

"I see," Dominik said, and there was a different sort of darkness in his voice then. "You are not sexual, you tell me with great confidence, but you are in love with your boss. How does that work, exactly?"

"I'm not in…" She couldn't finish the sentence, so horrified was she. "And I would never…" She wanted to roll down the window, let the cool air in and find her breath again, but she couldn't seem to move. Her limbs weren't obeying her commands. "Matteo Combe is one of the finest men I have ever known. I enjoy working for him, that's all."

She would never have said that she was in love with him. And she would certainly never have thought about him in any kind of sexual way. That seemed like a violation of all the years they'd worked together.

All she wanted—all she'd ever wanted—was for him to appreciate her. As a woman. To see her as something more than his walking, talking calendar.

"And this paragon of a man cannot stir himself to return home to meet the brother you claim he is so dedicated to? Perhaps, Lauren, you do not know the man you love so much as well as you think."

"I know him as well as I need to."

"And I know he's never tasted you," Dominik said with all

his dark ruthlessness. It made her want to cry. It made her want to...*do something* with all that restlessness inside her. "Has he?"

Lauren could barely breathe. Her cheeks were so red she was sure they could light up the whole of the city on their own.

"Not answering the question is an answer all its own, little red," Dominik murmured, his face alight with what she very much feared was satisfaction.

And she was delighted—relieved beyond measure—that the car pulled up in front of the Combe Industries building before she was forced to come up with some kind of reply.

But she didn't pretend it was anything but a reprieve, and likely a temporary one, when she pushed open the door and threw herself out into the blessedly cool British evening.

Where she tried—and failed, again and again—to catch her breath and recover from the storm that was Dominik James.

CHAPTER SIX

THERE WAS NO doubt at all that the man on the video screen was Dominik's brother. It was obvious from the shape of his jaw to the gray of his eyes. His hair was shorter, and every detail about him proclaimed his wealth and high opinion of himself. The watch he wore that he wasn't even bothering to try to flash. The cut of his suit. The way he sat as if the mere presence of his posterior made wherever he rested it a throne.

This was the first blood relative Dominik had ever met, assuming a screen counted as a meeting. This…aristocrat.

He couldn't think of a creature more diametrically opposed to him. He, who had suffered and fought for every scrap he'd ever had, and a man who looked as if he'd never blinked without the full support of a trained staff.

They stared at each other for what seemed like another lifetime or two.

Dominik stood in Lauren's office, which was sprawling and modern and furnished in such a way to make certain everyone who entered it knew that she was very important in her own right—and even more so, presumably, as the gatekeeper to the even more massive and dramatically appointed office beyond.

Matteo Combe's office, Dominik did not have to be told.

His only brother, so far as he knew. The man who had received all the benefit of the blood they shared, while Dominik had been accorded all the shame.

Matteo Combe, the man whose bidding Lauren did without question.

Dominik decided he disliked the man on the screen before him. Intensely.

"I would have known you anywhere," Matteo said after they'd eyed each other a good long while.

It would have pained Dominik to admit that he would have known Matteo, too—it was the eyes they shared, first and foremost, and a certain similarity in the way they held themselves—so he chose not to admit it.

"Brother," Dominik replied instead, practically drawling out the word. Making it something closer to an insult. "What a pleasure to almost meet you."

And when Lauren showed him out of the office shortly after that tender reunion, Dominik took a seat in the waiting area that was done up like the nicest and most expensive doctor's office he'd ever seen, and reflected on how little he'd thought about this part. The actually having family, suddenly, part.

Because all he'd thought about since she'd walked into his clearing was Lauren.

When he'd searched for his parents, he'd quickly discovered that the young man who'd had the temerity to impregnate an heiress so far above his own station had died in an offshore oil rig accident when he was barely twenty. An oil rig he'd gone to work on because he couldn't remain in Europe, pursuing his studies, after his relationship with Alexandrina had been discovered.

And when Dominik had found all the Combes and San Giacomos with precious little effort—which, of course, meant they could have done the same—he'd had wanted nothing to do with them. Because he wanted nothing from them—look what they'd done to the boy who'd fathered him. They had gotten rid of both of them, in one way or another, and Dominik had risen from the trash heap where they'd discarded him despite that abandonment. His mother's new boy and girl, who had been pampered and coddled and cooed over all this time in his stead, were nothing to him. What was the point of meeting with them to discuss Alexandrina's sins?

He'd been perfectly content to excel on his own terms, without any connection to the great families who could have helped him out of the gutter, but hadn't. Likely because they'd been the ones to put him there.

But it hadn't occurred to him to prepare himself to look into another man's face and see…his own.

It was disconcerting, to put it mildly.

That they had different fathers was evident, but there was no getting around the fact that he and Matteo Combe shared blood. Dominik scowled at the notion, because it sat heavily. Too heavily.

And then he transferred that scowl back to the screen inside Lauren's office, where Matteo was still larger than life and Lauren stood before him, arguing.

He didn't have to be able to hear a word she said to know she was arguing. He knew some of her secrets now. He knew the different shapes she made with that mouth of hers and the crease between her brows that broadcast her irritation. He certainly knew what she looked like when she was agitated.

And he found he didn't much care for the notion that whatever she called it or didn't call it, she had a thing for her boss.

Her boss. His brother.

"Is he one of the ones you've experimented with?" he asked her when she came out of the office, the screen finally blank behind her.

She was frowning even more fiercely than before, which he really shouldn't have found entertaining, especially when he hadn't had the pleasure of causing it. He lounged back in his seat as if it had been crafted specifically for him and regarded her steadily until she blinked. In what looked like incomprehension.

"I already declined to dignify that question with a response."

"Because dignity is the foremost concern here. With your boss." He refused to call the man *Mr. Combe* the way she did. And calling him by his Christian name seemed to suggest that they had more of a personal relationship—or any personal relationship, for that matter—than Dominik was comfortable having with anyone who shared his blood. "I want to know if he was one of your kissing experiments."

Lauren maintained her blank expression for a moment.

But then, to his eternal delight, she went pink and he couldn't seem to keep from wondering about all the other, more exciting ways he could make her flush like that.

"Certainly not." Her voice was frigid, but he'd tasted her. He knew the ice she tried to hide behind was a lie. "I told you, I admire him. I enjoy the work we do together. I have never *kissed—*"

She cut herself off, then pulled herself up straight. It only made Dominik wonder what she might have said if she hadn't stopped herself. "You and I have far more serious things to talk about than kissing experiments, Mr. James."

"I have always found kissing very serious business indeed. Would you like me to demonstrate?"

That pink flush deepened and he wanted to know where it went. If it changed as it lowered to her breasts, and what color her nipples were. If it made it to her hips, her thighs. And all that sweetness in between. He wanted to peel off that soft silk blouse she wore and conduct his own experiments, at length.

And the fact that thinking about Lauren Clarke's naked body was far preferable to him than considering the fact he'd met his brother, more or less, did not escape him. Dominik rarely hid from himself.

But he had no need, and less desire, to tear himself open and seek out the lonely orphan inside.

"Mr. Combe thinks it best that we head to Combe Manor. It is the estate in Yorkshire where his father's family rose to prominence. He understands you are not a Combe. But he thinks it would cause more comment to bring you directly to any of the San Giacomo holdings in Italy at this point."

Dominik understood that *at this point* was the most important part of Lauren's little speech. That and the way she delivered it, still standing in her own doorway too stiffly, her voice a little too close to nervous. He studied her and watched her grow even more agitated—and then try to hide it.

It was the fact that she wanted to hide her reactions from him that made him happiest of all, he thought.

"I don't know who you think is paying such close attention to me," Dominik said after a moment. "No one has noticed that I bear more than a passing resemblance to a member of the San Giacomo family in my entire lifetime so far. I cannot imagine that will change all of a sudden."

"It will change in an instant should you be found in a San Giacomo residence, looking as you do, as the very ghost of San Giacomos past."

He inclined his head. Slightly. "I am very good at living my life away from prying eyes, little red. You may have noticed."

"Those days are over now." She stood even straighter, and he had the distinct impression she was working herself up to say something else. "You may not feel any sense of urgency, but I can tell you that the clock is ticking. It's only a matter of time before Alexandrina's will is leaked, because these things are always leaked. Once it is, the paparazzi will tear apart the earth to find you. We need to be prepared for when that happens."

"I feel more than prepared already. In the sense of not caring."

"There are a number of things it would make more sense for us to do now, before the world gets its teeth into you."

"How kinky," he murmured, just to please himself.

And better still, to make her caramel eyes flash with that temper he suspected was the most honest thing about her.

"First, we must make your exterior match the San Giacomo blood that runs in your veins."

He found his mouth curving. "Are you suggesting a make-over? Have I strayed into a fairy tale, after all?"

"I certainly wouldn't call it that. A bit of tailoring and a new wardrobe, that's all. Perhaps a lesson or two in minor comportment issues that might arise. And a haircut, definitely."

Dominik's grin was sharp and hot. "Why, Lauren. Be still my heart. Am I the Cinderella in this scenario? I believe that makes you my Princess Charming."

"There's no such thing as a Princess Charming." She sniffed. "And anyway, I believe my role here is really as more of a Fairy Godmother."

"I do not recall Cinderella and her Fairy Godmother ever being attached at the lips," he said silkily. "But perhaps your fairy tales are more exciting than mine ever were."

"I hate fairy tales," she threw at him. "They're strange little stories designed to make children meek and biddable and responsible for the things that happen to them when they're not. And also, we need to get married."

That sat there between them, loud and not a little mad.

Dominik's gaze was fused to hers and, sure enough, that flush was deepening. Darkening.

"I beg your pardon." He lingered over each word, almost as if he really was begging. Not that he had any experience with such things. And there was so much to focus on, but he had to choose. "All this urban commotion must be getting to me." He made a show of looking all around the empty office, then, because he had never been without a flair for the dramatic when it suited him—and this woman brought it out in him in spades. "Did you just ask me to marry you?"

"I'm not *asking* you, personally. I'm telling you that Mr. Combe thinks it's the best course of action. First, it will stop the inevitable flood of fortune hunters who will come out of the woodwork once they know you exist before they think to start. Second, it will instantly make you seem more approachable and civilized, because the world thinks married men are less dangerous, somehow, than unattached ones. Third, and most important, it needn't be real in any sense but the boring legalities. And we will divorce as soon as the furor settles."

Dominik only gazed back at her, still and watchful.

"Come now, Lauren. A man likes a little romance, not a bullet-pointed list. The very least you could do is bend a knee and mouth a sweet nothing or two."

"I'm not *proposing* to you!" Her veneer slipped at that, and her face reddened. "Mr. Combe thinks—"

"Will I be marrying my own brother?" He lay his hand over his heart in mock astonishment. "What sort of family *is* this?"

He thought her head might explode. He watched her hands curl into fists at her sides as if that alone could keep her together.

"You agreed to do whatever was asked of you," she reminded him, fiercely. "Don't tell me that you're the one who's going to break our deal. Now. After—"

After kissing him repeatedly, he knew she meant to say, but she stopped herself.

The more he stared back at her without saying a word, the more agitated she became. And the more he enjoyed himself, though perhaps that made him a worse man than even he'd imagined. And he'd spent a great quantity of time facing his less savory attributes head-on, thanks in part to the ministrations of the nuns who had taught him shame and how best to hate himself for existing. The army had taken care of the rest.

These days Dominik was merrily conversant on all his weaknesses, but Lauren made him…something else again.

But that was one more thing he didn't want to focus on.

"What would be the point of a marriage that wasn't real?" he asked idly. "The public will need to have reason to believe it's real for it to be worth bothering, no?"

The truth was that Dominik had never thought much about marriage one way or the other. Traditional family relationships weren't something he had ever seen modeled in the orphanage or on the streets in Spain. He had no particular feelings about the state of marriage in any personal sense, except that he found it a mystifying custom, this strange notion that two people should share their lives. Worse, themselves.

And odder still, call it love—of all things—while they did it.

What Dominik knew of love was what the nuns had doled out in such a miserly way, always shot through with disappointment, too many novenas and demands for better behavior. Love was indistinguishable from its unpleasant consequences and character assassinations, and Dominik had been much happier when he'd left all that mess and failure behind him.

He had grown used to thinking of himself as a solitary being, alone by choice rather than circumstance. He liked his own company. He was content to avoid others. And he enjoyed the peace and quiet that conducting his affairs to his own specifications, with no outside opinion and according to his own wishes and whims, afforded him. He was answerable to no one and chained to nothing.

The very notion of marrying anyone, for any reason, should have appalled him.

But it didn't.

Not while he gazed at this woman before him—

That pricked at him, certainly. But not enough to stop. Or leave, the way he should have already.

He told himself it was because this was a game, that was all. An amusement. What did he care about the San Giacomo reputation or public opinion? He didn't.

But he did like the way Lauren Clarke tasted when she melted against him. And it appeared he liked toying with her in between those meltings, too.

"What we're talking about is a publicity stunt, nothing more," she told him, frowning all the while. "You understand what that means, don't you? There's nothing real about it. It's entirely temporary. And when it ends, we will go our separate ways and pretend it never happened."

"You look distressed, little red," he murmured, because all

she seemed to do as she stood there before him was grow redder and stiffer, and far more nervous, if the way she wrung her hands together was any indication.

He didn't think she had the slightest idea what she was doing. Which was fair enough, as neither did he. Evidently. Since he was still sitting here, lounging about in the sort of stuffy corporate office he'd sworn off when he'd sold his company, as if he was obedient. When he was not. Actually subjecting himself to this charade.

Participating in it wholeheartedly, in point of fact, or he never would have invited her into his cabin. Much less left it in her company—then flown off to rainy, miserable England.

"I wouldn't call myself distressed." But her voice told him otherwise. "I don't generally find business concerns *distressing*. Occasionally challenging, certainly."

"And yet I am somehow unconvinced." He studied the way she stood. The way she bit at her lower lip. Those hands that telegraphed the feelings she claimed not to have. "Could it be that your Mr. Combe, that paragon of virtue and all that is wise and true in an employer by your reckoning, has finally pushed you too far?"

"Of course not." She seemed to notice what she was doing with her hands then, because she dropped them back to her sides. Then she drew herself up in that way she did, lifted her chin and met his gaze. With squared shoulders and full-on challenge in her caramel-colored eyes—which, really, he shouldn't have found quite as entertaining as he did. What was it about this woman? Why did he find her so difficult to resist? He, who had made a life out of resisting everything? "Perhaps you've already forgotten, but you promised that you would do whatever was asked of you."

He stopped trying to control his grin. "I recall my promises perfectly, thank you. I am shocked and appalled that you think so little of the institution of marriage that you would suggest wedding me in some kind of cold-blooded attempt to fool the general populace, all of whom you appear to imagine will be hanging on our every move."

He shook his head at her as if disappointed unto his very soul at what she had revealed here, and had the distinct pleasure of watching her grit her teeth.

"I find it difficult to believe that you care one way or the other," she said after a moment. "About fooling anyone for any reason. And, for that matter, about marriage."

"I don't." He tilted his head to one side. "But I suspect you do."

He thought he'd scored a hit. She stiffened further, then relaxed again in the next instant as if determined not to let him see it. And then her cheeks flamed with that telltale color, which assured him that yes, she cared.

But a better question was, why did he?

"I don't have any feelings about marriage at all," she declared in ringing tones he couldn't quite bring himself to believe. "It was never something I aspired to, personally, but I'm not opposed to it. I rarely think about it at all, to be honest. Are you telling me that you lie awake at night, consumed with fantasies about your own wedding, Mr. James?"

"Naturally," he replied. And would have to examine, at some point, why he enjoyed pretending to be someone completely other than who he was where this woman was concerned. Purely for the pleasure of getting under her skin. He smiled blandly. "Who among us has not dreamed of swanning down an expensive aisle, festooned in tulle and lace, for the entertainment of vague acquaintances?"

"Me," she retorted at once. And with something like triumph in her voice.

"Of course not, because you are devoid of feelings entirely, as you have taken such pains to remind me."

"I'm not sentimental." Except she looked so deeply pleased with herself just then it looked a whole lot like an emotion, whether she wanted to admit such things or not. "I apologize if you find that difficult to accept."

"You have no feelings about marriage. Sex. Even kissing, no matter how you react while doing it. You're an empty void, capable only of doing the bidding of your chosen master. I understand completely, Lauren."

That she didn't like that description was obvious by the way she narrowed her eyes, and the way she flattened her lips. Dominik smiled wider. Blander.

"How lucky your Mr. Combe is to have found such devotion, divorced of any inconvenient sentiment on your part. You might as well be a robot, cobbled together from spare parts for the singular purpose of serving his needs."

If her glare could have actually reached across the space between them and struck him then, Dominik was sure he would have sustained mortal blows. What he was less certain of was why everything in him objected to thinking of her as another man's. In any capacity.

"What I remember of my parents' marriage is best not discussed in polite company," she said, her voice tight. He wondered if she knew how the sound betrayed her. How it broadcast the very feelings she pretended not to possess. "They divorced when I was seven. And they were both remarried within the year, which I didn't understand until later meant that they had already moved on long before the ink was dry on their divorce decree. The truth is that they only stayed as long as they did because neither one wanted to take responsibility for me." She shook her head, but more as if she was shaking something off than negating it. "Believe me, I know better than anyone that most marriages are nothing but a sham. No matter how much tulle and expense there might be. That doesn't make me a robot. It makes me realistic."

Something in the way she said that clawed at him, though he couldn't have said why. Or didn't want to know why, more accurately, and accordingly shoved it aside.

"Wonderful," he said instead. "Then you will enjoy our sham of a marriage all the more, in all its shabby realism."

"Does that mean you'll do it, then?"

And he didn't understand why he wanted so badly to erase that brittleness in her tone. Why he wanted to reach out and touch her in ways that had nothing to do with the fire in him, but everything to do with that hint of vulnerability he doubted she knew was so visible. In the stark softness of her mouth. In the shadows in her eyes.

"I will do it," he heard himself say. "For you."

And every alarm he'd ever wired there inside him screeched an alert then, at full volume.

Because Dominik did not do things for other people. No one was close enough to him to ask for or expect that kind of favor. No one got close to him. And in return for what he'd always considered peace, he kept himself at a distance from everyone else. No obligations. No expectations.

But there was something about Lauren, and how hard she was clearly fighting to look unfazed in the face of her boss's latest outrageous suggestion. As if an order to marry the man's unknown half brother was at all reasonable.

You just agreed to it, a voice in him pointed out. *So does it matter if it's reasonable?*

One moment dragged on into another, and then it was too late to take the words back. To qualify his acceptance. To make it clear that no matter what he might have said, he hadn't meant it to stand as any form of obligation to this woman he barely knew.

Much less that boss of hers who shared his blood.

"For me?" she asked, and it was as if she, too, had suddenly tumbled into this strange, hushed space Dominik couldn't seem to snap out of.

He didn't want to call it sacred. But he wasn't sure what other word there was for it, when her caramel eyes gleamed like gold and his chest felt tight.

"For you," he said, and he had the sense that he was digging his own grave, shovelful by shovelful, whether he wanted it or not. But even that didn't stop him. He settled farther back against his chair, thrust his legs out another lazy inch and let one corner of his mouth crook. "But if you want me to marry you, little red, I'm afraid I will require a full, romantic proposal."

She blinked. Then swallowed.

"You can't be serious."

"I don't intend to make a habit of marrying. This will have to be perfect, the better to live on all my days." He nodded toward the polished wood at his feet. "Go on, then. On your knees, please."

And he was only a man. Not a very good one, as he'd acknowledged earlier. There was no possibility of issuing such an order without imagining all the other things she could do once she was there.

So he did. And had to shift slightly where he sat to accommodate the hungriest part of him.

"You agreed that any marriage between us will be a sham," she was saying, her voice a touch too husky for someone so dedicated to appearing unmoved. "You used that very word. It will be a publicity stunt, and only a publicity stunt, as I said."

"Whatever the marriage is or isn't, it begins right here." He ignored the demands that clamored inside him, greedy and still drunk on his last taste of her. "Where there is no public. No paparazzi. No overbearing employer who cannot stir himself to greet his long-lost brother in person."

She started to argue that but subsided when he shook his head.

"There are only two people who ever need to know how this marriage began, Lauren. And we are both right here, all alone, tucked away on an abandoned office floor where no one need ever be the wiser."

She rolled her eyes. "We can tell them there was kneeling all around, if that's really what you need."

"We can tell them anything you like, but I want to see a little effort. A little care, here between the two of us. A pretty, heartfelt proposal. Come now, Lauren." And he smiled at her then, daring her. "A man likes to be seduced."

Her cheeks had gone pale while he spoke, and as he watched, they flooded with bright new color.

"You don't want to be seduced. You want to humiliate me."

"Six of one, half dozen of another." He jutted his chin toward the floor again. "You need to demonstrate your commitment. Or how else will I know that my heart is safe in your hands?"

The color on her cheeks darkened, and her eyes flashed with temper. And he liked that a hell of a lot more than her robot impression.

"No one is talking about hearts, Mr. James," she snapped at him. "We're talking about damage control. Optics. PR."

"You and your Mr. Combe may be talking about all of those things," he said and shrugged. "But I am merely a hermit from a Hungarian hovel, too long-haired to make sense of your complicated corporate world. What do I know of such things? I'm a simple man, with simple needs." He reached up and dramatically clasped his chest, never shifting his gaze from hers. "If you want me, you must convince me. On your knees, little red."

She made a noise of sheer, undiluted frustration that nearly made him laugh. Especially when it seemed to make her face that much brighter.

He watched as she forced her knees to unlock. She took a breath in, then let it out. Slowly, as if it hurt, she took a step toward him. Then another.

And by the time she moved past his feet, then insinuated herself right where he wanted her, there between his outstretched legs, he didn't have the slightest urge to laugh any longer. Much less when she sank down on her knees before him, just as he'd imagined in all that glorious detail.

She knelt as prettily as she did everything else, and she filled his head as surely as his favorite Hungarian *palinka*. He couldn't seem to look away from her, gold and pink and that wide caramel gaze, peering up at him from between his own legs.

The sight of her very nearly unmanned him.

And he would never know, later, how he managed to keep his hands to himself.

"Dominik James," she said softly, looking up at him with eyes wide, filled with all those emotions she claimed she didn't feel—but he did, as if she was tossing them straight into the deepest part of him, "will you do me the honor of becoming my husband? For a while?"

He didn't understand why something in him kicked against that qualification. But he ignored it.

He indulged himself by reaching forward and fitting his palm to the curve of her cheek. He waited until her lips parted because he knew she felt it, too, that same heat that roared in him. That wildfire that was eating him alive.

"But of course," he said, and he had meant to sound sardonic. Darkly amused. But that wasn't how it came out, and he couldn't think of a way to stop it. "I can think of nothing I would like to do more than marry a woman I hardly know to serve the needs of a brother I have never met in the flesh, to save the reputation of a family that tossed me aside like so much trash."

There was a sheen in her gaze that he wanted to believe was connected to that strangely serious thing in him, not laughing at all. And the way her lips trembled, just slightly.

Just enough to make the taste of her haunt him all over again.

"I… I can't tell if that's a yes or no."

"It's a yes, little red," he said, though there was no earthly reason that he should agree to any of this.

There was no reason that he should even be here, so far away from the life he'd carved out to his specifications. The life he had fought so hard to win for himself.

But Lauren had walked into his cabin, fit too neatly into the chair that shouldn't have been sitting there, waiting for her, and now he couldn't seem to keep himself from finding out if she fit everywhere else, too.

A thought that was so antithetical to everything he was and everything he believed to be true about himself that Dominik wasn't sure why he didn't trust her away from him and leave. Right now.

But he didn't.

Worse, he didn't want to.

"It's a yes," he said, his voice grave as he betrayed himself, and for no reason, "but I'm afraid, as in most things, there will be a price. And you will be the one to pay it."

CHAPTER SEVEN

LAUREN DIDN'T UNDERSTAND anything that was happening.

She had been astounded when Matteo had suggested marriage, so offhandedly as if it was perfectly normal to run around marrying strangers on a whim because he thought that would look better in some theoretical tabloid.

"Marry him," he'd said, so casually, from the far side of the world. "You are a decent, hardworking sort and you've been connected to the family without incident for years."

"I think you mean employed by the family and therefore professional."

"You can take him in hand. Make sure he's up to the task. And by the time the shock fades over my mother's scandalous past, you'll have made him everything he needs to be to take his place as a San Giacomo."

"Will this new role come with combat pay?" she'd asked, with more heat than she normally used with her boss, no matter what was going on. But then, she wasn't normally dispatched into the hinterland, made to *hike*, and then kissed thoroughly and repeatedly. She was…not herself. "Or do you expect me to give up my actual life for the foreseeable future for my existing salary, no questions asked?"

She never spoke to Matteo that way. But he didn't normally

react the way he had then, either, with nothing but silence and what looked very much like sadness on his face. It made Lauren wish she hadn't said anything.

Not for the first time, she wondered exactly what had gone on between Matteo and the anger management consultant the Combe Industries board of directors had hired in a transparent attempt to take Matteo down. He'd gone off with her to Yorkshire, been unusually unreachable and then had set off on a round-the-world tour of all the Combe Industries holdings.

A less charitable person might wonder if he was attempting to take the geographic tour.

"You can name your price, Lauren," he said after what felt like a very long while, fraught with all the evidence she'd ever needed that though they might work very closely together, they had no personal relationship. Not like that. "All I ask is that you tame this brother of mine before we unleash him on the world. The board will not be pleased to have more scandal attached to the Combe name. And the least we can do is placate them a little."

And she'd agreed to ask Dominik, because what else could she do? For all Dominik's snide commentary, the truth was that she admired Matteo. He was not his father, who had always been willing to take the low road—and usually had. Matteo had integrity, something she knew because no matter how she might have longed for him to *see* her, he never had. He treated her as his personal assistant, not as a woman. It was why she felt safe while she wore her outrageously feminine heels. It was why she felt perfectly happy dedicating herself to him.

If he had looked at her the way Dominik did, even once, she would never have been able to work for him at all. She would never have been able to sort out what was an appropriate request and what wasn't, and would have lost herself somewhere in the process.

She'd been reeling from that revelation when she'd walked

out to pitch the marriage idea, fully expecting that Dominik would laugh at the very notion.

But he hadn't.

And she'd meant to present the whole thing as a very dry and dusty sort of business proposition, anyway. Just a different manner of merger, that was all. But instead of a board meeting of sorts, she was knelt down between his legs, gazing up at him from a position that made her whole body quiver.

And unless she was very much mistaken, he had actually agreed to marry her.

For a price.

Because with this man, there was always a price.

How lucky you want so badly to pay it, an insinuating, treacherous voice from deep inside her whispered. *Whatever it is.*

"What kind of price?" Lauren frowned at him as if that could make them both forget that she was kneeling before him like a supplicant. Or a lover. And that he was touching her as if at least one of those things was a foregone conclusion. "I have already promised to kiss you whenever you like. What more could you want?"

His palm was so hard and hot against the side of her face. She felt it everywhere, and she knew that seemingly easy touch was responsible for the flames she could feel licking at her. All over her skin, then deeper still, sweet and hot in her core.

Until she *throbbed* with it. With him.

"Do you think there are limits to what a man might want?" he asked quietly, and his voice was so low it set her to shattering, like a seismic event. Deep inside, where she was already molten and more than a little afraid that she might shake herself apart.

"You're talking about sex again," she said, and thought she sounded something like solemn. Or despairing. And neither helped with all that unbearable *heat.* "I don't know how many ways I can tell you—"

"That you are not sexual, yes, I am aware." He moved his thumb, dragging it gently across her lower lip, and his mouth crooked when she hissed in a breath. His eyes blazed when goose bumps rose along her neck and ran down her arms, and his voice was little more than a growl when he spoke again. "Not sexual at all."

Something in the way he said that made her frown harder, though she already knew it was futile. And it only seemed to make that terrible, knowing blaze in his gray eyes more pronounced.

And much, much hotter. Inside her, where she still couldn't tell if she hated it—or loved it.

"What do you want from me?" she asked, her voice barely above a whisper.

And she thought that whatever happened, she would always remember the way he smiled at her then, half wolf and all man. That it was tattooed inside her, branded into her flesh, forever a part of her. Whether she liked it or not.

"What I want from you, little red, is a wedding night."

That was another brand, another scar. And far more dangerous than before.

Lauren's throat was almost too dry to work. She wasn't sure it would. "You mean…?"

"I mean in the traditional sense, yes. With all that entails."

He shifted, and she had never felt smaller. In the sense of being delicate. *Precious*, something in her whispered, though she knew that was fanciful. And worse, foolish.

Dominik smoothed his free hand over her hair, and let it rest at the nape of her neck. And the way he held her face made something in her do more than melt.

She thought maybe it sobbed.

Or she did.

"Find a threshold, and I will carry you over it," he told her, his voice low and intent. And the look in his gray eyes so male, very nearly *possessive*, it made her ache. "I will lay you down on a bed and I will kiss you awhile, to see where it goes. And all I need from you is a promise that you will not tell me what you do and do not like until you try it. That's all, Lauren. What do you have to lose?"

And she couldn't have named the things she had to lose, because they were all the one thing—they were all *her*—and she was sure he would take them, anyway.

He would take everything.

Maybe she'd known that from the moment she'd seen the shadows become a man, there in that clearing so far from the rest of the world. There in those woods that had taunted her from the first, whispering of darkness and mystery in a thousand ways she hadn't wanted to hear.

Maybe it had always been leading straight here.

But between the heat of his hands and that shivering deep inside her, she couldn't seem to mind it as much as she should have.

As much as she suspected she would, once she survived this. *If* she survived this.

She should get up right this minute. She should move herself out of danger—out of arm's reach. She should tell Dominik she didn't care what he did with his newfound name and fortune, just as she should ring Matteo back and tell him she had no intention of marrying a stranger on command.

She knew she should do all those things. She *wanted* to do all those things.

But instead, she shivered. And in that moment, there at his feet with all his focus and intent settled on her, she surrendered.

If surrender was a cliff, Lauren leaped straight off it, out into nothing. She hadn't done anything so profoundly foolish since she was nine years old and had thought she could convince her parents to pay more attention to her by acting out. She'd earned herself instead an unpleasant summer in boarding school.

But surrendering here, to Dominik, didn't feel like that. It didn't feel like plummeting down into sharp rocks.

It felt far more like flying.

"I will give you a wedding night," she heard herself agree,

her voice very stern and matter-of-fact, as if that could mask the fact that she was capitulating. As if she could divert his attention from the great cliff she'd just flung herself over. "But that's all."

"Perhaps we will leave these intimate negotiations until after the night in question," Dominik said, that undercurrent of laughter in his voice. "You may find you very much want a honeymoon, little red. Who knows? Perhaps even an extended one. This may come as a surprise to you, but there are some women who would clamor for the opportunity to while away some time in my bed."

Wedding nights. Honeymoons. *Time in bed.* This was all a farce. It had to be.

But Lauren was on her knees in the offices of Combe Industries, and she had just proposed marriage to a man she'd only met this morning.

So perhaps *farce* wasn't quite the right word to describe what was happening.

Something traitorous inside her wanted to lean in closer, and that terrified her, so she took it as an opportunity to pull away. Cliff or no cliff.

Except he didn't let her.

That hand at her nape held her fast, and something about that…lit her up. It was as if she didn't know what she was doing any longer. Or at all. But maybe he did.

And suddenly she was kneeling up higher, her hands flat on his thighs, her face tilted toward his in a manner she could have called all kinds of names.

All of them not the least bit her. Not the person she was or had ever been.

But maybe she was tired of Lauren Isadora Clarke. And everything she'd made herself become while she was so busy not feeling things.

Like this. Like him.

"It's not a real proposal until there's a kiss, Lauren," Dominik told her. Gruffly, she thought. "Even you must know this."

"Isn't it enough that I promised you a wedding night?" she asked, and she might have been horrified at the way her voice cracked at that, but there were so many horrors to sift through. Too many.

And all of them seemed to catch fire and burn brighter as she knelt there between his legs, not sure if she felt helpless or far more alarming, *alive*.

Alive straight through, which only made it clear that she never had been before. Not really.

"Kiss me, little red," he ordered her, almost idly. But there was no mistaking the command in his voice all the same. "Keep your promise."

His voice might have been soft, but it was ruthless. And his gray eyes were pitiless.

And he didn't seem to mind in the least when she scowled at him, because it was the only thing she knew how to do.

"Now, please," he murmured in that same demanding way. "Before you hurt my feelings."

She doubted very much that his feelings had anything to do with this, but she didn't say that. She didn't want to give him more opportunity to comment on hers. Or call her a robot again.

"I don't understand why you would want to kiss someone who doesn't wish to kiss you," she threw at him in desperation.

"I wouldn't." Those gray eyes laughed at her. "But that description doesn't apply to either one of us, does it?"

"One of us is under duress."

"One of us, Lauren, is a liar."

She could feel the heat that told her that her cheeks were red, and she had the terrible notion that meant he was right. And worse, that he could see it all over her face.

She had no idea.

In a panic, she mimicked him, hooking one hand around the hard column of his neck and pulling his mouth to hers.

This man who had agreed to marry her. To pretend, anyway, and there was no reason that should work in her the way it did, like a powder keg on the verge of exploding. Like need and loss and yearning, tangled all together in an angry knot inside her.

And she was almost used to this now. The delirious slide, the glorious fire, of their mouths together.

He let her kiss him, let her control the angle and the depth, and she made herself shiver as she licked her way into his mouth. All the while telling herself that she didn't like this. That she didn't want this.

And knowing with every drugging slide of his tongue against hers that he'd been right all along.

She was a liar.

Maybe that was why, when his hands moved to trace their way down her back, she moaned at the sensation instead of fighting it. And when he pulled her blouse from the waistband of her formal trousers, she only made a deeper noise, consumed with the glory of his mouth.

And the way he kissed her and kissed her, endless and intoxicating.

But then his bare hand was on her skin, moving around to the front of her and then finally—finally, as if she'd never wanted anything more when she'd never wanted it in the first place, when it had never occurred to her to imagine such a thing—closing over the swell of one breast.

And everything went white around the edges.

Her breast seemed to swell, filling his palm, with her nipple high and hard.

And every time he moved his palm, she felt it like another deep lick—

But this time in the hottest, wildest, most molten place of all between her legs.

She could feel his other hand in her hair, cradling the back of her head and holding her mouth where he wanted it, making absolutely no bones about the fact that he was in charge.

And it was thrilling.

Lauren arched her back, giving him more of her, and it still wasn't enough.

The kiss was wild and maddening at the same time, and she strained to get closer to him, desperate for something she couldn't name. Something just out of reach—

And when he set her away from him, with a dark little laugh, she thought she might die.

Then thought that death would be an excellent escape when reality hit her.

Because she was a disheveled mess on the floor of her office, staring up at the man who'd made her this way.

Perilously close to begging for things she couldn't even put into words.

She expected him to taunt her. To tell her she was a liar again, and remind her of all the ways he just proved it.

But Dominik stayed where he was, those gray eyes of his shuttered as he gazed back at her.

And she knew it was as good as admitting a weakness out loud, but she lifted her fingers and pressed them to her lips, not sure how she'd spent so many years on this earth without recognizing the way her own flesh could be used against her. And then tingle in the aftermath, like it wasn't enough.

As if she was sexual, after all.

"The company maintains a small number of corporate flats in this building," she managed to tell him when she'd composed herself a little, and she didn't sound like herself. She sounded like a prerecorded version of the woman she'd been when she'd left these offices to fly to Hungary. She wasn't sure she had access to that woman anymore. She wasn't sure she knew what had become of her.

But she was very sure that the creature she was now, right there at his feet, would be the undoing of her.

Assuming it wasn't already too late.

She climbed off the floor with as much dignity as she could muster. For the first time in her life, she cursed the fact that she wore such ridiculous shoes, with such high heels, that it was impossible to feel steady even when she was standing.

Right, a little voice inside her murmured archly. *Blame the shoes. It's definitely the* shoes.

"Corporate flats," he repeated after another long moment, that dark gaze all over her. "How…antiseptic."

But when she called down to the security desk to have one of the guards come and escort him there, he didn't argue.

Lauren told herself that she liked the space he left behind him. That it wasn't any kind of emptiness, but room for her to breathe.

And once she was alone, there was no one to see her when she sank down into her chair behind her desk, where she had always felt the most competent. There was no one to watch as she buried her face in her hands—still too hot, and no doubt too revealing—and let all those emotions she refused to look at and couldn't name spill down her cheeks at last.

CHAPTER EIGHT

BY MORNING SHE'D pulled herself together. The tears of the night before seemed to have happened to someone else. Someone far more fragile than Lauren had ever been, particularly in the crisp light of day. She showered in the bathroom off the executive suite, rinsing away any leftover emotion as well as the very long previous day, and changed into one of the complete outfits she kept at the office precisely for mornings like this.

Well. Perhaps not *precisely* like this. She didn't often plan and execute her own wedding. She'd worn her highest, most impractical pair of heels as a kind of tribute. And she was absolutely not thinking—much less overthinking—about the many questionable bargains she'd made with the strange man she'd found in the forest.

She knocked briskly on the door to the corporate flat at half nine on the dot, aware as she did that she didn't expect him to answer. A man as feral as Dominik was as likely to have disappeared in the night as a stray cat, surely—

But the door swung open. And Dominik stood there, dressed in nothing but a pair of casual trousers slung low on his hips, showing off acres and acres of...*him*.

For a moment—or possibly an hour—Lauren couldn't seem to do anything but gape at him.

"Did you imagine I would run off in the night?" he asked, reading her mind yet again. And not the most embarrassing part, for a change. She tried to swallow past the dryness in her throat. She tried to stop staring at all those ridges and planes and astonishing displays of honed male flesh. "I might have, of course, but there were restrictions in place."

She followed him inside the flat, down the small hall to the efficient kitchen, bright in the morning's summer sunlight. "You mean the security guards?"

He rounded the small counter and then regarded her over his coffee, strong enough that she could smell the rich aroma and blacker than sin. "I mean, Lauren, the fact I gave you my word."

Lauren had allowed sensation and emotion and all that non-sense to get the best of her last night, but that was over now. It had to be, no matter how steady that gray gaze of his was. Or the brushfires it kicked up inside her, from the knot in her belly to the heat in her cheeks. So she cleared her throat and waved the tablet she carried in his direction, completely ignoring the tiny little hint of something bright like shame that wiggled around in all the knots she seemed to be made of today.

"I've sorted everything out," she told him, aware that she sounded as pinched and knotted as she felt. "We will marry in an hour."

Dominik didn't change expression and still, she felt as if he was laughing at her.

"And me without my pretty dress," he drawled.

"The vicar is a friend of the Combe family," she said as if she hadn't heard him. And she had to order herself not to fuss with her own dress, a simple little shift that was perfect for the office. And would do for a fake wedding, as well. "I took the liberty of claiming that ours is a deep and abiding love that requires a special license and speed, so it would be best all round if you do not dispute that."

"I had no intention of disputing it," Dominik said in that dark, sardonic voice of his that made her feel singed. "After all, I am nothing but a simple, lonely hermit, good for nothing but following the orders of wealthy aristocrats who cannot be bothered to attend the fake weddings they insisted occur in the first place. I am beside myself with joy and anticipation that I, too, can serve your master from afar in whatever way he sees fit. Truly, this is the family I dreamed of when I was a child in the orphanage."

He displayed his joy and anticipation by letting that impossible mouth of his crook, very slightly, in one corner, and Lauren hated that it felt like a punch. Directly into her gut.

"It is the romance of it all that makes my heart beat faster, little red," Dominik continued, sounding very nearly merry. If she overlooked that hard gleam in his eyes. "If you listen, I am certain you can hear it."

Lauren placed her tablet down on the marble countertop in a manner that could only be described as pointed. Or perhaps aggressive. But she kept her eyes on Dominik as if he really was some kind of wolf. As if looking away—for even an instant—could be the death of her.

And it wasn't his heart that she could hear, pounding loud enough to take down the nearest wall. It was hers.

"Could you take this seriously?" she demanded. "Could you at least try?"

He studied her for another moment as he lifted his coffee to his mouth and took a deep pull. "I didn't run off in the night as I assure you I could have done if I wished, regardless of what laughable corporate security you think was in place. The vicar bears down on us even as we speak. How much more seriously do you imagine I can take this?"

"You agreed to do this, repeatedly. I'm not sure that *I* agreed to submit myself to your…commentary."

She didn't expect that smile of his, bright and fierce. "Believe me, Lauren, there are all manner of things you might find yourself submitting to over the course of this day. Do not sell yourself short."

And she hated when he did that. When he said things in that voice of his, and they swirled around inside her—heat and madness and something like hope—making it clear that he was referring to all those dark and thorny things that she didn't understand.

That she didn't *want* to understand, she told herself stoutly.

"I've already agreed," she reminded him, with more ferocity than was strictly required. But she couldn't seem to bite it back. She had always been in such control of herself that she'd never learned how to *take* control of herself. If there were steps toward becoming composed, she didn't know them, and she could blame that on Dominik, too. "There's no need for all these insinuations."

"You've agreed? I thought it was I who agreed. To everything. Like a house pet on a chain."

His voice was mild but his gaze was…not.

"You asked me for a wedding night," she reminded him, her heart still pounding like it wanted to knock her flat. "And you know that I keep my promises. Every time you've asked to kiss me, I've allowed it."

"Surrendered to it, one might even say, with notable enthusiasm. Once you get started."

"My point," she said through her teeth, not certain why she was suddenly so angry, only that she couldn't seem to keep it inside her, where she was shaky and too hot and not the least bit *composed*, "is that you don't have to continue with all the veiled references. Or even the euphemisms. You demanded sex in return for marrying me, and I agreed to give it to you. The end."

It was a simple statement of fact, she thought. There was no reason at all that he should stare at her that way as if he was stripping all the air from the flat. From the world.

"If it is so distasteful to you, Lauren, don't."

But his voice was too smooth. Too silky. And all she could hear was the undercurrent beneath it, which roared through her like an impenetrable wall of flame.

"Don't?" she managed to echo. "Is that an option?"

"While you are busy marinating in the injustice of it all, remind yourself that it is not I who tracked you down in the middle of a forest, then dragged you back to England. If I wish to go through with a sham marriage for the sheer pleasure of the wedding night you will provide me as lure, that is my business." Dominik tilted his head slightly to one side. "Perhaps you should ask yourself what you are willing to do for a paycheck. And why."

"It's a little more complicated than that."

"Is it? Maybe it is time you ask yourself what you *wouldn't* do if your Mr. Combe asked it. You may find the answers illuminating."

"You obviously enjoy keeping to yourself." Lauren wasn't sure why all that breathless fury wound around and around inside her, or why she wanted nothing more than to throw it at him. She only wished she could be sure of her aim. "But some people prefer to be on a team."

"The team that is currently enjoying a holiday in scenic Australia? Or the one left here with a list of instructions and a heretofore unknown half brother to civilize through the glorious institution of marriage?" He smirked. "Go team."

Her jaw ached and she realized, belatedly, that she was clenching her teeth. *"You agreed."*

"So I did." And all he was doing was standing there across a block of marble, so there was no reason he should make her feel so…dizzy. "But then again, so did you. Is that what this is about, little red? Are you so terrified of the things you promised me?"

That took the wind out of her as surely as if she'd fallen hard and landed worse.

"What does it matter if I'm terrified or not?" She only realized after she'd said it that it was as good as an admission. "Would it change your mind?"

"It might change my approach," he said, that gleaming, dark thing in his gaze again, and she didn't understand how or why it connected to all that breathlessness inside her. Almost as if it wasn't *fury* at all. "Then again, it might not."

"In any case, congratulations are in order," she managed to say, feeling battered for no good reason at all. "In short order you will have a wife. And shortly after that, a wedding night sacrifice, like something out of the history books."

He laughed, rich and deep, and deeper when she scowled at him. "Do you think to shame me, Lauren? There are any number of men who might stand before you and thunder this way and that about how they dislike the taste of martyrdom in their beds, but not me."

"I am somehow unsurprised."

Dominik didn't move and yet, again, Lauren felt as if he surrounded her. As if those hands of his might as well have been all over her. She felt as if they were.

"You're not terrified of me," he said with a quiet certainty that made her shake. "You're terrified of yourself. And all those things you told yourself you don't know how to feel." That laughter was still all over his face, but his gray gaze made her feel pinned to the floor where she stood. "You're terrified that you'll wake up tomorrow so alive with feeling you won't know who you are."

"Either that or even more bored than I am right now," she said, though her throat felt scraped raw with all the things she didn't say. Or scream.

"Yes, so deeply bored," he said, and laughed again. Then he leaned forward until he rested his elbows on the countertop between them, making it impossible to pretend she didn't see the play of his muscles beneath the acres and acres of smooth male skin that he'd clearly shared with the sun in that Hungarian clearing. "But tell me this, Lauren. Does your boredom make you wet?"

For a moment she couldn't process the question. She couldn't understand it.

Then she did, and a tide of red washed over her, igniting her from the very top of her head to the tender spaces between her toes. No one had ever asked her a question like that. She hadn't known, until right now, that people really discussed such things in the course of an otherwise more or less regular day. She told herself she was horrified. Disgusted. She told herself she didn't even know what he meant, only that it was vile. That *he* was.

But she did know what he meant.

And she was molten straight through, red hot and flush with it, and decidedly not bored.

"You have twenty minutes," she told him when she could be sure her voice was clipped and cold again. "I trust you will be ready?"

"I will take that as a yes," he rumbled at her, entirely too male and much too sure of himself. "You are so wet you can hardly stand still. Don't worry, little red. You might not know what to do about that. But I do."

He straightened, then rounded the counter. Lauren pulled herself taut and rigid as if he was launching an attack—then told herself it was sheer relief that wound its way through her when he made no move toward her at all. He headed toward the flat's bedroom instead.

"You're welcome to join me in the shower," he said over his shoulder, and she didn't have to see his face to know he was laughing at her. "If you dare."

And she was still standing right where he'd left her when she heard the water go on. Frozen solid at the edge of the counter with her hands in fists, curled up so tight her nails were digging into her palms.

She made herself uncurl her fingers, one at a time. She made herself breathe, shoving back the temper and the fury until she could see what was beneath it.

And see that once again, he was right. It was fear.

Not of him. But of herself.

And how very much she wanted to see, at last, what it was she'd been missing all this time.

That was the thought that had kept sneaking into her head over the course of the long night.

She'd hardly slept, there on that couch in her office where she spent more time than she ever had in the flat she shared with Mary. And Lauren had always prided herself on not feeling the things that others did. She'd congratulated herself on not being dragged into the same emotional quagmires they always were. It made her better at doing her job. It made it easier to navigate the corporate world.

But Dominik had forced her to face the fact that she *could* feel all kinds of things, she just…hadn't.

Lauren had spent so long assuring herself she didn't want the things she couldn't feel. Or couldn't have. Her parents' love, the happy families they made without her, the sorts of romantic and sexual relationships all her friends and colleagues were forever falling in and out of with such abandon. She'd told anyone who asked that she wasn't built for those sorts of entanglements.

Secretly, she'd always believed she was above them. That she was better than all that mess and regret.

But one day of kissing Dominik James on demand and she was forced to wonder—if it wasn't about better or worse, but about meeting someone who made her feel things she hadn't thought she could, where did that leave her except woefully inexperienced? And frozen in amber on a shelf of her own making?

Lauren didn't like that thought at all. She ran her hands over her sensible shift dress, her usual office wear, and tried to pretend that she wasn't shaking.

But what if you melted? whispered a voice deep inside her that she'd never heard before, layered with insinuation and something she was terribly afraid might be grief. *What if you let Dominik melt you as he pleased?*

She let out a breath she hadn't known she was holding. And she swayed on her feet, yet knew full well it wasn't because of the skyscraper height of her shoes.

And she entertained a revolutionary thought. If she had to

do this, anyway—if she was going to marry this man, and stay married to him for as long as it took to ride out the public's interest in yet another family scandal—shouldn't she take it as an opportunity?

She already knew that Dominik could make her feel things that she never had before. And yes, that was overwhelming. A mad, wild whirl that she hardly knew how to process. Especially when she'd been certain, all her life, that she wasn't capable of such things.

Maybe she didn't know how to want. But it had never occurred to her before now that she hadn't been born that way. That maybe, just maybe, that was because no one had ever wanted her—especially the people who should have wanted her the most.

She didn't know why Dominik wanted to play these games with her, but he did. He clearly did, or he wouldn't be here. Lauren was persuasive, but she knew full well she couldn't have forced that man to do a single thing he didn't want to do.

So why shouldn't she benefit, too?

She had spent a lot of time and energy telling herself that she didn't care that she was so clearly different from everyone else she met. That she was somehow set apart from the rest of the human race, unmoved by their passions and their baser needs. But what if she wasn't?

What if she wasn't an alien, after all?

That was what one of her kissing experiments had called her when she had declined his offer to take their experiment in a more horizontal direction. Among other, less savory names and accusations.

Just as Dominik had called her a robot.

What if she...wasn't?

What if she melted, after all?

Lauren waited until he reemerged from his bedchamber, dressed in a crisp, dark suit that confused her, it was so well-made. His hair was tamed, pushed back from his face, and he'd even shaved, showing off the cut line of his ruthlessly masculine jaw. He looked like what he was—the eldest son of the current generation of San Giacomos. But she couldn't concentrate on any of the surprisingly sophisticated male beauty he threw around him like light, because she knew that if she didn't say what she wanted right here and now, she never would.

"I will give you a wedding night," she told him.

"So we have already agreed," he said in that silky way of his that made her whole body turn to jelly. And her stomach doing flips inside her didn't exactly help. "Is this a renegotiation of terms?"

"If it takes more than one night, that's all right," she forced herself to tell him, though it made her feel queasy. And lightheaded. Especially when he stopped tugging at his shirt cuffs and transferred all his considerable attention to her. "I want to learn."

"Learn what?"

And maybe his voice wasn't particularly, dangerously quiet. Maybe it just sounded like that in her head, next to all that roaring.

"Everyone has all this sex," she said, the words crashing through her and out of her. She couldn't control them. She couldn't do anything but throw them across the room like bombs. "People walk around *consumed* by it, and I want to know why. I don't just mean I want you to take my virginity, though you will. And that's fine."

"I'm delighted to hear you're on board," he said drily, though it was the arrested sort of gleam in his eyes that she couldn't seem to look away from. Because it made her feel as if a great wind was blowing, directly at her, and there was nothing she could do to stop it. "No one likes an unenthusiastic deflowering. Gardening metaphors aside, it's really not all that much fun. Anyone who tells you otherwise has never had the pleasure. Or any pleasure, I can only assume."

"I have no idea what you're on about." He looked even more

taken aback by that, and she moved toward him—then thought better of it, as putting herself in arm's reach of this man had yet to end well for her. Even if that was her current goal. "I want to understand why people *yearn*. I want to understand what all the fuss is about. Why people—you among them—look at me like something's wrong with me if I say I'm not interested in it. Can you do that, Dominik?"

Maybe it was the first time she'd called him by his name. She wasn't sure, but she felt as if it was. And he looked at her as if she'd struck him.

"I've spent my whole life never quite understanding the people around me." And Lauren knew she would be horrified— later—that her voice broke then, showing her hand. Telling him even more than she'd wanted. "Never really getting the joke. Or the small, underlying assumptions that people make about the world because of these feelings they cart about with them wherever they go. I never got those, either. Just once I want to know what the big secret is. I want to know what all the songs are about. I want to know what so many parents feel they need to protect their children from. I want to *know*."

"Lauren…"

And she didn't recognize that look on his face then. Gone was the mocking, sardonic gleam in his eyes. The theatrics, the danger. The challenge.

She was terribly afraid that what she was seeing was pity, and she thought that might kill her.

"I know this is all a game to you," she said hurriedly, before he could crush her, and had that out-of-body feeling again. As if she was watching herself from far away, and couldn't do a single thing to stop the words that kept pouring out of her mouth. "Maybe you have your own dark reasons for wanting to do what Mr. Combe wants, and I don't blame you. Family dynamics are difficult enough when you've known the players all your life. But you said that there could be certain things that were between the two of us. That are only ours. And I want this to be one of them." Her heart was in her throat and she couldn't swallow it down. She could only hope she didn't choke on it. "I want to know *why*."

He straightened then, and she couldn't read the expression he wore. Arrested, still. But there was a different light in those near-silver eyes of his. He held out his hand, that gray gaze steady on hers, as if that alone could hold her up.

She believed it.

Lauren was tempted to call the way he was looking at her *kind*. And she had absolutely no idea why that should make her want to cry. Or how she managed to keep from doing just that when her sight blurred.

"Come," Dominik said, his voice gruff and sure as if he was already reciting his vows before the vicar. And more shocking by far, as if those vows meant something to him. "Marry me, little red, and I will teach you."

CHAPTER NINE

WHEN HE LOOKED back on this episode and cataloged his mistakes—something Dominik knew he would get to as surely as night followed day—he would trace it all back to the fatal decision to step outside his cabin and wait for the Englishwoman the innkeeper had called from town to tell him was headed his way.

It had seemed so innocuous at the time. No one ever visited his cabin, with or without an invitation, and he hadn't known what would come of entertaining the whims of the one woman who had dared come find him. He'd been curious. Especially when he'd seen her, gold hair gleaming and that red cloak flowing around her like a premonition.

How could he have known?

And now Dominik found himself in exactly the sort of stuffy, sprawling, stately home he most despised, with no one to blame but himself. Combe Manor sat high on a ridge overlooking the Yorkshire village that had once housed the mills that had provided the men who'd lived in this house a one-way ticket out of their humble beginnings.

They had built Combe Manor and started Combe Industries. Dominik had also fought his way out of a rocky, unpleasant start…but he'd chosen to hoard his wealth and live off by himself in the middle of the woods.

Dominik felt like an imposter. Because he was an imposter.

He might have shared blood with the distant aristocrat he'd seen on the screen in a London office, but he didn't share…this. Ancient houses filled with the kind of art and antiques that spoke of wealth that went far beyond the bank. It was nearly two centuries of having more. Of having everything, for that matter. It was generations of men who had stood where he did now, staring out the windows in a library filled with books only exquisitely educated men read, staring down at the village where, once upon a time, other men scurried about adding to the Combe coffers.

And he knew that the Combe family was brand-spanking-new in terms of wealth when stood next to the might and historic reach of the San Giacomos.

Dominik might share that blood, but he was an orphan. A street kid who'd lived rough for years and had done what was necessary to feed himself, keep himself clothed and find shelter. A soldier who had done his duty and followed his orders, and had found himself in situations he never mentioned when civilians were near.

Blood was nothing next to the life he'd lived. And he was surprised this fancy, up-itself house didn't fall down around his ears.

But when he heard the soft click of much too high heels against the floor behind him, he turned.

Almost as if he couldn't help himself.

Because the house still stood despite the fact he was here, polluting it. And more astonishing still, the woman who walked toward him, her blond hair shining and a wary look on her pretty face, was his wife.

His wife.

The ceremony, such as it was, had gone smoothly. The vicar had arrived right on time, and they had recited their vows in a pretty sort of boardroom high on top of the London building that housed his half brother's multinational business. Lauren had produced rings, proving that she did indeed think of everything, they had exchanged them and that was that.

Dominik was not an impulsive man. Yet, he had gone ahead and married a woman for the hell of it.

And he was having trouble remembering what *the hell of it* was, because all he could seem to think about was Lauren. And more specific, helping Lauren out of those impossible heels she wore. Peeling that sweet little dress off her curves, and then finally—*finally*—doing something about this intense, unreasonable hunger for her that had been dogging him since the moment he'd laid eyes on her.

The moment he'd stepped out of the shadows of his own porch and had put all of this into motion.

There had been no reception. Lauren had taken a detour to her office that had turned into several hours of work. Afterward she had herded him into another sleek, black car, then back to the same plane, which they'd flown for a brief little hop to the north of England. Another car ride from the airfield and here they were in an echoing old mausoleum that had been erected to celebrate and flatter the kinds of men Dominik had always hated.

It had never crossed his mind that he was one of them. He'd never wanted to be one of them.

And the fact he'd found out he was the very thing he loathed didn't change a thing. He couldn't erase the life he'd led up to this point. He couldn't pretend he'd had a different life now that he was being offered his rich mother's guilt in the form of an identity that meant nothing to him.

But it was difficult to remember the hard line he planned to take when this woman—his *wife*, to add another impossibility to the pile—stood before him.

"I have just spoken to Mr. Combe," she began, because, of course, she'd been off the moment they'd set foot in this house. Dominik had welcomed the opportunity to ask himself what on earth he was doing here while she'd busied herself with more calls and emails and tasks that apparently needed doing *at once*.

And Dominik had made any number of mistakes already. There was the speaking to her in the first place that he would have to unpack at some later date, when all of this was behind him. Besides, he'd compounded that error, time and again. He should never have touched her. He should certainly never have kissed her. He should have let her fly off back to London on her own, and he certainly, without any doubt, should never have married her.

The situation would almost be funny if it wasn't so…preposterous.

But one thing Dominik knew beyond a shadow of any doubt. He did not want to hear about his damned brother again. Not tonight.

"Do me this one favor, please," he said in a voice that came out as more of a growl than he'd intended. Or maybe it was exactly the growl that was called for, he thought, when her eyes widened. "This is our wedding night. We have a great many things to accomplish, you and I. Why don't we leave your Mr. Combe where he belongs—across the planet, doing whatever it is he does that requires you to do five times as much in support."

He expected her to argue. He was sure he could see the start of it kicking up all over her lovely face and in the way she held her shoulders so tight and high.

But she surprised him.

She held his gaze, folded her hands in front of her and inclined her head.

Giving him what he wanted.

And the same demon that had spurred him on from the start—pushing him to walk out onto that porch and start all of this in the first place—sat up inside him, clearly not as intimidated by a stately library and a grand old house the way he was.

"What's this?" he asked quietly. "Is that all it took to tame you, little red? A ring on your finger and a few vows in front of the vicar? That's all that was required to make you soft? Yield-ing? Obedient?"

She made a sound that could as easily have been a cough as a laugh. "I am not certain I would call myself any of those things, no matter what jewelry I wear on my fingers. But I agreed to the wedding night. And…whatever else. I have every intention of going through with it."

"You make it sound so appealing." He eyed her, not sure if he was looking for her weaknesses or better yet, the places she was likely to be most sensitive. "You could do worse than a lit-tle softness. Yielding will make it sweeter for the both of us. And obedience, well…"

He grinned at that, as one image after the next chased through his head.

"I've never been much good at that, either, I'm afraid." She said it with such confidence, tipping her chin up to go with it. And more than that, pride. "If you're looking for obedience, I'm afraid you're in for some disappointment."

"You cannot truly believe you are not obedient." He moved toward her, leaving the window—and its view of the ruins of the mills that had built this place—behind him. "You obey one man because he pays you. What will it take, I wonder, for you to obey your husband with even a portion of that dedication?"

And he had the distinct pleasure of watching her shiver, goose bumps telling him her secrets as they rippled to life on her skin.

He was so hard he thought it might hurt him.

Dominik crossed the vast expanse of the library floor until he was in front of her, and then he kept moving, wandering in a lazy circle around her as if she was on an auction block and he was the buyer.

Another image that pulsed in him like need.

"I asked you to teach me." And he could hear all the nerves crackling in her voice. As obvious as the goose bumps down the length of her arms. "Does that come with extra doses of humiliation or is that merely an add-on extra?"

"It's my lesson to teach, Lauren. Why don't you stop trying to top from the bottom?"

He'd made a full circle around her then, and faced her once more. And he reveled in the look on her face. Wariness and expectation. That sweet pink flush.

And a certain hectic awareness in her caramel-colored eyes.

She was without doubt the most beautiful woman he had ever seen. And she was his.

She had made herself his.

"What do you want me to do?" Lauren asked, her voice the softest he'd ever heard it.

He reached out to smooth his hand over all her gleaming blond hair, still pulled back in that sleek, professional ponytail. He considered that tidy ponytail part of her armor.

And he wanted none of that armor between them. Not tonight.

"It's time to play Rapunzel," he told her. When she only stared back at him, he tugged on the ponytail, just sharp enough to make her hitch in a breath. "Let down your hair, little red."

He watched the pulse in her throat kick into high gear. Her flush deepened, and he was fairly certain she'd moved into holding her breath.

But she obeyed him all the same, reaching back to tug the elastic out of her hair. When it was loose she ran her free hand through the mass of it, letting it fall where it would, thick and gold and smelling of apples.

She kept saying she didn't believe in fairy tales, but Dominik was sure he'd ended up in the midst of one all the same. And he knew the price of taking a bite out of a sweet morsel like Lauren, a golden-haired princess as innocent as she was sweet to look upon, but he didn't care. Bake him into a pie, turn him into stone—he meant to have this woman.

He made a low, rumbling sound of approval, because with her hair down she looked different. Less sharp. Less sleek. More accessible. The hair tumbled over her shoulders and made her seem…very nearly romantic.

Dominik remembered the things he'd promised her, and that ache in him grew sharper and more insistent by the second, so he simply bent and scooped her up into his arms.

She let out the breath she'd been holding in a kind of gasp, but he was already moving. He held her high against his chest, a soft, sweet weight in his arms, and after a startled moment she snuck her arms around his neck.

And that very nearly undid him.

The sort of massive, theatrical staircase that had never made sense to him dominated the front hall, and he took the left side, heading upstairs.

"Oh, the guest suites are actually—" she began, shifting in his arms and showing him that frown of hers he liked far too much.

"Is anyone else here?"

He already knew the answer. She had told him the house was empty when they'd landed in Yorkshire. She'd told him a lot of information about the house, the grounds, the village, the distant moors and mountains—as if she'd believed what he truly wanted today was a travelogue and a lecture on the Combe family.

"You know that Mr. Combe is in Australia, and his sister, Pia—" She cut herself off, her gaze locking to his. "Well. She's your sister, too, of course. And she is currently in the kingdom of Atilia."

"The island."

"Yes, it's actually several islands in the Ionian Sea—"

"I don't care." He didn't. Not about Matteo Combe or Pia Combe or anything at all but the woman in his arms. "How many beds are there in a house like this?"

"Fifteen," she replied, her gaze searching his. Then widening as he smiled.

"Never fear, Lauren. I intend to christen them all."

He took the first door he found, carrying her into a sprawling sitting room that led, eventually, into an actual bedroom. The bed itself was a massive thing, as if they'd chopped down trees that could have been the masts of ships to make all four posters, but Dominik found his normal disgust about class issues faded in the face of all the lovely possibilities.

There were just so many things an imaginative man could do with bedposts and a willing woman.

He set her down at the side of the bed and smiled wider when she had to reach out to steady herself. "Those shoes may well be the death of you. It is the shoes, is it not? And not something else entirely that leaves you so...unbalanced?"

She shot him a look, but she didn't say anything. She reached down, fiddled with the buckle around one delicate ankle, then kicked her shoe off. She repeated it on the other side, and when she was done she was nearly a foot shorter.

And then she smiled up at him, her gaze as full of challenge as it was of wariness.

"I didn't realize all the witty banter came as part of the package. I thought it would just be, you know, straight to it. No discussion."

"You could have gotten that in any pub you've ever set foot in with precious little effort on your part."

He shrugged out of the formal suit jacket he'd been wearing all day, like the trained monkey he'd allowed himself to become. And he was well aware of the convulsive way she swallowed, her gaze following his shoulders as if she couldn't bring herself to look away from him.

Dominik liked that a little too much. "Why didn't you?"

He started on his buttons then, one after the next, unable to keep his lips from quirking as she followed his fingers as they moved down his chest. And took much too long to raise her gaze back to his.

"Pardon?"

"If you were curious about experimenting with your nonsexual nature, Lauren, why not get off with a stranger after a few drinks? I think you'll find it's a tried and true method employed by people everywhere."

"As appealing as that sounds, I was never curious before. I was never curious before—"

She looked stricken the moment the words were out. And the word she'd been about to say hung between them as surely as if she'd shouted it. *You.*

I was never curious before you.

And Dominik felt...hushed. Something like humbled.

"Don't worry," he found himself saying, though his voice was gruff and he'd planned to be so much more smooth, more in control, hadn't he? "I promise you will enjoy this far more than a drunken fumble in the toilets after too much liquid courage and a pair of beer goggles."

She blinked as if she was imagining that, and Dominik didn't want a single thing in her head but him.

He tossed his shirt aside, then nodded at her. "Your dress, wife. Take it off."

Her breath shuddered out of her, and her hands trembled when she reached down to grip the hem of the shift dress she wore. She had to wiggle as she lifted it, peeling it up and off and displaying herself to him as she went.

Inch by luscious inch.

At last, he thought as she tossed the dress aside and stood there before him wearing nothing but a delicate lace bra that cupped her perfect breasts, and a pair of pale pink panties that gleamed a bit in the last of the light of the waning summer afternoon.

She made his mouth water.

And God, how she made him ache.

He reached over and put his hands on her, finally. He drew her hair over her shoulders, then followed the line of each arm. Down to find her fingers, particularly the one that wore his ring, then back up again. He found the throat where her pulse pounded out a rhythm he could feel in the hardest part of him, and each soft swell of her breast above the fabric that covered them and held them aloft.

She was like poured cream, sweet and rich, and so soft to the touch he had to bite back a groan. He traced his way over the tempting curve of her belly, her hips made for his hands, and then behind to her pert bottom.

She was warm already, but she became hot beneath his palms. And he was delighted to find that when she flushed, she turned bright red all the way down to her navel. Better by far than he'd imagined.

He dropped to his knees, wrapped his arms around her and dropped his mouth to a spot just below her navel, smiling when she jolted against him.

Because touching her wasn't enough. He wanted to taste her.

First, he retraced his steps, putting his mouth everywhere he could reach, relishing each shocked and greedy little noise she made. The way she widened her stance, then sagged back against the high bed as if her knees could no longer hold her. She buried her hands in his hair, but either she didn't know how to guide him, or didn't want to, so he made his own path.

And when her eyes looked blind with need, he reached up and unhooked her bra, carefully removing it so he could expose her breasts to his view.

Perfect. She was perfect, and he leaned in close so he could take his fill of her. He pulled one nipple deep into his mouth, sucking until she cried out.

And Dominik thought it was the most glorious sound he had ever heard.

When he was finished with both nipples, they stood harder and more proud. And she was gripping the bed sheets behind her, her head tipped back so all of her golden hair spread around her like a halo.

He shifted forward, lifting her up and setting her back on the bed so he could peel the panties from her hips.

As he pulled them down her satiny legs, she panted. And was making the slightest high-pitched sounds in the back of her throat, if he wasn't mistaken.

She only got louder when he lifted up her legs and set them on his shoulders so they dangled down his back, and then he lost himself in the fact he had full, unfettered access to all that molten sweetness between her legs.

The scent of her arousal roared in him, making him crazy.

Making him as close to desperate as he'd ever been.

He looked up and let his lips curve when he found her gazing back at him, a look of wonder on her face.

And something like disbelief in her eyes.

"You... My legs..." She hardly sounded like herself.

"All the better to eat you with, my dear," he said, dark and greedy.

And then he set his mouth to the core of her, and showed her exactly how real the fairy tales were, after all.

CHAPTER TEN

IT HIT HER like a punch, thick and deep, setting Lauren alight from the inside out.

It made her go rigid, then shake.

But that didn't stop Dominik.

Her husband.

He was licking into her as if he planned to go on forever. He was using the edge of his teeth, his wicked tongue and the scrape of his jaw. His shoulders kept her thighs apart, and he didn't seem to care that her hands were buried in his hair. And tugging.

And after the first punch, there was a different, deeper fire. A kind of dancing flame she hardly knew how to name, and then there was more.

A shattering.

As if there were new ways to burn, and Dominik was intent on showing her each and every one of them.

The third time she exploded, he pulled his mouth away from her, pressing his lips against her inner thigh so she could feel him smile.

He stood, hauling her with him as he went, and then somehow they were both in the middle of a giant bed in one of the family's suites she had never dared enter on her previous trips to Combe Manor.

He rolled over her, and Lauren realized she must have lost time somewhere, because he was naked, too. She had no memory of him stripping off his trousers.

Not that she cared.

Because she could feel him everywhere, muscled legs between her, and the heat of his skin. All that lean weight of his. The crispness of the hair that dusted his decidedly male body. His eyes were like silver, hot and indulgent at once, and he braced himself over her as she ran her hands down all the planes and ridges of his beautiful chest, the way she'd wanted to since he'd opened the door this morning.

It was finally her turn to touch him. And she was determined to touch *all* of him, with all the fascination she hadn't know she held inside her. But there was no denying it as she followed her fingers wherever they wanted to go. There was no pretending it didn't swell and dance inside her.

"I don't understand how a man can be so beautiful," she whispered, and if that was betraying herself the way she feared it was, she couldn't bring herself to care about that.

Because he took her mouth then, a hard, mad claiming, and it thrilled her.

She surged against him, unable to get close enough. Unable to process each and every sensation that rolled over her, spiraled around inside her and made her want nothing more than to press every part of her against every part of him.

And she could feel it then. The hardest part of him, there between them. Velvet and steel, insistent against the soft skin of her belly.

It made her shudder all over again.

He slanted his mouth over hers, and then his hands were working magic between them. She heard the faint sound of foil, and then he settled himself between her legs as if all this time, her whole life, she had been made to hold him just like this.

Dominik had asked her if she was wet before. And now she knew what he meant in an entirely different way.

But he growled his approval as his fingers found the neediest part of her, playing with her until she bucked against him, her head thrashing back against the mattress.

He lifted her knees, then settled himself even more completely between them, so he was flush against her.

"Tell me if you don't feel anything," he said, his voice nearly unrecognizable, there at her ear.

"If I don't..." she began.

But then she could feel him, there at her center.

He pressed against the resistance he found; her body protested enough to make her wince, and then it was over.

Or just beginning, really.

Because he kept pressing. In and in, and there was too much. She couldn't name the things she felt; she could barely experience them as they happened—

"Remember," and his voice was a growl again. "You are nonsexual, little red. You do not feel what others do. Is that how this feels?"

But she couldn't answer him.

She couldn't do anything but dig her fingers into his shoulders as he opened her, pressed deeper and stretched her farther still.

Then finally, and yet too soon, he stopped.

And for a moment he only gazed down at her, propped up on his elbows with nothing but silver in his gaze and that very nearly stern set to his mouth.

While he was buried completely within her body.

And the knowledge of that, mixed with the exquisite sensation, so full and so deep, made her break apart all over again.

Less like a fist this time, and more like a wave. Over and over, until it wore itself out against the shore.

And when she opened her eyes again, she could see Dominik's jaw clenched tight and something harder in his gaze. Determination, perhaps.

"You're killing me," he gritted out.

She tried to catch her breath. "Am I doing it wrong?"

And he let out a kind of sigh, or maybe it was a groan, and he dropped down to gather her even more firmly beneath him.

"No, little red, you're not doing it wrong."

But she thought he sounded tortured as he said it.

Then Lauren couldn't care about that, either, because he began to move.

And it was everything she'd never known she wanted. She had never known she could want at all. It was the difference between a dark, cloudy sky, and a canopy of stars.

And she couldn't breathe. She couldn't *think*. She could only feel.

She was all sensation. All greed and passion, longing and desire, and all of it focused on the man who moved within her, teaching her with every thrust.

About need. About want.

About everything she had been missing, all these lonely years.

He taught her about hope, and he taught her about wonder, and still he kept on.

Lesson after lesson, as each thrust made it worse. Better.

As he made her undeniably human, flesh and passion made real, as surely as any kiss in a fairy tale story.

Until there was nothing between them but fire.

The glory of flames that danced and consumed them, made them one, and changed everything.

And when she exploded that time, he went with her.

He shouldn't have gone out on that porch, Dominik thought grimly a long while later as the sky outside darkened to a mysterious deep blue, and Lauren lay sprawled against his chest, her breathing even and her eyes closed.

He should have stayed in Hungary. He should have laughed off the notion that he was an heir to anything.

And he never, ever should have suggested that they make this marriage real.

He felt…wrecked.

And yet he couldn't seem to bring himself to shift her off him. It would be easy enough to do. A little roll, and he could leave her here. He could leave behind this great house and all its obnoxious history. He could pretend he truly didn't care about the woman who'd rid herself of him, then later chosen this.

But he had promised to take part in this whole charade, hadn't he? He'd promised not only to marry Lauren, but to subject himself to the rest of it, too. Hadn't she mentioned comportment? The press?

It was his own fault that he'd ended up here. He accepted that.

But he could honestly say that it had never occurred to him that sex with Lauren could possibly be this…ruinous.

Devastating, something in him whispered.

He hadn't imagined that anything could get to him. Nothing had in years. And no woman had ever come close.

Dominik had never experienced the overwhelming sensation that he wasn't only naked in the sense of having no clothes on—he was naked in every sense. Transparent with it, so anyone who happened by could see all the things in him he'd learned to pack away, out of view. First, as an orphan who had to try his best to act perfect for prospective parents. Then as a kid on the street who had to act tough enough to be left alone. Then as a soldier who had to act as if nothing he was ordered to do stayed with him.

And he couldn't say he much cared for the sensation now.

He needed to get up and leave this bed. He needed to go for a long, punishing run to clear his head. He needed to do something physical until he took the edge off all the odd things swirling around inside him, showing too much as if she'd knocked down every last boundary he had, and Dominik certainly couldn't allow that—

But she stirred then, shifting all that smooth, soft heat against him, and a new wave of intense heat washed over him.

She let out a sigh that sounded like his name, and what was he supposed to do with that?

Despite himself, he held on to her.

Especially when she lifted her head, piled her hands beneath her chin and blinked up at him.

And the things he wanted to say appalled him.

He cleared his throat. "Do you feel sufficiently indoctrinated into the sport?"

He hardly recognized his own voice. Or that note in it that he was fairly certain was...playfulness? And his hands were on her curves as if he needed to assure himself that they were real. That she was.

"Is it a sport? I thought of it more as a pastime. A habit, perhaps." She considered it, and what was wrong with him that he enjoyed watching a woman *think*? "Or for some, I suppose, an addiction."

"There are always hobbyists and amateurs, little red," he found himself saying, a certain...*warmth* in his voice that he wanted to rip out with his own fingers. But he didn't know where to start. "But I have never counted myself among them."

He meant to leave, and yet his hands were on her, smoothing their way down her back, then cupping her bottom. He knew he needed to let her go and make sure this never happened again, but she was smiling.

And he hardly knew her. Gone was all that sharpness, and in its place was a kind of soft, almost dreamy expression that made his chest hurt.

As if she was the one teaching him a lesson here.

"I beg your pardon. I didn't realize I was addressing such a renowned star of the bedroom," she said, and her lovely eyes danced with laughter.

It only served to remind him that she didn't laugh nearly enough.

"I will excuse it," he told her. "Once."

He needed to put distance between them. Now. Dominik

knew that the way he knew every other fact of his existence. He knew it like every single memory he had of the nuns. The streets. The missions he'd been sent on.

He wasn't a man built for connection. He didn't want to be the kind of man who could connect with people, because people were what was wrong with the world. People had built this house. A person had given him away. He wanted nothing to do with *people*, or he never would have taken himself off into the woods in the first place.

But this pretty, impossible person was looking at him as if he was the whole world, her cheeks heating into red blazes he couldn't keep from touching. He ran his knuckles over one, then the other, silky smooth and wildly hot.

"It is still our wedding night," she pointed out.

"So it is."

Lauren lowered her lashes, then traced a small pattern against his chest with one fingertip.

"I don't know how this works. Or if you can. Physically, I mean. But I wondered… I mean, I hoped…" She blew out a breath. "Was that the whole of the lesson?"

And Dominik was only a man, after all, no matter how he'd tried to make himself into a monster, out there in his forest. And the part of him that had been greedy for her since the moment he'd seen her could never be happy with so small a taste.

Will you ever be satisfied? a voice in him asked. *Or will you always want more?*

That should have sent him racing for the door. He needed to leave, right now, but he found himself lifting her against him instead. He drew her up on her knees so she straddled him, and watched as she looked down between them, blinked and then smiled.

Wickedly, God help him.

"By all means," he encouraged her, his hands on her hips. "Allow me to teach you something else I feel certain you won't feel, as shut off and uninterested in these things as you are."

She found him then, wrapping her hands around the hardest expression of his need and guiding him to the center of her heat.

As if she'd been born for this. For him.

"No," she murmured breathlessly. And then smiled as she took him inside her as if he'd been made to fit her so perfectly, just like that. "I don't expect I'll feel anything at all."

And there was nothing for it. There was no holding back.

Dominik gave himself over to his doom.

CHAPTER ELEVEN

THE SITUATION DID not improve as the days slid by and turned inevitably into weeks.

Dominik needed to put a stop to the madness. There was no debate on that topic. The pressing need to leave the mess he'd made here, get the hell out of England, and away from the woman he never should have married, beat in him like a drum. It was the first thing he thought of when he woke. It dogged him through the long summer days. It even wormed its way into his dreams.

But one day led into the next, and he went nowhere. He didn't even try to leave as if he was the one who'd wandered into the wrong forest and found himself under some kind of spell he couldn't break.

Meanwhile, they traded lesson for lesson.

"I know how to use utensils, little red," he told her darkly one morning after he'd come back from a punishing run—yet not punishing enough, clearly, as he'd returned to Combe Manor—and had showered and changed only to find the formal dining room set with acres of silver on either side of each plate. There was a mess of glasses and extra plates everywhere he looked.

And Lauren sat there with her hair pulled back into the

smooth ponytail he took personally and that prissy look on her face.

The very same prissy look that made him hard and greedy for her, instantly.

"This won't be a lesson about basic competence with a fork, which I'll go ahead and assume you mastered some time ago," she told him tartly. Her gaze swept over him, making him feel as if he was still that grubby-faced orphan, never quite good enough. He gritted his teeth against it, because that was the last thing he needed. The present was complicated enough without dragging in the past. "This will be about formal manners for formal dinners."

"Alternatively, I could cook for myself, eat with own my fingers if I so desire and continue to have the exact same blood in my veins that I've always had with no one the least bit interested either way. None of this matters."

He expected her to come back at him, sharp and amusing, but she didn't. She studied him for a moment instead, and he still didn't know how to handle the way she looked at him these days. It was softer. Warmer.

It was too dangerous. It scraped at him until he felt raw and he could never get enough of it, all the same.

"It depends on your perspective, I suppose," she said. "It's not rocket science, of course. The fate of the world doesn't hang in the balance. History books won't be written about what fork you use at a banquet. But the funny thing about manners is that they can often stand in for the things you lack."

"And what is it I lack, exactly? Be specific, please. I dare you."

"I'm talking about me, Dominik. Not you."

And when she smiled, the world stopped.

He told himself it was one more sign he needed to get away from her. Instead, he took the seat opposite her at the table as if he really was under her spell.

Why couldn't he break it?

"When I was nine my parents had been divorced for two years, which means each of them was married again. My stepmother was pregnant. I didn't know it at the time, but my mother was, too. I still thought that they should all be spending a great deal more time with me. So one day I decided I'd run away, thereby forcing them to worry about me, and then act like parents."

She smiled as if at the memory, but it wasn't a happy smile. And later Dominik would have to reflect on how and why he knew the difference between her *smiles*, God help him. As if he'd made a study against his will, when he wasn't entirely paying attention.

"I rode the buses around and around, well into the evening," she said with that same smile. "And they came together, just as I'd hoped, but only so they could blame each other for what a disaster I was. Within an hour of my return they'd agreed to send me off to boarding school for the summer, so others could deal with me and they wouldn't have to do it themselves."

"I understand that not all parents are good ones," Dominik said, his voice low. "But I would caution you against complaining about your disengaged, yet present, parents while in the presence of a man who had none. Ever. Disengaged or otherwise."

"I'm not complaining about them," Lauren replied quietly. "They are who they are. I'm telling you how I came to be at a very posh school for summer. It was entirely filled with children nobody wanted."

"Pampered children, then. I can assure you no orphanage is *posh*."

"Yes. Someone, somewhere, paid handsomely to send us all to that school. But it would have been hard to tell a lonely nine-year-old, who knew she was at that school because her parents didn't want anything to do with her, that she was *pampered*. Mostly, I'm afraid, I was just scared."

Dominik stared back at her, telling himself he felt nothing. Because he ought to have felt nothing. He had taught her that sensation was real and that she could feel it, but he wanted none of it himself. No sensation. No emotion.

None of this scraping, aching thing that lived in him now that he worried might crack his ribs open from the inside. Any minute now.

"They taught us manners," Lauren told him in the same soft, insistent tone. "Comportment. Dancing. And it all seemed as stupid to me as I'm sure it does to you right now, but I will tell you this. I have spent many an evening since that summer feeling out of place. Unlike everyone else my age at university, for example, with all their romantic intrigue. These days I'm often trotted off to a formal affair where I am expected to both act as an emblem for Combe Industries as well as blend into the background. All at once. And do you know what allows me to do that? The knowledge that no matter what, I can handle myself in any social situation. People agonize over which fork to choose and which plate is theirs while I sit there, listening to conversations I shouldn't be hearing, ready and able to do my job."

"Heaven forbid anything prevent you from doing your job."

"I like my job."

"Do you? Or do you like imagining that your Mr. Combe cannot make it through a day without you?" He shrugged when she glared at him. "We are all of us dark creatures in our hearts, little red. Think of the story from the wolf's point of view next time. Our Red Riding Hood doesn't come off well, does she?"

He thought she had quite a few things to say to that, but she nodded toward the silverware before them instead. "We'll work from the outside in, and as we go we'll work on appropriate dinner conversation at formal occasions, which does not include obsessive references to fairy tales."

Dominik couldn't quite bring himself to tell her that he already knew how to handle a formal dinner, thank you. Not when she thought she was giving him a tool he could use to *save himself*, no less.

Just as he couldn't bring himself—allow himself—to tell

her all those messy things that sloshed around inside him at the thought of her as a scared nine-year-old, abandoned by her parents and left to make *manners* her sword and shield.

He showed her instead, pulling her onto his lap before one of the interminable courses and imparting his own lesson. Until they were both breathing too heavily to care that much whether they used the correct fork—especially when his fingers were so talented.

He meant to leave the following day, but there was dancing, which meant he got to hold Lauren in his arms and then sweep her away upstairs to teach her what those bed posts were for. He meant to leave the day after that, but she'd had videos made of all the San Giacomo holdings.

There was something every day. Presentations on all manner of topics. Lessons of every description, from comportment to conversation and back again. Meetings with the unctuous, overly solicitous tailors, who he wanted to hate until they returned with beautiful clothes even he could tell made him look like the aristocrat he wasn't.

Which he should have hated—but couldn't, not when Lauren looked at him as if he was some kind of king.

He needed to get out of there, but he had spent an entire childhood making up stories about his imaginary family in his head. And he didn't have it in him to walk away from the first person he'd ever met who could tell him new stories. Real stories, this time.

Because Lauren also spent a significant part of every day teaching him the history of the San Giacomos, making sure he knew everything there was to know about their rise to power centuries ago. Their wealth and consequence across the ages.

And how it had likely come to pass that a sixteen-year-old heiress had been forced to give up her illegitimate baby, whether she wanted to or not.

He found that part the hardest to get his head around—likely because he so badly wanted to believe it.

"You must have known her," he said one day as summer rain danced against the windows where he stood.

They were back in the library, surrounded by all those gleaming, gold-spined books that had never been put on their self-important shelves for a man like him, no matter what blood ran in his veins. Lauren sat with her tablet before her, stacks of photo albums arrayed on the table, and binders filled with articles on the San Giacomo family. All of them stories that were now his, she told him time and time again. And all those stories about a family that was now his, too.

Dominik couldn't quite believe in any of it.

He'd spent his childhood thirsty for even a hint of a real story to tell about his family. About himself. Then he'd spent his adulthood resolved not to care about any of it, because he was making his own damned story.

He couldn't help thinking that this was all…too late. That the very thing that might have saved him as a child was little more than a bedtime story to him now, with about as much impact on his life.

"Alexandrina," he elaborated when Lauren frowned at him. "You must have known my mother while she was still alive."

And he didn't know how to tell her how strange those words felt in his mouth. *My mother.* Bitter and sweet. Awkward. Unreal. *My mother* was a dream he'd tortured himself with as a boy. Not a real person. Not a real woman with a life, hopes and dreams and possibly even *reasons.*

It had never occurred to him that his anger was a gift. Take that away and he had nothing but the urge to find compassion in him somewhere…and how was a man meant to build his life on that?

"I did know her," Lauren said. "A little."

"Was she…?"

But he didn't know what to ask. And he wasn't sure he wanted to know the answers.

"I couldn't possibly be a good judge." Lauren was choosing her words carefully. And Dominik didn't know when he'd become so delicate that she might imagine he needed special handling. "I worked for her son, so we were never more than distantly polite the few times we met. I don't know that any impression I gleaned of her would be the least bit worthwhile."

"It is better than no impressions, which is what I have."

Lauren nodded at that. "She was very beautiful."

"That tells me very little about her character, as I think you know."

"She could be impatient. She could be funny." Lauren thought a moment. "I think she was very conscious of her position."

"Meaning she was a terrible snob."

"No, I don't think so. Not the way you mean it. I never saw her treat anyone badly. But she had certain standards that she expected to have met." She smiled. "If she was a man, people would say she knew her own mind, that's all."

"I've read about her." And he had, though he had found it impossible to see anything of him in the impossibly glamorous creature who'd laughed and pouted for the cameras, and inspired so many articles about her *style*, which Dominik suspected was a way to talk about a high-class woman's looks without causing offense. "She seemed entirely defined by her love affairs and scandals."

"My abiding impression of her was that she had learned how to be pretty. And how to use that prettiness to live up to the promise of both the grand families she was a part of. But I don't think it ever occurred to her that she could be happy."

"Could she?" Dominik asked, sardonic straight through. "I didn't realize that was on offer."

"It should always be on offer," Lauren replied with a certain quiet conviction that Dominik refused to admit got to him. Because it shouldn't have. "Isn't that the point?"

"The point of what, exactly?"

"Everything, Dominik."

"You sound like an American advertisement," Dominik said

after a moment, from between his teeth. "No one is owed happiness. And certainly, precious few find it."

He hadn't meant to move from the windows, but he had. And he was suddenly standing in front of that sofa, looking down at Lauren.

Who gazed straight back at him, that same softness on her face. It connected directly to that knot inside him he'd been carrying for weeks now. That ache. That infernal clamoring on the inside of his ribs that demanded he leave, yet wouldn't let him go.

"Maybe if we anticipated happiness we might find a little along the way." Her voice was like honey, and he knew it boded ill. He knew it was bad for him. Because he had no defenses against that kind of sweetness. Caramel eyes and honey voice— and he was a goner. "Why not try?"

"I had no idea that our shabby little marriage of convenience would turn so swiftly into an encounter group," he heard himself growl. When she didn't blanch at that the way he'd expected she would, he pushed on. "So-called happiness is the last refuge and resort of the dim-witted. And those who don't know any better, which I suppose is redundant. I think you'll find the real world is a little too complicated for platitudes and whistling as you work."

Lauren lifted one shoulder, then dropped it. "I don't believe that."

And it was the way she said it that seemed to punch holes straight through Dominik's chest. There was no defiant tilt to her chin. There was no angry flash of temper in her lovely eyes. It was a simple statement, more powerful somehow for its softness than for any attempt at a show of strength.

And there was no reason he should feel it shake in him like a storm.

"You don't believe that the world is a terrible place, as complicated as it is harsh, desperate people careening about from greed to self-interest and back again? Ignoring their children or abandoning them in orphanages as they see fit?"

"The fact that people can be awful and scared only means that when we happen upon it, we should cling to what happiness we can."

"Let me guess. You think I should be more grateful that after all this time, the woman who clearly knew where I was all along told others where to find me. But only after her death, so they could tell me sad stories about how she *might* have given me away against her will. You want me to conclude that I ended up here all the same, so why dwell on what was lost in the interim? You will have to forgive me if I do not see all this as the gift you do."

"The world won't end if you allow the faintest little gleam of optimism into your life," Lauren said with that same soft conviction that got to him in ways he couldn't explain. And didn't particularly want to analyze. "And who knows? You could even allow yourself to hope for something. Anything. It's not dimwitted and it's not because a person doesn't see the world as it is." Her gaze was locked to his. "Hope takes strength, Dominik. Happiness takes work. And I choose to believe it's worth it."

"What do you know of either?" he demanded. "You, who locked yourself away from the world and convinced yourself you disliked basic human needs. You are the poster child for happiness?"

"I know because of you."

The words were so simple.

And they might as well have been a tornado, tearing him up.

"Me." He shook his head as if he didn't understand the word. As if she'd used it to bludgeon him. "If I bring you *happiness*, little red, I fear you've gone and lost yourself in a deep, dark woods from which you will never return."

She stood up then, and he was seized with the need to stop her somehow. As if he knew what she was going to say when of course, he couldn't know. He refused to know.

He should have left before this happened.

He should have left.

His gaze moved over her, and it struck him that while he'd certainly paid close attention to her, he hadn't truly *looked* at her since they'd arrived here weeks ago. Not while she was dressed. She wasn't wearing the same sharp, pointedly professional clothing any longer—and he couldn't recall the last time she had. Today she wore a pair of trousers he knew were soft like butter, and as sweetly easy to remove. She wore a flowing sort of top that drooped down over one shoulder, which he liked primarily because it gave him access to the lushness beneath.

Both of those things were clues, but he ignored them.

It was the hair that was impossible to pretend hadn't changed.

Gone was the sleek ponytail, all that blond silk ruthlessly tamed and controlled. She wore it loose now, tumbling around her shoulders, because he liked his hands in it.

Had he not been paying attention? Or had he not wanted to see?

"Yes, you," she said, answering the question he'd asked, and all the ones he hadn't. "You make me happy, Dominik. And hopeful. I'm sorry if that's not what you want to hear."

She kept her gaze trained on his, and he didn't know what astounded him more. That she kept saying these terrible, impossible things. Or that she looked so fearless as she did it, despite the color in her cheeks.

He wanted to tell her to stop, but he couldn't seem to move.

And she kept right on going. "I thought I knew myself, but I didn't. I thought I knew what I needed, but I had no idea. I asked you to teach me and I meant very specifically about sex. And you did that, but you taught me so much more. You taught me everything." She smiled then, a smile he'd never seen before, so tremulous and full of hope—and it actually hurt him. "I think you made me whole, Dominik, and I had no idea I wasn't already."

If she had thrust a sword into the center of his chest, then slammed it home, he could not have felt more betrayed.

"I did none of those things," he managed to grit out. "Sex is not happiness. It is not hope. And it is certainly no way to go looking for yourself, Lauren."

"And yet that's who I found." And she was still aiming that smile at him, clearly unaware that she was killing him. "Follow the bread crumbs long enough, even into a terrible forest teeming with scary creatures and wolves like men, and there's no telling what you'll find at the other end."

"I know exactly what you'll find on the other end. Nothing. Because there's no witch in a gingerbread house. There's no Big Bad Wolf. You were sent to find me by a man who was executing a duty, nothing more. And I came along with you because—"

"Because why, exactly?" Again, it was the very softness and certainty in her voice that hit him like a gut punch. "You certainly didn't have to invite me into your cabin. But you did."

"Something I will be questioning for some time to come, I imagine." Dominik slashed a hand through the air, but he didn't know if it was aimed at her—or him. "But this is over, Lauren. You had your experiment and now it's done."

"Because I like it too much?" She had the audacity to laugh. "Surely, you've done this before, Dominik. Surely, you knew the risks. If you open someone up, chances are, they're going to like it. Isn't that what you wanted? Me to fall head over heels in love with you like every virgin cliché ever? Why else would you have dedicated yourself to *my experiment* the way you did?"

He actually backed away from her then. As if the word she'd used was poison. Worse than that. A toxic bomb that could block out the sun.

It felt as if she'd blinded him already.

"There is no risk whatsoever of anyone falling in love with me," he told her harshly.

"I think you know that isn't true." She studied him as if he'd disappointed her, as if he was *currently* letting her down, right there in full view of all the smug volumes of fancy books he'd never read and never would. "I assumed that was why you stayed all this time."

"I stayed all this time because that was the deal we made."

"The deal we made was for a wedding night, Dominik. Maybe a day or so after. It's been nearly two months."

"It doesn't matter how long it's been. It doesn't matter why. I'm glad that you decided you can feel all these emotions." But he wasn't glad. He was something far, far away from *glad*. "But I don't. I won't."

"But you do." And that was the worst yet. Another betrayal, another weapon. Because it was so matter-of-fact. Because she stared right back at him as if she knew things about him he didn't, and that was unbearable. Dominik had never been *known*. He wanted nothing to do with it. "I think you do."

And Dominik never knew what he might have said to that— how he might have raged or, more terrifying, how he might not have—because the doors to the library were pushed open then, and one of Combe Manor's quietly competent staff members stood there, frowning.

"I'm sorry to interrupt," she said, looking back and forth between them. "But something's happened, I'm afraid." She gestured in the direction of the long drive out front. "There are reporters. Everywhere. Cameras, microphones and shouting."

The maid's eyes moved to Dominik, and he thought she looked apologetic. When all he could feel was that emptiness inside him that had always been there and always would. Even if now, thanks to Lauren, it ached.

The maid cleared her throat. "They're calling for you, sir. By name."

CHAPTER TWELVE

IN THE END, Lauren was forced to call the Yorkshire Police to encourage the paparazzi to move off the property, down to the bottom of the long drive that led to Combe Manor from the village proper and away from the front of the house itself.

But the damage was done. The will had been leaked, as Lauren had known it would be eventually, and Dominik had been identified. That he had quietly married his half brother's longtime personal assistant had made the twenty-four-hour news cycle.

She quickly discovered that she was nothing but a shameless gold digger. There was arch speculation that Matteo had dispatched her to corral Dominik, marry him under false pretenses and then…work him to Matteo's advantage somehow.

It was both close to the truth and nothing like the truth at all, but any impulse she might have had to laugh at it dissipated in the face of Dominik's response.

Which was to disappear.

First, he disappeared without actually going anywhere. It was like looking into a void. One moment she'd been having a conversation—admittedly, not the most pleasant conversation—with him. The next, it was as if the Dominik she'd come to know was gone and a stranger had taken his place.

A dark, brooding stranger, who looked at her with icy disinterest. And as far as she could tell, viewed the paparazzi outside the same. He didn't call her *little red* again, and she would have said she didn't even like the nickname.

But she liked it even less when he stopped using it.

Her mobile rang and rang, but she ignored the calls. From unknown numbers she assumed meant more reporters. From Pia, who had likely discovered that she had another brother from the news, which made Lauren feel guilty for not insisting Matteo tell her earlier. And from the various members of the Combe Industries Board of Directors, which she was more than happy to send straight to voice mail.

"It's Mr. Combe," she said when it rang another time. "At last."

"You must take that, of course," Dominik said, standing at the windows again, glaring off into the distance. "Heaven forfend you do not leap to attention the moment your master summons you."

And Lauren couldn't say she liked the way he said that. But she didn't know what to do about it, either.

"We always knew this day would come," she told him, briskly, when she'd finished having a quick damage control conversation with Matteo. "It's actually surprising that didn't happen sooner."

"We have been gilding this lily for weeks now," Dominik replied, his voice that dark growl that made everything in her shiver—and not entirely from delight. "We have played every possible Pygmalion game there is. There is nothing more to be accomplished here."

"Where would you like to go instead?" She had opened up the cabinet and turned on the television earlier, so they could watch the breathless news reports and the endless scroll of accusation and speculation at the bottom of the screen. Now she turned the volume up again so she could hear what they were saying. About her. "I suppose we should plan some kind of function to introduce you to—"

"No."

"No? No, you don't want to be introduced to society? Or no, you don't want—"

"You fulfilled your role perfectly, Lauren." But the way he said it was no compliment. It was…dangerous. "Your Mr. Combe will be so proud, I am sure. You have acted as my jailer. My babysitter. And you have kept me out of public view for very nearly two months, which must be longer than any of you thought possible. You have my congratulations. I very nearly forgot your purpose in this."

His voice didn't change when he said that. And he didn't actually reach out and strike her.

But it felt as if he did.

"I thought this would happen sooner, as a matter of fact," Lauren managed to say, her heart beating much too wildly in her chest. Her head spinning a little from the hit that hadn't happened. "And my brief was to give you a little polish and a whole lot of history, Dominik. That's all. I found a hermit in a hut. All Mr. Combe asked me to do was make you a San Giacomo."

"And now I am as useless as any one of them. You've done your job well. You are clearly worth every penny he pays you."

It was harder to keep her cool than it should have been. Because she knew too much now. He was acting like a stranger, but her body still wanted him the way it always did. He had woken her this morning by surging deep inside her, catapulting her from dreams tinged with the things he did to her straight into the delirious reality.

She didn't know how to handle this. The distance between them. The fury in his dark gaze. The harsh undercurrent to everything he said, and the way he looked at her as if she had been the enemy all along.

She should have known that the price of tasting happiness—of imagining she could—meant that the lack of it would hurt her.

More than hurt her. Looking at him and seeing a stranger made her feel a whole lot closer to broken.

She should have known better than to let herself *feel*.

"I know this feels like a personal attack," she said, carefully, though she rather thought she'd been the one personally attacked. "But this is about how the San Giacomo and Combe families are perceived. And more, how Matteo and his sister have been portrayed in the press in the wake of their father's death. No one wanted you to be caught up in that."

"And yet here I am."

"Dominik. Please. This is just damage control. That's the only reason Mr. Combe didn't proclaim your existence far and wide the moment he knew of you."

That gaze of his swung to her and held. Hard, like another blow. It made her want to cry—but she knew, somehow, that would only make it worse.

"You cannot control damage, Lauren. I would think you, of all people, would know this. You can only do your best to survive it."

And she had no time to recover from that.

Because that was when the self-satisfied newscaster on the television screen started talking about who Dominik James really was.

"We've just been made aware that Dominik James is not merely the long-lost heir to two of Europe's most prominent families," the man said. "Our sources tell us he is also a self-made billionaire who ran his own security company until he sold it recently for what is believed to be a small fortune in its own right. Dominik himself has been widely sought after by celebrities and kings alike, and a number of governments besides."

Then they flashed pictures of him, in case Lauren had somehow missed the implications. There were shots of Dominik in three-piece suits, his hair cropped close to his head, shaking hands with powerful, recognizable men. In and out of formal balls, charity events and boardrooms.

Nothing like a feral hermit at all.

"Oh, dear," Dominik said when the newscast cut to some

inane commercial, too much darkness in his voice. "Your table settings will not save you now, Lauren. It has all been a lie. I am not at all who you thought I was. Why don't you tell me more about how happy you are?"

And Lauren remembered exactly why she'd decided emotion wasn't for her. She had been nine years old and sent off to a terrifying stone building filled with strangers. She'd stayed awake the whole of that first night, sobbing into her pillow so her roommate didn't hear her.

Since then, she'd forgotten that these terrible emotions could sit on a person like this. Crushing her with their weight. Suffocating her, yet never quite killing her.

Making her own heartbeat feel like an attack.

"You didn't need me at all," she managed to say, parts of her breaking apart on the inside like so many earthquakes, stitched together into a single catastrophe she wasn't sure she would survive. No matter what he'd said about damage.

But she didn't want to let him see it.

"No," Dominik said, and there was something terrible there in his gray eyes that made her want to reach out to him. Soothe him somehow. But his voice was so cold. Something like cruel, and she didn't dare. "I never needed you."

"This was a game, then." She didn't know how she was speaking when she couldn't feel her own face. Her outsides had gone numb, but that paralysis did not extend inside, where she was desperately trying to figure out what to do with all that raw upheaval before it broke her into actual pieces. "You were just playing a game. I can understand that you wanted to find out who your family really was. But you were playing the game with me."

And maybe later she would think about how he stood there, so straight and tall and bruised somehow, that it made her ache. With that look on his face that made her want to cry.

But all she could do at the moment was fight to stay on her feet, without showing him how much he was hurting her. It was crucial that she swallow that down, hide it away, even as it threatened to cut her down.

"Life is damage, Lauren," he said in that same dark, cold way. "Not hope. Not happiness. Those are stories fools tell to trick themselves into imagining otherwise. The true opiate of the masses. The reality is that people lie. They deceive you. They abandon you whenever possible, and may use you to serve their own ends. I never needed you to polish me. But you're welcome all the same. Someday you'll thank me for disabusing you of all these damaging notions."

Her mobile rang again, Matteo's name flashing on her screen.

And for the first time in as long as she could remember, Lauren didn't want to answer. She wanted to fling her mobile across the room and watch it shatter against the wall. Part of her wanted very much to throw it at Dominik, and see if it would shatter that wall.

But she did neither.

She looked down at the mobile, let her thoughts turn violent, and when she looked up again Dominik was gone.

And she sat where she was for a very long time, there on a Combe family sofa before a television screen that repeated lie after lie about who she was until she was tempted to believe it herself.

Her mobile rang. It rang and rang, and she let it.

Outside, the endless summer day edged into night, and still Lauren sat where she was.

She felt hollowed out. And yet swollen somehow. As if all those unwieldy, overwhelming emotions she'd successfully locked away since she was a child had swept back into her, all at once, until she thought they might break her wide open.

It was the first time in almost as long that she didn't have the slightest idea what to do. How to fix this. Or even if she wanted to.

All she knew was that even now, even though Dominik had looked at her the way he had, and said those things to her, he was still the one she wanted to go to. It was his arms she longed for. His heat, his strength.

How could she want him to comfort her when he was the one who had hurt her?

But she wasn't going to get an answer to that question.

Because when she went looking for him, determined to figure at least some part of this out, she discovered that Dominik hadn't simply disappeared while he'd stood there before her.

He'd actually gone.

He'd packed up his things, clearly, as there was nothing to suggest he'd been here at all. And then he must have let himself out while she'd been sitting there in the library where he'd left her, trying her best not to fall apart.

And she didn't have to chase after him to know he had no intention of coming back.

Because she had fallen for him, head over heels. But he had only ever been playing a game.

And Lauren would have to learn to live with that, too.

Lauren launched herself back into her life.

Her real life, which did not include mysterious men with hidden fortunes who lived off in the Hungarian woods. The life she had built all by herself, with no support from anyone.

The life that she was sure she remembered loving, or at least finding only a few months ago.

"You still love it," she snapped at herself one morning, bustling around her flat on her way to work. "You love every last part of it."

"You know when you start talking to yourself," Mary said serenely, splashing the last of the milk into her tea, "that's when the stress has really won."

Lauren eyed her roommate and the empty jug of milk. "Is that your mobile ringing?"

And as Mary hurried out of the room, she told herself that she was fine. Good.

Happy and hopeful, as a matter of fact, because neither one of those things had anything to do with the surly, angry man who'd done exactly what she'd asked him to do and then left after staying much longer than she'd expected he would.

She had what she wanted. She knew what other people felt. She understood why they went to such great lengths to have sex whenever possible. And she was now free to go out on the pull whenever she pleased. She could do as Dominik had once suggested and take herself off to a local pub, where she could continue conducting the glorious experiment in her own sexual awakening. On her own.

He didn't need her. And she certainly didn't need him.

Lauren decided she'd get stuck into it, no pun intended, that very night.

She thought about it all day long. She made her usual assenting, supportive sounds during the video conference from wherever Matteo was in the world today, but what she was really thinking about was the debauchery that awaited her. Because Dominik had been no more than a means to an end, she told herself. Merely a stepping-stone to a glorious sensual feast.

She left work early—which was to say, on time for once—and charged into the first pub she saw.

Where she remained for the five minutes it took to look around, see all the men who weren't Dominik and want to cry.

Because it turned out that the only kind of awakening she wanted was with him.

Only and ever with him, something in her said with a kind of finality that she felt knit itself inside her like bone.

And maybe that was why, some six weeks after the tabloids had discovered Dominik—when all that bone had grown and gotten strong—she reacted to what ought to have been a perfectly simple request from Matteo the way she did.

"I'll be landing in San Francisco shortly," he told her from his jet.

"And then headed home, presumably," she interjected. "To attend to your empire."

"Yes, yes," he said in a way that she knew meant, *or perhaps not.* "But what I need you to do is work on that marriage."

Lauren had him on the computer monitor at her desk so she could work more easily on her laptop as he fired his usual instructions at her.

But she stopped what she was doing at that and swiveled in her chair, so she could gaze at him directly.

"Which marriage would that be?" she asked. Tartly, she could admit. "Your sister's? You must know that she and her prince are playing a very specific cat and mouse game—"

Matteo was rifling through papers, frowning at something off screen, and she knew that his sister's romantic life was a sore point for him. Was that why she'd brought it up? When she knew that wasn't the marriage he meant?

"I mean your marriage, Lauren," he said in that distracted way of his. She knew what that meant, too. That her boss had other, more important things on his mind. Something she had always accepted as his assistant, because that was her job— to fade into his background and make certain he could focus on anything he wished. But he was talking about *her.* And the marriage he'd suggested, and she'd actually gone ahead and done on his command. "There's a gala in Rome next week. Do you think your husband is sufficiently tamed? Can he handle a public appearance?"

"Well, he's not actually a trained bear," she found herself replying with more snap in her voice than necessary. "And he was handling public appearances just fine before he condescended to come to Combe Manor. So no need to fear he might snap his chain and devour the guests, I think."

"You can field the inevitable questions from paparazzi," Matteo said, frowning down at the phone in his hand. The way he often did—so there was no reason for it to prick at Lauren the way it did. *Maybe it is time you ask yourself what you* wouldn't *do if your Mr. Combe asked it,* Dominik had said. *You may find the answers illuminating.* But what about what Matteo wouldn't do for her? Like pay attention to the fact she was an actual person, not a bit of machinery? "You know the drill."

"Indeed I do. I know all the drills."

She'd created the drills, for that matter. And she wasn't sure why she wanted to remind Matteo of that.

"Just make sure it looks good," Matteo said, and he looked at her then. "You know what I mean. I want a quiet, calm appearance that makes it clear to all that the San Giacomo scandal is fully handled. I want to keep the board happy."

"And whether the brother you have yet to meet is happy with all these revelations about the family he never knew is of secondary interest, of course. Or perhaps of no interest at all."

She was sure she'd meant to say that. But there it was, out there between them as surely as if she'd hauled off and slapped her boss in the face.

Matteo blinked, and it seemed to Lauren as if it took a thousand years for him to focus on her.

"Is my brother unhappy?" he asked. Eventually.

"You will have to ask him yourself," she replied. And then, because she couldn't seem to stop herself, "He's your brother, not mine."

"He is your husband, Lauren."

"Do you think it is the role of a wife to report on her husband to her boss? One begins to understand why you remain unmarried."

Something flashed over his face then, and she didn't understand why she wasn't already apologizing. Why she wasn't hurrying to set things right.

"You knew the role when you took it." Matteo frowned. "Forgive me, but am I missing something?"

And just like that, something in Lauren snapped.

"I am your personal assistant, Mr. Combe," she shot at him. "That can and has included such things as sorting out your wardrobe. Making your travel arrangements. Involving myself more than I'd like in your personal life. But it should never have included you asking me to marry someone on your behalf."

"If you had objections you should have raised them before you went ahead and married him, then. It's a bit late now, don't you think?"

"When have I ever been permitted to have objections in this job?" She shook her head, that cold look on Dominik's face flashing through her head. And the way he'd said *your master*. "When have I ever said no to you?"

Matteo's frown deepened, but not because he was having any kind of emotional response. She knew that. She could see that he was baffled.

"I value you, Lauren, if that's what this is about. You know that."

But Lauren wasn't the same person she had been. It wasn't the value Matteo assigned to her ability to do her job that mattered to her. Not anymore.

She could look back and see how all of this had happened. How she, who had never been wanted by anyone, threw herself into being needed instead. She'd known she was doing it. She'd given it her all. And she'd been hired by Matteo straight out of university, so it had felt like some kind of cure of all the things that ailed her to make sure she not only met his needs, but anticipated them, too.

She had thought they were a team. They had been, all these years. While he'd had to work around his father and now he was in charge.

But Dominik had taught her something vastly different than how to make herself indispensable to the person who paid her.

He had taught her how to value herself.

He'd taught her how to want. How to *be wanted*.

And in return, he'd taught her how to want *more*.

Because that was the trouble with allowing herself to want anything at all when she'd done without for so long. She wasn't satisfied with half measures, or a life spent giving everything she had to a man who not only couldn't return it, but whom she didn't want anything from.

She didn't want to sacrifice herself. It turned out that despite her choice of profession, she wasn't a martyr. Or she didn't want to be one.

Not anymore.

She knew what she wanted. Because she knew what it felt like now to be wanted desperately in return—no matter that Dominik might not have admitted that. She still knew.

He had stayed so long at Combe Manor. He had showed her things that she'd never dared dream about before. And he had taken her, over and over again, like a man possessed.

Like a man who feared losing her the same way she'd feared losing him.

If he hadn't cared, he wouldn't have snuck away. She knew that, too.

Lauren looked around the office that was more her home than her flat had ever been. The couch where she'd slept so many nights—including the night before her wedding. The windows that looked out over the city she'd loved so desperately not because she required its concrete and buildings, she understood now, but because it had been her constant. The one kind of parent that wouldn't turn its back on her.

But she didn't need any of these things any longer.

Lauren already had everything she needed. Maybe she always had, but she knew it now. And it was time instead to focus on what she *wanted*.

"And I have valued these years, Mr. Combe," she said now, lifting her head and looking Matteo in the eye. "More than you know. But it's time for me to move on." She smiled when he started to protest. "Please consider this my notice. I will train my replacement. I'll find her myself and make certain she is up to your standards. Never fear."

"Lauren." His voice was kind then.

But it wasn't his kindness she wanted.

"I'm sorry," she said quietly. "But I can't do this anymore."

And that night she lay in her bed in the flat she paid for but hardly knew. She stared at her ceiling, and when that grew old, she moved to look out the window instead.

There was concrete everywhere. London rooftops, telephone wires and the sound of traffic in the distance. The home she'd made. The parent she'd needed. London had been all things to her, but in the end, it was only a city. Her favorite city, true. But if it was any more than that, she'd made it that way.

And she didn't want that any longer. She didn't need it. She craved…something else. Something different.

Something wild, a voice in her whispered.

Lauren thought about want. About need. About the crucial distinction between the two, and why it had taken her so long to see it.

And the next morning she set off for Hungary again.

By the time she made it to the mountain village nestled there at the edge of the forest it was well into the afternoon.

But she didn't let that stop her. She left the hired car near the inn she'd stayed in on the last night of her life before she'd met Dominik and everything changed, and she began to walk.

She didn't mind the growing dark, down there on the forest floor. The temperature dropped as she walked, but she had her red wrap and she pulled it closer around her.

The path was just as she remembered it, clear and easy to follow, if hard going against the high, delicate heels she wore. Because of course she wore them.

Lauren might have felt like a new woman. But that didn't mean she intended to betray herself with sensible shoes.

On she walked.

And she thought about fairy tales. About girls who found their way into forests and thought they were lost, but found their way out no matter what rose up to stop them. Especially if what tried to stop them was themselves.

It was only a deep, dark forest if she didn't know where she was going, she told herself. But she did. And all around her were pretty trees, fresh air and a path to walk upon.

No bread crumbs. No sharp teeth and wolves. No witches masquerading as friends, tucked up in enchanted cottages with monstrous roses and questionable pies.

No foreboding, no wicked spells.

There was only Lauren.

And she knew exactly what she wanted.

When she reached the clearing this time, she marched straight through it. There was no one lurking in the shadows on the front porch, but she hadn't really expected there would be. She walked up, anyway, went straight to the front door and let herself in.

The cabin was just as she remembered it. Shockingly cozy and inviting, and entirely too nice. It was a clue, had she bothered to pay attention to it, that the man she'd come to find—her husband—wasn't the mountain man she'd expected he would be.

Best of all, that same man sat before the fire now, watching her with eyes like rain.

"Turn around, Lauren," he said, his voice like gravel. "If you leave now, you'll make it back to the village before full dark. I wouldn't want to be wandering around the woods at night. Not in those shoes. You have no idea what you might encounter."

"I know exactly what I'll find in these woods," she replied. And she let her gaze go where it liked, from that too-long inky-black hair he'd never gotten around to cutting to her specifications to that stern mouth of his she'd felt on every inch of her body. "And look. There you are."

He shook his head. "You shouldn't have come here."

"And yet I did. Without your permission. Much as you ran off from Combe Manor without so much as a hastily penned note."

"I'm sure whatever mission you're on now is just as important as the last one that brought you here to storm about in my forest," he said, and something like temper flashed over his face—though it was darker. Much, much darker. "But I don't care what your Mr. Combe—"

"He didn't send me. I don't work for him anymore, as a matter of fact." She held his gaze and let the storm in it wash over her, too. "This is between you and me, Dominik."

The air between them shifted. Tightened, somehow.

"There is no you and me."

"You may have married me as a joke," she said softly, "but you did marry me. That makes me your wife."

"I need a wife about as much as I need a brother. I don't do family, Lauren. Or jokes. I want nothing to do with any of it."

"That is a shame." She crossed her arms over her chest and she stared him down as if he didn't intimidate her at all. "But I didn't ask you if you needed a wife. I reminded you that you already have one."

"You're wasting your time."

She smiled at him, and enjoyed it when he blinked at that as if it was a weapon she'd had tucked away in her arsenal all this time.

God, she hoped it was a weapon. Because she needed all of those she could find.

And she had no qualms about using each and every one she put her hands on.

"Here's the thing, Dominik," she said, and she wanted to touch him. She wanted to bury her face in the crook of his neck. She wanted to wake up with him tangled all around her. She wanted him, however she could get him. She wanted whatever a life with him looked like. "You taught me how to want. And don't you see? What I want is you."

CHAPTER THIRTEEN

"YOU CAN'T HAVE ME," Dominik growled at her, because that was what he'd decided. It was what made sense. "I never was a toy for you to pick up and put down at will, Lauren. I assumed that was finally clear."

And yet all he wanted to do was get his hands on her.

He knew he couldn't allow that. Even if he was having trouble remembering the *why* of that at the moment, now that she was here. Right here, in front of him, where he'd imagined her no less than a thousand times a night since he'd left England.

But he didn't. Because touching her—losing himself in all that pink and gold sweetness of hers—was where all of this had gone wrong from the start.

"I introduced you to sex, that's all," he said through gritted teeth, because he didn't want to think about that introduction. The way she'd yielded completely, innocent and eager and so hot he could still feel it. As if he carried her inside him. "This is the way of things. You think it means more than it does. But I don't."

"I tested that theory," she told him, and it landed on him like a punch, directly into his gut. "You told me I could walk into any pub in England and have whatever sex I wanted."

"Lauren." And he was surprised he didn't snap a few teeth

off, his jaw was so tight. "I would strongly advise you not to stand here in my cabin and brag to me about your sexual exploits."

"Why would you care? If you don't want me?" She smiled at him again, self-possessed and entirely too calm. "But no need to issue warnings or threats. I walked in, took a look around and left. I don't want sexual exploits, Dominik. I told you. I want you."

"No," he growled, despite the way that ache in his chest intensified. "You don't."

"I assure you, I know my own mind."

"Perhaps, but you don't know me."

And he didn't wait for her to take that on board. He surged to his feet, prowling toward her, because she had to understand. She had to understand, and she had to leave, and he had to get on with spending the rest of his life trying to fit the pieces back together.

After she'd torn him up, crumpled him and left him in this mess in the first place.

Because you let her, the voice in him he'd tried to ignore since he'd met her—and certainly since he'd left her—chimed in.

"I thought at first it was the media attention that got to you, but you obviously don't mind that. You've had it before. Why should this be any different?"

And she didn't remind him of his lies of omission. They rose there between them like so much heat and smoke, and still, the only thing he could see was her.

"I don't care about attention." He wanted things he couldn't have. He wanted to *do* something, but when he reached out his hand, all he did was fit it to her soft, warm cheek.

Just to remind himself.

And then he dropped his hand to his side, but that didn't make it better, because she felt even better than he remembered.

"Dominik. I know that you feel—"

"You don't know what I feel." His voice was harsh, but his

palm was on fire. As if touching her had branded him, and he was disfigured with it. And maybe it was the fact she couldn't seem to see it that spurred him on. "You don't have great parents, so you think you know, but you don't. There's no doubt that it's your parents who are the problem, not you. You must know this."

"They are limited people," she said, looking taken aback. But she rallied. "I can't deny that I still find it hurtful, but I'm not a little girl anymore. And to be honest, I think they're the ones who are missing out."

"That sounds very adult. Very mature. I commend you. But I'm not you. This is what I'm trying to tell you." And then he said the thing he had always known, since he was a tiny child. The thing he'd never said out loud before. The thing he had never imagined he even needed to put into words, it was so obvious. "There's something wrong with me, Lauren."

Her eyes grew bright. And he saw her hands curl into fists at her sides.

"Oh, Dominik." And he would remember the way she said his name. Long after she was gone, he would replay it again and again, something to warm him when the weather turned cold. It lodged inside him, hot and shining where his heart should have been. "There's nothing wrong with you. Nothing."

"This is not opinion. This is fact." He shook his head, harshly, when she made to reach for him. "I was six days old when I arrived in the orphanage. And brand-new babies never stay long in orphanages, because there are always those who want them. A clean slate. A new start. A child they can pretend they birthed themselves, if they want. But no one wanted me. Ever."

She was still shaking her head, so fiercely it threatened the hair she'd put in that damned ponytail as if it was her mission to poke at him.

"Maybe the nuns are the ones who wanted you, Dominik. Did you ever think of that? Maybe they couldn't bear to give you up."

He laughed at that, though it was a hollow sound, and not

only because her words had dislodged old memories he hadn't looked at in years. The smiling face of the nun they'd called Sister Maria Ana, who had treated him kindly when he was little, until cancer stole her away when he was five. How had he forgotten that?

But he didn't want to think about that now. The possibility that someone had been kind to him didn't change the course of his life.

"Nobody wanted me. Ever. With one or two people in your life, even if they are your parents, this could be coincidence. Happenstance. But when I tell you that there is not one person on this earth who has ever truly wanted me, I am not exaggerating." He shoved those strange old memories aside. "There's something wrong with me inside, Lauren. And it doesn't go anywhere. If you can't see it, you will. In time. I see no point in putting us both through that."

Because he knew that if he let her stay, if he let her do this, he would never, ever let her go. He knew it.

"Dominik," she began.

"You showed me binders full of San Giacomos," he growled at her. "Century upon century of people obsessed with themselves and their bloodlines. They cataloged every last San Giacomo ever born. But they threw me away. *She* threw me away."

"She was sixteen," Lauren said fiercely, her red cloak all around her and emotion he didn't want to see wetting her cheeks. But he couldn't look away. "She was a scared girl who did what her overbearing father ordered her to do, by all accounts. I'm not excusing her for not doing something later, when she could have. But you know that whatever else happened, she never forgot you. She knew your name and possibly even where you lived. I can't speak for a dead woman, Dominik, but I think that proves she cared."

"You cannot care for something you throw away like trash," he threw at her.

And her face changed. It…crumpled, and he thought it broke his heart.

"You mean the way you did to me?" she asked.

"I left you before it was made perfectly obvious to you and the rest of the world that I don't belong in a place like that. I'm an orphan. I was a street kid. I joined the army because I wanted to die for a purpose, Lauren. I never meant for it to save me."

"All of that is who you were, perhaps," she said with more of that same ferocity that worked in him like a shudder. "But now you are a San Giacomo. You are a self-made man of no little power in your own right. And you are my husband."

And he didn't understand why he moved closer to her when he wanted to step away. When he wanted—needed—to put distance between them.

Instead, his hands found their way to her upper arms and held her there.

He noticed the way she fit him, in those absurd shoes she wore just as well as when she was barefoot. The way her caramel-colored eyes locked to his, seeing far too much.

"I don't have the slightest idea how to be a husband."

"Whereas my experience with being a wife is so extensive?" she shot right back.

"I don't—"

"Dominik." And she seemed to flow against him until she was there against his chest, her head tipped back so there was nothing else in the whole of the world but this. Her. "You either love me or you don't."

He knew what he should say. If he could spit out the words he could break her heart, and his, and free her from this.

He could go back to his quiet life, here in the forest where no one could disappoint him and he couldn't prove, yet again, how little he was wanted.

Dominik knew exactly what he should say.

But he didn't say it.

Because she was so warm, and he had never understood how

cold he was before she'd found him here. She was like light and sunshine, even here in the darkest part of the forest.

And he hadn't gone with her to England because she was an emissary from his past. He certainly hadn't married her because she could tell him things he could have found out on his own about the family that wanted to claim him all of a sudden.

The last time Dominik had done something he didn't want to do, simply because someone else told him to do it, he'd been in the army.

He could tell himself any lie at all, if he liked—and Lord knew he was better at that by the day—but he hadn't married this woman for any reason at all save one.

He'd wanted to.

"What if I do?" he demanded, his fingers gripping her—but whether to hold her close or keep her that crucial few inches away, he didn't know. "What do either one of us know about love, of all things?"

"You don't have to know a thing about love." And she was right there before him, wrapping her arms around his neck as if she belonged there. And fitting into place as if they'd been puzzle pieces, all this time, meant to interlock just like this. "Think about fairy tales. Happy-ever-after is guaranteed by one thing and one thing only."

"Magic?" he supplied. But his hands were moving. He tugged the elastic from her gleaming blond hair and tossed it aside. "Terrible spells, angry witches and monsters beneath the bed?"

"What big worries you have," she murmured, and she was smiling again. And he found he was, too.

"All the better to save you with, little red," he said. "If you'll let me."

"I won't." She brushed his mouth with hers. "Why don't we save each other?"

"I don't know how."

"You do." And when he frowned at her, she held him even closer, until that ache in his chest shifted over to something sweeter. Hotter. And felt a lot like forever. "Happy-ever-after is saving each other, Dominik. All it takes is a kiss."

And this was what she'd been talking about in that sprawling house in Yorkshire.

Hope. The possibility of happiness.

Things he'd never believed in before. But it was different, with her.

Everything was different with her.

So he gathered her in his arms, and he swept her back into the grandest kiss he could give her, right there in their enchanted cottage in the deep, dark woods.

And sure enough, they lived happily ever after.

Just like a fairy tale.

Twelve years later Dominik stood on a balcony that overlooked the Grand Canal in Venice as night fell on a late summer evening. The San Giacomo villa was quiet behind him, though he knew it was a peace that wouldn't last.

His mouth curved as he imagined the chaos his ten-year-old son could unleash at any moment, wholly unconcerned about the disapproving glares of the ancient San Giacomos who lurked in every dour portrait that graced the walls of this place.

To say nothing of his five-year-old baby girls, a set of the twins that apparently ran in the family, that neither he nor Lauren had anticipated when she'd fallen pregnant the second time.

But now he couldn't imagine living without them. All of them—and well did he remember that he was the man who had planned to live out his days as a hermit, all alone in his forest.

The truth was, he had liked his own company. But he exulted in the family he and Lauren had made together.

The chaos and the glory. The mad rush of family life, mixed in with that enduring fairy tale he hadn't believed in at first—but he'd wanted to. Oh, how he'd wanted to. And so he'd jumped into, feet first, willing to do anything as long as she was with him.

Because she was the only one who had ever wanted him, and she wanted him still.

And he wanted her right back.

Every damned day.

They had built their happy-ever-after, brick by brick and stone by stone, with their own hands.

He had met his sister shortly after Lauren had come and found him in the forest. Pia had burst into that hotel suite in Athens, greeted him as if she'd imagined him into being herself—or had known of him, somehow, in her heart of hearts all this time—until he very nearly believed it himself.

And he'd finally met his brother—in the flesh—sometime after that.

After a perfectly pleasant dinner in one of the Combe family residences—this one in New York City—he and Matteo had stood out on one of the wraparound terraces that offered a sweeping view of all that Manhattan sparkle and shine.

"I don't know how to be a brother," Dominik had told him.

"My sister would tell you that I don't, either," Matteo had replied.

And they'd smiled at each other, and that was when Dominik had started to believe that it might work. This strange new family he would have said he didn't want. But that he had, anyway.

His feelings about Matteo had been complicated, but he'd realized quickly that most of that had to do with the fact Lauren had admired him so much and for so long. Something Matteo put to rest quickly, first by marrying the psychiatrist who had been tasked with his anger management counseling, who also happened to be pregnant with his twin boys. But then he'd redeemed himself entirely in Dominik's eyes by telling Lauren that Combe Industries couldn't function without her.

And then hiring her back, not as his assistant, but as a vice president.

Dominik couldn't have been prouder. And as Lauren grew into her new role in the company she'd given so much of her time and energy, he entertained himself by taking on the duties of the eldest San Giacomo. He found that his brother and sister welcomed the opportunity to allow him to be the face of their ancient family. A role he hadn't realized anyone needed to play, but one it shocked him to realize he was…actually very good at.

He heard the click of very high heels on the marble behind him, and felt his mouth curve.

Moments later his beautiful wife appeared. She'd taken some or other call in the room set aside in the villa for office purposes, and she was already tugging her hair out of the sleek ponytail she always wore when she had her professional hat on. She smiled back at him as the faint breeze from the water caught her hair, still gleaming gold and bright.

"You look very pleased with yourself," she said. "I can only hope that means you've somehow encouraged the children to sleep. For a thousand hours, give or take."

"That will be my next trick." He shifted so he could pull her into his arms, and both of them let out a small sigh. Because they still fit. Because their puzzle pieces connected even better as time passed. "I was thinking about the banquet last night. And how it was clearly my confident use of the correct spoon midway through that won the assembled patrons of the arts over to my side."

Lauren laughed at that and shook her head at him. "I think what you meant to say was thank you. And you're very welcome. No one knows how difficult it was to civilize you."

He kissed her then, because every kiss was another pretty end with the happy-ever-after that went with it. And better yet, another beginning, stretching new, sweeter stories out before them.

And he wanted nothing more than to lift her into his arms and carry off to the bed they shared here—another four-poster affair that he deeply enjoyed indulging himself in—but he couldn't. Not yet, anyway.

Because it wasn't only the two of them anymore. And he

knew his daughters liked it best when their mama read them stories before bed.

He held her hand in his as they walked through the halls of this ancient place, amazed to realize that he felt as if he belonged here. And he imagined what it might have been like to be raised like this. With two parents who loved him and cared for him and set aside whatever it was they might have been doing to do something like read him a bedtime story.

He couldn't imagine himself in that kind of family. But he'd imagined it for his own kids, and then created it, and he had to think that was better. It was the future.

It was his belief made real, every time his children smiled.

"I love you," Lauren said softly when they reached the girls' room as if she could read every bittersweet line in his heart.

And he knew she could. She always had.

"I love you, too, little red," he told her.

More than he had back then, he thought. More all the time.

And then he stood in the doorway as she swept into the room where her daughters waited. He watched, aware by now that his heart wouldn't actually burst—it would only feel like it might— as his two perfect little girls settled themselves on either side of their gorgeous mother. One with her thumb stuck deep in her mouth. The other with her mother's beautiful smile.

And when his son came up beside him, a disdainful look on his face because he was ten years old and considered himself quite a man of the world, Dominik tossed an arm over the boy's narrow shoulders.

"I'm going to read you a fairy tale," Lauren told the girls.

"Fairy tales aren't real," their son replied. He shrugged when his sisters protested. "Well, they're not."

Lauren lifted her gaze to meet Dominik's, her caramel-colored eyes dancing.

And every time Dominik thought he'd hit his limit, that he couldn't possibly love her more—that it was a physical and emotional impossibility—she raised the bar.

He felt certain that she would keep right on doing it until the day they both died.

And he thought that was what happy-ever-after was all about, in the end.

Not a single kiss, but all the kisses. Down through the years. One after the next, linking this glorious little life of theirs together. Knitting them into one, over and over and over again.

Hope. Happiness. And the inevitable splashes of darkness in between, because life was life, that made him appreciate the light all the more.

And no light shined brighter than his beautiful wife. His own little red.

The love of his life.

"Of course fairy tales are real," he told his son. And his two wide-eyed little girls. Because he was living proof, wasn't he? "Haven't I told you the story of how your mother and I met?"

He ruffled his son's hair. And he kept his eyes on the best thing that had ever wandered into the deep, dark woods, and then straight into his heart.

"Once upon a time, in a land far, far away, a beautiful blonde in a bright red cloak walked into a forest," he said.

"And it turned out," Lauren chimed in, "that the big bad wolf she'd been expecting wasn't so bad, after all."

And that was how they told their favorite story, trading one line for the next and laughing as they went, for the rest of their lives.

* * * * *

Chosen For His Desert Throne

CHAPTER ONE

SHEIKH TAREK BIN ALZALAM had accomplished a remarkable amount in his first year as undisputed ruler of his small, mighty country.

He had accomplished more than he'd lost.

This was not only his opinion, he thought as he greeted the one-year anniversary of his father's death. It was fact, law, and would become legend.

He stood at the window of the royal bedchamber, gazing out on the ancient, prosperous walled capital city that was now his own. The city—and the desert beyond—that he had fought so hard for.

That he would always fight for, he asserted to himself as the newly risen desert sun bathed his naked body in its light, playing over the scars he bore from this past year of unrest. The scars he would always wear as they faded from red wounds to white badges of honor—the physical manifestation of what he was willing to do for his people.

His father's death had been sad, if not unexpected after his long illness, twelve months ago. Tarek was his eldest son and had been groomed since birth to step into power. He had grieved the loss of his father as a good son should, but he had been ready to take his rightful place at the head of the kingdom.

But his brother Rafiq had let his ambition get the best of him. Tarek hadn't seen the danger until it was too late—and it was his younger brother's bloody attempt to grab power no matter the cost that had required Tarek to begin his reign as more warrior than King. In the tradition of those who had carved this kingdom from the mighty desert centuries ago, one rebellion after another.

Or so he told himself. Because his was not the only brother in the history of this kingdom who had turned treacherous. There was something about being close to the throne yet never destined to rule that drove some men mad.

As King, he could almost understand it.

As a brother, he would never understand it—but he rarely allowed himself to think of that darkness. That betrayal.

Because nothing could come of it, save pain.

His mother had always told him that love was for the weak. Tarek would not make that mistake again. Ever. His blind love for Rafiq had nearly cost him the kingdom.

And his life.

But now his brother's misguided and petty revolution was over. Tarek's rule was both established and accepted across the land—celebrated, even—and he chose to think of the past year's turmoil as more good than bad.

Some rulers never had the opportunity to prove to their people who they were.

Tarek, by contrast, had introduced himself to his subjects. With distinction.

He had shown them his judgment and his mercy in one, for he had not cut down his younger brother when he could have. And when he knew full well—little as he wished to know such things—that had Rafiq accomplished his dirty little coup he would have hung Tarek's body from the highest minaret in the capital city and let it rot.

Tarek could have reacted with all the passion and anguish

that had howled within him, but he preferred to play a longer game. He was a king, not a child.

He had made Rafiq's trial swift and public. He'd wanted the whole of the kingdom to watch and tally up for themselves his once beloved brother's many crimes against Tarek—and more important, against them. He had not taken out his feelings of betrayal on his brother, though that, too, would have been seen as a perfectly reasonable response to the kind of treachery Rafiq had attempted.

His brother had tried to kill him, yet lived.

Rafiq had been remanded to a jail cell, not the executioners block.

"*Behold my mercy,*" Tarek had said to him on the day of his sentencing. There in the highest court of the land, staring at his younger brother but seeing the traitor. Or trying to see nothing but the traitor his younger brother had become. "*I do not require your blood, brother. Only your penance.*"

The papers had run with it. A Bright and New Day Has Dawned in the Kingdom! they'd cried, and now, standing in the cleansing, pure heat of the desert's newest sun, Tarek finally felt as if he, too, was bright straight through.

Now the dust was settled. His brother's mess had been well and truly handled, cleaned away, and countered. It was time to set down sword and war machine alike and turn his thoughts toward more domestic matters.

And while you're at it, think no more of what has been lost, he ordered himself.

He sighed a bit as he turned from the embrace of the sun. He did not need to look at all the portraits on his walls, particularly in the various salons that made up his royal apartments. Kings stretching back to medieval times, warlords and tyrants, beloved rulers and local saints alike. What all those men had in common with Tarek, aside from their blood, was that their domestic matters had dynastic implications.

If Tarek had no issue and his brother's co-conspirators rose again, and this time managed to succeed in an assassination attempt, Rafiq could call himself the rightful King of Alzalam. Many would agree.

It was time to marry.

Like it or not.

After his usual morning routine, Tarek made his way through the halls of the palace. The royal seat of Alzalam's royal family was a sixteenth-century showpiece that generations of his ancestors had tended to, lavishing more love upon the timeless elegance of the place than they ever had upon their wives or children.

"The palace is a symbol of what can be," his wise father had told him long ago. *"It is aspirational. You must never forget that at best, the King should be, too."*

Tarek was not as transported by architecture as some of his blood had been in the past but he, too, took pride in the great palace that spoke not only of Alzalam's military might, but the artistic passion of its people. Like many countries in the region, packed tight on the Arabian Peninsula, his people were a mix of desert tribesmen and canny oil profiteers. His people craved their old ways even as they embraced the new, and Tarek understood that his role was to be the bridge between the two.

His father had prepared him. And before his death, the old King had arranged a sensible marriage for his son and heir that would allow Tarek to best lead the people into a future that would have to connect desert and oil, past and present.

Tarek tried and failed to pull to his mind details of his bride-to-be as he crossed the legendary central courtyard, a soothing oasis in the middle of the palace, and headed toward his offices. Where he daily left behind the fairy-tale King and was instead the London School of Economics educated CEO of this country. He could not have said which role he valued more, but he could admit, as the courtyard performed its usual magic in him, that he was pleased he could finally set aside the other role that had claimed the bulk of his attention this last year. That of warlord and general.

Everything was finally as he wished it. There had been no unrest in the kingdom since his brother had surrendered. And with him locked away at last, the kingdom could once again enjoy its prosperity. No war, no civil unrest, no reason at all not to start concentrating on making his own heirs. The more the better.

He inclined his head as he passed members of his staff, all of whom either stood at attention or bowed low at the sight of him. But he smiled at his senior aide as he entered his office suite, because Ahmed had not only proved his loyalty to the crown repeatedly in the last year—he had made it more than clear that he supported Tarek personally, too.

"Good morning, Sire," Ahmed said, executing a low bow. "The kingdom wakes peaceful today. All is well."

"I'm happy to hear it." Tarek paused as he accepted the stack of messages his aide handed him. "Ahmed, I think the time has come."

"The time, Sire?"

Tarek nodded, the decision made. "Invite my betrothed's father to wait attendance upon me this afternoon. I'm ready to make the settlements."

"As you wish, Sire," Ahmed murmured, bowing his way out of the room.

Tarek could have sworn his typically unflappable aide looked...apprehensive. He couldn't think why.

Again, Tarek tried to recall the girl in question. He knew he had known them once—if only briefly. His father had presented him with a number of choices and he had a vague memory of a certain turn of cheek—then again, perhaps that had been one of his mistresses. His father had died not long after, Rafiq had attempted his coup, and Tarek had not allowed himself the distraction of women in a long while.

It was a measure of how calm things were that he allowed it now.

Tarek tossed the stack of messages onto the imposing desk that had taken up the better part of one side of the royal office for as long as he could remember. He crossed instead to the wall of glass before him, sweeping windows and arched doors that led out to what was known as the King's Overlook. It was an ancient balcony that allowed him to look down over his beloved fortress of a city yet again. These stones raised up from sand that his family had always protected and ever would.

He nodded, pleased.

For he would raise sons here. He would hold each one aloft, here where his father had held him, and show them what mattered. The people, the walls. The desert sun and the insistent sands. He would teach them to be good men, better rulers, excellent businessmen, and great warriors.

He would teach them, first and foremost, how to be brothers who would protect each other—not rise up against each other.

If he had to produce thirty sons himself to make certain the kingdom remained peaceful, he would do it.

"So I vow," he said then, out loud, to the watching, waiting desert. To the kingdom at his feet that he served more than he ruled, and ever would. "So it shall be."

But later that day he stared at the man who was meant to become his father-in-law before him without comprehension.

"Say that again," he suggested, sitting behind his desk as if the chair was its own throne. No doubt with an expression on his face to match his lack of comprehension. "I cannot believe I heard you correctly."

This was no servant who stood across from him. Mahmoud Al Jazeer was one of the richest men in the kingdom, from an ancient line that had once held royal aspirations. Tarek's own father had considered the man a close, personal friend.

It was very unlikely that the man had ever bent a knee to anyone, but here, today, he wrung his hands. And folded himself in half, assuming a servile position that would have been astounding—even amusing—in any other circumstances.

Had not what Mahmoud just told his King been impossible. On every level.

"I cannot explain this turn of events, Sire," the older man said, his voice perilously close to a wail—also astonishing. "I am humiliated. My family will bear the black mark of this shame forever. But I cannot pretend it has not happened."

Tarek sat back in his chair, studying Mahmoud. And letting the insult of what the other man had confessed sit there between them, unadorned.

"What you are telling me is that you have no control over your own family," he said with a soft menace. "No ability to keep the promises you made yourself. You are proclaiming aloud that your word is worthless. Is that what you are telling your King?"

The other man looked ill. "Nabeeha has always been a head-strong girl. I must confess that I spoiled her all her life, as her mother has long been the favorite of all my wives. My sons warned me of this danger, but I did not listen. The fault is mine."

"The betrothal was agreed upon," Tarek reminded him. "Vows were made and witnessed while my father yet lived."

He remembered the signing of all those documents, here in this very room. His father, already weak, had been thrilled that his son's future was settled. Mahmoud had been delighted that he would take a place of even greater prominence in the king-dom. But it had taken Ahmed's presentation of the dossier the palace kept on the woman who was to be his Queen to refresh his recollection of the girl in question, who had not been pres-ent that day, as it was not her signature that mattered.

Perhaps that had been an oversight.

"I would have her keep those vows," Mahmoud said hur-riedly. "She was only meant to get an education. A little bit of polish, the better to acquit herself on your arm, Sire. That was the only reason I agreed to let her go overseas. It was all in ser-vice to your greater glory."

"Those are pretty words, but they are only words. Meanwhile, my betrothed is…what? At large in North America? Never to be heard from again?"

"I am humiliated by her actions," Mahmoud cried, and this time, it was definitely a wail. And well he should wail, Tarek thought. For his daughter's defection was not only an embarrassment—it would cost his family dear. "But she has asked for asylum in Canada. And worse, received it."

"This gets better and better." Tarek shook his head, and even laughed, though the sound seemed to hit the other man like a bullet. "On what grounds does the pampered daughter of an international businessman, fiancée of a king, seek asylum?"

"I cannot possibly understand the workings of the Western governments," the man hedged. "Can anyone?"

Tarek's mouth curved. It was not a smile. "You do understand that I betrothed myself to your daughter as a favor to my father. An acknowledgment of the friendship he shared with you. But you and I? We do not share this same bond. And if your daughter does not respect it…"

He shrugged. The other man quailed and shook.

"Sire, I beg of you…"

"If your daughter does not wish to marry her King, I will not force her." Tarek kept his gaze on his father's friend, and did not attempt to soften his tone. "I will find a girl with gratitude for the honor being done her, Mahmoud. Your daughter is welcome to enjoy her asylum as she sees fit."

Despite the increased wailing that occurred then, Tarek dismissed the older man before he was tempted to indulge his own sense of insult further.

"*You must take the part of the kingdom*," his father had always cautioned him. "*Your own feelings cannot matter when the country hangs in the balance.*"

He reminded himself of that as he looked at the photograph before him of the blandly smiling girl, a stranger to him, who had so disliked the notion of marrying him that she had thrown herself on the mercy of a foreign government. What was he to make of that?

Then, with a single barked command, he summoned Ahmed before him.

"Why have I not been made aware that the woman who was to become my bride has sought, and apparently received, political asylum in a foreign country?"

Ahmed did not dissemble. It was one reason Tarek trusted him. "It was a developing situation we hoped to solve, Sire. Preferably before you knew of it."

"Am I such an ineffectual monarch that I am to be kept in the dark about my own kingdom?" Tarek asked, his voice quiet. Lethal.

"We hoped to resolve the situation," Ahmed said calmly. No wailing. No shaking. "There was no wish to deceive and, if you do not mind my saying so, you had matters of far greater importance weighing upon you this last year. What was a tantrum of a spoiled girl next to an attempted coup?"

Tarek could see the truth in that. His sense of insult faded. "And can you explain to me, as her father could not, why it is that the girl would be granted political asylum in the first place? She was allowed to leave the kingdom to pursue her studies. Supported entirely by me and my government. She would face no reprisals of any kind were she to return. How does she qualify?"

Ahmed straightened, which was not a good sign. "I believe that there are some factions in the West who feel that you have... violated certain laws."

Tarek arched a brow. "I make the laws and therefore, by definition, cannot violate them."

"Not your laws, Sire." Ahmed bowed slightly, another warning. "There are allegations of human rights abuses."

"Against me?" Tarek was genuinely surprised. "They must mean my brother, surely."

He did try not to speak his brother's name. Not thinking it was more difficult.

"No, the complaint is against you. Your government, not his attempt at one."

"I had the option for capital punishment," Tarek argued. "I chose instead to demonstrate benevolence. Was this not clear?"

"It does not concern your brother or his treatment." Ahmed met Tarek's gaze, and held it. "It is about the doctors."

He might as well have said, *the unicorns.*

Tarek blinked. "I beg your pardon?"

"The doctors, Sire. They were picked up eight months ago after an illegal border crossing in the north."

"What sort of doctors?" But even as Tarek asked, a vague memory reasserted itself. "Wait. I remember now. It is that aid organization, isn't it? Traveling doctors, moving about from one war zone to another."

"They are viewed as heroes."

Tarek sighed. "Release these heroes, then. Why is this an issue?"

"The male doctors were released once you reclaimed your throne," Ahmed said without inflection, another one of his strengths. "As were all the political prisoners, according to your orders at the time. But there was one female doctor in the group. And because she was a Western woman, and because there are no facilities for female prisoners in the capital city, she was placed in the dungeon."

Tarek found himself sitting forward. "The dungeon. *My* dungeon? Here in the palace?"

"Yes, sire." Ahmed inclined his head. "And as you are aware, I am sure, prisoners cannot be released from the palace dungeons except by your personal decree."

Tarek slowly climbed to his feet, his blood pumping through him as if he found himself in another battle. Much like the ones he had fought in his own halls on that bloody night Rafiq and his men had come. The ones he wore still on his body and always would.

"Ahmed." The lash of his voice would have felled a lesser

man, but Ahmed stood tall. "Am I to understand that after the lengths I went to, to show the world that I am a merciful and just ruler of this kingdom…this whole time, there has been not merely a Western woman locked beneath my feet, but a *doctor*? A do-gooder who roams the planet, healing others as she goes?"

Ahmed nodded. "I am afraid so."

"I might as well have locked up a saint. No wonder an otherwise pointless girl, who should have considered herself lucky to be chosen as my bride, has instead thrown herself on the tender mercies of the Canadians. I am tempted to do the same."

"It was an oversight, Sire. Nothing more. There was so much upheaval. And then the trial. And then, I think, it was assumed that you were pleased to keep things as they were."

The worst part was that Tarek could blame no one but himself, much as he might have liked to. This was his kingdom. His palace, his prisoners. He might not have ordered the woman jailed, but he hadn't asked after the status of any state prisoners, had he?

He would not make that mistake again. He could feel the scars on his body, throbbing as if they were new. This was on him.

Tarek did not waste any more time talking. He set off through the palace again, grimly this time. He bypassed graceful halls of marble and delicate, filigreed details enhancing each and every archway. He crossed the main courtyard and then the smaller, more private one. This one a pageant of flowers, the next symphony of fountains.

He marched through to the oldest part of the palace, the medieval keep. And the ancient dungeons that had been built beneath it by men long dead and gone.

The guards standing at the huge main door did double takes that would have been comical had Tarek been in a lighter mood. They leaped aside, flinging open the iron doors, and Tarek strode within. He was aware that not only Ahmed, but a parade of staff scurried behind him, as if clinging to the hem of his robes that towed them all along with the force of his displeasure.

He had played in these dungeons as a child, though it had been expressly forbidden by his various tutors. But there had never been any actual prisoners here in his lifetime. The dungeons were a threat, nothing more. The bogeyman the adults in his life had trotted out to convince a headstrong child to behave.

Tarek expected to find them dark and grim, like something out of an old movie.

But it turned out there were lights. An upgrade from torches set in the thick walls, but it was still a place of grim stone and despair. His temper pounded through him as he walked ancient halls he hadn't visited since he was a child. He tried to look at this from all angles, determined to figure out a way to play this public relations disaster to his advantage.

Before he worried about that, however, he would have to tend to the prisoner herself. See her pampered, cared for, made well again. And he had no idea what he would find.

It occurred to him to wonder, for the first time, what it was his guards did in his name.

"Where is she?" he growled at the man in uniform who rushed to bow before him, clearly the head of this dungeon guard he hadn't known he possessed.

"She is in the Queen's Cell," the man replied.

The Queen's Cell. So named for the treacherous wife of an ancient king who had been too prominent to execute. The King she had betrayed had built her a cell of her very own down here in these cold, dark stones. Tarek's memory of it was the same stone walls and iron bars as any other cell, but fitted with a great many tightly barred windows, too.

So she could look out and mourn the world she would never be a part of again.

This was where he—for it was his responsibility and no matter that he hadn't known—had locked away a Western *doctor*, God help him.

But Tarek had been fighting more dangerous battles for a year. He did not waste time girding his loins. He dove in. He rounded the last corner and marched himself up to the mouth of the cell.

And then stopped dead.

Because the human misery he had been expecting…wasn't on display.

The cell was no longer bare and imposing, the way it was in Tarek's memory. There was a rug on the floor. Books on shelves that newly-lined the walls. And the bed—a cot in place of a pallet on the stone floor—was piled high with linens. Perhaps not the finest linens he'd ever beheld, but clearly there with an eye toward comfort.

And curled up on the bed—neither in chains nor in a broken heap on the floor—was a woman.

She wore a long tunic and pants, a typical outfit for a local woman, and the garments did not look ragged or torn. They were loose, but clean. Her dark hair was long and fell about her shoulders, but it too looked perfectly clean and even brushed. She was lean, but not the sort of skinny that would indicate she'd been in any way malnourished. And try as he might, Tarek could not see a single bruise or injury.

He assessed the whole of her, twice, then found her eyes.

They were dark and clever. A bit astonished, he thought, but the longer she stared back at him, the less he was tempted to imagine it was the awe he usually inspired. And the longer he gazed at her, the more he noticed more things about her than simply the welfare of her body.

Like the fact she was young. Much younger than he'd imagined, he realized. He'd expected to find an older woman who suited the image of a *doctor* in his head. Gray-haired, lined cheeks… But this doctor not only showed no obvious signs of mistreatment, she was…

Pretty.

"You look important," the woman said, shocking Tarek by using his native tongue.

"I expected you to speak English," he replied, in the same language, though Ahmed had only said she was Western, not English speaking. She could have been French. German. Spanish.

"We can do that," she replied. And she was still lounging there on the bed, whatever book she'd been reading still open before her as if he was an annoyance, nothing more. It took Tarek a moment, once he got past the insolent tone, to realize she'd switched languages. And was American. "You don't really look like a prison guard. Too shiny."

Tarek knew that his staff had filed in behind him at the shocked sounds they all made. He lifted a finger, and there was silence.

And he watched as the woman tracked that, smirked, and then raised her gaze to his again. As if they were equals.

"Important *and* you have a magic finger," she said.

Tarek was not accustomed to insolence. From anyone—and certainly not from women, who spent the better part of any time in his presence attempting to curry his favor, by whatever means available to them.

He waited, but this woman only gazed back at him, expectantly.

As if he was here to wait upon her.

He reminded himself, grudgingly, that he was. That he had not fought a war, against his own brother, so that the world could sit back and judge him harshly.

At least not for things he had not done deliberately.

"I am Tarek bin Alzalam," he informed her, as behind him, all the men bowed their heads in appropriate deference. The woman did not. He continued, then. "I am the ruler of this kingdom."

The doctor blinked, but if that was deference, it was insufficient. And gone in a flash. "You're the Sheikh?"

"I am."

She sat up then, pushing her hair back from her face, though she did not rise fully from her bed. Nor fall to her knees before him, her mouth alive with songs of praise.

In point of fact, she smirked again. And her eyes flashed.

"I've been waiting to meet you for eight long months," she said, the slap of her voice so disrespectful it made Tarek's eyes widen.

Around him, his men made audible noises of dismay.

Once again, he quieted them. Once again, she tracked the movement of his finger and looked upon him with insolence.

"And so you have," Tarek gritted out.

There was still no sign of deference. No hint that she might wish to plead for her freedom.

"I'm Dr. Anya Turner, emergency medicine." Again, her dark eyes flashed. "I'm a doctor. I help people. While you're nothing but a tiny little man who thinks his dungeon and his armed guards make him something other than a pig."

CHAPTER TWO

ANYA HAD EXPECTED this moment to be sweet and satisfying, if it ever came, but it went off better than she'd imagined.

And she'd done very little else *but* imagine it.

For months.

The Sheikh of Alzalam himself stood before her. The man who every guard she'd encountered had spoken of in terms of such overwrought awe and glory that they'd made it a certainty that Anya would have loathed him on sight.

Even if she wasn't incarcerated in his personal prison.

She didn't much care for arrogant men at the best of times, which this obviously was not. Between her own father and every male doctor she'd ever met—not to mention the surgeons, who could teach arrogance to kings like this one and would not need an invitation to do so—Anya was full up on condescending males. An eight-month holiday in the company of these prison guards had not helped any.

And the way the Sheikh stared back at her, as if *dumbstruck* that she wasn't even now weeping at his feet, did not exactly inspire her to change her mind about the male ego.

The stunned silence went on.

Anya found herself sitting a little straighter, a little taller, as if that would protect her if the Sheikh had finally turned up only to go medieval on her. It occurred to her that, perhaps, she should have tried to get herself out of the dungeon before shooting off her mouth.

A lesson she never seemed to learn, did she?

After all these months, she'd figured she already knew how bad things could get here. She'd decided that sharing her unbridled feelings couldn't make things *worse*. What was worse than finding herself locked away in a literal dungeon in a country she wasn't even supposed to be in—separated from her colleagues who were very possibly dead and being kept alive for reasons no one had seen fit to share with her?

But as she stared back at the tall, ferocious, and obviously powerful man on the other side of her cell door, she was terribly afraid he might have a few answers to that question she wouldn't like.

Anya held her breath, but he didn't move. He only stared her down, inviting her to do the same.

There was a wall of other men behind him, staring at her in shock and disapproval, but *he* looked like he was attempting to crawl inside her head.

Anya didn't know what was wrong with her that she wanted to let him. Just because staring at him made her feel alive again. Just because it was different.

It had been *eight months*. Some two hundred and forty days, give or take. At first she'd intended to scratch each day into the walls, because wasn't that what people did? But she'd quickly discovered that someone—quite a few someones, or so she hoped, given the number of slash marks she'd found—had beaten her to it. She'd found that depressing. So depressing that she'd covered up the marks once the guards started permitting her furniture.

She had already cycled through fear. Despair. Over and over again, in those early days, until the panic faded.

Because that was the funny thing about time. It had a flattening effect. The human body couldn't maintain adrenaline that long. Sooner or later, routine took over. And with routine, a tacit acceptance.

She'd become friendly with her guards, though never *too* friendly. She'd learned the language, because that meant she was less in the dark. They'd made her comfortable, and over time, it became more and more clear that they had no intention of hurting her. Or no immediate plans to try, anyway.

Anya would have said she didn't have much fear left. She would have meant it.

Though the longer she stared at the man before her, stern and forbidding and focused intently on her, the more it reintroduced itself to the back of her neck. Then began tracing its way down her spine.

Maybe that's not entirely fear, something inside her suggested.

But she dismissed that. Because it was crazy.

And she had no intention of losing her mind in here, no matter how tempting it was. No matter how much she thought she might like a little touch of oblivion to make the time pass.

Okay, yes, she told herself impatiently. *He is remarkably attractive for a pig.*

Though *attractive* was an understatement.

He was dressed all in white, and in a contrast to the variously colored robes all the men wore around him, his fit him more closely. And more, were edged in gold. She probably should have known from that alone that he was the man in charge.

Sheikh. Ruler. King. Whatever they called him, he looked like the love child of the desert sun and some sort of bird of prey. A falcon, maybe, cast in bronze and inhabiting the big, brawny body of an extraordinarily fit man.

She was holding her breath again, but it was different. It was—

Stop it, Anya ordered herself.

This was no time to pay attention to something as altogether pointless as how physically fit the man was. So what if he had wide shoulders and narrow hips, all of it made of muscle. So what if he made gilt-edged robes look better than three-piece suits.

What mattered was that he'd thrown her into his dungeon and, as far she could tell, had thrown away the key, too. Anya had done a lot of dumb things in her lifetime—from allowing her father to bully her into medical school to focusing on emergency medicine because he'd told she was unsuited for it, to accepting the job that had brought her here, mostly to escape the job she'd left behind in Houston—but surely sudden-onset Stockholm syndrome would catapult her straight past dumb into unpardonably stupid.

She was sure she saw temper glitter in his dark, dark eyes. She would have sworn that same temper made that muscle in his jaw flex.

She *did not* feel an echo of those things inside. She refused to feel a thing.

"Please accept my humblest apologies," he said, and now that she wasn't gearing up to tell him what she thought of him, there was no escaping the richness of his voice. He spoke English with a British intonation, and she told herself it was adrenaline that raced through her, then. She'd forgotten what it felt like, that was all. "There has been great unrest in the kingdom. It is unfortunate that your presence here was not made known to me until now."

That was not at all what Anya had been expecting.

It felt a lot as if she'd flung herself against the walls—something she had, in fact, done repeatedly in the early days—only to find instead of the expected stone and pitiless bars, there was nothing but paper. She suddenly felt as if she was teetering on the edge of a sharp, steep cliff, arms pinwheeling as she fought to find her balance.

Something knotted up in her solar plexus.

It was a familiar knot, to her dismay. That same knot had been her constant companion and her greatest enemy over the last few years. It had grown bigger and thornier as she'd grown increasingly less capable of managing her own stress.

When here she'd been all of five minutes ago, feeling something like self-congratulatory that no matter what else was happening—or not happening, as was the case with whiling away a life behind bars—she was no longer one panic attack away from the embarrassing end of her medical career.

Thinking of her medical career made that knot swell. She rubbed at it, then wished she hadn't, because the Sheikh's dark gaze dropped to her hand. A lot like he thought she was touching herself *for* him.

Which made that prickle of sensation tracing its way down her spine seem to bloom. Into something Anya couldn't quite convince herself was fear.

"Are you apologizing for putting me in your dungeon or for *forgetting* you put me in your dungeon?" she asked, a little more forcefully than she'd intended. But she lifted her chin, straightened her shoulders, and went with it. "And regardless of which it is, do you really think eight months of imprisonment is something an apology can fix?"

He shifted slightly, barely inclining his head at the man beside him, who Anya knew was in charge of these dungeons. As the round little toad had pompously informed her of that fact, repeatedly. And she watched, astonished, as the keys were produced immediately, her cell was unlocked, and then the door flung wide.

The Sheikh inclined his head again. This time at her.

"I can only apologize again for your ordeal," he said in that low voice of his that made her far too aware of how powerful he was. Because it *hummed* in her. "I invite you to leave this prison behind and become, instead, my honored guest."

Anya didn't move. Not even a muscle. She eyed the obvious predator before her as if, should she breathe too loudly, he might attack in all that ivory and gold. "Is there a difference?"

The man before her did not shout. She could see temper and

arrogance in his gaze, but he did not give in to them. Though there were men all around him, many of them scowling at her as if she was nothing short of appalling, he did not do the same.

Instead, he held her gaze, and she could not have said what it was about him that made something in her quiver. Why she felt, suddenly, as if she could tip forward off of that cliff, fall and fall and fall, and never reach the depths of his dark eyes.

Then, clearly to the astonishment and bewilderment of the phalanx of men around him, Sheikh Tarek bin Alzalam held out his hand.

"Come," he said again, an intense urging. "You will be safe. You have my word."

And later, Anya would have no idea why that worked. Why she should take the word of a strange man whose fault it was, whether he'd known it or not, that she'd been locked away for eight long months.

Maybe it was as simple as the fact that he was beautiful. Not the way the men back home were sometimes, mousse in their hair and their T-shirt sleeves rolled *just so*. But in the same stark and overwhelming way the city outside these windows was, a gold stone fortress that was, nonetheless, impossibly beautiful. Desert sunrises and sunsets. The achingly beautiful blue sky. The songs that hung over the city sometimes, bringing her to tears.

He was harsh and stern and still, the only word that echoed inside her wasn't *pig*. It was *beautiful*.

Anya didn't have it in her to resist.

Not after nearly three seasons of cold stone and iron bars.

Before she could think better of it—or talk herself out of it—she rose. She crossed the floor of her cell as if his gaze was a tractor beam and she was unable to fight it. As if she was his to command.

Almost without meaning to, she slipped her hand into his.

Heat punched into her as his fingers closed over hers. Anya was surprised to find them hard and faintly rough, as if this man—this King—regularly performed some kind of actual labor that left calluses there.

Snips of overheard conversations between guards echoed inside her, then. Tales of a king who had risen from his bed and held off the enemy with his own two hands and an ancient sword, like something out of a myth.

Surely not, Anya thought.

She saw a flicker of something in his dark eyes, then. That same heat that should have embarrassed her, yes, but something else, too.

Maybe it was surprise that there was this *storm* between them, as if a simple touch could change the weather.

Indoors.

You have been locked up too long, Anya snapped at herself.

He did something with his head that was not a bow of any kind, but made her think of a deep, formal bow all the same.

Then, still gripping her hand and holding it out before him—like something out of an old storybook, wholly heedless of the way sensation lashed at her like rain—the King led her out of the dungeon.

And despite herself—despite every furious story she'd told herself over the past months, every scenario she'd imagined and reimagined in her head—as they emerged from the steep stone steps into what was clearly the main part of the palace, Anya was charmed.

She told herself it was as simple as moving from darkness into light. Anyone would be dazzled, she assured herself, after so many months below ground. Especially when she'd been brought here that terrifying night they'd been captured, hustled through lines of scary men with weapons, certain that the fact she'd been separated from her colleagues meant only terrible things.

Today Anya still had no idea what she was walking into, but at least it was pretty.

More than pretty. Everything seemed to be made of marble

or mosaic, inlaid with gold and precious stones or carved into glorious patterns. It was all gleaming white or the sparkling blue water of the fountains. There were splashes of color, exultant flowers, and the impossibly blue sky there above her in wide-open courtyards, like a gift.

She found herself tipping back her face to let the sun move over it, even though she knew that gave too much away. That it made her much too vulnerable.

But if he was only taking her from one cell to another, she intended to enjoy it.

Anya had learned the language, but still, she didn't understand what Tarek muttered to a specific man who strode directly behind him. The rest of the men fell away. There were more impossibly graceful halls, statues and art that made a deep, old longing inside her swell into being, and then this blade of a king led her into a room so dizzy with light that she found herself blinking as she looked around.

The light bounced off all the surfaces, gleaming so hard it almost hurt, but Anya loved it. Even when her eyes teared up, she loved it.

Tarek dropped her hand, then beckoned for her to take a seat in one of the low couches she belatedly realized formed a circle in the center of the room. But how could she notice the brightly patterned cushions and seats when the walls were encrusted in jewels and the room opened up on to a long, white terrace? She thought she saw the hint of a pool. And off to one side, more chairs, low tables, and lush green trees for shade.

"This is your suite and your salon," he told her. "I'm going to ask you some questions, and then I will leave you to reacclimate. You will be provided with whatever you need. Clothes to choose from, a bath with whatever accessories you require, and, of course, access to your loved ones using whatever medium you wish. My servants are even now assembling outside this room, ready to wait on you hand and foot. In the meantime, as I cannot imagine that the food in the dungeon speaks well of Alzalam and because I am afraid I must ask you these questions, I've taken the liberty of requesting a small tea service."

"A tea service," Anya repeated, and had to choke back the urge to burst out laughing. She coughed. "That is…the most insane and yet perfect thing you could possibly have said. *A tea service.*"

She suspected she was hysterical. Or about to be, because she was clearly in shock and attempting to process it, when that was likely impossible. She was out of her cell, and that was what mattered. More, she did not think that Tarek had chosen this room bursting with light and open to the great outdoors by accident.

Yet somehow, she thought that after all of this, she might not survive if she broke apart like that. Here, now, when it seemed she might actually have made it through.

She would never forgive herself if she fell apart now.

When he was sitting opposite her, all his ivory and gold seeming a part of the light that she was suddenly bathed in. As if he was another jeweled thing, precious and impossible.

If she cried now, she would die.

And as if to taunt her, that knotted horror in her solar plexus pulled tight.

"You do not have to eat, of course," he said with a kind of matter-of-fact gentleness that made the knot ache and, lower, something deep in her belly begin to melt. "Nor am I suggesting that a few pastries can make up for what was done to you. Consider it the first of many gifts I intend to bestow upon you, as an apology for what has happened to you here."

Anya didn't really know how she was expected to respond to that. Because the fact was, she was still here and she couldn't quite believe what was happening. She shifted in her plush, soft seat and dug her fingernails into her thigh, hard. It hurt, but she didn't wake up to find herself in her cell. She'd had so many of those dreams at first, and still had them now and again. They were all so heartbreakingly realistic and every time, the shock of waking to find herself still stuck in that cell felt like the kind of blow she couldn't get up from.

Slowly, she released her painful grip on her own thigh and assessed her situation.

She hadn't been tossed on a truck headed for the border, or shot in the back of the head, or sent back to the States so she could throw herself off the plane to kiss the ground—not that she thought an airport floor would inspire her to do any such thing.

If this was truly freedom, or the start of it, she was still a long way off from having to sort through what remained of the life she'd left behind.

That was not a happy thought.

When the door swung open again, servants streamed inside bearing platters and pushing a cart. Her stomach rumbled at the sight. Plate after plate of delicacies were delivered to the low table between her and the King. Nuts and dates, the promised pastries, meats and spreads, breads and cheeses. Cakes and yogurts and what she thought was a take on baklava, drenched in a rich honey she could smell from where she sat. Bowls filled with savory dishes she couldn't identify, all of which looked beautiful and smelled even better. Pitchers of water, sparking and still. Tea in one silver carafe and in another, rich, dark coffee.

Anya might not trust her own happiness, or what was happening around her, but she could eat her fill for the first time in months, and for the moment that felt like the same thing. Because there were flavors again, as bright as the sun that careened around this room. Flavors and textures, each one a revelation, like colors on her tongue.

She glutted herself, happily, and didn't care if it made her sick.

While across from her, the Sheikh lounged in his seat and drank only coffee. Black.

Anya told herself there was no reason she should take that as some kind of warning.

When her belly was deliciously full, she sat back and took a very deep breath. And for the first time in a long while, Anya was aware of herself as a woman again. Not a prisoner. Not a doctor.

A woman, that was all, who had just engaged in the deeply sensual act of enjoying her food.

Perhaps it was because Tarek was so harshly, inarguably, a man. Here in the dizzy brightness and jeweled quiet of this room, there was no doubt in her mind that he was a king. Mythic or otherwise, and everything that entailed. It was the way he sat there, waiting for her—yet not precisely waiting. Because she could feel the power in him. It was unmistakable.

He filled the room, hotter than the sunshine that poured in from outside. Richer than the coffee and more intense than the sugar and butter, tartness and spice on her tongue.

And his gaze only seemed darker the longer he studied her.

Waiting her out, she understood then. Because he was in control, not her. Yet in a different way than her guards had been in control below, or the cell itself had contained her. Tarek did not need to place her behind bars.

Not when he could look at her and make her wonder why she couldn't stay right where she was, forever, if that would please him—

Get a grip, Anya, she ordered herself.

She'd thought him beautiful in the dungeons, but here, he was worse. Much worse. There was no getting away from the stark sensuality of his features, with that face like a hawk's that she wouldn't have been surprised to find stamped on old coins.

Anya felt distinctly grubby by comparison. She was suddenly entirely too aware that she had not had access to decent products in a long, long time. Her hair felt like straw. Her prison-issue clothes had suited her fine in the cell she'd eventually made, if not cozy, livable. But the gray drabness of the clothes she'd lived in for so long felt like an affront now. Here where this man watched her with an expression that, no matter what pretty words he spouted, did not strike her as remotely apologetic.

"You said you had questions for me," she said, when it became clear to her that he was perfectly willing to sit there in silence. Watching her eat.

Making her feel as caged as if he held her between his hands.

It only made her feel more like a bedraggled piece of trash someone had flung onto his pristine marble floors. That, in turn, made her think of her long, quiet, painful childhood in her father's house. Her succession of stepmothers, each younger and prettier than the last.

Anya had never been a pretty girl. Not like her stepmothers. She'd never wanted to do the kind of work they did to remain so. And her father had always frowned and asked her why she would lower herself to worries about her appearance when she was supposedly intelligent, like him, thereby making certain Anya and the stepmother *du jour* were little better than enemies.

And sometimes a whole lot worse than that.

That didn't mean she wasn't aware of the ways she could use her appearance as a springboard toward confidence, upon occasion, when she wasn't feeling it internally. She didn't need a gown, or whatever it was the ladies wore in a place like this. But she wouldn't have minded a shower and some conditioner.

Still, he'd said he had his questions and Anya didn't know what would happen if she refused. Would it be straight back into the dungeon with her?

"Tell me how you came to be in my country," he invited her, though she felt the truth of that invitation impress itself against her spine as the order it was. "In the middle of a minor revolution."

"Minor?"

The Sheikh did something with his chin that she might have called a shrug, had he been a lesser man. "Loss of life was minimal. My brother anticipated a quiet coup and was surprised when that was not what he got. He lives on in prison, an emblem to all of his own bad decisions and my mercy. Despite his best efforts, the country did not descend into chaos."

Anya didn't have a brother, but doubted she would sound so remote about a coup attempt if she did. "I guess you must not have been out there in the thick of it."

His lips thinned. "You are mistaken."

Anya blinked at that, and found herself clearing her throat. Unnecessarily. And more because of that storm in her than anything in her throat. A storm that wound around and around, then shifted into more of that melting that should have horrified her.

She told herself it was shock. This was all shock. Her whole body kept *reacting* to this man and she didn't like it, but it wasn't him.

You're not yourself, she told herself, but it didn't feel like an excuse.

It felt a lot more like permission.

But Anya had trained in emergency medicine. Then had trained more by flinging herself into the deep end, in and out of some of the worst places on the planet and usually with very little in the way of backup.

She could handle tea with a king, surely.

There were fewer bodily fluids, for one thing.

"Crossing into Alzalam was accidental," she told him. She'd gone over it a thousand times. Then a thousand more. "We were working in one of the refugee camps over the border. You know that civil war has been going on for a generation."

"Yes," the man across from her said quietly. "And it has ever been a horror."

As if he felt that horror deeply. Personally.

Her heart jolted, then thudded loudly.

"I'm surprised you think so," she said without thinking, and watched a royal eyebrow arch high on his ferociously stark brow. "That you are even aware of the scope of that kind of disaster from..." She glanced around. "Here."

"Because I am no different from a tyrant who rules by fear." His voice was soft, but she did not mistake the threat in it. "We are all the same, we desert men in our ancient kingdoms."

Her heart and that knot in her chest pulsed in concert, and she thought she might be shaking. God, she hoped she wasn't *shaking*, showing her weaknesses, letting him see how easily he intimidated her.

"To be fair," she managed to say, "my experience of desert kings has pretty much been nothing but death, disease, and dungeons. Not to discount the pastries, of course."

She was holding her breath again. His gaze was so dark, so merciless, that she was sure that if she dared look away—if she dared look down—she would find he'd made her into some of that filigree that lined his archways. An insubstantial lace, even if carved from bone.

And then, to her astonishment, the most dangerous man she'd ever met, who could lock her up for the rest of her life with a wave of one finger—or worse—

Smiled.

CHAPTER THREE

TAREK HAD NEVER before considered food erotic. It was fuel. It was sometimes a necessary evil. It could, upon occasion, be a form of communion.

But watching the doctor eat with abandon, as if every bite she put in her mouth was a new, sensual delight, was a revelation. She had him hard and ready. Intensely focused on her and the unbridled passion she displayed as if she was performing her joy for him alone.

He could not recall ever experiencing anything quite like it.

And certainly not because of a captive still in her prison attire.

Still, Tarek smiled at her as if none of this was happening. He reminded himself—perhaps a bit sternly—that honey attracted more bees than vinegar. And that even a king could allow himself to act sweet if it suited him. It helped that his plan of how to handle the world's reaction to her incarceration began to take form in his head.

But she did not look particularly pleased to receive a smile from him. On the contrary, she looked... poleaxed.

"Perhaps this is not the time to ask you these questions," he said after a moment, when she only stared back at him. Her passionate eating on pause.

Tarek tried to let consideration and concern shine forth from within him, and it wasn't entirely an act for her benefit. He liked to think he was a compassionate man. Had he not proved it this dark year? He was certainly the most compassionate King the country had ever seen.

Surely the life he'd led had given him ample opportunity to practice.

Anya straightened her shoulders, a slight, deliberate jerk that he'd watched her do several times now. As if she was snapping herself to attention. And when she did, her brown eyes sharpened on him and he wondered, idly enough, if this was the doctor in her. That focus. That intensity.

That, too, made his sex heavy.

Later, Tarek promised himself, he would take a moment to ask himself why, exactly, he found himself attracted to a prisoner only recently released from his dungeon. Surely that spoke to issues within himself he ought to resolve. Especially if he truly thought himself compassionate in some way.

"I'm happy to answer questions now," she said, with a certain bluntness that made Tarek blink.

He wondered if it was simply that she was a Western woman, doctor or no. They were different from the women of his kingdom; he knew that already. Anya Turner was forthright, even so recently liberated from her prison cell. She appeared to have no trouble whatever meeting his gaze and more, holding it. The women of his country played far different games. They were masters of the soft sigh, the submissively lowered eyes, all to hide their warrior hearts and ambitions—usually to become his Queen and rule the kingdom in their own ways.

Not so this doctor, who had clearly never heard the word *submissive* in her life.

It was an adjustment, certainly.

"I had no idea you were being held here," Tarek told her. He lifted his mobile as if she could read the documents Ahmed had sent him while she ate. "But I have read your file."

"Would anything have been different if you had known?" she asked, and it wasn't precisely an interruption. He had paused.

Still. That, too, was different.

He reminded himself, with a touch of acid, that this was the woman who had cheerfully called him a pig while still behind bars. Unaware that he had come to liberate her, not punish her further.

Perhaps *blunt* and *forthright* did not quite cover it.

"I cannot alter the past, much as I would like to," he said. He studied her, and the easy way she held his gaze. As if she was the one measuring him, instead of the other way round. "Do you know why you were imprisoned in the first place?"

She let out a sharp little laugh of disbelief. Not a noise others generally made in his presence. "Do you?"

Again, he indicated his mobile. He did not react to the disrespectful tone. Much. "I know what was written in your file when you were taken into custody."

Another deeply impolite sound, not quite a laugh, that he congratulated himself on ignoring. "I believe the pretext for our arrest was an illegal border crossing. The fact that we were administering humanitarian aid and were in no way dissidents fomenting rebellion or revolution did not impress your police force. Mostly there was a lot of shouting. And guns."

"That was an upsetting period here," he agreed. "There was an attempt at a coup, as I mentioned. Dissidents tried to take the palace and there were a few, targeted uprisings around the country."

If he had only listened to his mother, he might have armored himself against the unforgivable affection that had allowed him to minimize his brother's behavior over the years. He'd convinced himself Rafiq's bad behavior was not a pattern. And even if it was, that it wasn't serious.

"A man who will be King cannot allow love to make him a danger to his country," his mother had warned him. *"What a*

*man loves is his business. What a king loves can never be any-
thing but a weapon used against him."*

Tarek had never imagined that weapon would be a literal one.
Or that he would wish, deeply and surpassingly, that he had
listened more closely to his mother when he'd had the chance.

There was something about the sharp focus Anya trained on
him, complete with a faint frown between her brows, that he
liked a lot more than he should. When he knew he would consider it nothing short of an impertinence in anyone else. And
would likely react badly.

But even this doctor's *focus* felt like passion to him.

"A coup? In the palace?" She waited for his nod. "You mean
they came for you. Here."

"They did." He did not precisely smile. "More accurately,
they tried."

Rafiq had tried. Personally. A bitter wound that Tarek doubted
would ever truly heal.

Still, he had the strangest urge to show her his scars. An
urge he repressed. But he found himself watching the way her
expression changed, and telling himself there was a kind of respect there.

"You're lucky you have so many guards to protect you, then."

He opted not to analyze why that statement bothered him
so much.

"I am," Tarek agreed, his voice cooler than it should have
been, because it shouldn't have mattered to him what this woman
thought—of him or the kingdom or anything else. "Though they
were little help when my brother and his men tried to take me
after what was meant to be a quiet family meal commemorat-
ing the two-month anniversary of our father's death."

He did not like the memory. He resented that he was forced
to revisit it.

Yet Anya's expression didn't change and Tarek could feel
her...paying closer attention, somehow. With the same ferocity
she'd used while demolishing a plate of pastries earlier.

Why did that make him want her so desperately?

But even as he asked himself the question, he knew the answer. He could imagine, all too well, that fierce, intent focus of hers on his body. On what they could do together.

He wrestled himself under control and wasn't happy at how difficult it proved. "It was a confusing time. I regret that there were far more imprisonments than there should have been, and, indeed, your colleagues were released as soon as order was restored. But due to the vagaries of several archaic customs, you were not. I could explain why, but what matters is that the responsibility is mine."

She broke her intense scrutiny of him then, glancing away while her throat moved. "They were released? How long ago?"

"As I said, when order was restored to the kingdom."

She looked back at him, her eyes narrow. "Thank you. But is that a week ago? Seven months ago? Twenty-four hours after they were taken in?"

"I do not think they were incarcerated for very long." That was no more and no less than the truth, as far as he knew it. He should not have felt that strange sense that he'd betrayed her, somehow. By telling her? Or by allowing it to happen in the first place—not that he'd known? Tarek felt the uncharacteristic shift about in his seat like a recalcitrant child. He restrained it. "No more than two months, I am given to understand."

Across from him, Anya sat very still in her gray, faded tunic, that hair of hers tumbling all around her. She shook her head, faintly, as if she was trying to shake off a cloud. Or perhaps confusion. "I was forgotten about?"

Tarek held her gaze, surprised to discover he did not want to. He reminded himself that this was the foremost duty of any king, like it or not. Accountability.

It didn't matter that he hadn't known she existed, much less that she and her colleagues had been caught up in the troubles here. Just as it didn't matter that he hadn't known until this very afternoon that she had been languishing in his very own dungeon. He was responsible all the same.

He might as well have slammed shut the iron door and turned the key himself.

Tarek inclined his head. "I'm afraid so."

She nodded, blinking a bit. Then she cleared her throat. "Thank you for your honesty."

And for a moment, there was quiet. She did not reach for more food from the platters before her. She did not hold him in the intensity of her brown gaze, shot through with gold in the hectic light that filled this salon.

For a moment there was only the faint catch of her breath, hardly a sound at all. The sound of birds calling to each other outside. The lap of the fountain out on her terrace.

And the improbable beat of his own pulse, hard and heavy in his temples. His chest. His sex.

Tarek could not have said if it was longing…or shame.

He had so little experience with either.

"You should know that your presence here has created something of an international crisis," he said when he could take the pressing noise of the silence between them no longer. "Something else I'm embarrassed to say I was unaware of until today."

She smirked. "It's created a crisis for me, certainly. An unwanted and forced eight-month vacation from my life."

"I want to be clear about this," Tarek said. "Were you harmed in any way?"

"Define harm," she shot back. "I expected to be beaten. Abused."

"If this happened, you need only tell me and the perpetrators will be brought to justice. Harsh justice to suit their crimes. I swear this to you, here and now."

"None of those things happened," Anya said, but her voice was thicker than it had been before. "And maybe your plan is to throw me right back into that cell today, so let me assure you that it's an effective punishment. That cell is deceptively roomy, isn't it? It's still a cell, cut off from the world."

He leaned forward, searching her face. "But you were not harmed?"

Her lips pressed into a line. "How do you measure the harm of being captured, shouted at in a language you don't speak, separated from the rest of your colleagues, and then thrown into a cold stone cell? Then kept there for months, never knowing if today might be the day the real terror might begin? Or you might be trotted out for an execution? I don't know how to measure that. Do you?"

Tarek studied her closely. Looking for scars, perhaps. Or some hint of emotional fragility or tears, because that, he would understand. But instead, this woman looked at him as if she was also a warrior. As if she too had fought, in her own way.

He felt his own scars, hacked into his flesh in this very same palace, throbbing as if they were new.

"It is all unfortunate," he said quietly. "There are many ways to fight in a war, are there not? And so many of them are not what we would have chosen, had we been offered a choice."

"I'm a doctor," she replied, matching his tone. Her dark eyes tight on his. "When I go to war, it's to heal. Never to fight."

"We all fight, Doctor. With whatever tools we are given. Whether you choose to admit that or do not is between you and whatever it is you pray to."

And for another long, impossibly fraught moment, they only stared at each other. Here where the desert sun made the walls shimmer and dance. A fitting antidote to the dungeon, he thought. Abundant, unavoidable sunshine made into a thousand different colors, until the sheer volume of it all made breath itself feel new.

But as the silence wore on, he found the glare she leveled on him with those sharp, clever eyes of hers far more intriguing.

Another thing he did not plan to look at too closely.

"Do you have more questions?" she asked. Eventually. "I

find the longer I'm out of that cell, the harder it is not to want to scrub myself clean of the experience. Assuming, that is, that this isn't all a great ruse."

Tarek understood, then, how easy it would be if this was the trick she thought it was. His brother, for example, would have thought nothing of fabricating some explanation for keeping this woman locked up—a law she'd broken that no one could prove she hadn't—and then tossing her back down in the dungeon to rot. His treatment of his own staff had been the despair of the palace. Rafiq would not have cared about international opinion. If things grew tense, he would have closed the American embassy, shut the Alzalam borders, and continued to do as he pleased.

But Tarek was not his grasping, morally vacant younger brother. His vision of the kingdom did not involve petty tyrannies, no matter the inconvenience to him, personally.

"I am not the kind of man who plays games," he told her, which should have gone without saying. He accepted that she was unlikely to know this about him. "Ruses of any kind do not impress me nor appeal to me. You will not be returning to that cell, or any other cell in my kingdom."

"Because you say so?"

"Because I am the King and so decree it."

"That sounds impressive." She did not sound impressed.

He shoved that aside. "But should you choose to reach out to the outside world, I would have you recognize that the moment I knew of your imprisonment, you were released."

She blinked again. Tarek wondered if he was watching her *think*. And sure enough, her gaze sharpened even further in the next moment. "Wait. My imprisonment is your crisis? Not my *presence*. But the actual fact that I've been locked away for eight months."

There were so many things he could have said to that. He entertained them all, then dismissed them, one by one.

"Yes."

Anya's lips quirked. "What level of crisis are we talking about here?"

"I have not had time to study it in any detail, I am afraid. As I was more focused on removing you from the dungeon as quickly as possible."

"Your mercy knows no bounds, I'm sure."

These were extraordinary circumstances and she was the victim in this, so Tarek ignored the insolent tone. Though it caused him physical pain to do so.

Or perhaps you only wish for an excuse to touch her, something insidious and too warm within him whispered.

"My understanding is that your imprisonment is considered a humanitarian crisis in many Western countries. And as our papers have only recently begun discussing the outside world again, after this long year of unrest, it has gone on far longer than it should have."

Anya nodded. "And I'm not a thoughtless tourist smuggling in drugs in a stranger's teddy bear, am I? That can't look good for you."

Tarek unclenched his jaw. "As a token of my embarrassment and a gesture of goodwill, I will throw a dinner this very night. We will invite your ambassador. You can assure him, in your own words, that you are safe and well."

That little smirk of hers deepened. "And what if I'm neither safe nor well?"

Tarek wanted to argue. She had eaten, she was sparring with him—*him*—and a glance at her cell had told him that she had not been suffering unduly while in custody. There were far greater ills. As a doctor, she should know that.

But he thought better of saying such things. What did he know about Americans? Perhaps the harm she'd spoken of was real enough. She could not possibly have been raised as hardy as the local women. Equal to sandstorms and blazing heat alike, all while keeping themselves looking soft and yielding.

It was only kind to make allowances for her upbringing.

"Then you may tell the ambassador of your suffering," he said instead of what he wanted to say. Magnanimously, he thought. "You may tell him whatever you wish."

"You will have to forgive me," Anya said, sounding almost careful. It was a marked contrast to how she'd spoken to him before, with such familiarity. "But I can't quite wrap my head around this. I expect to be seized again at any moment and dragged back to the dungeon. I certainly can't quite believe that the King of Alzalam is perfectly happy to give me carte blanche to tell any story I like to an ambassador. Or to anyone else."

Tarek made his decision then and there. The plan that was forming in his head was outrageous. Absurd on too many levels to count. But the more it settled in him, the more he liked it.

It was simple, really. Elegant.

And while bracing honesty was not something he had ever imagined would factor into his usual relationships with women, such as his betrothal, this woman was different. If she wasn't, she would not have ended up in his dungeon. She would certainly not have been here, telling him to his face that she doubted what he said to her. His word, which was law.

He ought to have been outraged. Instead, he accepted that he had to treat his doctor…differently.

It wouldn't be the first time in this long and difficult year that he'd had to change strategy on the fly. To set aside old plans and come up with new ones, then implement them immediately. Tarek liked to think he'd developed a talent for it.

The kingdom was ancient. Yet the King could not be similarly made of stone, or he would be the first to crumble. His father had taught him that, his mother had tried to warn him, but Tarek had lived it.

"Of course I wish that I could control what it is you might say about your time here," he told her, and watched the shock of that hit her, making her fall back in her seat. "I have no wish to be thought a monster, and I would love nothing more than to present your emancipation…carefully and in a way that brings, if not honor to the kingdom, no greater shame. But that is not up to me."

If Tarek was not mistaken, that dazed light in her eyes meant he had succeeded in being...disarming. Imagine that.

He continued in the same vein. "I will leave it up to you. You have no reason to trust me, so I will not ask such a thing of you. I would request only this. That if asked, you make it known that the very moment I learned that you were here, I freed you myself."

That dazed light faded, replaced by something far sharper.

"You want me to be your press release," she said softly.

"I would love you to be my press release." He even laughed, and as he did, it occurred to him that he wasn't faking this. "If there exists any possibility that you will sing wide the glory of the kingdom, I would be delighted."

Her head tilted slightly to one side, and Tarek still wasn't used to her direct gaze. To the way she unapologetically *considered* him, right where he could see her do it. "I can't speak to any possibilities or press releases, I'm afraid. I haven't taken a proper shower in eight months. Much less soaked myself in a good, long bath. Or used moisturizer. Or any of a thousand other everyday things that now seem luxurious to me."

"I understand, of course." Tarek smiled, again astonished to discover it was not a forced smile. He did not think of honey or vinegar, bees or business. Only what he could do to make her look at him without suspicion. "You must do what you feel is right."

He should not have taken pleasure in the way she looked at him, as if he wasn't quite what she expected. Surely he should not have introduced *pleasure* into this in the first place, no matter how tempting she was when she ate so recklessly, so heedlessly.

Tarek could not help but wonder how else she might approach her appetites. How else she might choose to sate them.

That is enough for now, he snapped at himself.

He stood, inclining his head to her in what he doubted she would realize was more of an apology than anything he might have said. Or would say.

"I will leave you to your luxuries, Doctor," he said. He nodded toward the door. "As I mentioned before, my staff waits outside to attend to you, should you wish it. This suite has both indoor and outdoor spaces, so you need not feel confined. Should you have need of me, personally, I will make myself available to you. You need only ask."

Her eyes darted around the room as if she was looking for a way out. Or for a lie. "Um. Yes. Thank you."

And Tarek left her then, aware as he strode from the room that he was battling the most unusual sensation.

Not fury at the circumstances.

Not distaste at what fate had thrown before him on this day, just as he'd imagined he was over the worst of this complicated year and ready to settle into a brighter future.

Not the usual bitterness that surged in him when he thought of his brother's betrayal.

But the exceptionally unusual feeling that, even though all she was doing was fencing words with him—with an insolence Tarek would have permitted from no other—he would have preferred to stay.

CHAPTER FOUR

THE BATHROOM ALONE was at least three times the size of her cell, and Anya intended to enjoy every inch of it.

She spent a long while in the vast shower, with its numerous jets and showerheads, offering her every possible water experience imaginable. She conditioned her hair three separate times. She slathered herself in all the shower creams and gels and soaps available. When she was done, having scrubbed every inch of her body to get the dungeon off, she drew a bath in a freestanding tub. She filled it with salts that felt like silk against her skin and she sat in the water for a long while, letting emotion work itself through her in waves. She stared out the windows, sank down deeper into the embrace of the water, and let whatever was inside her work its way through her while she breathed.

And pretended it was the steam on her cheeks, nothing more.

After her bath, she wrapped herself in one of the exultantly thick robes that hung on the wall, and sat at the vanity piled high with every hair implement she'd ever dreamed of. And a great many more she'd never seen before. Then she thought of absolutely nothing while she blew out her hair, then put in a few well-placed curls, until the woman who looked back at her from the mirror was actually...her again.

"Me," she whispered out loud.

Her chest felt so tight it hurt to breathe, but she made herself do it anyway—long and deep—trying to keep that knotted thing below her breastbone at bay.

Anya got up then, snuggling deeper into the lush embrace of the robe. Now that she was so clean she was pickled, she let herself explore. She enjoyed her bare feet against the cool stone floors, or sunk deep into the thick rugs. She wandered the halls, going in and out of each of the bright rooms, then out onto the wide terrace so she could stand beneath the sky.

She hadn't invited any staff inside, because that felt too much like more guards. Instead, she wandered around all on her own, as thrilled with the fact she was alone as anything else. All alone. No one was watching her. No one was listening to her. It amazed her how much she'd missed the simple freedom of walking through a room unobserved.

Through all the rooms. A media center with screens of all descriptions. There was that brightly colored room she'd sat in with Tarek, and three other salons, one for every mood or hint of weather. She had her own little courtyard, filled with flowers, plants, and a fountain that spilled into a pretty pool. There was a fully outfitted gym, two different office spaces, each with a different view, and a small library.

There was also a selection of bedchambers. Anya went into each, testing the softness of the mattresses and sitting in the chairs or lounging on the chaises, because she could. And because it made her feel like Goldilocks. But she knew the moment she entered the master suite. There was the foyer of mosaic. The art on the walls.

In the bedchamber itself, she found a glorious, four-poster bed that could sleep ten, which made her feel emotional all over again.

And laid out on top of the brightly colored bed linens, a rugged-looking canvas bag that she stared at as if it was a ghost.

Because it was. The last time Anya had seen it, the police had taken it from her.

Suddenly trembling, she moved to the end of the bed, staring at her bag as if she thought it might…explode. Or she might. And then, making strange noises as if her body couldn't decide if she was breathing or sobbing, she pulled her bag toward her. Beneath it she found the jeans, T-shirt, and overtunic she'd been wearing that night. The scarf she'd had wrapped around her head. And inside the bag, her personal medical kit, her passport, and her mobile.

Charged, she saw when she switched it on. Anya stayed frozen where she was, staring at the phone in her hand and the now unfamiliar weight of it. Her voice mailbox was full. There were thousands of emails waiting. Notifications from apps she'd all but forgotten about.

The outside world in a tiny little box in her palm. And after all this time—all the days and nights she'd made long and complicated lists of all the people she would contact first, all the calls she would make, all the messages she would send—what she did was drop the mobile back down onto the bed.

And then back away as if it was a snake.

Her heart began to race. Nausea bloomed, then worked its way through her. Her breath picked up, and then the panic slammed straight into her.

It didn't matter what she told herself. It never had mattered. Anya sank down onto her knees and then, when that wasn't sufficiently low enough, collapsed onto her belly. And as it had so many times before, the panic took control.

"You are not dying," she chanted at herself. "It only feels like it."

Her heart pounded so hard, so loud, it seemed impossible to her that she wasn't having a major cardiac event. She ordered herself to stop hyperventilating, because the doctor in her knew that made it worse, but that didn't work. It never worked.

Anya cried then, soundless, shaking sobs. Because it felt like she was dying, and she couldn't bear it—not when she'd only just escaped that dungeon.

But she knew that there was no fighting these panic attacks when they came. That was the horror of them. There was only surrendering, and she had never been any good at that.

It felt like an eternity. Eventually, she managed to breathe better, slowing each breath and using her nose more than her mouth. Slowly, her heart beat less frantically.

Slowly, slowly, the clench of nausea dissipated.

But she still had to crawl across the floor on her hands and knees. Back into the bathroom, where she had to lie for a while on the cold marble floor. Just to make sure that *this time* it really wasn't the sudden onset of a horrible influenza.

As she lay there, staring balefully at the literally palatial toilet before her, it occurred to her that in all the months she'd been imprisoned, she'd never once had one of these attacks. If asked, Anya would have said that her whole life had taken place on a level of intense stress and fear. Especially before she'd begun to learn the language, and had been forced to exist in a swirl of uncomprehending terror.

Stress, fear, and terror, sure. But she hadn't had one of these vicious little panic attacks, had she?

And in fact, it was only when she thought about the world contained on her mobile—and the inevitable messages she would find from her father—that her heart kicked at her again. And another queasy jolt hit her straight in the belly. She could feel her shoulders seem to tie themselves into dramatic shapes above her head, and apparently, it was here on the bathroom floor of a grand palace in Alzalam that Anya might just have to face the fact that it wasn't her eight-month imprisonment that really stressed her out.

It was the life she'd put on hold while stuck in that cell.

"That's ridiculous," she muttered at herself as she pulled herself up and onto her feet, feeling brittle and significantly older than she had before.

When she staggered back out of the bathroom, she didn't head for her bag again. Or her mobile, God forbid. She went instead through the far archway and found herself in an expansive dressing room, stocked full of clothing, just as the forbidding and beautiful Tarek had promised.

Anya told herself that she was erring on the side of caution. But she suspected it was more that she didn't want to be alone any longer, stuck with nothing but her panic, too many voice mail messages she didn't want to listen to, and the horror of her inbox.

Whatever it was, she went out and called in the servants.

"I am to have dinner with the Sheikh and the American ambassador," she told the two women who waited for her, both of them smiling as if they'd waited their entire lives for this opportunity.

"Yes, madam," one of them said. "Such an honor."

Anya had not considered it an honor. Should she have? When Tarek had made it clear that it was likely damage control? Maybe she really did need to sit down with her mobile, get online, and read the story of what had happened to her as told by people she'd never met. But the thought of picking up that phone again made something cold roll down her spine.

She smiled back at the women. "I'm hoping you can help me. I've never attended a formal dinner in your country and I have been...indisposed for so long."

"Don't you worry, madam," said the other woman, smiling even brighter. "We will make you shine."

And that was what they did.

They spared no detail. They buffed Anya's fingernails and her toenails, then added polish. They clucked disapprovingly over her brows, and then, as far she could tell, removed every errant piece of hair from her entire body. There was a salt scrub, because they did not feel that her long shower, or deep soak in the bath, was up to par.

Nor were they impressed with her hair, and when they were finished restyling it, she could see why. Anya looked luminous. Soft, pampered, and something like happy.

They had rimmed her eyes with dark mascara. They'd slicked a soft gloss over her lips. And when she looked in the set of full-length mirrors in the dressing room, she found herself resplendent in a bright tunic and matching trousers, flowing and lovely. Topped off with a long scarf with a pretty, jeweled edge that complemented the outfit and made her seem like someone else. The kind of woman who dined with ambassadors and kings, maybe.

"Thank you," she said to the women when they were done. "You've worked miracles here tonight."

Anya found herself smiling when they led her out of her rooms, then through the halls of the palace.

Night was falling outside, but the palace was still filled with light. She could see the last of the sun creep away a bit more every time they walked across a courtyard. And when they reached the grand central courtyard—that she vaguely remembered studying on the plane out of Houston a lifetime ago, because she'd known she was heading into the region—she paused for a moment as the night took over the sky.

Because she wasn't in the cell. There was nothing between her and the stars, save the palace walls that stood, then, at a distance. As if they understood, the women seemed content to wait while she stood there, her head tipped back and the half-wild notion that if she jumped, she would float straight off into the galaxy.

But she didn't. And when she came back to earth, the servants led her into a smaller room off the courtyard that was filled with Americans.

"His Excellency wishes you to speak with your countrymen for long as you desire," the woman closest to her said, not in English. "Only when you are satisfied will the formal dinner begin."

"Thank you," Anya said quietly.

"You learned the language?" asked one of the men who

waited for her, slick and polished in his suit and shiny shoes, with a sharp smile to match. "Smart move, Dr. Turner."

Anya heard the door close behind her, and surely she should have felt…something different, now. Some sense of triumph, or victory. Instead, she felt almost as if she was back in one of the hospitals she'd worked in before she'd come abroad, forced to contend with competitive doctors and high-stakes medical issues alike.

There were too many men in suits in the room and somehow, what she wanted was a different man. One in ivory and gold, with a predator's sharp gaze, and the quiet, inarguable presence of heavy stone.

"Was it smart?" she asked, smiling faintly because she thought she should. "Or survival?"

"It's an honor to meet you, Dr. Turner," said the most polished of the men, his face creased with wisdom and his smile encouraging. "I'm Ambassador Pomeroy, and I have to tell you, I can't wait to take you home."

Home. That word echoed around inside of her. And as the circle of men tightened around her, all of them making soothing noises and asking about her state of mind and general welfare, she told herself it was joy.

Because it had to be joy.

But it wasn't until she walked into the dining room that had been prepared for them—another triumph of mosaic and marble, beautifully lit and welcoming—that she breathed easy again.

Because Tarek waited there, lounging with seeming carelessness at the head of a long table. His gaze was hooded and dark, a clear indication of the power he was choosing not to wield, so obvious to Anya that it made her feel hollowed out with a kind of shiver. He was wearing a different set of robes that should have made him look silly compared to the pack of American diplomats in their business suits. But didn't.

At all.

"Welcome," the King said, his voice a ruthless scrape across the pretty room. "I thank you for joining me in this celebration of—" and Anya could have sworn that he looked only at her, then "—resilience and grace."

"Hear, hear," cried the men, a bit too brightly for strangers.

And despite how she'd feasted earlier, and how sure she'd been that she couldn't eat another bite, she found when she was seated at Tarek's right hand that she was starving. So while the men engaged in the sort of elegantly poisonous dinner conversation that she supposed was the hallmark of international diplomacy, or perhaps of tedious dinner parties, Anya indulged herself. Again.

It was only when she was quietly marveling at the tenderness of the chicken she was eating—simmered to tear-jerking tenderness on a bed of fragrant rice and doused in a thick, spicy sauce with so many *flavors*—that Anya realized that the Sheikh was not paying any attention to the arch wordplay of the ambassador and his aides.

Instead, Tarek was focused on her.

"The food in the dungeon wasn't terrible," she told him, realizing only as she smiled at him that she was… not embarrassed, exactly. But something in her heated up and stayed hot at the notion he was watching her again. "Just, you know. Bland."

"That is unpardonable."

Was she imagining the heat in his gaze? The faint trace of humor in that dark voice of his?

"How did you find your ambassador?" he asked, doing something with his chin that brought one of the waiting servants over to place more delicacies in front of her. "Appropriately outraged on your behalf, I trust?"

"Are you asking if I issued that press release?" she heard herself ask, in a tone she was terribly afraid was more flirtatious than not.

Good lord. Maybe when she'd had that panic attack, she'd hit her head on the stone floor. That was the only explanation. She dropped her gaze to her plate.

But she could still feel Tarek beside her. The burn of his attention all over her.

"I have a far more interesting question to ask you than what you did or did not tell a career diplomat," he said, all quiet force and the dark beneath. Like the night sky she'd wanted to float away in, ripe with stars. "Who will tell his own tales to suit himself, let me assure you."

Anya's heart was picking up speed again, but this time, without all the other telltale signs that she was descending into a panic attack. Because she wasn't.

She recognized the heat. And what felt an awful lot like need, curling inside her, like flame.

It had been there from the moment she'd first seen him. And now, buffed and plucked and polished to please, she understood that it had been for him as much as for her. She'd felt pretty in her mirror.

But when Tarek looked at her, she felt alive.

It was crazy. Maybe *she* was crazy. At the very least, she needed to leave this country and sort out what had happened to her—and how she felt about it—far, far away from the very dungeon where she'd been held all this time. This was likely nothing more than PTSD.

But tell that to the softest part of her, that melted as she sat there.

"You appear to be filled with questions," she said. Less flirtatiously, to her credit.

"I have spent a long year as a man of action, primarily," he said, and she made a note to look up the coup he'd mentioned. And what he'd done to combat it when his brother had been involved. "But I have always found that intellectual rigor is the true measure of a person. For without it, what separates us from the beasts?"

Anya forgot the plates piled high before her. "Some would say a soul."

"What would you say?"

She was dimly aware that they were not alone. That the ambassador and his aides were still at the same table, sharing the same meal. But she couldn't have said where they were seated. Or what they were talking about. Or even what any of them looked like.

It was as if there was only Tarek.

"I think that when everything is taken from you, what's left is the soul," she said quietly. "And it is up to you if that sustains you or scares you, I suppose."

There was a different, considering light in his gaze then. "What did you find, then?"

Something in her trembled, though she knew it wasn't fear. But it was as if some kind of foreboding kept her from answering him, all the same. Instead, she made herself smile to break the sudden tension between them. She reminded herself that they were not alone in this room, no matter how it felt.

And that he might have told her that he intended to be honest, but that didn't make it true. He was a very powerful, very canny king who had proved that he was more than capable of holding on to his throne, the ambassador had told her earlier.

"*He is not to be underestimated,*" the man had said.

Anya spread open her hands, shrugging. "Here I am. I suppose that means that I found a way to sustain myself, whatever it took."

Tarek lifted the glass before him, sitting back in his chair. He looked every inch the monarch. Currently indulgent, but with that severity lurking beneath.

She should certainly not have found him remotely compelling.

She told herself that of course she didn't.

Yet as the dinner wore on, she admitted privately that something about this man seemed to be lodged beneath her skin. She might have told herself it was simply because he was the first truly, inarguably beautiful man she'd seen since her ordeal had begun. But a glance around the table put paid to that idea.

Because the ambassador's men were all perfectly attractive. She could see that...but she didn't *feel* it. Her body didn't care at all about these bland men with their overly wide smiles and targeted geniality.

But the brooding, dangerous Sheikh who could have them all executed with one of those tiny flicks of his finger made her pulse pound.

Anya made a mental note to seek out psychiatric help the moment she returned to American soil.

"We're prepared to take you to the embassy tonight," the ambassador said at the end of the meal. "You must be anxious to leave the palace behind."

His smile was slick and aimed directly at Tarek.

Tarek looked faintly bored, as if these discussions were beneath him. "Dr. Turner is, of course, welcome to do as she pleases."

Anya thought that what would have pleased Dr. Turner the most would have been to remain full and happy again, without the unmistakable tension that filled the room. Especially because she doubted very much that any of the diplomats particularly cared about her feelings in this. She was a figure. A cause.

She was tired of being something other than a woman.

"I thought I made this clear before dinner," she said, as if she was concerned that the ambassador had gotten the wrong end of the stick when she knew very well he hadn't. "I'm not being *held* here. Not anymore."

Though it took everything she had in her not to look at Tarek when she said that, to see if that was actually true.

"I know it suits you to think of me as your pet barbarian," Tarek said to the ambassador, in a voice of silk and peril. "But I am nothing so interesting as a monster, I am afraid. Some things are regrettable mistakes, nothing more."

"Then there should be no trouble removing Dr. Turner from your custody," Ambassador Pomeroy replied with a toothy smile. "The American people would breathe a little easier, knowing she was safe at last."

"That is entirely up to Dr. Turner," Tarek replied. "As I have said."

Anya thought of her mobile, still on her bed back in her suite. She thought of the life that waited for her, in that phone and back in the States. Of the time she'd spent in Houston. Of her father.

Mostly she thought of Tarek, the heat in his dark gaze, and the question he had yet to ask her.

Because she knew he hadn't forgotten. Neither had she.

She picked up the linen napkin in her lap and dabbed gently at the corner of her mouth. "I would love to put the American people at ease. And I appreciate your assistance, Ambassador." She smiled, as punctuation. Or performance, maybe. It was hard to tell with so much molten heat making her ache. "But I spent eight months locked beneath this palace. I'm going to spend at least one night sleeping like a princess before I go. It's literally the very least this palace can do for me."

There were protestations. Some dire mutterings from the ambassador and far louder commentary from his aides. Still, eventually, they left her to the fate she was almost certain she already regretted choosing.

Yet Anya didn't open up her mouth and change that fate, even though she knew she could. And almost certainly should.

When the palace staff retreated after the Americans had left, she found herself once again alone in a room with this obviously ruthless man who really should not have fascinated her the way he did.

Especially when he took a long, simmering sort of look at her, setting fire to the quiet between them.

"I take it your rooms are to your liking, then," Tarek said, almost idly. "And though I am glad of it, surely you must be in a great hurry to resume your life. To see your family, your friends. To pick up where you left off eight months ago."

Anya felt that knot in her chest tighten a painful inch or two. "The funny thing about spending so long locked away is how little some things seem to matter, in the end. My friends are scattered all over the globe. I miss them, but we're used to not seeing each other. And my life had become nomadic. I haven't truly *lived* in a place since I left my last hospital job in Houston."

He was watching her almost too closely. "And your family?"

"It's only my father and his wife." She could feel herself getting tighter, everywhere, and was horrified at the idea she might collapse into panic here. With him. "We aren't close."

Anya didn't want to talk to him about accommodations or her lonely little life. Not now they were alone. Not now he seemed looser as he sat there. Lazier, almost, though she did not for one second mistake that leashed power in him for anything else. She could feel it as if it was a third presence in the room.

She could feel it inside her, turning her to flame.

Anya frowned at him. "Is that the question you wanted to ask me?"

He laughed at that, as if it was funny, when she felt so sure that it was crucial that he ask her his question. That it was *fate*.

But he was laughing. And Anya took the opportunity to ask herself what she was doing here. Why wasn't she on her way to the American embassy right now? And if she really wanted to sleep in that glorious bed—which she truly did, after a prison cot—why wasn't she up in that suite right now, continuing to pamper herself?

Why was she sitting here next to Tarek, imprisoning herself by choice, as if he was cupping her between his palms?

Worse still, she had the distinct sensation that he knew it.

"It is more a proposition than a question," he told her.

And Anya did not need to let that word kick around inside her, leaving trails of dangerous sparks behind. But she didn't do a thing to stop it. "Do you often proposition your former captives?"

"Not quite like this, Doctor." He didn't smile then, though she thought his eyes gleamed. And she felt the molten heat of it, the wild flame. She thought she saw stars again, but it was only Tarek, gazing back at her. "I want you to marry me."

CHAPTER FIVE

"*MARRY YOU?*" HIS suspicious doctor echoed.

Notably not in tones of awe and gratitude, which Tarek would have expected as his due from any other woman not currently seeking asylum in the Canadian provinces.

But then, that somehow felt to Tarek like confirmation that this woman was the correct choice for this complicated moment in Alzalam's history. And for him, because she was...different. A challenge, when women had always been an afterthought at best for him.

"It is an easy solution to a thorny problem." He watched, fascinated, as a hint of color asserted itself on her fine cheeks. "I assume you acquainted yourself with the media coverage of your case before dinner."

Her color deepened. "I did not."

He lifted his brows. "Did you not? I find that surprising."

She moved her shoulders, but it was less a straightening, or even a shrug. It was more...discomfort, he thought. And he found he liked the idea that she was not immune to him, to this. That he was not the only one wrestling with entirely too much sensation.

"I haven't had access to the internet for a long time," she said after a moment. "It seemed almost too much, really. I'm sure that will pass and I'll find myself addicted to scrolling aimlessly again. Isn't everyone?"

Tarek did not allow himself the weakness of addiction. But he did not say this here, now. He liked, perhaps too much, that she had not raced off to look herself up. That the stories others told about her—and about him—had not been her first priority.

That she was in no hurry to resume her old life could only support his proposition, surely.

He should not have let that notion work in him like heat. "I assume your ambassador and his men shared with you that you have become something of a cause célèbre."

Anya didn't meet his gaze. And though he hadn't known her long at all, it was clear that looking away was not usual for this woman. She was all about her directness. She was forthright and pointed. A scalpel, not a soft veil.

That, too, was its own heat inside him.

"I don't exactly know how to process the notion that anyone knows who I am," she said after a moment. "I know some people enjoy being talked about like that, but I'm not one of them."

"Allow me to recap," Tarek offered, sitting back in his chair so he would not indulge himself and touch her. Though he marveled at how much he wished to do so. "Because I did spend the evening catching up on the sad tale of the American doctor we so cruelly imprisoned here while handling a small, inconsequential revolution. After she illegally crossed our border."

Her gaze snapped to his then, and Tarek wondered why it was he preferred her temper when he would not have tolerated it from anyone else.

"Careful," she said softly. "The mocking tone doesn't help your case."

"Forgive me. It is only that looking at you, it is hard to imagine that you suffered at all." She looked too ripe. She glowed. She was… *You must remain calm*, he ordered himself, when he could not recall the last time he was not calm. Supernaturally calm, his brother had once claimed. It was only now that Tarek understood that had been a warning he should have heeded. "I know, of course, that is not the case."

"You're always welcome to lock yourself away for eight months and see how you enjoy the experience." Her smile was sharp. "I wonder how you'd look at the end of it."

He felt his lips curve despite himself. "Touché. Consider me adequately chastened."

Her smiled lost its sharpness. "You were telling me my story."

"Indeed. The fact is, while there was certainly interest in all the doctors disappearing that night, when the male doctors were returned but you were not, it created…consternation."

She looked amused. "Consternation?"

"Concern," he amended. "The news reports have been increasingly more frantic as time has gone on."

"I'm surprised the ambassador didn't insist upon seeing me sooner, then." Her gaze darkened. "Or at all."

"There is no possibility that the ambassador could have visited you before now," Tarek assured her, not pleased with that sudden darkness. Not pleased at all. "At the best of times, the palace does not comment on internal matters and therefore, never confirmed nor denied that you were held here. And during the troubles, the palace was locked down completely. There was no access. Regrettably, what that meant was that as far as the world knew, you went into the same prison as your colleagues, then disappeared."

She toyed with the gleaming edge of her scarf. "That does sound dramatic."

"Had I been less preoccupied with putting down a coup and suffering through the very public trial of my own brother for high treason, I would have paid more attention to international headlines myself."

"I am moved, truly, by this non-apology."

Again, he found himself moved to smile when surely he should rage. "Alas, my focus was on putting my kingdom back together. That brings us to today and your immediate release once I learned of your incarceration."

"And your solution to this tale of the world's cruel mischaracterization of your perseverance is…marriage?" Anya laughed, and even though Tarek knew the laugh was directed at him, he found himself…entertained. Or not furious, anyway, which amounted to the same thing. "Maybe you can explain to me why the King of Alzalam, who surely could marry anyone, would want to marry a woman he quite literally lifted out of a cell."

"It is practical," he told her, though the heat in him was surely nothing of the kind. "You could not have suffered any great abuses here, could you, if you end up marrying me. Your experience will be seen as romantic."

"A romantic imprisonment." Her tone was dubious. "I don't think that's a thing."

Tarek only smiled. "Is it not?"

She flushed again, and he felt that too distinctly. Like her hands on him.

He took pity on her. "Western audiences live for romantic love. They insert it into the most unlikely scenarios. You must know this is so. How many stalkers do you suppose are heralded as romantic heroes? I can think of dozens and I am no particular aficionado of your Western stories, no matter the media."

"I think you underestimate the difference between fiction and reality," she replied, no longer looking or sounding the least bit flustered. "And hard as it might be for you to imagine, the average Western woman is perfectly capable of judging the difference between the two."

"But is the average Western journalist capable of the same?" Tarek shrugged. "I do not think so."

Anya nodded slowly, as if taking it all on board. "This is all a bit out of left field, but I understand where you're coming from. It even makes a kind of sense. But what can you imagine is in it for me?"

The answer should have been self-evident, but Tarek could

not allow himself to dwell on the day's indignities. "That is where it comes in handy that I am the King."

"I see that more as a detracting factor, to be honest, given my people gave up on kings in the seventeen hundreds."

"Ah, yes, the lure of independence. So attractive." He waved a hand. "But this is not practical, Anya. You can find independence anywhere. Meanwhile, I am a very powerful, very wealthy man. A sheikh and a king who can, if I desire, make my wishes into law. Tell me what you want and I will make it so. Anything at all."

"For all you know I'm going to ask for a spaceship."

"Then one shall be built for you." He bit back his smile. "Is that what you want? I assumed it would be more along the lines of wishing to practice medicine here in the capital city, even once you become Queen."

But to his surprise, she paled at that.

He didn't know quite how to feel about it when she blew out a breath, then met his gaze once more as if she hadn't had that extreme reaction. "You say that as if a female doctor is as fantastical as a spaceship."

But Tarek found he liked her spiky voice better than watching her pale before him.

"Alzalam is not in the Stone Age, Doctor," he murmured. "No matter what foreign publications may imagine. We have a great many female doctors. But what we do not have, and never have had, are queens who work. Perhaps that is an oversight."

Anya huffed out another breath, as if she couldn't comprehend that. "I have to tell you, of all the endings I imagined to my time in prison, talk of queens did not enter into it."

She was too pretty, he thought. And getting more so by the moment, to his mind. Because he liked her bold. He liked how little she seemed in awe of him. He could not deny that he also liked the hint of vulnerability he saw now.

Did he want to give her a throne or did he simply want to take her to bed?

Tarek found he couldn't answer the question. Normally, that would have been all the convincing he needed that he was headed down the wrong path. He had never let a woman turn his head and he would have sworn on Alzalam itself that he never would.

But then, when it came to his doctor, there were practical considerations that outweighed everything else. Trade implications, for example, and potential sanctions. He could weather those, as his ancestors had upon occasion, but if there was no need to put himself in bed with only those economies who did not fear the taint of a regime considered monstrous, why would he condemn his country to such a struggle?

That he found himself longing to taste her was a problem when his country was at stake. Tarek tried to focus. "You have yet to tell me what it is you want most, Anya."

Had he said her name aloud before? He couldn't recall it. But it sizzled there, on his tongue. It felt far more intimate than it should. And in case he was tempted to imagine that it was only he who felt these things, he saw her eyes widen—her pupils dilating—as she sat there within reach.

But he did not use his hands. Not yet.

"I'm going to tell you something I've never told anyone before," Anya said, her voice softer than he had ever heard it. She leaned forward, the flowing scarf she wore making even the way she breathed look like a dance. She propped her elbows on the table and smiled at him over the top of the fingers she linked together. "I don't know why. Maybe it's because you're a stranger. A stranger who asked me to marry him after locking me up. If I can't tell you my secrets, who can I tell?"

"Tell me your secrets, Anya," he found himself saying, when he shouldn't. When he ought to have known better. "And I will show you my scars."

He was fascinated by watching her *think*. He watched her blink, then her head tilted slightly to one side as her gaze moved all over him. "Are your scars secret?"

"Naturally." Tarek kept his tone careless when he felt anything but. "Who wishes to see that their King is little more than a mortal man, frail and easily wounded?"

It seemed to take her longer than usual to swallow. "But surely the point of a king is that he is a man first."

"A king is only a man when he fails," Tarek bit out. He gazed at her until he saw, once more, that telltale heat stain her cheeks. "But first you must tell me your secrets. That is the bargain."

"My father is a doctor," she said, and he had the notion the words tumbled from her, as if she'd loosed a dam of some kind and could no more control them than if they'd been a rush of water. "Not only a doctor, mind you. He's one of the foremost neurosurgeons in the country. Possibly the world. He would tell you that he is *the* foremost neurosurgeon, full stop. Even now, years past what others consider their prime, his hands are like steel. He's deeply proud of that."

"Is this secret you plan to tell me actually his secret? I will confess I find myself less interested in the deep, dark secrets of a man I have never met."

Anya sighed. "Surgeons are a very particular type of doctor. A very particular type of person, really. They don't think that they're God. They know it."

"My father was a king, Anya. I am familiar with the type."

Her smile flashed, an unexpected gift. "And look at you, not only happy to be your father's heir but apparently prepared to fight off a revolution so you can assume your throne after him, as planned."

It was tempting to thunder at her about duty and blood, but Tarek did not. He thought instead of what it was she was implying with her words. None of it having to do with him.

He chose to simply sit and watch her. To wait.

"There was never any question that I would become a doctor as well," Anya said, her voice something like careful. "To be honest, I don't know if I would have been permitted to imagine a different path for myself. My mother died when I was small and I wish I could remember what my father was like with her, but I don't. After she was gone I had a succession of stepmothers, each younger and more beautiful than the last. My father liked to praise their beauty while making a point of letting me know that the only thing he was interested in from me was my intellect. It never occurred to me to rebel. Or even to question. It was what he wanted that mattered. But then, for a long time, I wanted it as well. I wanted to show him that I could be smart like him, not merely a pretty plaything, easily ignored, like the stepmothers he replaced so easily. I wanted to make certain I was *special*."

Tarek waited still, his gaze on her and the storm in her eyes.

"But when it came time to pick my specialty in medical school," she said quietly, "I failed him."

"I do not understand." Tarek lifted a brow. "You are a doctor, are you not?"

"My father likes to refer to emergency medicine as fast food," Anya said. She shook her head. "Where's the art? Where's the glory? It's all triage, addicts, and Band-Aids slapped over broken limbs while bureaucrats count beds. That's a quote."

"But you knew his opinion and you did it anyway."

Anya smiled again, though it was a sad curve that didn't quite reach her eyes. "That was my form of rebellion. My father accused me of being afraid of the responsibility a surgeon must assume. He's not wrong."

Tarek was baffled. "Surely handling emergencies requires you to save lives. Potentially more lives than a brain surgeon, if we are to count volume alone."

"Sometimes he would sneer that it was ego. Mine. That I was afraid to enter into the same arena as him because he was so clearly superior to me. And that might have had something to do with my choices, I can't deny it. But mostly, I didn't want to compete with him." She took a breath. "It took a long while for me to recognize that it wasn't that I didn't want to be a surgeon. It's that really, I never wanted to be a doctor."

Tarek noticed her fingers were trembling, as if she'd just confessed to treason. He supposed, by her metric, she had.

"I couldn't tell him this," she continued, her voice shaking along with her fingers. "I couldn't tell anybody this. After all those years of study. All that work. All that knowledge stuck in my head forever. People are *called* to be doctors—isn't that what everyone wants to believe? You're supposed to want to help others, always. Even if it means sacrificing yourself." She paused to take another shaky breath. "My father is unpleasant in a great many ways, but day in and day out, he saves lives no one else can. How could I tell him that having already failed to live up to his example, I was actually, deep down, not even a shell of a decent person because I didn't want to anymore?"

Tarek waited, but he no longer felt the least bit lazy. Or even indulgent. He was coiled too tight, because he could see the turmoil in Anya's gaze. All over her face. And she was gripping her hands together, so tight that he could see her knuckles turn white.

"I couldn't tell him any of that," she said, answering herself. "I simply quit. I walked out of my job and refused to go back. I signed up for the charity the next day, ensuring that I couldn't have gone back even if I'd wanted to. And I don't know why I didn't tell him everything then, because believe me, Dr. Preston Turner was not on board with me heading off to what he called *sleep-away camp for doctors*."

"I am fascinated by this man," Tarek drawled, sounding dangerous to his own ears. "It's not as if you joined the circus, is it?"

"He knew that I was putting myself at risk," Anya said softly. "He thought I was doing it because I was too foolish to see the potential consequences of my decision. By which he didn't mean an eight-month stint in a dungeon. He assumed I would get killed."

Tarek thought of his own father, and the expectations he had placed on his heir. "He does not have much faith in you."

Anya smiled again, edgily. "The responsibility of bearing his name comes with a requirement to help others. And surely the best way to do that is in controlled circumstances, like a surgical theater. Emergency rooms can be rowdy enough. But to risk myself in the middle of other people's wars? He disdained these choices."

"Surely the risk makes the help you give that much more critical."

"I would love to sit here, agree with you, and puff myself up with self-righteousness." Anya's gaze was direct again, then. And this time it made his chest feel tight. "But it wasn't as if I felt some glorious calling to immerse myself in dangerous places, all to help people who needed it. I know the difference, because every single one of my colleagues felt that call. But not me."

"Then why?" Tarek asked, though he had the distinct impression he did not wish to know the answer. The twist of her lips told him so. "Why did you do it?"

Anya let out a faint sort of laugh, and looked away. She loosened her grip on her own fingers. "You have no idea what it's like. The pressure. The endless stress. The expectation that no matter what's happening in your own life, or to you physically, you will always operate with the total recall of everything you learned in medical school, be able to apply it, and never make a mistake. It's a high-wire act and there is no soft landing. It's day in, day out, brutal and grueling and all-consuming. And that's just the emergency room."

"As it happens," Tarek said quietly, "I might have some idea."

Her gaze slid back to him. "All that gets worse in a war zone. You have to do all of the same things faster and more accurately, with or without any support staff. All while knowing that any moment you could be caught up in the crossfire."

"You say you were not called to do these things, but you did them," Tarek pointed out. "Maybe the call you were looking for does not feel the way you imagine it will."

He knew that well enough. Because it was one thing to spend

a life preparing for duty, honoring the call from his own blood and history. And it was something else to stand beside the body of a man who had been both his King and his father, and know that no matter how he might wish to grieve, he had instead to step into his new role. At once.

Then to do it.

Even in the face of his own brother's betrayal.

"I didn't have a death wish, necessarily," Anya told him, as if she was confessing her sins to him. "But I took risks the others didn't because deep down? I wanted something to happen to me."

He felt everything in him sharpen. "You mean you wished to be hurt?"

"Just enough." She looked haunted, hectic. He could see how she was breathing, hard and deep, making her whole chest heave. "Just so I wouldn't have to do it anymore."

"Courage is not the absence of fear, Anya," Tarek said, his gaze on hers, something hot and hard inside his chest. "It is not somehow rising above self-pity, wild imaginings, or bitter fantasies that you might be struck down into oblivion so you need not handle what is before you. I'm afraid courage is simply doing what you must, no matter how you happen to feel about it."

She sat back in her chair, her eyes much too bright. "Thank you," she whispered. "But I know exactly how much of a coward I am. Because I also know that there was a part of me that actually enjoyed eight months of rest. When no one could possibly expect me to pick up a stethoscope or try to make them feel better. I got to rest for the first time since I entered a premed program at Cornell."

Tarek was riveted, despite himself. When surely, he ought to wrest control of this conversation. Of her. Instead, his blood was a roar within him. And he could not seem to make himself look away.

"So, yes," Anya said softly. "I will marry you. But I have two conditions."

"Conditions," he repeated, provoked that easily. He made a show of blinking, as if he had never heard the word. "It is almost as if I am any man at all. Not the King of Alzalam. Upon whom no conditions have ever been applied."

"If you want a press release, there are conditions."

Tarek tamped down the sudden surge of his temper, telling himself that this was good. If she'd leaped into this, heedless and foolish, surely it would have been proof that she would be a terrible queen. He could not have that.

"Very well then," he said, through gritted teeth. "Tell me what it is you want. I promised I would give it to you."

"First," Anya said, searching his face, "promise me that I will never have to be a doctor."

"Done. And the second condition?"

He was fascinated to watch her cheeks heat up again. "Well," she said, her voice stilted. "It's a bit more...indelicate."

"Was there delicacy in these discussions?" His voice was sardonic. "I must have missed it."

"I want a night," she blurted out. "With you. To see whether or not..."

And Tarek did not plan to ever admit, even to himself, what it cost him to simply...wait.

When everything inside him was too hot, too intent. Too hungry.

Anya cleared her throat. "To see whether or not this is real chemistry. Or if it's because you were the first man I interacted with outside that cell. I...need to know the difference."

A good man might have pointed out that it seemed likely this was all yet another attempt at self-immolation on her part.

But then, Tarek had no problem being her fire.

"Come," he said, reaching out his hand as he had at the mouth of the prison cell, his gaze hot enough to burn. "Let us find out."

CHAPTER SIX

A WISE WOMAN would have questioned her own sanity, Anya thought. Or certainly her motives.

Wise or foolish, Anya hadn't stopped trembling for some time. Deep inside, where every part of her that shook was connected to the heat that seemed to blaze between her and Tarek, and that aching, slick fire between her legs.

She told herself that what mattered was that it all made sense in her own head.

He wanted a queen. A press release and the performance that would go with it.

And she wanted a different life. With the clarity she'd gotten in the dungeon, Anya knew she could never go back. Not to who she'd been, destroying herself with stress, locking herself away when the panic hit, terrified that she was moments away from being found out for the fraud she truly was. She couldn't keep moving from one way of administering medicine to another, until she started hoping that mortar fire might take her out and save her from her inability to walk away from the life she'd spent so long—too long—building.

Maybe if she was the Queen of a faraway country she could do more good than she'd ever managed as a doctor riddled with her own guilt and shame.

And somehow, all of that seemed tied together with Tarek himself. Not the King, but the man.

Too beautiful. Too intense.

And unless she was mistaken, feeling all the same fire that she was.

Anya didn't want to be mistaken. But she also wanted to feel *alive*.

She didn't need a primer on all the ways it could go badly for her to marry this man on a whim. All the ways it could turn out to be a far worse prison than the one she'd just left.

She wanted one night. One night, just the two of them, to see.

"No kings, no queens," she said, looking up at him as he rose to stand there before her, his hand extended. "Just a woman and a man, until dawn."

"Come," he said again, with all that power and confidence. Heat and promise.

Anya took her time getting to her feet, not sure her legs would hold her up. But they did. And as she had hours ago, she reached over and slid her hand into his.

Once more, the heat punched through her. She pulled in a swift breath, but that only made it worse. His hand was too hard. His grip was too sure.

And the way he watched her, those dark eyes fixed on her, made her quiver.

She expected him to bear her off again, marching her through the palace with the same courtly formality he'd shown earlier.

Instead, Tarek pulled her closer to him.

With an offhanded display of strength that had her sprawling against the hard wall of his chest, and gasping a bit while she did it.

Because it had been one thing to say she wanted this. And something else to be so close to another person.

To him.

Her pulse skyrocketed as she gazed up at him. If it was possible, Tarek was even more beautiful up close. Even more compelling. He smoothed his hands over her head, sliding that scarf out of his way.

And she watched, transfixed, as he pulled a long, glossy strand of her hair between two fingers. Looking down at it, very seriously, as if it held the mysteries of the universe.

Then he shifted that look to her.

"Tarek—" she began.

His hard mouth curved. "I like my name in your mouth. But I have other priorities."

Then he bent his head and put that stern mouth of his on her hers.

Everything inside of Anya, all that fire and need, exploded.

Tarek gripped her head, he angled his jaw, and then he swept her away.

His kiss was a hard claiming. He possessed her, challenged her and dared her. Anya surged forward, pressing her palms harder against the glory that was his hard chest as if she could disappear into all his heat.

And she kissed him back, pouring everything she had into it. Into him.

Again and again.

He made a low, gloriously male sound, then tore his mouth from hers.

"No," Anya breathed, heedless and needy. "Don't stop."

He laughed. Deep, dark, rich. It rolled through her, setting her alight all over again.

Anya felt swollen and desperate straight through, and he was still laughing.

"Order me around, Doctor," he suggested, his voice moving inside her as if it was a part of her. As if it was the sun, even now, in the dark of night. "Tell me what to do and see how that works for you."

But before she could try, mostly to see what he would do, Tarek bent slightly to sweep her into his arms.

Anya knew that none of this made sense. That she should have left with the American ambassador when she'd had the chance. That she certainly shouldn't have exposed herself to this man, telling him secrets she'd never breathed to another living soul.

Yet she had.

What was another vulnerability to add to the list? Maybe she was lucky she hadn't become a psychiatrist. She doubted she would enjoy knowing the inner workings of her own mind. Not when there was a king gazing down at her, his expression stern and possessive, sending a spiral of delight all the way through her.

Maybe, finally, it was time to stop thinking altogether. And to let herself feel instead.

Because she already knew what it was like to sit frozen in the dark. Literally.

Tonight, Anya intended to shine. And live. And feel everything—every last drop of sensation she was capable of feeling. Every touch, every sigh, every searing bit of flame she could hoard and call her own.

It took her a moment to realize that Tarek was moving. His powerful body was all around her, those arms of his holding her aloft as if she weighed little more than a notion. The granite wall of his chest. The tempting hollow at the base of his throat. His scent, a faint hint of smoke and what she assumed gold might smell like, warmed through and made male.

She assumed he would carry her off to his bed, wherever that was in this sprawling place, but instead he headed out through the grand, windowed doors that led outside. Anya caught a glimpse of the lights of the old city, gleaming soft against the desert night. Then he was setting her down, and it took her a moment to get her bearings, to find herself out on one of the palace's many balconies.

This one was made for comfort. He placed her on one of many low, bright couches, ringed all around with torches, and a canopy far above. There was a thick rug tossed across the ground at her feet and lanterns scattered across the table, making her think of long-ago stories she'd read as a child.

Tarek stood before her, gazing down at her as if she was the spoils of the war he'd fought, and he intended to fully immerse himself in the plunder.

Her entire body reacted to that thought as if she'd been doused in kerosene. She was too hot. She had too many clothes on. She was *burning alive*.

Looking at him was like a panic attack, except inside out. Anya's heart pounded. She could feel herself grow far too warm. And she felt a little dizzy, a little unsure.

But what was laced through all of that wasn't fear.

There was only him.

And how deeply, how wantonly and impossibly, she wanted him.

As she watched, Tarek began to remove those robes of his, casting them aside in a flutter of ivory and gold. He kept going until he stood before her, magnificently naked.

And when he made no move toward her, she felt a moment's confusion—

But then, as her gaze moved over his body, roped with muscle and impossibly powerful, she found the red, raised scars. One crossed the flat slab of his left pectoral muscle. Another cut deep across his torso, all along one half of the V that marked where his ridged wonder of an abdomen gave way to all the relentless masculinity beneath. Those were the biggest, most shocking scars—but there were more. Smaller ones, crisscrossing here and there.

Anya realized she was holding her breath.

And she thought he realized it too, because with no more than a simmering look, he turned so she could see the ones on his back.

"Your scars," she whispered.

"They came in the night like the cowards they were," Tarek

told her, slowly turning back to face her. "But let me assure you, their wounds were far greater than mine."

"Wounds are wounds," Anya said. And she wondered what lay beneath his. What it must have felt like for him, with his own brother involved in the plot against him. "And the marks we carry on our skin is the least of it, I think."

"Perhaps." He inclined his head in that way of his. So arrogant, every inch of him the absolute ruler he was, that she didn't know whether to scream or launch herself at him. "But what matters is that I won."

Anya had spent hours with this man by now. And had thought only of herself. Rightly so, maybe, given what had happened to her.

But she thought of his words from earlier. *Tell me your secrets, and I will show you my scars.* She thought of the fact that he hid them in the first place.

That he clearly had no intention of discussing his *feelings*, God forbid.

And it occurred to her, in a flash that felt a lot like need, that though he stood before her, the very picture of male arrogance, what he was showing her was vulnerability.

This was how this man, this King who had fought off his enemies and protected his throne and his people with his own hands, showed anything like vulnerability.

Anya understood, then. If she showed him softness, it would insult him. If she cried for the insult done to his beautiful body, she would do nothing but court his temper.

Tarek was not a soft man. And he did not require her tears.

So she responded the only way she could.

She flowed forward, moving from the edge of the cushion where she sat to her knees before him. She tipped her head back to look up at him, catching the harshness of his gaze. Matching it with her own.

Bracing her hands on either side of his hips, Anya took the hard, proud length of him deep into her mouth.

He tasted like rain. A hint of salt, that driving heat, and beneath it, something fresh and bright and male.

She had never tasted anything so good in her life.

Anya sucked him in as far as she could, then wrapped her hand around the base of him to make up for what she couldn't fit in her mouth.

And then, using her mouth and her hands together and his hard length like steel, she taught herself what it was to live again.

His hands fisted in her hair. Anya thrilled at the twin pulls *this close* to pain that arrowed straight to where she ached the most. Sensations stormed through her as she took him deep, then played with the thick, wide head, using her tongue. And then suction. And anything else that felt good.

He groaned, and that sent bolt after bolt of that wildfire sensation streaking through her body to lodge itself in her soft heat, where it pulsed.

Tarek was muttering, dirty words in several languages, and Anya loved that, too.

She wanted all of him. She wanted, desperately, for him to flood her mouth so she could swallow him whole. So she could take some part of him—of this—inside her and hold on to it, forever.

And this time, she was the one who groaned when he pulled her away from him. It took her a few jagged breaths to recognize that the man who looked down at her then was not the King. Not the indulgent monarch.

He looked like a man.

A man at the end of his rope. And he was somehow more beautiful for that wildness.

Tarek hauled her up to her feet.

"You will be the death of me," he growled at her.

"But a good death," Anya replied, though her mouth felt like his, because he was all she could taste. "Isn't that the point?"

"I have no intention of dying," Tarek told her fiercely. His hands were busy, and she felt too limp, too ravaged by lust and need, to do anything but stand there as he stripped her of her tunic, her trousers, her silky underthings. "Certainly not before I had tasted every inch of you, *habibti*."

And when he bore her down to the soft cushions behind her, they were both gloriously undressed at last.

Anya felt as if she'd been waiting a lifetime for this. For him.

At first it was almost like a fight, as they each wrestled to taste more. To consume each other whole.

She kissed his scars, one after the next, until he flipped her over and set about his own tasting. Each breast. Her nipples. The trail he made himself down the length of her abdomen, until he could take a long, deep drink from between her legs.

But even though she bucked against him, on the edge of shattering, he only laughed. That dark, rich sound that seemed to pulse in her. Then he nipped at the inside of her thigh.

"Not so fast, *habibti*," he said, climbing back up her body. "I wish to watch you come apart. So deep inside you that neither one of us can breathe. So there can be no mistake that no matter what else happens in the course of my reign, no matter what we find in this practical arrangement of ours, we will always have this."

And before she could react to that, he twisted his hips and drove himself, hard and huge, deep inside of her.

Anya simply…snapped.

She arched up, shattering all around him with that single stroke that was almost too much. Almost too deep.

She rocked herself against him, over and over, as the storm of it took her apart, shaking her again and again until she forgot who she was.

And as she came back, she was gradually aware that Tarek waited, smoke and gold and dark eyes trained on her face, as if he was drinking in every last moment.

He was still so hard. Still so deep inside her she could feel him when she breathed. He braced himself above her, that beautiful predator's gaze trained on her. And the sight of all that barely contained ferocity above her while he was planted within her made the heat inside her flare all over again.

"This is not a hallucination brought on by a prison cell," he told her, his voice no more than a growl.

"No," she agreed, breathlessly. She wrapped her legs around him because she knew, somehow, that she needed to hold on tight. "This is who we are."

And Tarek smiled at her, though it was a fierce thing, all teeth and sensual promise.

Only then did he begin to move.

It was like coming home.

He wasn't gentle. She wasn't sweet. It was a clashing of bodies, pleasure so intense it made her scream.

Tarek pounded into her, his mouth against her neck. They flipped over once and she found herself astride him. She braced herself against his chest as she worked her hips to get *more*, to ride that line between pleasure and pain when it was all part of the same glory.

To make them one, to make them *this*.

Then they flipped again and he was on his knees, lifting her so he could wrap his arms around her hips and let her arch back as she wished. She did, lifting her breasts to his mouth for him to feast upon while he worked her against him, over and over.

Until she couldn't tell if he pounded into her or she surged against him. It was all one.

Finally, Tarek gathered her beneath him again. He reached down between them while still he surged into her, that same furious pace, and pinched the place where she needed him most.

Hard enough to make her scream.

And while she screamed for him, explode.

Anya sobbed as he kept pounding into her, again and again, aware that she felt like she was flying. Like she was finally free.

She felt him empty himself inside her with a shout as they both catapulted straight into the eye of the storm they'd made.

And shook together, until it was done.

For a long while, Anya knew very little.

Slowly, she became aware of herself again, but barely. And only when Tarek shifted, pulling out of the clutch of her body, but moving only far enough to stretch out beside her. He shifted her to his chest and she breathed there while the night air washed over her body, cooling her down slowly.

Anya thought she really ought to spend some time analyzing what had just happened. If it was possible to analyze...all that. She should consider what to do now. Now that she knew. Now that there was no going back from that knowing.

But that felt far too ambitious.

Instead, she rested her cheek against his chest. She could feel the ridge of his scar and beneath it, the thunder of his heart. It felt a lot like poetry. She watched the torches set at intervals around them dance and flicker. From where they lay, stretched out on the wide sofa, she could see the tallest spires of the city in the distance. Rising up above them as if they were keeping watch while the desert breeze played lazily with the canopy far above.

Anya was wrecked. Undone.

And she had never felt so alive, so fully herself, in all her days.

"Well?" came Tarek's voice, from above and beneath her at once.

He sounded different, she thought, as she shifted so she could look at him. And though he gazed at her with all his usual arrogance, there was an indulgent quirk to his fine, sensual lips.

She hungered for him, all over again, her body heating anew.

It should have scared her, these postprison appetites. But she knew that what charged through her was nothing so simple as fear.

Fear left her sprawled out on bathroom floors, gasping for her breath. It didn't make her feel sunlight in a desert night, or as if she'd discovered wings she'd never known were there. Fear reduced her into nothing but a set of symptoms she couldn't think through. It created nothing, taught her nothing, and never left her anything like sated.

Anya had never considered it before, but fear was simple.

What stormed in her because of Tarek, *with* Tarek, was complicated. Possibly insane, yes. But there were too many layers in it for her to count. Too many contradictions and connections. Scar tissue and the stars above, and that delirious heat, too.

"And if I say that I have never been so disappointed?" she asked, though she couldn't keep herself from smiling.

His smile did not change his face, it made him more of what he was. *Like a hawk*, she thought, as she had from the first. He made her shiver with a single look. But he also held her there, tight against his body, as if he would never let go.

"Then I will call you a liar," he said, dark and sure. "Which is no way to begin a marriage, I think."

He waited, that fierce gaze of his on her. Stark and certain. And yet Anya knew that all she needed to do was roll away from him. Thank him, perhaps, and he would let her go.

She could be back in the States before she knew it. Back to whatever her life was going to look like, on the other side of this. And by *this* she wasn't sure she meant the dungeon so much as the fact she'd finally admitted all those dark, secret things in her heart. She had finally said them out loud.

How could she go back from that?

"Be my Queen, Anya," Tarek urged her, his voice a dark, royal command. She could feel it in every part of her, particularly when he shifted so he could bend over her once more, bringing his mouth almost close enough to hers. Almost. "Marry me."

He was holding her tight, yet she felt set free.

Whatever else happened, surely that was what mattered.

"I take it you want a real marriage," she said as if the idea was distasteful to her, when it was nothing of the kind. "Not one of those 'for show' ones royals supposedly have. For the people and the press releases and what have you."

And this time, she could feel his smile against her mouth. "I will insist."

"All right then," Anya muttered, trying to sound grumpy when she was smiling too. "I suppose I'll marry you, Tarek."

From captive to Queen, in the course of one evening.

It made her dizzy.

Then he did, when he took her mouth in a kiss so possessive she almost thought it might leave a bruise.

Anya wished it would.

And she told herself, as she melted against him all over again, that Tarek might be a king. That the King might have his practical reasons for this most bizarre of marriages. That the man who had fought his own family and wore their marks on his skin might have all kinds of reasons for the things he did, and he might not have told her half of them.

But that she was the one claiming him, even so.

CHAPTER SEVEN

LIFE IN THE DUNGEON was slow. One day crawled by, then the next, on and into eternity, every one of them the same. The world outside the windows turned. Changed. Seasons came and went, but the dungeon stayed the same.

But after Anya agreed to marry Tarek, everything sped up.

"First," said Ahmed, the King's dignified, intimidating aide and personal assistant in one, a few days after she and Tarek had come to terms, "I believe there is the issue of press releases to local and international outlets alike."

"Oh," Anya said after a moment, staring back at the man. "You mean real ones."

"Indeed, madam. They would otherwise be somewhat ineffective, would they not?"

She was seated in the King's vast office, trying to look appropriately queenly. Trying also not to second-guess herself and the choices she'd made. But she'd snuck a look at Tarek then. "We wouldn't want that."

And she'd taken it as a personal victory when the stern, uncompromising King of Alzalam, sitting like a forbidding statue behind his appropriately commanding desk, had visibly bit back a smile.

If Anya was fully honest she didn't really want to face the

outside world. Every time she thought of her overly full mobile, she shuddered. But she also knew that as much as she might have liked to do absolutely nothing but lose herself in the passion she had never felt before in her life, that slick and sweet glory only Tarek seemed to provide, that wasn't the bargain they'd made.

She was going to have to face the real world sooner or later, she reasoned. That might as well be under the aegis of the palace, so they could control the message. And help shelter her from the response.

"Timing is an issue," Tarek said after a moment, no trace of laughter in his voice. "We would not wish to suggest that there was any romance conducted while you were more or less in chains."

"A king romancing a captive can really only occur within a certain window," Anya agreed merrily. "Lest we all forget ourselves and start fretting about upsetting power dynamics."

"No one who has met you, Doctor," Tarek murmured then, "would have the slightest doubt where the power lay."

And though Ahmed looked at her as if that was meant to be an insult, Anya knew it wasn't.

Because when they weren't discussing media campaigns, wedding arrangements, or thorny issues of which family members to invite—what with her father being her father, and a number of Tarek's relatives being in jail for attempting to kill him—they were exploring that fire that only seemed to blaze hotter between them.

Tarek, it turned out, hid a sensualist of the highest order beneath his stern exterior.

"You are always hungry," he mused one night as Anya happily polished off yet another feast. They'd taken to eating in one of the private rooms in her apartments, the two of them sitting cross-legged on the floor where it was far easier to reach for each other when a different sort of hunger took control.

She paused in the act of pressing her linen napkin to her lips, waiting for a comment like that to turn dark. For Tarek to make her feel bad the way her father always had, with snide little remarks like knives.

But instead, he smiled. "I take pleasure in sating each and every one of your hunger pangs."

And he made good on that at once, tugging the napkin from her fingers and laying her out flat before him on the scattered pillows. He drew the hem of the long, lustrous skirt she wore up the length of her legs. Then he lifted her hips and settled his mouth at her core, licking his way into her molten heat.

Only when he had her bucking against him, shattering and sobbing out his name, did Tarek sit back again. Then sedately returned to his dinner, merely lifting an arrogant brow when she cursed him weakly, lying there amongst the pillows in complete disarray.

"I do not wait for my dessert," he told her, as if he was discussing matters of state. "If I wish to indulge myself, I do so immediately."

"As you wish, Your Majesty," she panted.

It took Anya a full week to face up to the reality of what awaited her on her mobile, much less the repeated requests for appointments with the American embassy. Not to mention the press releases—more a press junket, Ahmed informed her solemnly—that she'd promised Tarek.

A week to face her new reality and another week to decide that she was well enough prepared to handle it. Or if not prepared, not likely to suffer irreparable harm when subjecting herself to reporters and their intrusive questions.

She did the biggest interviews first, sitting in a room of the palace that seemed like an anachronism. It was tucked away next to an ancient courtyard that a small plaque announced had existed in one form or another even before the palace had been fully built. Truly medieval, yet it invited any who entered to breathe deep and forget about the passage of time.

But inside the media room, it was very clear what century

Anya was in. It was all monitors and lights, cameras and green screens. The palace's senior press secretary ushered her through the roster of engagements, where all Anya had to do was tell her story.

And more critically, her reasons for remaining in Alzalam now she'd been freed.

"It's hard to imagine what would keep you there," said one anchorwoman. She wrinkled her brow as if in concern—or tried. "Surely most people in your position would try to get home as quickly as possible."

"I don't know that many people in my position," Anya replied. She reminded herself to smile, because if she didn't, people asked why she was *so mad*. "Captured, held, then released into a royal palace. Maybe I think that having spent so much time in the kingdom, it might be nice to explore it a little."

And then, on the heels of a morning filled with interviews from all over the world, she marched herself back to her rooms, dug her phone out of her bag, and forced herself to deal with all of her messages and voice mails.

It took hours. But when she was done, she felt both more emotional than she'd anticipated, and less panicky. A good number of the voice mail messages were from an array of journalists, some of whom she'd already spoken to. A few friends had called over the past eight months, claiming they only wanted to hear her voice and letting her know they'd been thinking of her during her ordeal. She took a surprising amount of pleasure in discovering that a bulk of her email was, as always, online catalogs she couldn't remember shopping from in the first place.

It made her feel as if, no matter what, life went on.

Better still, Anya felt somewhat better about the fact she still hadn't called her father, because he had neither written nor called her. Not once in all the time she'd been held in the dungeon. And, of course, not before that either, because he hadn't approved of her wasting her time in an aid organization when she could do something of much greater status and import.

Maybe it told her something about herself—or him—that she felt a bit triumphant when she finally dialed the number of the house she'd grown up in. She knew the number by heart, still, even though the house and the number attached to it hadn't been hers in a long while. Since long before she'd left it, in fact.

She stood in her elegant suite, looking out the window as yet another desert sky stretched out before her. Impossibly blue to the horizon and beyond. Looking out at so much sky, so much sand, made her feel as if she was just as expansive. As if, should she gather up enough courage, she might run through these windows, out to her terrace, and launch herself straight into the wind. Then fly.

It made her heart ache in a good way.

Anya had never felt that way in the excruciatingly tidy Victorian house on a Seattle hill where her father still lived. More care had been put into the gardens than her feelings. She had grown up guilty. Because she barely recalled her own mother. Because she was forever disturbing her father. Because she didn't usually like the women he married and presented to her as so much furniture. Because they mostly didn't care for her, either—and as the window between her age and the current stepmother's age narrowed, she felt even guiltier at how relieved she was to stop pretending.

She had left for college and had never returned for more than a brief visit over the holidays. She would have said that she barely remembered the place that her father's cleaners kept so pristine that it was sometimes hard to believe people actually lived there. Even when she'd been one of them.

But she could see it all too clearly, now.

As if all this time away forced her to look at it face on, at last. Not the house itself, but the fact it had never been a home.

The dungeon beneath this palace, hewn of cold, hard stone, had been cozier. Happier, even. She had catapulted herself out of her father's house as quickly as she could. The urgency to get it behind her—the kind of urgency the anchorwoman thought

Anya should feel about Alzalam—had guided her every move after she'd graduated high school. But it wasn't as if she'd ever made herself a home elsewhere.

She'd been moving from place to place ever since, concentrating on school, then her job, then how much she hated her job. She'd never settled anywhere, she'd only endured wherever she'd found herself.

Until the dungeon had settled on her.

First she'd despaired, as anyone would. Then she'd tried to make someone tell her how long she could expect to be left there. But after the despair and the bargaining, there was only time.

When she'd told Tarek that prison had been a kind of holiday, she'd meant it. Now she had the unsettling realization that it had also felt a whole lot more like a home than any other place she'd ever lived. No expectations. No demands.

Just time.

What was Anya supposed to do with that?

"Oh," came the breathy voice of her latest stepmother when she picked up the phone. For a moment, Anya couldn't remember her name. Or more precisely, she remembered a name, but wasn't sure it was the right one. It had been eight months, after all. "Anya. My goodness. You've been all over the news."

Charisma, Anya thought then, recognizing her voice. That was this stepmother's name. It was, of course, a deeply ironic name for a creature with all the natural charisma of a signpost. But Charisma was young. Anya's exact age, if she was remembering right, which said all kinds of things about Dr. Preston Turner that Anya preferred not to think about too closely.

Charisma was not smart, according to Anya's father. He liked to say this in Charisma's hearing, and she always proved his hypothesis to his satisfaction by giggling as if that was an endearment. Charisma was blonde in that silky way that seemed to require endless flipping of the straw-colored mass of it over one shoulder, then the other. Her hobbies involved numerous appointments at beauty salons and sitting by the pool in a microscopic bikini.

Charisma also managed to make it sound as if Anya had gone on the news in a deliberate attempt to provoke her father. As if she was indulging in attention-seeking behavior by telling her story.

Anya didn't have the heart to tell this woman that she'd given up on attempting to get Preston Turner's attention a long time ago. Or that she should do the same.

"I would prefer not to be on the news," Anya said, proud of how steady she kept her voice. With a hint of self-deprecation, even. "But apparently you become a person of interest when you're snatched up in a foreign country, thrown into prison, and then disappear for eight months. I don't see the appeal myself."

Charisma made a breathy, sighing sort of sound. "Your father's at the hospital," she said. "Do you want me to tell him that you called? He's very upset."

"He's been worried about me?" Anya asked, in complete disbelief.

"There have been a lot of questions," Charisma hedged. "And you know how your father is. When he's at the country club he really doesn't like to be approached or recognized. So."

"So," Anya echoed. She did not point out that the entire purpose of her father's snooty country club was to be recognized. What would be the point? "What I think you're telling me, Charisma, is that my imprisonment was an inconvenience."

"It was just all those questions," her stepmother said airily. "He would have appreciated it if you'd given him a little warning, maybe."

Anya's good intentions deserted her. "Funnily enough, they didn't offer me the opportunity to make a lot of phone calls," she said, and her voice was not even. It was inarguably sharp. "I was thrown in a dungeon. And then kept there, without any contact with the outside world, for the better part of the year."

"Well, I'm not going to tell him *that*." Charisma laughed. "You know how he gets. You can tell him that if you want."

"I'll go ahead and do that," Anya said, already furious at herself for showing emotion. When she knew Charisma would report it back to her father and it would only give him more ammunition to disdain her. "The next time he calls."

Which would be never.

After she ended the call she stayed where she was, standing still in the bright glare of the desert sun, trying to make sense of all the competing feelings that stormed around inside her.

She could feel that sharp pain in her chest, that knotted thing pulling tight again. Anya rubbed at it with the heel of her hand, then wheeled around, heading toward that bright, happy room Tarek had showed her that first day. She liked how dizzy the light made her, still. She liked that if it became too much, she could go out and dunk herself in that infinity pool. It soothed her to float there, folding her arms over the lip of it while she gazed out across the city to the desert, always waiting beyond.

Before now, Anya had always considered herself an ocean sort of person. She'd always love the sea, its immensity and pull. She'd grown up in a city surrounded by water, and had imagined she would always live where she could see it, or access it, because it was what she knew. But she hadn't.

And something about the desert stirred her, deep inside. It was like the ocean inside out. It was a reminder, always, that no matter what was happening to her, something far greater and more powerful than petty human concerns stood just there. Watching. Waiting. And perfectly capable of wiping it all away.

She supposed other people might not find that comforting.

But then, when had Anya ever been like other people? If she was anything like other people, she might have remained a doctor in the emergency room of her busy hospital in Houston, Texas. She might have felt called to medicine like so many of her fellow doctors. Or even called to money and prestige, like her father.

Instead, she found as the days passed that becoming a queen gave her far more opportunities to truly help people. Without having to run triage, check vitals, or desperately operate a crash cart.

Even thinking about those things made her blood pressure rise.

She sat down with her own aides, who showed up one day at Tarek's order. They discussed different sorts of charity work. Initiatives Anya could undertake. Both the traditional province of Alzalam queens, and new ideas about the sorts of things she, as the most untraditional Queen in the kingdom's long history, could attempt.

A month after Tarek had appeared at the door of her cell, they announced their engagement.

But they did it in the traditional Alzalam fashion.

Meaning, the announcement was made and the nation launched itself into a week-long celebration that would culminate in the wedding itself.

"Your people do not waste any time," Anya said, standing out on a balcony Tarek had told her was built for precisely this purpose. The King and his chosen bride together, waving at the cheering crowd gathered below. "What's the rush? Are you afraid the bride will change her mind?"

"Historically yes." He shot her a narrow look, laced with that amusement she had come to crave. Because she knew it was only hers. "Many brides were kidnapped from an enemy tribe, and it was always best not to leave too much time between taking her and claiming her, in case the warriors from her tribe came to collect her."

"Romantic," Anya murmured. "Practically to Western levels, really."

She was rewarded for that with the bark of his laughter.

And she was starting to get used to how deeply she craved such things. His touch. His laughter. *Him.*

Not that she dared say such things to Tarek.

It wouldn't do to throw too much emotion into their very practical arrangement. She knew that. And no matter that she found it harder and harder to pretend her feelings weren't involved.

Anya sobbed out his name regularly, but kept her feelings to herself.

Just as she decided it was best not to tell this man of stone that sometimes, her own panic dropped her to the floor. Because that might not only involve emotions—Tarek's response to such a weakness might spark an attack.

She had spent hours in fittings over the past month, as packs of the kingdom's finest seamstresses descended upon her, determined to make sure that everything she wore—whether traditional or Western, depending on which day of the wedding week it was—reflected the glory of the King.

"And accents your own beauty of course, my lady," the head seamstress had murmured at one point, after there had been quite a lot of carrying on about Tarek and the honor due him from the women assembled in the room.

With more than a few speculative looks thrown her way, not all of them as friendly as they could have been.

But she understood.

"Of course," Anya had replied. "But I must only be an accent. It is the King who must shine."

That had changed the mood in the room. Considerably.

And it was not until later that Anya—who would once have ripped off heads if anyone had suggested she was an *accent* to a man—realized that somehow…she meant that.

The realization hit her like a blow as she stood in her glorious shower, and when her heart kicked in, she froze. She expected the panic to rush at her, to take her to the shower floor. She expected to sit there, naked and wet and miserable, until it finished with her.

But the panic didn't come.

No nausea, no hyperventilating, no worries that she might aspirate her own saliva and choke while unable to help herself.

The hot water rained down upon her. Anya pressed the heel of her hand into that tightness in her solar plexus, hard.

But still, though she could feel that she was *agitated*, there was no panic.

"Because I chose this," she whispered out loud. "I chose him."

It was hardly a thread of sound, her voice. She could barely hear herself over the sound of the water.

But it rang in her, loud and true, and kept ringing long after she left the shower and dried herself off.

The night they announced their engagement, Tarek did not eat dinner with her the way he'd been doing, too caught up was he in matters of state. Anya ate alone, enjoying her solitude now that it was not enforced. She read a book. She caught up with her far-flung friends, many of whom could not make it to this remote kingdom on such short notice, no matter how they wished they could. She let herself...be part of the world again.

After she ate, she sat outside. She found she couldn't get enough of the desert evenings. The sunsets were spectacular, a riot of colors that never failed to make her catch her breath. And even in the dark, she could feel the desert itself, stretching on and on in all directions, almost as if it called to her. She wrapped herself up in a blanket when she grew cold and stayed tucked up under the heaters, watching the magical old city bloom as the lights came on. Her aides had taken her on a guided tour of the narrow streets, the ancient buildings stacked high, and the more she saw of it, the more she loved it.

A mystery around every corner. History in every step. And wherever she turned, the people who smiled at her and called out their support of Tarek. Making her foolish heart swell every time she heard it.

They were not the only ones who adored him.

She didn't think she fell asleep, but one moment she was gazing out at the city and the next, he was there. As if she'd conjured him from the spires and lights that spread out behind him.

Anya smiled, then studied that face of his, sensual and harsh at once. "What's the matter?"

She was learning how to read him now, this man she would marry in seven days. He was always fierce. He was always, without question, the King. But there were different levels of ferocity in him, and tonight it seemed…darker.

Something inside her curled up tight in a kind of warning. The knot inside her grew three sizes.

But she kept her gaze on Tarek, and ignored them both.

"Nothing is the matter," he told her, standing there at the foot of the chaise where she was curled up. In a voice that was little more than a growl. "Save my own weakness."

"You have a weakness?" Anya asked lightly. "Quick, tell me what it is, so I might exploit it."

Tarek didn't laugh at that. His hard mouth did not betray the faintest curve. Anya ordered herself not to panic, or note that it felt too much like loss.

Or worse, ask herself how she could feel the things she felt after so little time.

"I spent the night in tense negotiations," Tarek said, staring down at her as if he couldn't quite make sense of her. Or as if Anya had *done something* to him. "It is the kind of diplomacy that I abhor. Snide remarks masquerading as communication. All employed by men who would never last a moment on any kind of real battlefield. Still, these things are part of what I am called to do. As such, they deserve my full attention."

"I'm sure you give everything your full attention."

As it happened, Anya had become something like obsessed with the force of Tarek's full attention. With the sorts of things he could do with all that *focus*. Her body shivered into readiness at once, her nipples forming hard peaks, her belly tightening, and the soft, yearning place where she wanted him most like fire.

The ways she hungered for this man never ceased to surprise

her. But the way he looked at her now did. As if she'd betrayed him in some way.

"The only thing I could think about was you," he told her, his voice a rough scrape against the dark.

It was not a declaration of feelings. It was an accusation.

An outrage.

For a moment, Anya froze, feeling as if he'd kicked her. That terrible knot grew teeth. But in the next moment, she breathed out. And again, as she had the night he showed her his scars, Anya understood that this was not something she could laugh away. She couldn't show him her first reaction. Once again, it was not softness or emotion he needed.

Maybe, something in her whispered, *all that medical training was not to keep your cool in an emergency room. Maybe it was so you could stare down a king no matter his mood, and be what he needs. Whether or not he knows how to ask for it.*

Not because she was losing herself in him, as one article she'd read about herself tonight had suggested. But because he wasn't simply a man, who a woman might argue with about domestic arrangements or respect or any number of things.

His people needed him to rule above all else. They had told her so themselves, out in the winding streets of this age-old city. And if she wanted to marry him, to be his Queen as well as his woman, she needed to support the King first.

Only once the ruler was handled could she tend to the man.

Because she was the only one who got both.

"You're welcome," Anya said, neither gently nor particularly apologetically.

He blinked at that, a slow show of arrogant disbelief that made her pulse pick up. "I beg your pardon?"

She didn't quite shrug. "Tedious negotiations with terrible people, you say? How lucky you must feel to know that I'll be waiting for you at the end of it." Anya nodded regally toward the foot of her chaise. "And you are even more lucky that I find myself in the mood for a king."

"Are you suggesting that it is possible that you might ever *not* be in the mood for your King?" Tarek was gazing down at her as if thunderstruck. Far better than the look that had been in his eyes before, by any reckoning. "An impossibility, surely. Or treason. You may take your pick."

"I am the Queen of this land," she told him grandly, and only just kept herself from waving an imaginary scepter in the air between them.

Tarek's dark eyes gleamed with the fire she knew best. "Not yet, Anya. Not quite yet."

"I will be the Queen in a week, and you are trying my patience." She sniffed haughtily. "Daring to come before me and speak to me of petty concerns when you could be pleasuring me, even now."

She was sure she could see him waver there. He looked torn between the sort of erotic outrage she was going for or more of whatever temper had brought him here, too much like a storm cloud for her liking.

Anya held her breath. She waited. And she could see exactly when that hunger that never seemed to wane between them won.

"You may not like the way I worship you, my Queen," Tarek told her then, his voice deep, suggestive, and a kind of dark threat that made her shiver, happily. "But I will."

Then he fell upon her. Both of them ravenous, both of them wild.

And when he held her before him, on her hands and knees so he could take her as he liked, Anya gloried in it, in him. The impossible iron length of him was a wildfire inside her. A gorgeous catastrophe of sensation and need. She was bared entirely to his gaze and to the desert sky, vulnerable and invulnerable at once, while he surged deep inside of her and made her scream.

It was quickly becoming her favorite melody.

A song she wanted to sing out, heedless and loud, for the rest of her days.

But Tarek wasn't done. And as he pounded them both sweet

again, until they were *them* again, Anya gave herself over to the only form of wedding vow she thought she'd ever need.

Again and again and again.

CHAPTER EIGHT

THE WEDDING GUESTS began to pour in the day after their announcement.

From near and far they came. Tarek welcomed in men who had fought with him, relatives and business allies, foreign heads of state and an inevitable selection of celebrities. He pretended he did not know which of his guests had spoken against him over the course of the last year and which had given him nothing but their quiet support.

But he knew. And they knew. And there was a power in the invitation to his would-be enemies, to permit them to witness how wrong they'd been about him up close. It was the logical extension of the press junket he and Anya had undertaken and Tarek could not pretend he didn't enjoy it.

There was a grand party that night to kick off the traditional week of celebrations. It was also the first opportunity for Anya to prove to the international crowd that she was not under duress. And for the people of Alzalam, that she was worthy of the role she was to assume at the end of the week.

"No pressure, then," she'd said earlier in the flippant manner only she dared employ in his presence.

Tarek had found he had to have her, in a slick rush of need, even if it meant that her aides would have to reapply all the beauty enhancements—to his mind, wholly unnecessary—that they'd used on her to prepare her for the evening.

"You will be a natural."

"Because you say so?" She had been slumped in a delicious sort of ruin where he'd left her, bonelessly draped over an ottoman in her bedchamber.

"Yes, because I say so," he'd replied. "Am I not the King?"

Anya had smiled at him, the way he liked best. Dreamy and sweet. Private.

The Anya who appeared in public never looked that soft. That was for him alone.

And as he stood in the middle of the grand party in one of the palace's ballrooms that night, Tarek found himself thinking about that smile more than he should.

Just as he thought about her more than he should, when he knew better.

Because while it turned out that the former prisoner he was marrying for purely practical reasons was remarkably good at distracting him from the things he brooded about, that didn't change the truth of them.

Like the fact he was obsessed with this woman.

Tarek knew better than that. The history of his kingdom was filled with examples of why romantic obsession was a scourge. Nothing but a curse. Many of his ancestors had been endlessly derailed by theatrics in the harem. Favorite wives seemed to lead inevitably to catastrophes—witness his former betrothed and the shame she had brought to her family. Tarek had always vowed he would never succumb to such pettiness.

He had already paid dearly for the affection he'd held for his younger brother. He could not afford a far worse blindness. He would never forgive himself.

"*Imagine my surprise,*" Anya had said at dinner one day after she'd finally got a comprehensive tour of the Royal Palace. "*I thought the dungeon was the scariest place in this building. But you actually have a harem.*"

Tarek had been feeling expansive and relaxed. He had eaten, then spread his woman out on the table. He had eaten his dessert from her skin—sweets from the sweet—before burying himself inside her to the hilt. Then they'd gone out to the tiled tub on her balcony and sunk into the hot water. He had smiled at Anya's wide eyes and scandalized tone.

"I was raised in the harem," he told her. *"My mother was only the first of my father's many wives."*

And he was not a nice man, and nothing like a good one, because he had greatly enjoyed Anya's look of horror.

"The only words we've discussed were wife and queen," she'd said then. Her shoulders had straightened with a sharp jerk, enough to make the water slosh around them. *"Wife was never plural. And neither was* queen."

"I enjoyed my childhood," Tarek had told her, reaching over to pull her to him, settling her before him, her back to his front. *"My brother and I were doted upon and when our half siblings arrived, they were, too. We all grew up together. We had maternal attention from all sides, and therefore felt that any attention we received from our father was a gift."*

He had not wanted to think about those years. When he and Rafiq had been so close. When it would have seemed laughable to him that anything could ever change that.

Even now, he sometimes forgot what had happened and thought to call his brother. Only to remember it all over again, with a sickening sort of lurch.

Anya's shoulders were no longer braced for an attack. She'd softened against him, and he liked that better.

"It's so hard to imagine that he could grow up and...do what he did," she said quietly.

Tarek tensed, and hated that she could feel it. *"When it comes to my brother, I do not imagine anything but his prison sentence."*

And his voice was so forbidding he could actually watch her

respond to it. Her shoulders had risen all over again. Her breath went shallow.

He told himself he did not, could not mind it. His brother had no place here. Childhood memories were one thing, but he would have no...*imagining.*

"*I think you would love the harem,*" he had continued after a moment. He'd tried to sound relaxed again, looking over her head toward the city before them. The sky above, the lights below. And Anya between. It made something in him...settle. "*It would certainly be one way to make friends in the kingdom.*"

He'd wondered if she would nurse her upset. If she would act as if he'd bruised her—

But this was Anya.

All she did was twist around to glare at him as if his brother had never been mentioned.

"*That, right there, is why I have no intention of filling my harem with all the wives I can support, though I certainly could. It is not worth all the fighting. The jealousy, the petty attacks, the attempts at power grabs.*" He'd shaken his head, thinking of those years. Thinking of his father's wives, not Rafiq. "*My father always acted as if he was unaware of such things, but I've never seen greater personal viciousness than I did then. It was never directed at me, but that didn't mean I didn't see it.*"

"*Thank you for this lesson on the historical use of harems here,*" Anya had said darkly. "*I have no desire to be in one, thank you. I would rather become a neurosurgeon.*"

"*The same accuracy and skill is needed to rise to power within one, I assure you.*" He'd laughed. It had been a shade more hollow a laugh than it might have been otherwise, but it had still been a laugh. "*I might assemble one for the sheer pleasure of forcing your hand. I suspect you would rule with an iron fist.*"

She had sniffed. She had not mentioned his brother again. "*You can try.*"

Tarek had a different way of trying. He'd pulled her astride him, pushing his way inside her again. Then he'd watched as she wriggled to accommodate him. It was his favorite show and no matter how many times he watched, it never grew old. Her indrawn breath, especially when she was already faintly swollen from before. The way she bit down on her lower lip. Her marvelous hips and how they moved against his as she adjusted to his length, his girth. The way she rocked slightly until it felt good.

And all the while she softened around him, drenching him with her fire.

Until there were no memories left to haunt him.

Until there was only Anya.

There was no way around it, he thought now, only half attending to the deeply boring world leaders standing around him. He was obsessed.

And he couldn't be any such thing. He was the King.

The country was the only obsession he allowed himself. The only memories he permitted. How else could he have fought off Rafiq? How else would he rule?

Against his will, he found Anya in the crowd. He didn't know what he wanted. To assure himself he was not obsessed or to feed that obsession? But whatever dark thoughts he might have had in either direction, when he located her he was instantly struck by the way she was holding herself.

Anya was wearing a glorious gown in a Western style for this first celebration of the week. It was a sweeping number that left her collarbone bare, a perfect place for the jewels he'd placed there himself when he'd finished wringing them both dry earlier. The rest of the dress was a glorious fall to the floor in a deep aubergine shade that made her glow. Her glossy hair was swept up so the whole world might see the elegance of her neck, the delicate sweep of her jaw, and all of that was nothing next to the sophistication she seemed to carry in her bones.

She looked like a queen. His Queen.

But she was staring at the woman before her in a manner Tarek recognized all too well. Her shoulders were tight and her chin was tilted up at a belligerent angle that Tarek knew was a tell. It was outward evidence of her ferocity.

It should not have been happening at a party in her honor.

And certainly not in the presence of so many cameras. Though that particular consideration was an afterthought—another indication that Tarek was not in his right mind where this woman was concerned. Surely, with the international press present at this party, his only thoughts should have been on their joint performance instead of her feelings.

You are a king, he reminded himself icily. *Perhaps act like one.*

He excused himself and crossed to her, moving swiftly through the great hall. The crowd of guests parted before him as he moved, and he did not waste his time nodding greetings or allowing anyone to catch his eye. He bore down upon his betrothed.

And Anya alone did not instinctively move out of his way. She stayed where she was, only glancing his way—with a frown—when he appeared beside her.

"I do not care for the look on your face, *habibti*," Tarek told her. In his language, because the froth of a blonde woman before her and the older man beside her who looked as if he smelled something rank were clearly American.

Anya's gaze softened. Her frown smoothed out, and Tarek thought he saw something like relief there. He took his time shifting to gaze directly at the people who dared upset her. Here in the royal palace, right beneath his nose.

"Your Excellency," Anya murmured in formal greeting. She smiled at the couple. "Dad, Charisma, I would like to introduce you to Tarek bin Alzalam, the King of this country and my fiancé." Then she looked at him again. "Tarek, this is my father, Dr. Preston Turner, and his wife, Charisma Turner."

"Ah, yes." Tarek neither smiled nor offered his hand, as was his right as sovereign. That it also made the man before him *tut* in outrage was merely a bonus. "The doctor, yes?"

It was possible he made *doctor* sound a great deal like *snake*.

But then, Anya's father did not look sufficiently honored to find himself in the presence of a king. Nor particularly pleased to reunite with his only child after such a long separation—that had included said child's incarceration. Tarek did not expect or want an emotional display, certainly, but surely there should have been something other than the haughty expression on the older man's face.

"I was telling my daughter that I was forced to reschedule several surgeries," the man said, as if relaying an outrage. "In order to fly across the world at a moment's notice."

Then he waited, as if he expected Tarek to react to that.

And Tarek did. He gazed down at the man the way he imagined he might look at an insect, should it dare to begin buzzing at him. Right before he squashed it.

Beside him, Anya made a soft sound that he thought was a suppressed laugh.

"My father is referring to his schedule at the hospital," she said quickly. "He is…distressed that he had to alter it to come here for these celebrations. I explained to him that he could have come in later in the week, of course."

"You may not care what people think of you, Anya," her father said, making no apparent attempt to curtail the snide lash in his words. "But I'm afraid I do. However inconvenient it might be, I can hardly pretend this hasty wedding isn't happening. It's been all over the news."

"Your daughter is my choice of bride," Tarek said, without comprehension. "She is about to become the Queen of Alzalam, the toast of the kingdom. Yet you speak of your convenience?"

The man bristled in obvious affront. Tarek did not reply in kind, an example of his benevolence he suspected was lost on this small and unpleasant man.

"Rescheduling is such a nightmare," the blonde on his arm breathed, her eyes on her husband.

"Excuse us." Tarek's tone was dark as he took Anya's arm. "Let us leave you to contemplate your calendar. We will continue with the celebration."

He steered Anya away from her scowling father, doing his best not to scowl himself, as that would only cause general agitation in the crowds all around.

"I cannot comprehend the fact I found you discussing your father's *inconvenience*," he said in a low voice. "As if he was not standing in the ancient palace of Alzalam's kings, in the presence of a daughter who will become Queen. He should have been stretched out at your feet, begging your favor."

And would have been even a generation ago, but the wider world tended to frown upon such things in these supposedly enlightened times.

Anya looked philosophical. Was Tarek the only one who could see the hurt beneath? And because he could see it, he could see nothing else.

"I suppose I should be grateful that no matter what he's doing, no matter where he finds himself or who he speaks to, my father is always...exactly the same," she said.

Tarek found himself even less philosophical as the night—and the week—wore on.

The kingdom overflowed with wedding guests and those who merely wished to use their King's wedding as an opportunity to celebrate, now that the troubles of the past year were well and truly over. There were celebrations in and out of the palace, all over the capital city and in the farthest villages alike, as the people celebrated not just Tarek and the bride he was taking, but this new era of the kingdom.

Tarek was deeply conscious of this. He had promised them a new world, a bright future, and this was the first happy bit of proof that he planned to deliver. And in a far different way than any of his ancestors would have. His brother was in jail, the insurgents had been fought back, and Tarek had no fear of the world's condemnation or attention—or he would not have been marrying this woman.

Now was a time for hope. His new Queen was the beacon of that hope.

Love grows in the most unlikely of places… the more easily swayed papers sighed, from London to Sydney and back again.

From Convict to Queen! shouted the more salacious.

But either way, choosing this thoroughly American career woman—all previously considered epithets to his people—was having precisely the effect on Alzalam's image that Tarek had hoped it would. She was a success and their supposed love story even more so. All was going to plan, save his unfortunate obsession with the woman in question that he would far rather have coldly used as a pawn.

Yet no matter where he found himself in these endless parties, dinners, and the more traditional rituals prized by his people, and no matter the current state of his insatiable hunger for Anya herself, Tarek couldn't keep himself from noticing that Anya's father behaved more as if he was being tortured than welcomed into the royal, ruling family of an ancient kingdom.

"I told you," Anya said one night, looping her arms around his neck as he carried her from her terrace into her bedroom. He had not yet moved her things into the King's suite, in a gesture toward tradition—even if he did not intend to install her in the usual harem quarters. He wanted her much closer. "My father believes there is no greater more noble calling than his. What are kings and queens next to *the foremost neurosurgeon in all the land.*"

Tarek threw her on her bed and followed her down. "He acts as if it is an insult that he is here at all."

Anya had sighed as if it didn't matter to her, yet Tarek was sure he'd seen a shadow move over her face. He hated it. "He has always been easily insulted. The real truth, I think, is that he's used to being the center of attention. That's really all there is to it."

"At his own daughter's wedding?"

"In fairness, if I was marrying almost anyone else he really would be the center of attention. Because the father of the bride commands a different part of the wedding where we come from. At the very least he would have stacked the guest list with his friends and associates, all of whom would be far more impressed with him than a collection of royals."

"Anya," Tarek had said, not exactly softly. "Why do you feel the need to treat this man with fairness when he feels no compunction to extend the same to you?"

She had looked stricken, then kissed him instead of answering.

Tarek understood that was an answer all its own.

Today there had been a gathering earlier for a wide swathe of guests, but the night featured a dinner for family only. Given the size of Tarek's immediate family, this meant a formal meal in one of the larger dining rooms, with all of Tarek's half siblings, their mothers, and their spouses invited to make merry. Compared to the other celebrations that had occurred this week, it was an intimate gathering. Tarek should have enjoyed introducing his bride to all his sisters and brothers—save the one, who no one dared mention.

But it was Anya's father who once again had Tarek's attention.

"It is a delight to welcome your daughter to the family," said Tarek's oldest half sister, Nur, smiling at the sour-faced doctor. Tarek wasn't surprised that his sister admired his choice of bride. Nur had not taken the princess route as many of their other half sisters had. She had a postdoctoral degree at Cambridge, she had married a highly ranked Alzalamian aristocrat who also happened to be a scientist, and she had never been remotely interested in or impressed by poor Nabeeha, at large in

Canada. "A real doctor in the palace at last. I fear I am merely a doctor of philosophy, myself."

Anya smiled. "You're very kind."

Beside her, her father snorted.

That was objectionable enough. But Tarek found himself watching Anya. At the way she lowered her gaze and threaded her fingers together in her lap, as if she was trying to calm herself down. Or as if her father had not merely made himself look foolish, but had hurt her in some way.

Unacceptable, Tarek thought.

"I wouldn't call Anya a real doctor," her father said with a sniff. "There is such a thing as a waste of a medical degree. And for what? To wear pretty dresses and play Cinderella games? What a travesty."

Nur drew back, appalled. Anya's chin was set, her gaze still on her hands in her lap.

Tarek found he'd had enough.

"You forget yourself," he said softly from his place at the head of the table. Though he did not project his voice on the length of it, he knew that the rest of his family heard him.

A stillness fell over the room.

The doctor was staring at Tarek. "I beg your pardon?"

"It is denied," Tarek retorted. He leaned forward in his chair. "I do not know where it is you imagine you are, but let me enlighten you. This is the kingdom of Alzalam. *My* kingdom, which I have bled to defend." There was a chorus of cheers at that, startling the older man. "You are sitting at my table. The woman you insult will be my wife the day after tomorrow. Men have died for lesser insults."

There was more murmuring down the length of the table, rumbles of support from his family.

But Anya's father only blinked at him. "Anya would be the first to tell you that she hasn't quite lived up to expectations. She was raised to make a difference, not to…"

"Not to what?" Tarek asked.

Dangerously.

He shouldn't have been doing this, he knew. Not because there was any weakness in a man defending his woman—quite the opposite. A man who did not happily and thoroughly defend his woman, in Tarek's opinion, was no man at all. But because Anya would likely not thank him for complicating her family affairs.

But it was too late.

"Preston," said the man's wife, fluttering helplessly beside him. "You haven't even touched your food."

"Don't insert yourself into things you don't understand, Charisma," he replied in a cutting tone that made his wife—and daughter—flinch. "The adults are talking."

"Dad," Anya said then, in a fierce undertone. "This is not the time or the place."

"My daughter is a smart girl," the doctor said, glaring at Tarek. "I had high hopes that she might lead with her intellect. Make the right choices. But instead, this spectacle." He shook his head and looked at Anya. Pityingly, Tarek was astonished to note. "I told you what would happen if you joined that traveling aid organization. I even dared to hope that prison might get your head on straight for a change."

Anya shook her head at him. "You say that as if you were actually aware that I was in a dungeon all that time. I was under the impression you were maintaining plausible deniability so as not to make golf at the club too awkward."

"Of course I knew you were in prison, Anya," her father snapped at her. "I can hardly avoid camera crews on my front lawn. What I don't understand is how you could come out of an experience like that and decide to make your life even less intelligible. What do you intend to do? Sit on a throne as you while your days away? Useless in every regard?"

Tarek did not like the way that Anya flushed at that, flashing a look at her stepmother. He remembered what she'd told him. That her stepmothers were allowed to be pretty and useless while she was meant to be smart. And it was clearly a downgrade to move from one column to the other.

"You will stop speaking, now," he decreed, and though the older man's eyes widened as if he planned to sputter out his indignation, he didn't make a sound. Like the coward he clearly was. "I will not bar you from your daughter's wedding, but one more word and I will have you deported."

Nur, sitting across from the Americans, did not applaud. Neither did her husband. But down the table, their other half siblings were not so circumspect.

"Tarek," Anya murmured. "Please."

Tarek kept his gaze trained on the man before him. The man who'd put shadows on his bride's face on what should have been a joyous occasion. More than once.

This was unforgivable as far as he was concerned.

"You and I know the truth, do we not?" Tarek did not look at Nur when she made a soft sound of agreement. Or at Anya, though he could sense her tension. "Your daughter is smart. Far smarter than you, evidently, which I imagine has scared you from the start. You wanted to control her, but you couldn't. And now look at you. A tiny little rooster of a man, prancing around a palace and acting as if it is his very own barnyard. It is not. I am a king. You are a doctor whose worth lies only in the steadiness of his hands. And your daughter has saved countless lives and will now save more in a different role, because that is real power. Not ego—"

The older man opened his mouth.

Tarek lifted a brow. "I do not make idle threats."

He waited as Anya's father turned an alarming shade of red. Tarek shot a look at Nur, who started up the conversation anew, and then Tarek sat back and stopped paying the older man the attention he did not deserve.

And it was only when the room filled with warmth and laughter again that Anya looked over at him and smiled.

Then mouthed her thanks.

Tarek had received gratitude before in the form of treaties. Surrenders. Invaluable gifts too innumerable to name, many of which were displayed with pride in this very palace.

But Anya's simple *thank you* lodged inside him like a heartbeat.

Until his chest felt filled with it—with her. Until it threatened to take his breath.

Until he wondered what he was going to do with this.

How was he going handle this woman he needed to be his Queen when she made him *feel*?

And not like the King he was—but like the regular man he could not permit himself to become.

Because Tarek knew well the cost of forgetting himself.

Rafiq had been the only person alive Tarek had felt he could truly be himself with. They had been so close. Tarek had depended on him. And Rafiq had used that affection to stab Tarek in the back.

Literally.

"*You cannot permit yourself the failings and petty feelings of common men,*" his mother had told him time and time again. "*In a king these are fatal flaws, Tarek. Remember that.*"

He remembered her words too well.

What was he going to *do*?

CHAPTER NINE

THE DAY OF the wedding dawned at last.

Anya had been waiting for the sun to rise for hours, unable to sleep.

She had been ceremoniously escorted to her bedchamber the night before by Tarek's sisters and aunts. It was tradition for the groom's relatives to guard the bride and so they had, though the royal family's version of "guarding" had included more laughter and abundant food. They had told Anya involved tales about Tarek as a child, omitting any mention of his treacherous brother. They had painted her pictures of what he'd been like as an adolescent, too aware of the weight he would one day carry.

All with a kind of easy, warm familiarity that Anya had never experienced before. She hardly knew what to call it.

It wasn't until she'd gone and stretched out in her bed with only the moon for company that she realized it was…family. They were a family. More, they acted the way she had always imagined a family should. Teasing, laughing. Gestures of quiet support when more serious topics were addressed. The very fact they'd all gathered together to celebrate Anya when all they really knew about her was that she was Tarek's choice of bride.

But they loved him, so that was all they needed.

Anya had stared out at the moon and accepted a hard truth. She had long told herself that she didn't need the connections that other people took for granted. She had her chilly father, she'd told people when the subject came up, and that was more than enough family for her, thank you. She had friends, though she didn't see them often enough.

But Tarek's family wasn't the Turner version of family. It was the version she realized now that she'd always imagined in her head—but had assured herself didn't exist.

It left her something like shaken to discover that she was wrong.

More, it made her miss Tarek.

The solid weight of his stare. The sheer perfection of his body and the things he could do with it. The fire that burned so bright between them that she found she didn't want to live without it, not even for a night.

She suspected she knew what words she could use to describe all the things she felt about the man she was marrying, and none of them were *practical*. None of them were appropriate press releases.

But they were right there on her tongue. Dangerously close to spilling out at the slightest provocation.

"Until tomorrow," Tarek had murmured much earlier that night, out in the desert where they had taken part in rituals he told her his people had considered holy since the earth was young.

It had felt more than holy to Anya.

The sand and the sky. The stars.

The two of them in a circle of fire while the elders sang over them.

Anya sighed now, remembering the stark beauty all around them. The press of the songs and chants against her skin, winding all around their clasped hands.

"If I hadn't ended up in your prison, I never would have

known," she'd whispered to Tarek. "*How much beauty there is in the world. Particularly here.*"

Particularly you, she'd thought, perilously close to letting those words she shouldn't say spill out to join the rest of the night's magic.

"*Tomorrow, habibti*," he'd said, his dark eyes gleaming.

Out on her favorite chaise, Anya waited as the sun rose. The city below her shook itself to life in preparation. Songs filled the air, alive with the sweetness of the coming day. She pulled her throw tighter around her, breathing in the desert air mixed with the palace's usual *bakhoor*, a smoky scent that would always be Tarek to her. She sighed as the first tendrils of light and color snuck across the sky while she watched. Yellows and oranges. A glorious purple.

As the sun climbed, the air warmed.

Anya did, too.

And the light danced all over her, reminding her that she was still free. That stone cells were a thing of the past. That what lay before her might not look like anything she'd thought she wanted—or should want—but made her feel, finally, that it might actually be possible to be happy.

A revolution, she thought.

Only then did she get up and head inside to begin the long process of getting ready for her wedding. Her royal wedding that would be broadcast around the world as part of the press release portion of the bargain she'd made with Tarek.

And in Alzalam, wedding preparations were a largely public affair. Her seamstresses swept in and out. All of Tarek's family returned, flooding in as if the dressing of the bride was a party they were throwing—more for themselves than her.

Once Anya was dressed in her finery and several thousand photographs had been taken, men were allowed in as well. Trays of food were brought in while the guests mingled all throughout the sprawling suite. Anya stood in one of the smaller salons, catching glimpses of herself in the enormous mirror propped against the wall while she thanked the guests for coming, one after the next, until it was all little more than a blur.

She looked like something out of a dream she hadn't known she'd had. Her dressmakers had truly outdone themselves, somehow managing to fuse both Tarek's world and hers into the sweep of the long white gown. She looked exactly as she should—like a beacon of a kind of hope.

Like the future she imagined here, bright beyond measure.

And then, perhaps inevitably, her father walked in.

She could tell by the way he marched into the salon, holding his body sharply and crisply, that he was still in high dudgeon from the other night. That he was *deeply offended* hung around him like a cloud, likely discernible even to those who hadn't spent a lifetime parsing his moods. The way he snapped the door shut behind him only underscored it.

That he wanted her to apologize to him—even though he'd had an entire day to get over what had happened at that dinner, having not been part of yesterday's rituals—was clear by the imperious way he glared at her as he stood there, Charisma standing to one side and slightly behind him, as if he didn't notice his only daughter on a dais before him.

In a bridal gown, with jewels in her hair.

Tarek's sister Nur had teared up when she'd seen Anya. "*You look like everything my brother deserves*," she'd said.

But her own father looked at her and saw only himself.

Anya kept herself from sighing, barely, because that wasn't anything new, was it?

"It's so nice of you to come and wish me health and happiness, Dad," she said, and she imagined she saw Charisma wince a bit. "Thank you."

Dr. Preston Turner did not wince. He hardly reacted.

"This is a low, even for you," he told her, the force of his outrage making his voice even crisper and more precise than usual. "It's not enough that you should humiliate yourself in this way and on such a grand scale when you are clearly in no fit state to make decisions of this magnitude. Look at the mess you've already made of your life. But that you should sit silently by and allow me to suffer such attacks..."

His voice trailed off. Anya mused, almost idly, that she had never seen her father at a loss for words in all her life. Not until now.

Point to Tarek, she couldn't help but think.

Sadly, he recovered. With a furious glare. "I thought I couldn't be more disappointed in you, Anya. Trust you to go ahead and prove me wrong yet again."

Anya looked at this man who she had tried and failed to please for her entire life. This man whose expectations sat so heavily upon her that she had found a dungeon preferable to the weight of them.

She knew she favored her mother in looks, but she had always imagined that there were similarities between her and her father anyway. Not his famous hands, maybe. Not his drive. But certain expressions. The color of their eyes.

But today she looked at him and saw a stranger.

No, she corrected herself. *Not quite a stranger. Something worse than that.*

A father who had made himself a stranger to his only child. By choice.

"Your disappointment has nothing to do with me," she said, with a quiet force she knew her father did not miss. "I can't help you with it or save you from it."

Out of the corner of her eye, she could see her stepmother, fluttering as ever as she murmured something to Preston.

"For God's sake," her father snapped at her. "Just stand still, Charisma."

"She's not your lapdog, Dad." Anya shook her head at him. "I know you like to think she's stupid, but she's not. She knows exactly how to handle you, which is an art I certainly failed to master. You're lucky to have her."

"I'll thank you to keep your opinions about my marriage to yourself," her father barked.

Though next to him, Charisma blinked. Then smiled.

Anya smoothed her hands over the front of her dress, because it made her think of her wedding and the life she would live here, far away from her father's toxic disappointment. "I thought we were commenting on marriages today. Isn't that what you came to do? Tell me your opinions about the man I'm marrying in a few hours? Or did you miss that I'm standing here in a bridal gown?"

"I would advise you not to speak to me in such a disrespectful manner, Anya."

"Or what?" It was a genuine question. "I'm not a small child you can spank. Or one of your surgical residents or nurses you can bully. You're standing in a palace that is to be my home, in a kingdom I am to be Queen of in a few hours. Really, Dad. What do you plan to do to me if I don't obey you?"

"I'm your father," Preston thundered at her.

"And I'm your daughter." Anya felt the swell of something inside her, bigger than a wave. It crashed over her, into her, and she couldn't tell if it was drowning her or drawing her out to sea. But she found she didn't have it in her to care. "I'm your daughter and you treat me a lot worse than a lapdog. I've spent my whole life trying to make you proud of me, but I realize now that it's impossible. No one can make you happy, Dad. No one. You don't have it in you. And that has to do with you, not me. I can't make you a different man. What I can do is stop pretending that I'm someone I'm not when you don't even appreciate the effort."

She had been afraid of saying something like that her whole life. And now she had, and she didn't feel a burst of freedom and joy, the way she'd thought she would. Instead, she found she felt sad. Not for herself, but for him. For the relationship they'd never had.

"I have no idea what you mean," he was raging at her. "You

had every opportunity to do the right thing and you squandered it, each and every time. That's on you, Anya."

And Anya was already swimming far from land. This was already happening. Last night there had been too many stars to count, and here was her father, determined to ruin it.

She lifted her hands, then dropped them. Not a surrender, because it felt too...right.

Too long overdue.

"I don't want to be a doctor," she told him, the words she'd never dared say out loud falling from her lips as if it had always been easy to say them. As if she should have long ago. Because there was no sadness in this. There was only truth. "I never did."

Charisma actually gasped.

"Don't be ridiculous," her father snapped. "You have obviously let this awful place get to you. You need help, Anya. Psychological help. You've always been far too emotional and your ordeal has clearly put you over the edge."

What struck her then wasn't the dismissive tone her father used. Anya was used to that. It wasn't the contemptuous look on his face, because, of course, she was familiar with that, too.

But she wasn't the same woman she'd been the night she'd gotten arrested. Those eight months had changed her.

Yet she still paused for a moment, tried to look inside herself, to see if anything that he said had merit. After all, hadn't she wondered if she was suffering from some kind of psychiatric issue? Hadn't she made little jokes to herself—and her friends once she'd started using her mobile again—about Stockholm syndrome?

No, came a voice from inside her, deep and certain and undeniably her own. *That's your father talking. You know what you feel. You always have.*

"It doesn't matter what I want to do with my life," she said quietly. "In the end, it's really very simple. You either love me, Dad—or you don't."

And then she waited. She didn't look past him to the closed

door with the palace staff waiting on the other side. Guests and soon-to-be in-laws celebrating as her own father couldn't. She didn't look at her stepmother, who was still standing at Preston's side. She didn't fidget. She didn't look away.

Anya trained her gaze on her father, direct and open. And watched as something impatient moved over his face. With possibly more than a little distaste, mixed right in.

"My God, Anya," he said. And when he spoke, that distaste was unmistakable. He didn't quite recoil, but managed to give the impression that he might at any moment. "You've become completely unglued." His gaze, so much like her own, sharpened in a way she hoped hers never had. She found she was bracing herself, though she couldn't have said why when she knew him. There was no point bracing for the inevitable, was there? "Unglued, emotional, and pitiful. Just like your mother."

He meant it like a bomb, and it exploded inside her like a blinding flash of light. She stared back at him, seeing nothing but his gaze like a machete, aimed right at her.

Aimed to hurt. To leave wounds.

On some level, Anya was aware that her father, brimming with triumph at the blow he'd landed, had turned and was marching for the door. She met her stepmother's gaze, bright blue and stricken, but all either one of them could do was stare. Then Charisma, too, scurried for the exit.

And once the door was open, the room filled up again. There was laughter again, sunlight and brightness and that glorious sense of expectation and hope that Anya herself had felt so keenly earlier.

She was aware of all of it. She smiled for her photographs. She shook hands, smiled wider, and did her job as the Queen she would shortly become.

Yet all the while, the bomb her father had lobbed at her kept blowing up inside her. Over and over again.

But not, she thought, in the way he'd intended it to.

Because all she could seem to concentrate on were memories of her mother she'd have sworn she didn't have.

She'd been seven when her mother died. Anya wasn't one of those who had memories dating back to the cradle, but she did have memories. That was the point. When all this time she'd convinced herself she didn't.

"*You are brave, Anya*," her mother had used to whisper to her. She would gather Anya in her lap, tucked away in the corner of the house that was only theirs. Sometimes she would read books. Other times, she would have Anya tell stories about her day. About school, her friends, her teachers. Or perhaps her stuffed animals, if that was a mood Anya was in. "*You are brave and you are fierce. You can do anything you want to do, do you hear me?*"

"*I hear you, Mama*," Anya would reply.

What she remembered now was that when she'd thought of all the things she could do, it had never been becoming a doctor. She had been far more interested in learning how to fly, with or without wings, much less a plane. And dancing, which she had loved more than anything back then, despite her distinct lack of talent or ability. And the masterpieces she'd created with her crayons, that she'd secretly believed were the sort of thing she ought to do forever, if only as a gift to the world.

Anya remembered walking in the backyard holding tight to her mother's hand, listening intently as Mama had pointed out a bird here, a bug there. She had repeated the names of flowers and plants, all the trees that towered over them, then made up stories to explain the tracks in the dirt.

She remembered her mother's laugh, her joyful smile, and if she focused as hard as she could, she was convinced that she could almost remember the particular smell of her mother's skin, right in the crook of her neck where Anya liked to rest her face when she was sleepy. Or sick.

Or just because.

Once one memory returned to her, all the rest followed suit.

She was flooded with them. And it was clear to her, when it was finally time and she was led from her rooms, that somehow, this was her mother's way of being here today.

It was what her private moment with her father should have been, yet wasn't. All these memories dressed up more brightly now, and almost better for having been lost to her for so many years.

Because it felt like her mother was here. Right here. With her she walked through the palace halls, surrounded by Tarek's sisters and aunts. It was as if her mother was holding fast to her hand all over again, her simple presence making Anya feel safe. Happy.

And absolutely certain that there was nothing wrong with her. No psychological damage from her time in jail. Just hope.

Anya knew, then, that every step she took was right and good, and better still, her mother was beside her for all of it.

She waited outside the great ballroom, open today to the even grander courtyard beyond, and she knew something else, too. As surely and as fully as if the words were printed deep into her own flesh. As if they were scars like Tarek's, angry and red at first, then fading into silver with the passage of time.

But scars all the same.

Because her heart was pounding at her. Her stomach was fluttery. But she knew that none of that was panic.

She thought of her long-lost mother and the things she'd said so long ago. That Anya was brave and fierce, capable of choosing any life she wanted. Anya had believed her.

Anya believed her so hard, so completely, that when she was gone it was as if she'd taken all of that with her.

Without her, Anya had never felt brave. Or anything like fierce. And she hadn't known what she wanted, except her mother back.

But that was never on offer.

And without her mother there, there was nothing to temper her father's coldness. Back then, he'd been a different man. She could remember him, too. Never as warm as her mother had been, but he'd smiled then. He'd laughed. He'd danced with her mother in the backyard on warm summer nights, and held Anya between them, her bare feet on his shoes. In every way that mattered, she'd lost both her parents when her mother died.

Anya almost felt sympathy for him, in retrospect. But back then, as a little girl awash in grief, all she'd known was that she didn't want to cause her father more pain. She'd wanted him to love her. She'd wanted him to gather her up in his lap, tell her stories, and make her feel better. Dance with her in the yard while the summer night stretched out above them, warm and soft. But he didn't.

He never did.

So she'd made herself cold instead, to please him.

But she was not cold, no matter how hard she tried. And maybe, Anya thought, as she waited for a panic attack to hit her when surely it should—poised to walk down an aisle to marry a king in the full view of the better part of the planet— the panic attacks had been her actual, real feelings trying to get out all along.

The doors opened before her, then. And then it was happening.

She was walking toward Tarek. She could see him there, waiting for her at the end of the aisle, magnificent in every way.

But best of all, looking straight at her. Into her.

As if this thing between them was fate and they'd been meant for each other all along.

When she finally reached him, he took her hands and they began to speak old words. Ancient vows. Sharing who they were and becoming something else.

Husband and wife. King and Queen.

And so much more.

But inside, Anya made a different vow, there before the assembled throng. That she would not be cold another day in her life. That she would never again be buried in stone or locked away behind iron. That she would not allow herself to feel dead while she was alive.

Not with him. Not with this man who had freed her from a cell first, and then from the life she'd never really wanted.

So she married him, and then she lived.

She danced at the reception. She smiled until her cheeks hurt. And when Tarek finally stole her away, bundling her into a helicopter that raced across the desert, suspended between the shifting, undulating sands beneath and the heavens above, she loved him so much that she thought it might burst out of her like a comet. Another bomb, and a better one this time.

Anya didn't know how she kept it inside.

The helicopter dropped them in an oasis straight out of a fairy tale. The water in the many pools was an indigo silk, lapping gently against the sand as the breeze hit it. Palm trees rustled all around, while waterfalls tumbled over rocks like a song.

And a glorious, sprawling tent blazed with welcoming light, beckoning them in.

"Welcome, my Queen," Tarek said when the helicopter rose back into the air and the sound of its rotors faded away. He had led her into the vast living area of the tent, outfitted with a thousand pillows and low tables, like a desert fantasy. Now he smiled down at her. "This is the royal oasis. Some claim the water is sacred. Some believe it heals. We will have to test it, you and I."

Anya was sure that all the things she felt must be emblazoned on her face. But that wasn't enough. Nothing could be *enough*.

She reached up, placed her palms on either side of his beautiful face, and sighed a little as his strong arms came around her. She thought, *this is home*.

She was finally home.

"Tarek," she breathed, with her whole heart. With everything she had and everything she was. With all the bright hope inside her after this magical, beautiful day. "I love you."

And watched as his face turned to stone.

CHAPTER TEN

"YOU MUST BE TIRED," Tarek said, taking each of Anya's hands in his. He pulled them away from his face, as if that would erase the words she'd said.

The words that seemed to fill the tent and more, roll out over the desert like a storm, blanketing everything.

Burying him alive.

"Not particularly," she replied, that frown he liked too much appearing between her brows. "On the contrary, I've never felt more alive. And in love, Tarek."

In case he'd missed that the first time.

And there was that pressure in his chest. That pounding thing inside him that he thought was his heart, but it seemed too large. Too dangerous.

Too catastrophic.

"Come now, Doctor," he said, not sure he sounded like himself—but it was hard to know what it was he heard with that storm in him. "There are far more pleasurable things to do tonight than forget ourselves."

She was dressed in that gown that he had spent long hours today imagining taking off her, one centimeter at a time. Her hair was set with precious jewels, each representing a different facet of the kingdom. She was a vision, she was now his Queen, and the last thing in the world he wanted to talk about was love.

But Anya did not melt into him. She did not shake off the gathering storm. Instead, her hands found her hips.

"Forget ourselves?" she echoed.

This oasis was one of Tarek's favorite places in all the world, and yet he never came here enough. It had been years. There always seemed far too many things he needed to do in the city, far too many responsibilities in the palace alone. He had looked forward to the time he would spend here with Anya more than he should have.

It was his own fault. He accepted that. He'd allowed his obsession with her to get the better of him.

No wonder it had come to this.

"I take responsibility," he told her, as he had the day they'd met. When she had sat opposite him in her prison grays in a roomful of dizzy light.

When he had found himself stunned, the way he had been ever since.

His declaration did not have the effect on her that he'd been hoping it would. It was hard to say it had any effect at all. Anya only continued to stare up at him, still frowning, her hands still propped on her hips.

"I'm beginning to think that you say that as a way to deflect attention. It's nice that you want to take responsibility, Tarek. But no responsibility needs to be taken." She lifted her shoulders, then dropped them, a parody of a careless shrug when he could see the stubborn angle of her chin. "I'm in love with you."

"We are married," he ground out. "There is no need for… this."

"We can pretend that I married you because I was suddenly seized with the need for a throne." She actually rolled her eyes, something he would have taken exception to under any other circumstances. "But I think you and I both know that there are a great many more convenient ways to stop practicing medicine.

I could have simply…stopped. People do that. Who knows? I could have moved to a quiet little town and opened a charming bookshop, if I liked. There are a thousand better solutions to a career that makes me unhappy than marrying a sheikh. A king. And everything that goes with that."

"We discussed what this marriage is and isn't," he managed to say, aware that his voice was little better than a growl. "Romantic fantasies were never a part of this."

"Oh, right." Another eye roll, that Tarek liked no better than the first. "I should have realized. This is the part where you attempt to convince me that I don't know my own feelings. This is where you tell me that I've somehow confused love with something else. A bit too much of the bubbly stuff, perhaps? I can see how a person might mistake the two."

"I think," Tarek said, carefully, though he was not doing a good job at keeping that seething, furious note out of his voice, "that it is easy to let the pageant of a wedding…become confusing."

Anya aimed that smirk of hers at him. "Are you confused?"

"I warned you, did I not?" And he was less careful, then. The storm was too intense, too rough and wild. "You can't help yourself. You're culturally predisposed to romanticize everything."

Any other woman of his acquaintance would have backed down in a hurry, but this was Anya.

"I wasn't sitting in my jail cell, rhapsodizing about the possibility of being swept off into the arms of a desert king, thank you very much," she hurled at him. "If I fantasized about you at all back then, it was to imagine your comeuppance. And I don't think that I've romanticized what happened since. We had an agreement, sure. But we also had everything else."

Tarek wanted to touch her. And knew that if he did, it would be betraying everything he stood for. Everything he was.

And still he had to draw his hands back as they moved toward her, seemingly of their own accord.

"I do not believe in love." He said it with brutal finality, but he felt no joy in it when she flinched. "I should have made that clear from the start. I rather thought I did. Love has no place in an arrangement like this. How could it? I am a king, Anya."

"You are," she agreed. She shook her head as if she didn't understand. Or as if she didn't think *he* understood. "But you're also a man. And that man—"

"There is no difference between the two," he said gruffly. "Don't flatter yourself, Anya. I married you because it was convenient. Marrying a Western woman, a doctor who the world decided was a prisoner of conscience, was a calculated political move. It suggests things about me that I would like the world to believe. That I am progressive. That I am capable of softer feelings and fairy tales. That my regime and my kingdom are soft and cuddly in some way, or that I have a more accessible side. When none of those things are true."

Her hands had moved from her hips and were hanging on her sides, curled into fists now. Another gesture of disrespect he would accept from no one else in his presence. She'd gone pale, but she was still holding his gaze, no matter that her eyes were far brighter than before.

What she did not do was back down.

"I understand the nature of a press release," she said, from between her teeth. "But that's not the only thing that's between us."

Tarek roamed away from her then. The tent was expansive, this room in particular, but it was still only a tent. There was only so much distance he could put between them.

He heard her follow him, her dress rustling in a way that set fire to parts of his imagination he wished he could cut out. Or dig out with his own fingers, whatever worked, just to be… *himself* again.

This was not how he had imagined this evening going.

When Tarek had looked up and seen her—there at the other end of the aisle that his staff had made through the center of the crowd, laden with flower petals to mark her way—he'd worried that he might truly have died where he stood.

Right there, in full view of the world.

He felt as if the skies had opened up and rain had poured down on this stretch of ancient desert that was lucky to see water from above perhaps twice in a decade. More, he was sure he'd been struck by lightning.

Repeatedly.

If possible, she was even more beautiful than she'd been only the night before, when he'd been bound to her in the desert, the fires all around them flickering over her and making her glow.

Tarek had wondered how it could be that every time he looked at her it was as if he'd never seen her before. He felt that stunning jolt of recognition. His heart beat at him, hard. He felt the punch of it in his gut. And always, that heavy fire in his sex that was only hers.

It was not Alzalamian tradition for a father to walk a bride to her husband. It was rare that a bride's family had even been present in weddings of old, when brides had been used to end wars and make allies of enemies. Tarek had never been gladder that he was made of this place, these sands and these proud tribes, because even the sight of her dour father would have marred the perfection he'd seen moving toward him on her own.

A vision in white. Petals at her feet and glittering jewels in her hair.

His Queen. His woman. His Anya.

Her gaze was fixed on him as if he was the sun. She was smiling, brighter than the desert sky far above them in the grand courtyard.

There was a part of him that knew news organizations from around the world, set up around the courtyard with their cameras, would capture that smile. That it would sell their story better than anything else could. Tarek was aware of it the way he was aware of the sky, the heat, the crowd. All the inevitabilities, but he didn't care about it the way he should have. He didn't feel as if it was a job well done, that smile of hers, or as if he ought to sit around patting himself on the back for the show.

All he could think was that her smile was his.

His.

For the first time in as long as he could remember, possibly ever, Tarek had resented the fact that he was the King. That he could not enjoy Anya's joyful smile privately. That he could not keep this perfect, exquisite vision of his Anya walking toward him to marry him to himself.

I do not wish to share her, he had thought.

And when she finally reached him, he'd gazed down at her in a kind of shock, torn between what he wanted and what was.

Duty and desire, as always.

But there was only one winner in that fight, and ever had been.

Tarek knew that. He had always known that. And yet here he stood, engaged in futile battles inside himself while she looked at him with eyes so soft it made him ache, speaking of *love.*

"You can't really mean to tell me that you think there isn't more between us than a bargain we made," Anya said from behind him.

He turned and braced himself, but she didn't look the way he expected her to look. Her arms were folded and she was glaring at him. She was not cringing. She was certainly not frail and fainting. If she was awash in whatever emotions he'd seen in her eyes outside, he could see no trace of it on her.

This is your American doctor, he reminded himself. *In case you have forgotten.*

Not the sweetly pliant woman who smiled at him like he was a sunrise and ran all over him like the heat of the day.

"You're talking about sex," he said, harshly. "I won't pretend I don't enjoy it. But it is only sex."

Tarek meant that to hurt. To cut her in half, or at least stop this conversation. And he did not admire that he had that in him. That urge to cause pain that did not speak well of him or his ability to control himself no matter the situation. How had he imagined he'd been tested before? He clearly had not been.

But he didn't take those words back, either.

He should have known better. This was Anya.

She laughed.

And by the time she stopped, he found his teeth were gritted. His jaw clenched so hard he was surprised he didn't hear something break.

"Oh, Tarek." There was still laughter in her voice, and she shook her head a little as she said his name. "You can't really think that I'll suddenly and magically believe that what happened between us is *just sex*, because you say so. It doesn't work that way."

"You are mistaken," he said, though his mouth was full of glass, he was sure of it.

"I was there." It was as if she hadn't heard him speak. Her gaze never wavered. "I know better."

And something inside him was shaking. Shaking, crumbling, turning to ash and that bitter glass even as he stood there. Suggesting that what he'd taken to be the solid iron foundation of who he was, who he needed to be, had only ever been wishful thinking after all.

"I understand what it is you want," he told her, trying to sound less like broken pieces and more like a king. "But you cannot have it. Royal marriages have always been thus. Each one of us has very specific duties, Anya. I must rule the kingdom. You must support the throne. There will be heirs and they must be raised to respect the country, its people, the traditions that make us who we are, and the future we must make happen if we are to thrive."

"That sounds like a civics lesson," she threw at him. "I'm talking about our marriage."

"Our marriage has even more rules," he retorted. "How could you think otherwise? This is not one of your romances. This is a union that must produce the next King. You and I do not belong to each other, Anya. We are not lovers. I belong to the kingdom. And you must know your place."

"My place." Her eyes glittered with temper and something else Tarek didn't think he wished to define. "Maybe you'd better tell me exactly what you think that is."

"I have been telling you." His voice was an iron bar and he wished he still was, deep within. He wished she hadn't made him doubt he ever could be again. "What do you imagine this last month has been?"

She did not laugh at that, as he half expected she would, this woman who sobbed out her pleasure as if she might never recover and then faced him down as no man alive would dare. He saw something in that gaze of hers falter as she searched his face. He told himself he did not wish to know what she looked for. "This last month?"

"Yes, Anya." He started toward her then, the lanterns flickering all around them. The tent was lush, done up in deep colors, soft rugs, and everything that might make the cold of a desert night more comfortable. But it might as well have been a stark, empty cell for all he noticed. "What did you think? I have been teaching you how to be the Queen I want."

"I didn't realize that class was in session." There was that brightness in her eyes again, but she didn't give in to it. She stood taller, lifted her chin the way he thought she always would, and as ever with this woman, met his gaze.

Defiantly, he thought.

But Tarek was an expert at putting down rebellions. And he knew that if he did not stop this one before it started, it would sweep them both up. He had seen it happen.

He had spent his childhood surrounded by his father's wives. Some of them loved his father. Others loved his power. But love was always at the heart of the jealous wars that swept through the harem, pitting wife against wife and even half siblings against each other sometimes. All for love.

Practical wives, like his mother, kept themselves above the fray.

"A queen in love with the King is but a silly woman in love

with an inconstant man," his mother had told him long ago, in the dialect that marked her as a member of the fiercest of all the Alzalam tribes. He knew his father had been forced to fight for her—literally, in a bare-fisted battle against her eldest brother. Only when he won did his mother's people, and his mother, consider his proposal. "*The world is filled with such women in love with lesser men. But there is only one King of Alzalam. And I choose to be his Queen first, last, and always.*"

He had to make Anya see.

"I have taught you well," he said as he drew close, impressed as ever that she did not back down. Even when he stood over her, perfectly placed to put his hands on her in temper. In passion. In any way he liked, but she looked unmoved by his proximity. "I taught you the kinds of meals that I prefer and how I like to eat them. I taught you how to give me your surrender when I wish it. Each and every kind of release I prefer. And how to please me with your compliance."

She shook her head. "Silly me. I thought *I* taught *you* that there's nothing wrong with taking out your frustrations on a willing participant."

"There's nothing I don't like about you, Doctor," Tarek gritted out, because that was no more than the truth. "I like your sharp tongue. I like your temper and your brain. And I think you know I like the pleasures of your flesh. But you must never mistake the matter. Those are part of the bargain we have made. Love does not enter into it."

"I think," she said softly, her eyes glittering, "that His Majesty protests too much."

"There it is again. That maudlin belief that all things end up tied in a bow while something sentimental plays in the distance. I understand that you can't help it. You can't change where you came from." He sighed. "But it's not real, Anya. It will never be real."

"I don't believe you."

"You don't have to believe me. It makes no difference. Not

believing me won't make what I'm telling you any less true or real. It will only cause you heartache. Facts are facts whether you choose to believe them, or do not."

"Tarek," she began, a kind of storm in her eyes. "You must know that I can see—"

But he did not wish to know what she saw. He *could not* know what she saw.

He had only let his guard down once, and he bore the scars of that mistake.

He refused to do it again.

"Very well then," he bit off, wrapping his hands around her upper arms and jerking her toward him, as he should have done from the start. "Let me show you."

And he set his mouth to hers in a punishing kiss.

But as sensation stormed through him, lighting him up and making him yearn for things he knew better than to want, Tarek suspected that the real punishment was his, not hers.

CHAPTER ELEVEN

His kiss was electric.

Anya could feel it in every single inch of her body, tearing her up. Making her wonder how a person could function when they were nothing but pieces, scattered and torn and tossed to the wind. Burned alive, yet wanting nothing more than to keep burning.

She had half a mind to pull away. Slap him, maybe, not that she wanted to cause him pain. But she wanted to *wake him up*.

To prove to him that he was wrong about this and she was right.

That not only did she love him, but he loved her, too.

But Tarek was kissing her, and it didn't take much for her to forget that there was anything in the world but that.

All the things she'd been thinking all day seemed to course through her then, its own kind of power source. Until everything was something far hotter and brighter than electricity, and she could feel it inside her, twisting all around and then sinking down deep.

To where she would always run hot and soft for him. All for him.

"This is what we are," he gritted out, in her ear. "This is what I want from you."

She wanted to protest. She wanted to beat him away with her fists. Or her mind did, anyway.

Because her body wanted nothing more than to be close to him. To be devoured by him and to devour him in turn. To be wrapped around him, and then, gloriously, lifted up into his arms once more.

Where I belong, she couldn't help but think.

No matter how many times he tried to tell her otherwise.

He carried her through the tent, one section after the next. She had the impression of salons made of tapestries, delicately carved furnishing, and wide wooden trunks. But she only knew they'd reached a bedroom when he laid her down on a wide, soft bed. Lanterns lit up the brightly patterned walls and made their own shapes out of shadows.

But all Anya could really focus on was Tarek.

His robes were ivory and gold again, but there was far more gold tonight. The light caught at it, making him gleam. He was resplendent and beautiful, powerful and pitiless, and she loved him so much and so hard it made her feel lightheaded.

That in no way made her *less* mad at him.

Anya was panting as much from the force of the things she wanted to say to him as his deep, drugging kisses, and she pushed herself up on her elbows so she could glare at him with the full force of her displeasure.

But all he did was follow her down to the bed, making them both groan as their bodies came together. He wasted no time in getting his hands on her, up beneath skirts and then streaking up to her knees. He found her upper thighs, and took a moment to trace the place where her stockings were attached with clips. Then he moved on, finding the white-hot, molten truth of her. Of this.

Of them.

Tarek stroked her then, intent and deep. She fell back down into the soft embrace of bed, piled high with silk and linen and surrounded by the scent that rolled over her the way this man—

her *husband*, her King—did. She told herself to fight, but she was unable to do anything at all but lift her hips to take his clever fingers as they found their way into her slick, wet heat.

And she knew that she should be ashamed of this. That he could tell her there was nothing between them but sex, then prove it so easily. That she could claim she loved him and sex was the least of it, then succumb to his touch so wantonly.

But her hips lifted with abandon. Her back arched to give him better access. She was moaning out his name, even before he began to thrust his fingers deep inside her.

His other hand moved to her face, guiding her mouth to his all over again. Taking what he wanted. Showing her who she was.

Tarek kissed her, deep and hot, dark and demanding.

And when she broke apart, it was against his mouth. He groaned back as if he was consuming every last noise she made. As if she was his, and the sounds she made were his, and he was branding her mouth and sex alike.

But it was not love, he would claim. It was only sex, this mad possession.

Tarek moved over her and she could feel his hands working between them. A tug here, and adjustment there. Then the broad head of his hardness found her slick folds.

He waited.

Anya opened her eyes to meet his, stark and commanding.

"I love you," she whispered.

Tarek made a rough noise, then he was thrusting inside her, deep and hard. Reward or punishment, or both wrapped in the same shock of connection and belonging, hunger and dark delight—it was hard to tell.

She'd had him so many times by now. She knew his body so well. She knew his scent, his weight, the glory he could work with a twist of his hips or that merciless mouth of his.

She knew too much.

And this was different from what had come before. This was a storm all its own, a wildly different claiming.

It was raw, untamed, and just this side of *too much.*

It was like a fever. It was all those things she'd felt all day, whirling around and around, all of them a crisis.

And still he pounded into her, braced there above her, as he made her his in a new way to suit the new things they were to each other.

Husband and wife. King and Queen.

This.

He could call it what he liked. Anya knew better.

But still, when the explosion came rushing at her, she wasn't entirely sure she would survive it. Or even if she wished to.

Tarek let her fall apart first, but he kept going until she sobbed. His name, maybe. Or a cry for the mercy she both did and didn't want. Until her fingers dug so hard into the back of the robes he still wore that she felt a nail break.

Still he continued.

Proving a point, she was sure. Driving them both wild. Making her shake and shake, sensations roaring through her with such intensity it almost scared her.

"I love you," she cried out as she hurtled off a cliff she hadn't seen coming.

And only then did Tarek follow, with a roar she felt shake through her all over again, like a new kind of shattering.

And there was no drifting off into bliss. There was no oblivion.

Tarek lifted his head, shifting his weight to his elbows. Anya was too aware of how he was covering her then, that rangy body of his, heavy and muscled everywhere, pressing her down into the bed.

Another claim, she knew. Like the rings he'd put on her hand today. Like the title he'd bestowed upon her, the throne they now shared, the palace that was to be her home.

He had never looked more like a predator than he did then, the lanterns throwing odd shapes onto the walls of fabric all around them. He was stone and hawk, carved from granite and cast in metal.

And the way he looked at her broke her heart.

Tarek moved to wipe moisture from beneath her eyes. He used his thumbs, touching her carefully, but there was nothing gentle in the expression on his face.

Something inside her rolled over hard, then sank.

"That is a pleasurable duty," he said, horribly. Deliberately. "But it is a duty, Anya. Everything I do, everything I am, is that duty. Sex to me is about succession before it is anything else."

"Succession…" she repeated.

But she was winded. She could feel it as if he'd reached in, scraped her raw, and then sucked everything she was out.

And in return, what was left was that familiar knot in her chest.

It swelled, then pulsed.

"You are a doctor," he said in the same darkly calm way. Still lodged deep inside her, his shoulders wide enough to block the light, as if he'd taken over the whole world. As if he *was* the whole world. "Surely you must have noticed that we have never used anything that might prevent nature from taking its course."

And Anya's brain…blanked out at that, more or less. Still, she heard him. She knew that he was talking about birth control and that she ought to have thought about it.

Why hadn't she thought about it?

Because she hadn't. It had been a month, she was indeed a doctor, and she had never even raised the subject in her own mind. No matter how many times they came together like this. No matter how many times she'd felt him flood her with his release.

Why haven't I thought about it? she demanded silently.

But no answers presented themselves.

There was a curious look on his hard face. "You look so shocked. I assumed it was what you wanted. You surely knew, and when you did not raise the topic, neither did I."

She couldn't quite catch her breath. Or move. "Why would you...?"

"I told you I wanted to marry you." He did something with his jaw that might as well have been a shrug, though there was nothing careless in it. "I am not a man of half measures. Of course if I wished to marry you, that would mean children to follow. You can tell me that you did not know this, if you like. But between you and me, *wife*, I don't believe it."

And there was a truth in his words that she didn't like. Especially not now, when she felt as if he had stripped her of everything, leaving her with nothing.

Nothing but that terrible knot that seemed to grow twice its size in a moment. Then three times its size in the next.

Worse, it hurt.

"You told me I could have whatever I wanted. You promised that no matter what it was, you would make it happen." She shook her head, horrified when she felt tears spill over, but completely unable to do anything but let them. "What do you call this?"

"Practicality," he said, there against her mouth, a bitter kiss. "We can none of us be anything but what we are, Anya. Remember that. It will save you pain."

Then he was moving. Anya struggled to sit up, some part of her thinking she ought to leap to her feet, chase after him, *do* something.

But she couldn't seem to move.

"What if I'm not practical?" she demanded of him as he stood there beside the bed. "Will you throw me back into your dungeon? It is called the Queen's Cell, after all."

"Now I know why," he threw back at her. "You decide if you want to be my Queen or you wish to be my curse, *habibti*. And I will respond in kind."

And then she watched, in shocked disbelief, as he left her. On their wedding night.

When he had just finished telling her how little she truly meant to him.

She stayed where she was, trying to breathe. Trying to think of how best to keep fighting—

Until she heard the sound of a motor turning over outside, and she understood.

He wasn't simply leaving the room. He was leaving, full stop.

The message was clear. As long as she insisted on loving him, there could be no stopping him.

When the panic attack hit her that time, she honestly thought that it might kill her. Or maybe she wished it would, this time.

It came on all fronts, walloping her again and again.

She couldn't catch her breath. Her heart pounded so hard it frightened her. She was nauseated. Sweating. Hot, then cold. Then *this close* to bursting out of her skin—

And all the while the tent spun around and around and around, until she was so dizzy she was afraid she might fall down.

It took her a long while to realize that she was already lying flat.

Slowly, laboriously, she pulled herself up, but she couldn't stand. On and on it went, as if she was caught on some sort of horrid carnival ride. Eventually she made to the side of the wide bed, then to the floor, crawling on her hands and knees across priceless rugs, sure she would die there. Any moment.

There were too many things in her head. The certainty that this time, she really was going to die. That she'd minimized these attacks, called them *panic*, but this would be the end of her. Left behind in her wedding dress, on her hands and knees on the floor of a tent in a desert that even her emotionally va-cant father had warned her she'd only chosen to stay in because something was terribly, terribly wrong with her.

She was sobbing or she was gagging, or it was both at once. But still, Anya crawled until she found the bathroom.

And then she celebrated her first night as Queen of Alzalam

by curling up in a wretched ball next to yet another toilet, waiting for this violent death to claim her once and for all.

Which gave her ample time to think about all the things that Tarek had thrown at her tonight.

Her love. His horror that she would even use the word. His talk of duty, and her place.

She thought of the Queen's Cell and felt the panic rise all over again as she imagined him throwing her straight back in for another stint of cold stone walls and unyielding iron bars.

Not that it mattered, she thought miserably, there on the floor. Because wasn't this marriage just another kind of prison? Not the way she'd imagined it, but clearly the way Tarek intended.

A sick little repeat of her childhood and the life her mother had left her to, however unwillingly.

Anya already knew where that led.

To this, right here. To that throbbing, blaring knot in her chest and her in a ball on the floor, alone.

And then, through all of that noise and riot, nausea and anguish, she heard a voice as clearly as if someone stood over her.

She blinked, but she was still alone.

"*You are brave, Anya,*" said her mother in her head. In her heart. "*You are fiercer than you know. And you can make your life whatever you want it to be.*"

My life, she thought then. *And certainly my marriage.*

She pulled in a shaky breath, deep. Then let it out, and like magic, the panic disappeared with it.

As if it had never been.

Anya sat up carefully. Gingerly. Waiting for all of those terrible sensations to slam back into her and throw her straight back down into that miserable ball, writhing within reach of yet another toilet.

But it was still…gone.

"*You are the bravest girl I know,*" her mother whispered, deep inside, where Anya understood, then, she always would.

She pressed her hand to that place in the center of her chest, the place where that knot had always blazed at her, and felt her eyes fill anew.

But for a different reason this time.

She'd thought it earlier today, hadn't she? That the panic was her feelings all along. That all those things she'd locked up in her attempt to please her father had only ever waited for her there.

Now she understood that it was more than that.

It had come out medically, because that was the only thing she allowed herself. It had burst forth in symptoms, so she could catalog them. List them. Pretend she could clinically examine her own breakdowns.

Because medicine was the only emotional language she'd ever allowed herself.

But now... Now she knew.

It had been her mother all along, talking to her. Telling her. Showing her by making her stop. By making her listen.

By coming to Anya in the only way she would hear.

She laughed a little bit, there on the floor of a desert tent, still wearing her wedding gown as she crouched there in yet another bathroom.

Because it had worked.

She'd had a panic attack before she chose her specialty in medical school, and knew she wasn't going to choose neurosurgery. She'd another panic attack, a terrible one, the night before she'd taken her medical boards. She'd had them with regularity as a resident. Then, for a time, she'd thought she'd gotten them under control.

Until that last one she'd had while she was still an ER doctor. The one that had made her realize that if she didn't change something, radically, she very well might die of that pressure in her chest.

"Thanks, Mama," she said now, out loud, though her voice was scratchy. "You were pushing me where I needed to go all along."

"*Be brave, Anya,*" her mother had whispered the last time

Anya had seen her alive. She'd held her tight, though she'd been so thin by then. So frail. "*I will be with you, always. You only have to look.*"

Anya hadn't looked, but that was okay. Her mother had kept her promise just the same.

She wiped at her face. She took a breath.

And she knew, with a new sort of certainty that reached deep into every last part of her, that she was not going to have a panic attack again. Not ever again.

Because she'd finally cracked the code.

It was love. And who had ever said that love had to be all soft plush toys, big eyes and faint trembling? Anya loved a king who happened to also be a hard man, made of this desert in its formidable starkness.

Loving a man like Tarek was a challenge. Even a calling.

Her calling, she knew, without a shred of doubt.

And this time, Anya was choosing a calling because of love. Because her blood moved hot inside her and she had never felt so much all at once without it flattening her on cold, impersonal bathroom floors. Because she didn't fear him, she loved him, and that meant she could take whatever came. No matter what it was.

Even if what came for them was him.

She was not a soft and trembling thing herself, and that was why he'd chosen her. Tarek could say what he liked about practicality and duty and all the rest. But he'd chosen her all the same.

Just as Anya had chosen him. Because he was absolutely right. She hadn't spared a thought to the possibility they might make a child, and that was so unlike her it really should have been funny.

All along, no matter what they pretended—to themselves and each other—the two of them had been choosing each other.

Anya simply knew it. It was in her now, part of her DNA. And she could have stayed where she was, reveling in this new knowledge, but there was no time for that.

Because Tarek had given her golden opportunity to prove that she was truly his Queen. That she was deserving of the title, and that he might give her anything she wanted, but she would do better in return. She would give him what he needed.

If she had to walk all the way back to the palace, she would.

She staggered to her feet and wandered through room after room of this marvelous, plush palace that was something far more than a *tent*. She found the entrance and pushed her way out, stopping outside when the beauty of the oasis hit her.

The canopy of stars. The soft lights that showed her date trees dancing in the breeze, and set to glowing all the glorious pools set into the sand.

But most beautiful by far was the figure she saw standing near the water, looking into the indigo depths as if tortured.

Anya glanced to the side and saw a jeep pulled up beneath the palms. When she had been so sure he'd driven it off. That he'd left her here.

Because that was something, she realized, her father would do without a second thought.

And she decided, then and there. This was not her childhood. She was not that daughter her father had ignored—and she was not her mother, either.

Tarek was her husband. This was her marriage.

And Anya was brave. She was fierce. She would make their lives exactly what she wanted.

All she had to do was be the Queen he had chosen her to be, at last.

CHAPTER TWELVE

TAREK STOOD BY the ancient pools, looking for wisdom in the water that men of his blood had long called holy, but seeing only himself.

And the monster he had become.

He despised weakness, and yet it had taken hold of him. It had eaten away at him, leaving nothing behind but the hunger he could no more control than he could feed enough to sate himself.

Making it impossible for him to leave tonight, when he knew that's what he should have done.

To prove to her that what he said was true.

That there was nothing between them but duty. Because that was all that *should* have been between them.

He heard the rustle of her dress first, sounding like the desert breeze. Like the date palms that danced overhead.

And then she was there beside him, reflecting back at him from the water's surface. Tarek turned to look at her, expecting to find her in pieces and already kicking himself for breaking her, no matter how necessary.

But his heart did the kicking, hard against his ribs, because this was Anya. She did not look broken in the least.

"I did not expect you to come after me," he said.

When he could.

"Why?" Her tone was arch, and she did nothing to conceal the evidence that she'd been crying from him. She stood beside him as if it was her place, her right, and made him wonder why he thought she should conceal anything. "Because women of your acquaintance are more likely to fling themselves on the mercy of foreign countries than confront you personally? I apologize. I never did learn how to cower."

He admired her, and that was only one of the problems. That was only one of the ways she was tearing him apart, and all she was doing was standing there, watching him calmly.

As if she could see straight through him.

And had every intention of doing it forever.

Something in Tarek...broke.

It was not the duties and responsibilities that marked his life. It had not been the losses he suffered. His mother when he was twelve. His father last year. Worse still, the brother he had loved unconditionally, until the night he'd come to kill Tarek. And had laughed while he'd tried, betraying not only Tarek in that moment, but all of Tarek's memories of their childhood.

As if Rafiq had died that night and killed Tarek, too. Yet both of them had to live with it.

He had survived all of those things, if perhaps more scarred and furious than the cheerful boy he'd been once. He'd had no choice but to survive.

But he didn't know how he was meant to survive this.

It was this. It was her.

It was this woman he never should have met in the first place.

And it was something about being here, far away from the civilization of the city, the dampening influence of the palace, where he could never forget for a moment that he was the King. And what, therefore, he owed everyone around him, all the time.

But out here in the desert, he was only...a man.

With her he became the things he should not whether he wished it or did not.

With her he broke into pieces when he could not break. He tore open, when he needed to remain contained. Himself above all.

"*A broken man can rule, but only ever badly*," his mother had always told him. Well did Tarek know it. The history of the world was littered with broken men who ruled their countries straight into the dark.

He had always intended to find the light. Always.

"You knew the rules going in," he heard himself say, louder than he could recall ever speaking before. As if he howled to the moon and stars above. "You knew what this was."

"But rules are not who we are," Anya replied, with that impenetrable calm he found a challenge. More than a challenge—it bordered on an assault.

"Rules are what separate us from the beasts," he thundered at her. "And emotions are what separate kings from mere men. I have a country I must think of, Anya. Do you not understand this? I cannot have *feelings*."

Because that was what this was. He understood that now.

He had become the thing he'd sworn he never would.

All because of her. The woman who stood beside him, when he had never wanted that. He thought of that soft, inconsequential girl he had been betrothed to and knew full well that none of this would have happened, had she done her duty. He would have felt nothing. He would have married her, even bedded her, with courtesy and distance. He would have treated her with respect.

He never would have felt a thing.

And now, instead, Tarek felt everything.

Every star in the sky above him was bright and hot and still dull compared to what shined in him now, all because of this woman.

Anya turned to him then, looking at him straight on the way she always did. Direct, to the point.

Honest, something in him whispered.

Neither hiding the emotion he could see on her face nor flinging it at him.

And a great deal as if she was daring him to do the same.

Daring *him*, when no one else would brave such an endeavor.

"I understand," she said, so evenly he had the mad urge to *force her* to sound as uneven as he felt. As messy. As ruined. "If it was easy to fall in love, Tarek, we wouldn't call it falling, would we? If it wasn't overwhelming, we might say we stepped into it. Or slid into it, maybe. But everyone knows falling can only end one of two ways. Either you stick the landing or you don't, and either way, it's probably going to hurt."

That word echoed in his chest. In his head. It beat in him like a pulse.

Like a drum.

"I have spent my life in service to this country," he threw at her. Then his hands were on her again, somehow, holding her close. The look in her eyes was killing him. *She* was killing him, as surely as if she wielded a sword or gun. When all she was doing was looking back at him as if she already knew all the noise and clamor inside of him. As if she heard that same drum. "My entire life, everything I have learned and everything I became, I've done so to better serve and rule this kingdom. And not merely rule from afar, as so many do. I put my body into the fires of war to protect my people. I always will. This is who I am."

"Of course it is," she said softly. "No one doubts you are a great king, Tarek. How could they?"

"What you're asking me to do is—"

But he couldn't finish.

And all the while the drums grew louder.

"I'm asking you to love me," Anya said, but she didn't sound anguished. She sounded resolute. "I'm asking you to let me love you. I'm asking you to let us build a family, but not because it's our duty. Not only because of that and not only because we intend to raise them in your family's tradition, but because we want them to really understand what a family is."

"Anya..." he gritted out.

"You're right that I never mentioned protection," she said, and to his astonishment, she smiled. How could she *smile* when he was being torn asunder where he stood? "I didn't even think of it and I used to give lectures on the topic. How could I possibly have failed to think about something so important?"

She shook her head, still smiling. Still wrecking him without even seeming to try.

Tarek tried to gather himself, but it was no use.

"I'll tell you why," Anya continued. "Despite some reports, I didn't lose my mind in that cell. If anything, it clarified my life for me. And then there you were, with your hand outstretched, and I knew."

He shook his head at that as if he could ward it off—push her away—but even as he did, he held her close.

"I couldn't admit it to myself," she told him. "I didn't have the words. But I knew, Tarek. And I think that every choice I made that day was in service to this. *Us.* To building the family we were always meant to be."

"Anya. *Habibti.*"

But she didn't stop. "I don't want a family like the one I already have, Tarek. I don't want the coldness, the contempt. I think it's possible that my father knew how to love a long time ago, but I don't think it's in him any longer. I don't ever want a child of mine to feel the way that I have, all these years. And I don't believe that the man you are—the King you are—would tolerate treating his own child the way you saw my father treat me. You leaped to my defense. How could you visit that upon your own?"

He didn't understand what was happening in him. The earthquake that was ripping him open when he could see that the palms behind her stood tall.

"My mother warned against this," he managed to get out.

"She was never involved in the harem's squabbles, because she wasn't emotional. She thought that it made her a better queen that she did not love my father and I have always agreed. The less emotion, the better. But I neglected to guard against other kinds of love. I was reckless enough to love my brother so blindly I overlooked his flaws, and nearly died for that folly. I want no more emotion in my life, Anya. None."

"Your brother is a coward and a snake. He's precisely where he belongs, and you put him there. And loved him enough to let him live."

"It was an act of mercy, nothing more."

"Tarek. What is mercy if not love?"

He wanted to shout at her. He wanted to shout down the trees. He wanted to wrestle the stars, and beat them into darkness—but all he could do was stand there as this woman tore him apart.

"And maybe not loving her husband did make your mother a better queen." Anya held his gaze. "Maybe that was exactly what your father needed. But Tarek. Do you think I don't know who *you* are?"

And Tarek was a man who had always known who he was. From the day of his birth, his destiny was secure. He had never had a moment's doubt, never suffered from the trials of insecurity. How could he?

He knew who he was. What he was. What he would do, how he would do it, and how history would record him.

He had always known.

Now he gazed down at this woman, his wife and his Queen, who made his heart beat. Who made him want things he'd never considered possible or even desirable before.

And it suddenly became critical to him that he know who *she* thought he was.

"You don't need a cold queen, or a harem filled with women, none of whom love you so much as they love power," she told him when he didn't answer her question. Because he couldn't. "You need me and you know it."

And for perhaps the first time in his life, Tarek found himself appreciating the power of pure confidence in another. Because Anya wasn't asking him or begging him, she was telling him.

She kept going. "You would never have chosen a prisoner and elevated her as you did otherwise. You would never have defended me against my own father, in public. Or left me with your own family the way you did, with no worries whatever that I might embarrass you or act against you in some way. You need me, Tarek. The woman who loves you. The Queen who will defend you."

"Anya." And her name was that drumming thing, and that drumming was a song. He could hear it in the night all around them. In the wind and the sand. In him and between them. And, at last, Tarek stopped fighting it. "I fear...that want to though I might, I do not know how to love."

And her smile then was so bright it made the heavens dim.

"Then I will love you enough that you are forced to learn," she whispered.

This time, when Tarek broke, he understood it was nothing to fight. It was no surrender. It was no rebellion he needed to quell.

Unless he was very much mistaken...this was falling.

And she was right. It hurt.

But that hardly mattered. What was one more scar to add to his collection?

"And if I already love you," he managed to ask, though his heart ached. His temples were spikes of pain. He fell and he fell. "What then?"

Anya slid her arms around his waist, and tilted her head back to look him full in the face. "We will make our own rules, here and now. You and I. We can do as we like, Tarek. This is ours."

And he thought, then, of possibilities instead of problems. Of hope instead of tradition.

Of love—not instead of duty, but laced through it, making it glow.

He thought, *Have I loved her all along?*

And the thought itself seemed to fuse with that smile on her face, the stars all around them, and all the ways he fell. Until he was filled with a wild sense of wonder.

"I think I stuck the landing, *habibti*," he told her, and his reward was not only the way her smile widened and took the world with it. But the way it felt inside him, a wild rush that left him smiling, too.

"I love your scars, that you won in defending this kingdom even though it broke your heart," she said, moving her hands lightly over his chest, tracing one scar. Then the next. He felt it like light, though he still wore his robes. "I love your arrogance and your certainty, because it makes it so evident that you could never be anything but a king. I love my King, Tarek."

He wanted to speak, then, but he was filled with that wonder and a bright, almost painful *thing*—

It occurred to him, at last, that it had never been obsession. This was so much more than that. *She* was.

"And you deserve to love me back, King and man alike," she whispered fiercely. "You deserve a place where you can hide, Tarek. Where you can be who you are. No thrones or kingdoms or worries. No people. Just you and me. Just this."

Tarek felt washed clean. Made new. He held her face between his hands again, but this time there was no darkness in it.

Because there was none left in him.

For she was a light far brighter than the desert sun, and he could feel her inside him like the brightest, hottest midday.

"Just as you deserve a place where you can shine, Anya," he told her gruffly. "Queen always. *My* Queen, always. And whatever you want of me, you will have, as long as I draw breath."

"Tarek," Anya whispered. "I do love you. So much."

"I love you," he whispered back, because there was no other way to describe the tumult. The longing and the light. The fury and the fear. The endless need, the sharp joy.

Her. Anya.

It was falling and then falling more. It was a tumble from a height so high it made his whole body seize—

But the landing was worth the fall.

It was the way she smiled at him. It was the ferocity in her voice when she came to find him, wherever he'd gone. It was the way she'd knelt before him on a terrace long ago, taking him deep in her mouth and absolving him of the scars he wore, the wars he'd won.

It was the love in her eyes, then and now. Always.

"I love you," he said again, because it barely scratched the surface. It was too small a word, and yet it was everything.

"Tarek," she whispered. "I love you, too."

"Teach me how to love you," he demanded, urgently. "Teach me every day. And I promise you, Anya, I will give you the world."

She slid her hands up the length of his chest, then looped her arms around his neck. And then they were both falling, together, and that was no less overwhelming, but it was theirs.

This was all theirs.

And it was good. And Tarek intended to keep on falling, forever.

He was the King of Alzalam, and he would see to it personally.

"Don't you see?" Anya asked, breathlessly, still smiling as if she would never stop. "You already have."

And later, Tarek thought, he would think of that scene by the pools as the real moment they became husband and wife, man and woman.

Them.

Forever.

But here and now, he stopped wasting time, and kissed her.

CHAPTER THIRTEEN

TEN YEARS LATER, Anya waited for her husband near the pools at the oasis, on a night so like their wedding night that she found she couldn't stop smiling.

This time, she wore a shift dress and little else, sitting on a rock with her feet in the silky water. No bulky wedding gown that had required both of them to remove.

Eventually.

They had kept their promises to each other. There had been press releases and publicity tours, but that fell under the mantle of *duty*. They were both deeply dedicated to doing their duty.

But when they were alone, they were something more than a king and a queen, the embodiment of a kingdom's hopes and dreams.

They made their own hopes and dreams, together.

He told her stories of Rafiq and the childhood they'd shared, learning how to grieve what was lost without letting what had happened tarnish the good that had happened first. And because he'd trusted her with that, she told him about her panic attacks and her mother, and how she was reclaiming her own memories of the happy life she'd had when her mother was alive.

Because grief was love. And because they were together, there was no need to fear love, no matter how it presented itself.

Loving each other was the best antidote to fear that Anya could have imagined.

And it only grew with time.

Anya gave birth to Crown Prince Hakim before their first anniversary. She stood beside Tarek on the balcony called the King's Overlook where he'd taken her to announce their engagement, showing off the next generation to the crowds below.

"*You look so happy,*" she'd whispered, brought nearly to tears at the sight of this tiny creature they'd made tucked up safe and sound in his father's arms. And she didn't think it was entirely due to her new mother hormones, either.

It was him.

Tarek had turned to smile at her—the smile that was only for her, no matter where they happened to be.

"*I have long dreamed of this moment,*" he'd told her. "*But I find that now it is here, what I care about is you, by my side. My Queen outside these walls. My wife within. But most of all, mine.*"

"*Yours,*" she'd agreed. "*Always yours.*"

They'd made two more princes to keep Hakim company, then a brace of princesses. Each and every one of them a perfect bundle of dark eyes, dark hair, and a deep stubbornness they took pleasure in claiming came from the other.

"*Behold your work,*" Tarek had said one morning in the great courtyard, years back, shaking his head as his firstborn son and heir ran in circles. Naked. "*This is the future of my kingdom.*"

Anya had only laughed.

"*That sounds familiar, doesn't it?*" she'd asked him one afternoon, years later, when their tiny, perfect eldest daughter was found in one of the palace's public rooms.

And refused to leave.

"*No,*" she kept saying. "*No.*"

With all the consequence of a king.

Tarek had laughed too, but he'd also pulled Anya close and kissed her soundly.

They tended to their duties, they were deeply involved in the raising of their children, and at night they repaired to the King's royal suite and set themselves on fire.

Over and over and over again.

Year after year. Whether Anya was big with child or not. Whether they had fought for days or not.

They might not have always agreed with each other. They might have spent hours shouting. She was too direct and he was too arrogant and sometimes those things left bruises no matter how much they loved each other.

But they kissed each other's wounds, there in the dark of their big, wide bed. And when he moved inside her and she clung tight to him, they found their way back to each other. Sooner or later, they always found their way.

As the years passed, Tarek became a powerful new voice in the region. And Anya found ways to use the power he'd given her to truly do her best to make the world a better place. She and her sister-in-law Nur first became friends, then partners in a charitable initiative that promoted women's health and wellness.

"*Finally*," she told Tarek at the charity's inaugural ball. "*A use for all my medical knowledge.*"

"*You will always be my doctor, habibti,*" he'd told her, there in the center of the ballroom where his gaze told her what his hands and his mouth would, later. When they were alone and naked and making each other fall all over again.

Anya thought of her mother daily and never did have another panic attack, as she'd known she wouldn't. Instead, she pursued the dreams of that long-ago little girl. She danced often, because she was a queen and her husband was a king and there were an endless array of balls for them to attend. She had tried painting things as a hobby, but had found herself both terrible and bored.

Her true artistic genius was still in the medium of crayons, in her opinion—something she discovered by coloring things with her children and then festooning them about the bedroom for Tarek to find. Then find creative ways to both laugh at her and praise her at the same time.

Usually he chose to take her flying, without wings or a plane, as only he could.

The most surprising twist had happened back in Seattle. Charisma had left Alzalam a new woman. She had stopped fluttering and had laid down a series of ultimatums, the crux of which was that she no longer intended to be a lapdog of any kind.

Anya's father and his latest, youngest wife were still together, ten years later. With twins Preston doted on.

"Part of me wishes he could have been a better father to me," Anya had confessed to Tarek one night, after one of her father and Charisma's annual visits—something else her stepmother had insisted on. *"But if he had, would I be here now?"*

"That almost makes me like him," Tarek had growled.

She and her father were not close. He had never apologized and never would. She didn't understand him and never would. But they tried, in their way. And she and Charisma had become friends out of the bargain.

It was hard to imagine a better outcome.

And now a whole decade had passed, laced with its own share of disappointments, certainly. But brighter with hope, all the same. Stronger by far for the tests they'd faced along the way.

"Life is good, Mama," Anya whispered into the night. "Life is so good."

She heard Tarek come out of the tent, then. They liked to come here whenever they could, but that didn't mean he could always leave the palace behind. After their long, leisurely dinner in that bright and sprawling room where he'd once tried to put her in her place, he'd taken an urgent phone call.

Anya had checked in with the children and their nannies, had taken care of a pressing matter with her own doctor, and had come outside to wait for him.

She tilted her head, listening to the cadence of Tarek's voice and ready to be what he needed when he came to her. Sometimes he raged. Sometimes he grieved. Now and again he was lost.

He came to her as he was, however he was, and she held him. She challenged him. She was strong for her King and when he could be a man again, he was always hers.

Always and ever hers.

Tonight he sounded good. And then he ended the call and she heard him walk toward her.

And wasn't at all surprised when he simply lifted her up, turning her so he could hold her in his arms.

"Happy anniversary, my love," he said in a low voice, there against her mouth.

"Only a decade," Anya replied. "It seems like a week. And forever."

Tarek kissed her as he always did. As if it was the first time, desperate and needy.

And when she was panting against his mouth, he smiled. "Well?"

She laughed. "Why do you ask when you already know? You always know before I do."

Tarek moved back, then went to his knees before her. This big, strong man. This powerful King.

He slid his hands over her belly and kissed her there. Then grinned up at her.

"Every centimeter of you is precious, and mine," he said with all the dark arrogance she adored. "I know when something changes."

"Yes, I'm pregnant again," she said. "The doctor just confirmed it. But you knew that."

"I did." His grin faded, and something stark replaced it. Stark like the desert all around them, beautiful and vast. "You keep teaching me that no matter how much I love, there is always more. There is no end to it."

"There is never any end," she agreed, her eyes getting glassy. "Not as long as we're together."

Tarek stood them. He bent to scoop her into his arms and then he held her there, gazing down at her.

"Come, *habibti*," he said, the way he always did. The way he always would. "Let us fall the rest of the way together."

And then he carried her off into the night, falling sweetly into the rest of their beautiful lives.

* * * * *

My Bought Virgin Wife

CHAPTER ONE

Imogen

IN THE MORNING I was to marry a monster.

It did not matter what I wanted. It certainly did not matter what I felt. I was the youngest daughter of Dermot Fitzalan, bound in duty to my father's wishes as women in my family had been forever.

I had always known my fate.

But it turned out I was less resigned to it than I'd anticipated when I was younger and far more silly. And when my wedding had not loomed before me, beckoning like some kind of inevitable virus that nothing could keep at bay.

There were no home remedies for my father's wishes.

"You cannot let Father see you in this state, Imogen," my half sister, Celeste, told me briskly as she swept in. "It will only make things worse for you."

I knew she was right. The unfortunate truth was that Celeste was usually right about everything. Elegant, graceful Celeste, who had submitted to her duty with a smile on her face and every appearance of quiet joy. Stunning, universally adored Celeste, who had the willowy blond looks of her late mother and to whom I had forever been compared—and found lacking.

My own lost mother had been a titian-haired bombshell, pale of skin and mysteriously emerald of eye, but I resembled her only in the way a fractured reflection, beheld through a mist, might. Next to my half sister, I had always felt like the Fitzalan troll, better suited to a life beneath a bridge somewhere than the grand society life I'd been bred and trained for.

The life Celeste took to with such ease.

Even today, the day before my wedding when theoretically I would be the one looked at, Celeste looked poised and chic in her simple yet elegantly cut clothes. Her pale blond hair was twisted back into an effortless chignon and she'd applied only the faintest hint of cosmetics to enhance her eyes and dramatic cheekbones. While I had yet to change out of my pajamas though it was midday already and I knew without having to look that my curls were in their usual state of disarray.

All of these things seemed filled with more portent than usual, because the monster I was set to marry in the morning had wanted her first.

And likely still wanted her, everyone had whispered.

They had even whispered it to me, and it had surprised me how much it had stung. Because I knew better. My marriage wasn't romantic. I wasn't being chosen by anyone—I was the remaining Fitzalan heiress. My inheritance made me an attractive prospect no matter how irrepressible my hair might have been or how often I disappointed my father with my inability to enhance a room with my decorative presence. I was more likely to draw attention for the wrong reasons.

My laugh was too loud and always inappropriate. My clothes were always slightly askew. I preferred books to carefully vetted social occasions where I was expected to play at hostessing duties. And I had never convinced anyone that I was more fascinated by their interests than my own.

It was lucky, then, that my marriage was about convenience—my father's, not mine. I had never expected anything like a fairy tale.

"Fairy tales are for other families," my severe grandmother had always told us, slamming her marble-edged cane against the hard floors of this sprawling house in the French countryside, where, the story went, our family had been in residence in one form or another since sometime in the twelfth century. "Fitzalans have a higher purpose."

As a child, I'd imagined Celeste and me dressed in armor, riding out to gauzy battles beneath old standards, then slaying a dragon or two before our supper. That had seemed like the kind of higher purpose I could get behind. It had taken the austere Austrian nuns years to teach me that dragon slaying was not the primary occupation of girls from excruciatingly well-blooded old families who were sent away to be educated in remote convents. Special girls with impeccable pedigrees and ambitious fathers had a far different role to fill.

Girls like me, who had never been asked what they might like to do with their lives, because it had all been plotted out already without their input.

The word *pawn* was never used. I had always seen this as a shocking oversight—another opinion of mine that no one had ever solicited and no one wanted to hear.

"You must find purpose and peace in duty, Imogen," Mother Superior had told me, time and again, when I would find myself red-eyed and furious, gritting out another decade of the rosary to atone for my sins. Pride and unnatural self-regard chief among them. "You must cast aside these doubts and trust that those with your best interests at heart have made certain all is as it should be."

"Fitzalans have a higher purpose," Grand-Mère had always said.

By which, I had learned in time, she meant money. Fitzalans hoarded money and made more. This was what had set our family apart across the centuries. Fitzalans were never kings or courtiers. Fitzalans funded kingdoms they liked and overthrew regimes they disparaged, all in service to the expansion of their wealth. This was the grand and glorious purpose that surged in our blood.

"I am not 'in a state,'" I argued to Celeste now, but I didn't sit up or attempt to set myself to rights.

And Celeste did not dignify that with a response.

I had barred myself in the sitting room off my childhood bedchamber, the better to brood at the rain and entertain myself with my enduring fantasies of perfect, beautiful Frederick, who worked in my father's stables and had dreamy eyes of sweetest blue.

We had spoken once, some years ago. He had taken my horse's head and led us into the yard as if I'd required the assistance.

I had lived on the smile he'd given me that day for years.

It seemed unbearable to me that I should find myself staring down so many more years when I would have to do the same, but worse, in the company of a man—a *husband*—who was hated and feared in equal measure across Europe.

Today the historic Fitzalan estate felt like the prison it was. If I was honest, it had never been a home.

My mother had died when I was barely eight, and in my memories of her she was always crying. I had been left to the tender mercies of Grand-Mère, before her death, and my father, who was forever disappointed in me, but still my only remaining parent.

And Celeste, who was ten years older than me. And better at everything.

Having lost my mother, I held fast to what was left of my family, and no matter if that grip often felt a good deal more like a choke hold I was performing on myself. They were all I had.

"You must look to your sister as your guide," Grand-Mère had told me on more than one occasion. Usually when I'd been discovered running in the corridors of the old house, disheveled and embarrassing, when I should have been sitting decorously somewhere, learning how to cross my ankles and incline my head in sweet subservience.

I had tried. I truly had.

I had watched Celeste come of age before me, elegant and meek in ways I envied and yet failed to understand. She had done it all with grace and beauty, the way she did everything. She had been married on her twentieth birthday to a man closer in age to our father—a hereditary count who claimed the blood of famed kings on both sides, stretching deep into Europe's gloried past. A man who I had never seen crack so much as the faintest smile.

And in the years since, Celeste had presented her ever-glowering husband with two sons and a daughter. Because while I had been raised to do my duty and knew what was expected of me—despite the dark thoughts I had about it in private while dreaming of Frederick's blue eyes—Celeste had *bloomed* in her role as countess.

It was hard to look at all that blooming, I thought uncharitably now. Not the day before I turned twenty-two, came into my fortune, and—not coincidentally, I was well aware—married the man of my father's choosing, who I had never met. My father felt a meeting was unnecessary and no one argued with Dermot Fitzalan, least of all the daughters he used as disposable pawns.

Happy birthday to me, I told myself darkly.

I would celebrate with a forced march down the aisle with a man whose very name made even the servants in the manor house recoil in horror.

A man I knew all manner of terrible things about.

A man widely regarded as a devil in the flesh.

A man who was not even the member of some or other gentry, as I had expected my eventual husband would be, given my father's celestially high opinion of himself and all he felt his vaunted pedigree—and thus mine—demanded.

In contrast, Celeste's husband, the dour count, had a title

that ached with age—but had very few lands behind it. Or any money left over after all those centuries of aristocratic splendor, I had heard them whisper.

And this, I knew, was why my father had chosen a man for me who might have lacked gentility and pedigree, but more than made up for both with his astonishing wealth. Because this would surely add to the Fitzalan reach and financial might.

Genteel Celeste, so gentle and fragile, had been married carefully to a title that would sit well on her perfect brow. I was hardier. I could be sold off to a commoner whose coffers only seemed to swell by the year. In this way, my father could have his cake and eat it, merrily.

I knew this. But it didn't mean I liked it.

Celeste settled herself on the other end of the settee beneath the windows in my sitting room, where I had curled in a miserable ball this gray January day as if my brooding could make time stand still and save me from my fate.

"You will only make yourself ill," she told me, pragmatically. Or at least, that was how I interpreted the way she gazed at me then, down the length of the aristocratic nose she shared with our father. "And nothing will change either way. It is a wasted effort."

"I do not wish to marry him, Celeste."

Celeste let out that lilting laugh that I normally thought sounded like the finest music. Today it clawed at me.

"You do not *wish*?" She laughed again, and I wondered if I imagined the hardness in her gaze when it faded. "But who, pray, told you that your wishes mattered?"

I noted the year in as grim a tone as I could manage. "Surely my wishes should be consulted, at the very least. Even if nothing I want is taken into account."

"Fitzalans are not modern, Imogen," Celeste said with a hint of impatience, as I knew my father would. Though he would not *hint*. "If what you want is progress and self-determination, I'm afraid you were born into the wrong family."

"It was hardly my choice."

"Imogen. This is so childish. You have always known this day would come. You cannot possibly have imagined that *you*, somehow, would escape what waits for every Fitzalan from birth."

I turned that over and over in my head, noting it felt more bitter every time. More acrid.

The way she said *you*, with what sounded a great deal like scorn.

And the way she'd said *escape*, as if the very notion was fantastical.

It suggested she was neither as effortless nor as *joyfully blooming* as I had always imagined. And I didn't know quite how to process that possibility.

I shivered, here in these gloomy rooms built to impress fellow Norman invaders centuries ago en route to their sacking and pillaging of England, not to provide any semblance of comfort for the descendants of those invaders. I stared out the window at the deceptively quiet countryside spread out before me. The gardens that rolled this way and that, dead now, but still scrupulously maintained and manicured. I pretended I didn't know that the front of the house was decidedly less tranquil today as the family and guests gathered to cheer me on to my doom.

Celeste and her family in from Vienna, our shriveled great uncles from Paris, the impertinent cousins from Germany. My father's well-fed and sly business associates and rivals from all over the planet.

Not to mention the terrifying groom. The monster I was expected to marry in the morning.

"What is he like?" I asked, my voice cracking.

Celeste was quiet so long that I dragged my gaze from the window to study her expression.

I don't know what I expected. But it wasn't what I saw—my sister's mouth tilted up in the corners, like a cat in the cream.

An unpleasant jolt walloped me in the gut, then shivered through me. I endeavored to shake it off. Or better yet, ignore it.

"Are you sure you wish to know?" Celeste asked, after another long moment of nothing but that self-satisfied half smile that boded all manner of ill, I was sure. It shuddered through me like some kind of fear. "I am not certain that anything is gained by approaching an arranged marriage with an excess of knowledge about a man you must come to terms with, one way or another, no matter what you know ahead of time."

"You did not marry a monster," I retorted.

Though when I thought of the count and that expression of his that suggested he had never encountered a scent he did not abhor and never would, I wondered if the term *monster* might not have a variety of applications.

That smile of hers, if possible, grew ever more smug and made that shuddering thing in me all the more intense.

"He is not like anyone you have met, Imogen. It is impossible to prepare for the impact of him, really."

"I don't understand what that means."

Again, that tinkling laugh. "I must remind myself you are so young. Sheltered. Untouched, in every possible way."

"You were younger when you got married. And presumably, equally untouched and sheltered."

But the way she looked at me then made my heart stutter in my chest. Because if her sly, faintly pitying expression was to be believed, my half sister was not at all who I had believed her to be all this time.

And if Celeste was not Celeste…it was almost as if I forgot who I was, too.

The truth was, I didn't know what to make of it. I shoved it aside, thinking I'd take it out and look at it again when I could breathe normally again. Sometime in the dim future when I was married and settled and had somehow survived the monster who was already in this house, waiting for me.

"I feel sorry for you," Celeste murmured, after a moment, though her tone did not strike me as the sort one would use if that was true. "Truly, it isn't fair. How can a naive little thing like you be expected to handle a man like Javier Dos Santos?"

Even his name struck dread through the center of me. I told myself it had to be dread, that thick and too-hot sensation. It hit me in the chest, then spiraled down until it lodged itself low in my belly.

That, I told myself, was a measure of how much I loathed and feared him.

"I thought you hated him," I reminded my sister. "After what he did to you..."

I remembered the shouting. My father's deep voice echoing through the house. I remembered Celeste's sobs. Until now, it had been the only example I'd ever seen of something less than perfection in my half sister—and I had blamed the man who was the cause of it. I had held him responsible for the commotion. The jagged tear in the smooth inevitability that was our life here, so securely beneath our father's thumb.

More than this, I remembered the one glimpse I'd had of Javier Dos Santos in person. After another bout of screams and sobs and the sort of fighting I'd been taught Fitzalans were above, I had plastered myself to the window over the grand front entrance where I could hide myself in the drapery, and I had gazed down at this monster who had threatened to tear my family apart.

It had been years ago, but my memories remained as vivid as if it had happened yesterday.

He was dark like sin. A stain against the stones. His hair was glossy and black, so dark it looked nearly blue and reminded me of nothing so much as a raven's wing. His face was cruel and hard, so harsh it took my breath away. He had been made of muscle, hard and dangerous, a striking counterpoint to the genteel men I had been raised with. He was not elegant. He was not graceful.

He had no right to my beautiful sister, I had thought fiercely.

A sentiment my father had echoed in no uncertain terms. Celeste, he had bellowed throughout the manor house, was meant for better.

But it seemed Javier Dos Santos was good enough for me.

"Of course I do not hate him," Celeste said now, with more of that laughter that seemed to suggest I was very young and foolish. I didn't care for it, but I couldn't work out how to ask her to stop. "Where do you get such ideas?"

"From you. When you screamed that you hated him, and would hate him forever, and would never cheapen yourself by succumbing to the kind of dime-store forgiveness—"

"Here is what I can tell you about Javier," Celeste said, cutting me off. And pronouncing his name as if it was a meal. "He is not like other men. You should know this, going in. Throw out any preconceptions you might have."

"The only man I know is Father. A handful of priests. And your husband."

I had not meant to say those words the way I did. *Your husband.* As if I was pronouncing some kind of judgment.

But Celeste settled farther back against the settee as if she was relaxing. As if this was the moment she could finally retreat from her usual strict perfection and render herself boneless. "Javier is virile. Animalistic, even. He will take what he wants, and worse, you will happily debase yourself to give it to him."

I frowned. "I have no intention of debasing myself. Much less happily."

Celeste waved a hand. "You will. He will demean you, insult you, and likely make you cry. And you will thank him for it."

My heart was pounding so hard it made me feel dizzy. My throat was dry, and my tongue felt thick in my mouth. And that dread seemed to pulse in me, hotter and wilder by the second.

"Why are you telling me these things? The day before I must marry him?"

If Celeste was abashed, she didn't look it. At all. "I am merely trying to prepare you, Imogen."

"I already think he is a monster. I'm not certain why you

think talk of debasement and insults would improve the situation."

"You will have to watch that tongue of yours, of course," she said, almost sadly. "He won't put up with it. Or the way you run about heedlessly as if you are one of those common women on a treadmill somewhere, sweaty and red-faced."

Because she was naturally slim and beautiful, of course. She assumed that anyone who had to work for perfection didn't deserve it.

It had somehow never occurred to me before that this description might apply to me, too.

"You are very lucky, then, that you were spared this," I said softly. "That I am here to carry this burden for you. For the family."

I had never seen her look as she did then. Her face flushed with what I could only call some kind of temper. Her chin rose. And her eyes glittered. "Indeed. I count myself lucky daily."

I found my hands on the hem of my pajama top, fiddling with the fine cotton as if I could worry it into threads. Betraying my anxiety, I knew.

And as strangely as my sister was behaving today, she was still my sister. The only person who had never punished me for asking questions.

This was why I dared to ask the one thing that had worried me the most since my father had announced my engagement to me over Christmas dinner.

"Do you think...?" I cleared my throat. "Will he hurt me?"

For a long moment, Celeste did not speak. And when she did, there was a hard look in her eyes, her lips twisted, and she no longer looked the least bit relaxed.

"You will survive it," she told me, something bleak and ugly there between us. "You will always survive it, Imogen, for better or worse, and that is what you will hold on to. My advice to you is to get pregnant as quickly as possible. Men like this want heirs. In the end, that is all they want. The sooner you do your duty, the quicker they will leave you alone."

And long after she swept from my room, I stayed where I was, stricken. And unable to breathe. There was a constriction in my chest and that heavy dread in my gut, and I couldn't help but think that I had seen my half sister—truly seen her—for the first time today.

It filled me like a kind of grief.

But I was also filled with a kind of restlessness I didn't understand.

That was what got me up and onto my feet. I dashed the odd moisture from my eyes with hands I knew better than to keep in fists. I started for the door, then imagined—too vividly—my father's reaction should I be found wandering about the house when it was filled with important wedding guests, clad only in my pajamas with my hair obviously unbrushed.

I went into my bedroom and dressed quickly, pulling on the dress the maids had left out for me, wordlessly encouraging me to clothe myself the way my father preferred. Not to my own taste, which would never have run to dresses at this chilly time of year, no matter that this one was long-sleeved and made of a fine wool. I paired the dress with butter-soft knee-high leather boots, and then found myself in my mirror.

I had not transformed into elegance during my vigil on the settee.

Curls like mine always looked unkempt. Elegance was sleek and smooth, but my hair resisted any and all attempts to tame it. The nuns had done what they could, but even they had been unable to combat my hair's natural tendency to find its own shape. I ran my fingers through it as best I could, letting the curls do as they would because they always did.

My hair was the bane of my existence. Much as I was the bane of my father's.

Only then, when I could say that in all honesty I had at least tried to sort myself out into something resembling order, did I leave my room.

I made my way out into the hall in the family wing, then ducked into one of the servants' back stairs. My father would not approve of his daughter moving about the house like one of the help, but I had never thought that he needed to know how familiar I was with the secret passages in this old pile of stones. Knowing them made life here that much more bearable.

Knowing my way through the shadows allowed me to remain at large when there was a lecture brewing. It permitted me to come in from long walks on the grounds, muddy and disheveled, and make it to my own rooms before the sight of me caused the usual offense, outrage, and threats to curtail my exercise until I learned how to behave *like a lady*.

I carefully made my way over to the guest wing, skirting around the rooms I knew had been set aside for various family members and my father's overfed friends. I knew that there was only one possible place my father would have dared put a man as wealthy and powerful as Javier Dos Santos. Only one place suitable for a groom with such a formidable financial reputation.

My father might have turned Javier from the house ten years ago, but now that he was welcome and set to marry the right daughter, Dermot Fitzalan would spare him no possible luxury.

I headed for what was one of the newer additions to the grand old house, a two-story dwelling place appended to the end of the guest wing where my grandmother had lived out her final days. It was more a house all its own, with its own entrance and rooms, but I knew that I could access it on the second level and sneak my way along its private gallery.

I didn't ask myself why I was doing this. I only knew it was tied to the grief I felt for the sister it turned out I barely knew and that dread inside me that pulsed at me, spurring me on.

I eased my way through the servant's door that disappeared behind a tapestry at one end of the gallery. I flattened myself to the wall and did my best to keep my ears peeled for any signs of life.

And it was the voice I heard first.

His voice.

Commanding. Dark. Rich like dark chocolate and deep red wine, all wrapped in one.

Beautiful, something in me whispered.

I was horrified with myself. But I didn't back away.

He was speaking in rapid Spanish, liquid and lovely, out of sight on the floor below me. I inched forward, moving away from the gallery wall so I could look over the open side of the balcony to the great room below.

And for a moment, memory and reality seemed tangled up in each other. Once again, I was gazing down at Javier Dos Santos from afar. From above.

Once again, I was struck by how *physical* he seemed. Long ago, he had been dressed for the evening in a coat with tails that had only accentuated the simmering brutality he seemed to hold leashed there in his broad shoulders and his granite rock of a torso.

Today he stood in a button-down shirt tucked into trousers that did things I hardly understood to his powerful thighs. I only knew I couldn't look away.

Once again, my heart beat so hard and so fast I was worried I might be ill.

But I wasn't.

I knew I wasn't.

I watched him rake his fingers through that dark hair of his, as black and as glossy as I remembered it, as if even the years dared not defy him. He listened to the mobile he held at one ear for a moment, his head cocked to one side, then replied in another spate of the lyrical Spanish that seem to wind its way around me. Through me. Deep inside me, too.

With my functional Spanish I could pick up the sense of the

words, if not every nuance. Business concerns in Wales. Something about the States. And a fiercer debate by far about Japan.

He finished his call abruptly, then tossed his mobile onto the table next to him. It thunked against the hard wood, making me too aware of the silence.

And too conscious of my own breathing and my mad, clattering heart.

Javier Dos Santos stood there a moment, his attention on the papers before him, or possibly his tablet computer.

When he raised his head, he did it swiftly. His dark eyes were fierce and sure, pinning me where I stood. I understood in a sudden red haze of exposure and fear that he had known I was here all along.

He had known.

"Hello, Imogen," he said, switching to faintly accented English that made my name sound like some kind of incantation. Or terrible curse. "Do you plan to do something more than stare?"

CHAPTER TWO

Javier

I WAS A man built from lies.

My faithless father. My weak, codependent mother. The lies they had told—to each other, to the world, to me and my sisters—had made me the man I was today, for good or ill.

I allowed no room in the life I had crafted from nothing for lies like theirs. Not from my employees or associates. Not from my sisters, grown now and beholden to me. Not from a single soul on this earth.

And certainly not from myself.

So there was no hiding from the fact that my first glimpse of my future bride—the unfortunate Fitzalan sister, as she was known—did not strike me the way I had anticipated it would.

I had expected that she would do well enough. She was not Celeste, but she was a Fitzalan. It was her pedigree that mattered, that and the sweet, long-anticipated revenge of forcing her father to give me the very thing he had denied me once already.

I had never done well with denial. Ten years ago it had not taken me to my knees, as I suspected Dermot Fitzalan thought it would. On the contrary, it had led me to go bigger, to strive harder, to make absolutely certain that the next time I came for a Fitzalan daughter, their arrogant, self-satisfied father would not dare deny me.

I had expected that my return to this cold, gloomy mausoleum in the north of France would feel like a victory lap. Because it was.

What I did not expect was the kick of lust that slammed through me at the sight of her.

It made no sense. I had been raised in the gutters of Madrid, but I had always wanted better. Always. As I'd fought my way out of the circumstances of my birth, I'd coveted elegance and collected it wherever I could.

It had made sense for me to pursue Celeste. She was grace personified, elegant from the tips of her fingernails to the line of her neck, and nothing but ice straight through.

It had made sense that I had wanted her to adorn my collection.

The girl before me, who had dared try to sneak up on a man who had been raised in dire pits filled with snakes and jackals and now walked untroubled through packs of wolves dressed as aristocrats, was...unruly.

She had red-gold hair that slithered this way and that and stubborn curls she had made no apparent attempt to tame. There was a spray of freckles over her nose, and I knew that if I could see them from this distance, it likely meant that my eyes were not deceiving me and she had not, in fact, bothered with even the faintest hint of cosmetics in a nod toward civility.

On the one hand, that meant her dark, thick lashes and the berry shade of her full lips were deliciously natural.

But it also showed that she had little to no sense of propriety.

She was otherwise unadorned. She wore a navy blue dress that was unobjectionable enough, with classic lines that nodded toward her generous figure without making too much of it, and leather boots that covered her to her knees.

I could have forgiven the hair and even the lack of cosmetics—which suggested she had not prepared for her first meeting with me the way a woman who planned to make the perfect wife would have.

But it was the way she was scowling at me that suggested she was even less like her sister than I had imagined.

Celeste had never cracked. Not even when she'd been denied what she'd so prettily claimed she wanted. Oh, she'd caused a carefully prepared scene for her father, but there had never been anything but calculation in her gaze. Her mascara had never run. She had never presented anything but perfection, even in the midst of her performance.

The fact it still rankled made it a weakness. I thrust it aside.

"Surely that is not the expression you wish to show your future husband," I said quietly. "On this, the occasion of our first meeting."

I had heard her come in and creep along the strange balcony above me the butler had told me was a gallery. Not a very good gallery, I had thought with a derisive glance at the art displayed there. All stodgy old masters and boring ecclesiastical works. Nothing bold. Nothing new.

Until she'd come.

"I want to know why you wish to marry me." She belted that out, belligerent and bordering on rude. A glance confirmed that she was making fists at her sides. *Fists.*

I felt my brow raise. "I beg your pardon?"

Her scowl deepened. "I want to know why you want to marry me, when if you are even half as rich and powerful as they say, you could marry anyone."

I thrust my hands—not in anything resembling fists—into the pockets of my trousers, and considered her.

I should have been outraged. I told myself I was.

But the truth was, there was something about her that tempted me to smile. And I was not a man who smiled easily, if at all.

I told myself it was the very fact that she had come here, when our wedding was not until the morning. It was the fact she seemed to imagine she could put herself between her grasping, snobbish father and me when these were matters that could not possibly concern her. Daughters of men like Dermot Fitzalan always did what they were told, sooner or later.

Yet here she was.

It was the futility of it, I thought. My Don Quixote bride with her wild hair, tilting at windmills and scowling all the while. It made something in my chest tighten.

"I will answer any questions you have," I told her magnanimously, trying my best to contain my own ferocity. "But you must face me."

"I'm looking right at you."

I only raised a hand, then beckoned her to me with two languid fingers.

And then waited, aware that it had been a long time indeed since I had been in the presence of someone…unpredictable.

I saw her hands open, then close again at her sides. I saw the way her chest moved, telling me that she fought to keep her breath even.

I learned a lot about my future bride as the seconds ticked by, and all she did was stare down at me. I learned she was willful. Defiant.

But ultimately yielding.

Because when she moved, it was to the spiral stair that led her down to the stone floor where I stood.

Perhaps not yielding so much as curious, I amended as she drew near, folding her arms over her chest as if she was drawing armor around herself in order to face me.

I took a moment to consider her, this bride I had purchased outright. This girl who was my revenge and my prize, all in one.

She will do, I thought, pleased with myself.

"I suppose," I said after a moment, in the cool tone I used to reprimand my subordinates, "you cannot help the hair."

Imogen glowered at me. Her eyes were an unusual shade of brown that looked like old copper coins when they filled with temper, as they did now. It made me wonder how they would look when she was wild with passion instead.

That lust hit me again. Harder this time.

"It is much like being born without a title, I imagine," she retorted.

It took me a moment to process that. To understand that this messy, unruly girl had thrust such an old knife in so deftly, then twisted it.

I couldn't think of the last time that had happened. I couldn't think of the last person who had dared.

"Does it distress you that you must lower yourself to marry a man so far beneath you?" I asked, all silk and threat. "A man who is little more than a mongrel while you have been deliberately bred from blood kept blue enough to burn?"

I could not seem to help but notice that her skin was so fair it was like cream and made me...hungry. And when her eyes glittered, they gleamed copper.

"Does it distress you that I am not my sister?" she asked in return.

I hadn't expected that.

I felt myself move, only dimly aware that I was squaring my shoulders and changing my stance, as if I found myself engaged in hand-to-hand combat. I supposed I was.

"You cannot imagine that the two of you could be confused," I murmured, but I was looking at her differently. I was viewing her as less a pawn and more an opponent. First a knife, then a sucker punch.

So far, Imogen Fitzalan was proving to be far more interesting that I had anticipated.

I wasn't sure I knew where to put that.

"As far as I am aware," she said coolly, "you are the only one who has ever confused us."

"I assure you, I am not confused."

"Perhaps I am. I assume that purchasing my hand in marriage requires at least as much research as the average online dating profile. Did you not see a picture? Were you not made aware that my sister and I share only half our blood?"

"I cannot say I gave the matter of your appearance much thought," I said, and I expected that to set her back on her heels.

But instead, the odd creature laughed.

"A man like you, not concerned with his own wife's appearance? How out of character."

"I cannot imagine what you think you know of my character."

"I have drawn conclusions about your character based on the way you allow yourself to be photographed." Her brow lifted. "You are a man who prefers the company of a very particular shape of woman."

"It is not their shape that concerns me, but whether or not other men covet them." This was nothing but the truth, and yet something about the words seemed almost...oily. Weighted. As if I should be ashamed of saying such a thing out loud when I had said it many times before.

Though not, I amended, to a woman I intended to make my wife.

"You like a trophy," she said.

I inclined my head. "I am a collector, Imogen. I like only the finest things."

She smiled at me, but it struck me as more of a baring of teeth. "You must be disappointed indeed."

Though she looked as if the notion pleased her.

I moved then, closer to her, enjoying the way she stood fast instead of shrinking away. I could see the way her pulse beat too fast in her neck. I could see the way her copper eyes widened. I reached over and helped myself to one of those red-gold curls, expecting her hair to be coarse. Much as she was.

But the curl was silky against my fingers, sliding over my skin like a caress. And something about that fell through me like a sudden brush fire.

If I was a man who engaged in self-deception, I would have told myself that was not at all what I felt.

But I had built my life and my fortune, step by impossible step in the face of only overwhelming odds, on nothing short of brutal honesty. Toward myself and others, no matter the cost.

I knew I wanted her.

She reached up as if to bat my hand away, but appeared to think better of it, which raised her another notch or two in my estimation. "You have yet to answer the question. You can marry anyone you like. Why on earth would you choose me?"

"Perhaps I am so enamored of the Fitzalan name that I have hungered for nothing but the opportunity to align myself with your father since the day I met your sister. And you should know, Imogen, that I always get what I want."

She swallowed. I watched the pale column of her neck move when she did. "They say you are a monster."

I was so busy looking at her mouth and imagining how those plump lips would feel wrapped around the hungriest part of me that I almost missed the way she said that. And more, the look on her face when she did.

As if she was not playing a game, any longer.

As if she was actually afraid of me.

And I had dedicated my life to making certain that as many people as possible were afraid of me, because a healthy fear bred respect and I did not much care if they feared me so long as they respected me.

But somehow, I did not wish this to be true of Imogen Fitzalan. My bride, for her sins.

"Those who say I am a monster are usually poor losers," I told her, aware that I was too close to her. And yet neither she nor I moved to put more space between us. "It is in their best interests to call me a monster, because who could be expected to prevail against a creature of myth and lore? Their own short-comings and failures are of no consequence, you understand. Not if I am a monster instead of a man."

Her gaze searched my face. "You want to be a monster, then. You enjoy it."

"You can call me whatever you like. I will marry you all the same."

"Again. Why me?"

"Why does this upset you?" I didn't fight the urge that came over me then, to reach over and take her chin in my fingers and hold her face where I wanted it. Simply because I could. And because, though she stilled, she did not jerk away. "I know that you have spent your life preparing for this day. Why should it matter if it is me or anyone else?"

"It matters."

Her voice was fierce and quiet at once. And emotion gleamed in her lovely eyes, though I couldn't discern what, exactly, that sheen meant.

"Did you have your heart set on another?" I asked, aware as I did so that something I had never felt before stirred to life within me. "Is that why you dare come to me with all this belligerence?"

It was because she was mine, I told myself. That was why I felt that uncharacteristic surge of possessiveness. I had not felt it for a woman before, it was true. Despite how much I had wanted Celeste back in the day and how infuriated I had been when I had lost her to that aristocratic zombie of a count she called her husband.

I had wanted Celeste, yes.

But that was a different thing entirely than knowing she was meant to be mine.

Imogen was mine. There was no argument. I had paid for the privilege—or that was how her father planned to spin this match.

He and I knew the truth. I was a wealthy man, my power and might with few equals. I took care of my sisters and my mother because I prided myself on my honor and did my duty—not because they deserved that consideration. And because I did not want them to be weak links others could use to attack me.

But otherwise I had no ties or obligations, and had thus spent my days dedicating myself to the art of money.

The reality was that Dermot Fitzalan needed my wealth. And better still, my ability to make more with seeming ease. He needed these things far more than I needed his daughter's pedigree.

But I had decided long ago that I would marry a Fitzalan heiress, these daughters of men who had been the power behind every throne in Europe at one point or another. I had determined that I would make my babies on soft, well-bred thighs, fatten them on blue blood, and raise them not just rich, but cultured.

I had been so young when I had seen Celeste that first time. So raw and unformed. The animal they accused me of being in all the ways that mattered.

I had never seen a woman like her before. All clean lines and beauty. I had never imagined that a person could be…flawless.

It had taken me far longer than it should have—far longer than it would today, that was for certain—to see the truth of Celeste Fitzalan, now a countess of petty dreams and an angry old man's promises because that was what she had wanted far more than she had wanted me.

But my thirst for my legacy had only grown stronger.

"If there was another," my confounding betrothed said, a mulish set to that fine mouth and a rebellion in her gaze, "I would hardly be likely to tell you, would I?"

"You can tell me anything you like about others," I told her, all menace and steel. "Today. I would advise you to take advantage of this offer. Come the morning, I will take a far dimmer view of these things."

"It doesn't matter what I want," she threw at me, pulling her chin from my grasp.

I assumed we were both well aware that I allowed it.

"I never said that it did. You are the one who came here. Was it only to call me names? To ask me impertinent questions? Or perhaps you had another goal in mind?"

"I don't know why I came," Imogen said, and I could tell by the way her voice scraped into the air between us that she meant that.

But there was a fire in me. A need, dark and demanding, and I was not in the habit of denying myself the things I wanted.

More than this, she was to be my wife in the morning.

"Don't worry," I told her with all that heat and intent. "I know exactly why you came."

I hooked my hand around her neck, enjoying the heat of her skin beneath the cover of those wild curls. I pulled her toward me, watching her eyes go wide and her mouth drop open as if she couldn't help herself. As if she was that artless, that innocent.

I couldn't understand the things that worked in me. To take her, to possess her, to bury myself in her body when she looked nothing like the women that I usually amused myself with.

But none of that mattered.

Because I already owned her. All that remained was the claiming, and I wanted it. Desperately.

I dropped my mouth to hers.

CHAPTER THREE

Imogen

HE WAS KISSING ME.

The monster was kissing me.

And I hardly knew what to do.

His mouth was a bruising thing, powerful and hard. It should have hurt, surely. I should have wanted nothing more than to get away from all that intensity. I should have tried. But instead, I found myself pushing up on my toes and leaning toward him...

As if I wanted more.

He cradled the back of my head in one hand and moved his lips over mine.

And I *wanted*. I wanted...everything.

I had dreamed of kisses half my life. I had longed for a moment like this. A punishing kiss, perhaps. Or something sweet and filled with wonder. Any kind of kiss at all, if I was honest.

But nothing could have prepared me for Javier Dos Santos.

Nothing could have prepared me for this.

I felt his tongue against the seam of my lips, and couldn't help myself from opening up and giving him entry. And then I thought I would give him anything.

And even though I understood, on some distant level, what

he was doing to me—that his tongue was testing mine, dancing here, then retreating—all I could feel was the heat. *The heat.* Something greedy and wild and impossibly hot, thrilling to life inside me. What I had called dread had melted into something else entirely, something molten. It wound around and around inside my chest, knotted up in my belly, and dripped like honey even lower.

And still he kissed me.

His arms were a marvel. Heavy and hard, they wrapped around me, making me feel things I could hardly understand. Small, yet safe. Entirely surrounded, yet sweet, somehow.

Still Javier's mouth moved on mine. He bent me backward, over one strong arm. His heavy chest, all steel planes and granite, pressed hard against mine, until I felt my breasts seem to swell in response.

It was like a fever.

The ache was everywhere, prickling and hot, but I knew—somehow I knew—I wasn't ill.

He bent me back even farther and there was a glory in it. I felt weightless, too caught up in all that fire and honey to worry whether or not my feet still touched the ground.

And then I felt his fingers as they found their way beneath the hem of my dress, a scandalous caress that made my heart stutter. Yet he didn't stop. He tracked that same sweet flame along the length of my thigh, climbing ever higher.

My brain shorted out. The world went white-hot, then red-hot, then it became nothing at all but need.

His hand was a wonder. Not soft and manicured, like the hands of the very few men whose hands I'd shaken at some point or other, but hard and calloused. Big, and brutally masculine.

He traced some kind of pattern into my skin, and then laughed against my mouth when I shuddered in response.

His taste was like wine. It washed through me in the same way, leaving me flushed, giddy.

And then his fingers toyed with the edge of my panties, until I was sure I stopped breathing.

Not that I cared when he angled his head, taking the kiss deeper. Hotter.

While at the same time, his fingers moved with bold certainty to find my soft heat.

And then, to my wonder and shame, he began to stroke me, there below.

His tongue was in my mouth. His fingers were deep between my legs, and I couldn't remember why I had ever thought this man was a monster. Or maybe I thought he was a far greater monster than I'd ever imagined.

Either way, I surrendered. And my surrender felt like strength.

It was like some kind of dance. Parry, then retreat. His mouth and his hand, one and then the other, or both at once.

Before I knew it, that fever in me was spreading. I shook, everywhere. I could feel my own body grow stiff in his arms and I felt myself edging ever closer to crisis.

I would have pushed him away if I could. If I could make my hands do anything but grip the front of his shirt as I shook and stiffened and spun further and further off into that blazing need.

I lost myself somewhere between Javier's hot, hard mouth and his pitiless hand between my legs. I lost myself, and I followed that shaking, and I hardly understood why I was making those greedy, shameful noises in the back of my throat—

"Come apart for me, Imogen," he growled against my mouth, as if he owned even this. "Now."

And there was nothing in me but heat and surrender.

I exploded on cue.

And I was only dimly aware of it when Javier set me away from him. He settled me on the lip of the table behind us, ran his hands down my arms as if he was reminding me of the limits of my own body, and even smoothed the skirt of my dress back into place.

I was tempted to find it all sweet, however strange a word that seemed when applied to a man so widely regarded as a monster. A man I still thought of in those terms. But there was a tumult inside of me.

My head spun and everything inside me followed suit. I couldn't focus. I couldn't breathe. I couldn't make sense of what had happened.

And when my breathing finally slowed enough that I could think beyond it, Javier was waiting there. He stood in the same position he'd been standing before, his hands thrust into the pockets of the trousers I knew at a glance had been crafted by hand in an atelier in a place like Milan or Paris.

His might seemed more overwhelming now. I had a vague memory of the stable boy's dreamy blue eyes, but they seemed so insubstantial next to Javier's relentless masculinity. I felt it like a storm. It buffeted me, battering my skin, until I felt the electricity of it—of him—as if he had left some part of himself inside me.

I told myself I hated him for it.

"You look upset, *mi reina*," Javier murmured. I understood the words he used—Spanish for *my queen*—but stiffened at the dark current of mockery in it. "Surely not. I am certain someone must have prepared you for what goes on between a man and a woman no matter how hard your father has worked to keep you locked up in a tower."

I was not one of the sacrificial maidens ransomed out of this place in centuries past, despite appearances. I might have lived a sheltered life, but that life came with abundant internet access.

Still, I followed an urge inside of me, a dark insistence I didn't have it in me to resist.

"I prepared in the usual way," I told him. "Locked towers might work in fairy tales. They are harder to manage in real life, I think."

And when his dark gaze turned to fire and burned where it

touched me, I only held it. And practiced that half smile I had seen on my sister's face earlier.

"I will assume you mean that your preparation for marriage took place under the careful tutelage of disinterested nuns as they discussed biology."

I channeled Celeste. "Assume what you like."

Right there, before my eyes, Javier…changed. I had thought he was stone before, but he became something harder. Flint and granite, straight through.

I couldn't tell if the pulse that pounded in me then—in my wrists and my ears, my breasts and between my legs—was fear or something else. Something far more dangerous.

All I knew was that I wanted whatever Celeste had appeared to have on my settee. I wanted that confidence. I even wanted her smugness.

Because it seemed to me that was some measure of power.

I didn't want to be what they called me. The lesser Fitzalan sister. The unfortunate one. Not here. Not now.

I didn't want this man—who had broken me wide-open in ways I didn't know how to explain without, as far as I could tell, so much as breaking a sweat—to know how inexperienced I was. I didn't want to give him my innocence, particularly if he thought it was his by right.

Just once, I thought defiantly, I wanted to feel sophisticated.

Just once, I wanted to be the sleek one, the graceful one.

I wasn't sure I could fake my sister's effortlessness. But I knew that my smirk was getting to him. I could see it in all that stone and metal that made his face so harsh.

"All the better," Javier growled at me, though he didn't look anything like pleased. "You should know that I am a man of a great many needs, Imogen. That I will not have to tutor you how best to meet them can only be a boon."

I didn't believe him. I didn't know what it was that whispered to me that he minded a great deal more than he was saying, but I knew it all the same.

Or you want *to know it*, something whispered in me, leaving marks. *You want to affect him, somehow, after he took your breath away like this.*

I didn't want to think such things. I found myself frowning at him instead.

"Careful," Javier said with a soft menace that made me feel molten and shivery all over again. "If you do not want an example of the sort of appetites I mean, here and now, I'd suggest you go back wherever you came from. There is a wedding in the morning. And an entire marriage before us in which, I promise you, you will have ample time to learn what it is I want and expect. In bed and out."

And then I felt twisted. As if there was something wrong deep within me. Because the fact he was dismissing me stung, when I knew I should have been grateful for the reprieve. I flushed again, but this time it felt more like poison than that same impossible, irresistible heat.

I was only pretending to be like Celeste—and the look on Javier's harsh face suggested that I wasn't doing a particularly good job. I was certain that if he touched me again, I would never be able to keep it up.

And no matter that there was a part of me that shimmered with longing. That wanted nothing more than to feel his hands on me again. And more.

So much more.

I knew I had to take the escape hatch he had offered me—or lose myself even further.

Possibly even lose myself for good.

I slid off the table to find my feet, and fought to keep my expression from betraying how tender I felt where his hand had been between my legs. It felt as if my panties were somehow too tight, as if I was swollen, and I hardly knew how to walk on my own.

Yet I did. I managed it.

I skirted around him as if he was on fire, convinced that I

could feel that blistering heat of his from feet away. Convinced that he had branded me, somehow. And entirely too aware of his glittering, arrogant gaze.

But I had a long night ahead of me to fret over such things.

I only understood that I expected him to reach out and take hold of me again when he didn't. And when I made it to the spiral stair and ran up it as fast as I could on my rubbery legs, the clatter of my heart inside my chest was so loud I was surprised he didn't hear it and comment on it from below.

I made my way along the second-floor gallery, aware of his gaze on me like a heavy weight—or some kind of chain binding me to him already—but I didn't turn back. I didn't dare look back.

Maybe there was a part of me that feared if I did, I might go to him again. That I would sink into that fire of his and burn alive, until there was nothing left of me but ashes.

When I slipped back beneath the tapestry and into the servants' walkway, there was no relief. It was like I carried Javier with me, in all the places he had touched me and, worse by far, all the places I only wished he had.

It was as if I was already half-consumed by that fire of his I both feared and longed for.

But I would die before I let him know that he had taught me more in those wild, hot moments than I had learned in a lifetime.

The reality was, I thought about what a wedding night with this man might entail and I…thought I might die, full stop.

I knew that was melodramatic, but I indulged in it anyway as I made my way through the shadowy recesses of my father's house. Why had I gone to Javier in the first place? Why had I been so foolish? What had I imagined might happen? I wanted to sink into a bath and wash it all away, let the water soothe me and hide me. I simply wanted to be back in my rooms again, safe and protected.

Because a deep, feminine wisdom I hadn't known resided

there inside me whispered these final hours before my wedding might be the last bit of safety I would know.

I knew too much now, and none of it things I'd wanted to learn. I had found a magic and a fire, yes. But now I knew how easily I surrendered. I knew how my body betrayed me.

I knew, worst of all, that I wanted things I was terribly afraid only Javier Dos Santos could give me.

And I wasn't paying sufficient attention when I slipped out from the servants' hall. I was usually far more careful. I usually listened for a good few minutes, then used the carefully placed eyeholes to be certain that no one was in sight before I slipped back into the house's main corridors.

But Javier had done something to me. He had used my own body against me, as if he knew what it could do better than I did. He had made me feel as if I belonged to him instead of to myself. Even with all this distance between us, clear on the other side of the rambling old manor house, I could feel his hands on me. Those powerful arms closed around me. His harsh, cruel mouth while it mastered mine.

That was the only excuse I could think of when I stepped out and found myself face-to-face with my father.

For a long, terrible moment, there was nothing but silence between us and the far-off sound of rain against the roof.

Dermot Fitzalan was neither tall nor particularly physically imposing, but he made up for both with the scorn he held for literally every person alive who was not him.

To say nothing of the extra helping he kept in reserve for me.

"Pray tell me that I have taken leave of my senses." His voice was so cold it made the ancient stone house feel balmy in comparison. I felt goose bumps prickle to life down my arms. "I beg you, Imogen—tell me that I did not witness an heiress to the Fitzalan fortune emerge from the servants' quarters like an inept housemaid I would happily dismiss on the spot."

I had imagined myself brave, before. When I had taken off on a whim and found the man my father had chosen for me.

When I had tangled with a monster and walked away—changed, perhaps, but whole.

But I realized as I stood there, the focus of my father's withering scorn as I so often was, that when it counted I wasn't the least bit brave at all.

"I thought I heard a noise," I lied, desperately. "I only ducked my head in to see what it was."

"I beg your pardon." My father looked at me the way he always did, as if the sight of me was vaguely repulsive. "Why should a lady of this house, a daughter of the Fitzalan line, feel it is incumbent upon her to investigate strange noises? Are you unable to ring for assistance?"

"Father—"

He lifted a hand. That was all.

But that was all that was needed. It silenced me as surely as if he'd wrapped that hand around my throat and squeezed. The hard light in his dark gaze suggested it was not outside the realm of possibility.

"You are an enduring disappointment to me, Imogen." His voice was cold. Detached. And I already knew this to be so. There was no reason it should have felt like an unexpected slap when he took every opportunity to remind me how often and comprehensively I let him down. And yet my cheeks stung red as if he'd actually struck me. "I do not understand this...willfulness."

He meant my hair. He meant those curls that had never obeyed anyone. Not him and not me, certainly. Not the relentless nuns, not my old governesses, not the poor maids he hired to attack me with their formulas and their straight irons to no avail.

"You might almost be pretty, if distressingly rough around the edges, were it not for that mess you insist on flaunting."

My father glared at my curls with such ferocity that I was almost surprised he didn't reach out and try to tear them off with his hand.

"I can't help my hair, Father," I dared to say in a low voice.

It was a mistake.

That ferocious glare left my hair and settled on me. Hard.

"Let me make certain you are aware of how I expect this weekend to go," he said, his voice lowering in that way of his that made my stomach drop. "In less than twenty-four hours you will be another man's problem. He will be forced to handle these pointless rebellions of yours, and I wish him good luck. But you will exit this house, and my protection, as befits a Fitzalan."

I didn't need to know what, specifically, he meant by that. What I knew about my father was that whenever he began to rant on about the things that *befit* a member of this family, it always ended badly for me.

Still, I wasn't the same girl who had foolishly wandered off in search of my husband-to-be. I wasn't the silly creature who had sat on my own settee staring out at the rain and dreaming of a stable boy. She felt far away to me now, a dream I had once had.

Because Javier Dos Santos had branded me as surely as if he'd pressed hot iron against my skin, and I could still feel the shock of it. The burn.

"What do you suggest I do?" I asked, with the sort of spirit I knew my father would find offensive. I couldn't seem to help myself. "Shave it all off?"

My father bared his teeth and I shrank back, but it was no use. My back came up hard against the wall. There was nowhere for me to go.

And in any event, it was worse if I ran.

"I suspect you are well aware that I wish no such thing, Imogen." If possible, my father's voice dripped with further disdain. "I take it you imagine that your marriage will provide you with some measure of freedom. Perhaps you view it as an escape. If you know what is good for you, girl, you will readjust that attitude before tomorrow morning. Your new husband might not be of the blood, but I assure you, he expects total and complete obedience in all things."

"I never said—" I began.

My father actually smiled. It was chilling. "In fact, Dos Santos is nothing but a common, rutting creature who handles any and all conflict with the deftness you might expect from an uncivilized beast. I shudder to think how he will choose to handle these displays of yours."

I thought I had a good idea of how he might handle them now, but I dropped my gaze, terrified that my father might see all that need and fire Javier had taught me, written all over me. And because I didn't want to see the malicious glee I knew would be stamped all over my only living parent at the notion my husband would *handle* me.

I tried not to miss my mother as it did no good. But in moments like this I couldn't help myself. I knew that if she'd lived, she wouldn't have defied my father, either, but at least I'd had no doubt she loved me.

"Silence at last?" my father taunted me. "That will not help you, either. The die is cast, I am afraid. You will spend the rest of this day and evening locked in your rooms. But do not imagine you will have the opportunity to retreat into those books you love so much, unnatural as you are. I will send in your attendants and mark my words, Imogen. I do not care if it takes from now until the moment the ceremony begins tomorrow, but you will look like a proper Fitzalan for the first time in your life, I swear it. You will tame that mess you call hair. You will do something with your face, for a change. You will be manicured and pedicured and forced to look like the pride and joy of this house no matter what it takes."

"Father," I tried again, "none of this is necessary."

"You cannot be trusted," he seethed at me. "You are an embarrassment. I have never understood how a child of my loins could come out so slovenly. Quite apart from those curls, look at how you walk around my house knowing full well we have important guests who expect the Fitzalan name to connote nothing but grace and elegance, handed down over centuries." His scornful glare swept me from forehead to toes, then back again. "You look as common as he is."

That was the worst insult my father could think to hurl at me.

And the part of me that wished I could please him, no matter how well I knew that was an impossibility, recoiled.

But I didn't say a word. I stood there, letting him skewer me in every way possible, because it wasn't as if there was any way to stop him. There never had been.

When he was done, he straightened, though he already stood as if there was an iron pole where his spine should have been. He adjusted the cuffs of his jacket indignantly, as if my slovenliness was contagious.

"Go to your rooms at once," he told me, as if I was a small child. Which was how I felt when he looked at me. "You will sit there and you will await your attendants."

"Yes, Father." I tried to sound obliging and obedient.

He reached over and grabbed my arm, his fingers closing painfully over my biceps. But I knew better than to make any sound of protest.

"You have less than a day remaining in this house," he hissed. "Less than a day remaining to conduct yourself appropriately. And I warn you, Imogen. If you attempt to embarrass me further, you will not like how this wedding ceremony goes. Remember that all I require is your presence at the ceremony. It is utterly irrelevant to me if you are capable of speaking or even standing."

He left me there, marching off without so much as a backward glance, because he was certain that I would obey him. He was certain—and he was right.

I knew that none of his threats were idle. He would roll me into my own wedding ceremony strapped down to a stretcher if he wished, and not one guest would raise an eyebrow. I wasn't a person to them. I wasn't *me*. I was a Fitzalan heiress, nothing more and nothing less, and it was my father's right to do with me what he pleased. The guests here were as interested in my feelings on what happened in my life as they would be in the thoughts of any piece of livestock.

I could feel the fingerprints Father had left on me, bruising up on my arm already. I ducked my head down, frustration and fury making my eyes water, as I headed toward my rooms.

As ordered.

But the things my father had said to me had, perhaps, the opposite effect of what he'd intended.

Because I had been so focused on Javier. On the fact he was meant to be a monster. I had been so worried about marching myself down the aisle and straight on into my own doom.

I hadn't spent nearly enough time thinking about the fact that monster or not, Javier could only be an improvement on the monster I would be leaving behind.

I might never be free, but I would be free of my father.

And if the price of that was an unpleasant evening of attempts to beat me into submission and make of me the perfect Fitzalan bride to honor my father's vanity, I could only believe it was worth it.

CHAPTER FOUR

Javier

I WASN'T ENTIRELY surprised that my blushing bride was no-where to be seen at the tedious drinks affair Dermot Fitzalan threw that night.

After all, this was not the kind of wedding that got written up in the gossip pages or excessively photographed for the Style sections of various magazines across the globe, rife with planned events and excessive opportunities to celebrate the romantic idiocy of the marrying couple. My wedding was not a performance.

It was a contract and Imogen was incidental. I had paid for access. For a connection to the kings across time who lived in the Fitzalan name. For the pièce de résistance to add to my collection.

"Have you come with no family of your own, Dos Santos?" asked one of the wolves gathered for this occasion that I doubted anyone would call joyous. He was an overly titled idiot who had spent the last few moments risking his continuing health by standing too close to me and making a great show of looking around the room while he did it. He had obviously wished me to ask what he was doing. I had not. "What kind of man attends his own wedding solo?"

I raised my glass, but made no attempt to wrestle my expression into anything approaching polite. "A man who is well aware that he is making a business acquisition, which I am perfectly capable of doing without an entourage."

The other man brayed with laughter, and I was already bored. I left him without another word, making my way through the high-ceilinged room that had been set up to host this supposedly genial cocktail hour ahead of what promised to be an even duller banquet. I knew Fitzalan was showing off, the way he always did. The guests were meant to be in awe of this historical monument he called a house, me most of all. I was meant to be cowed into reverence by the medieval flourishes and the history in every ostentatious antique.

I was meant to feel small.

Sadly for Fitzalan and his self-regard, I felt quite the opposite.

I couldn't get my bride-to-be and her wild, wholly irreverent red-gold curls out of my head.

Imogen Fitzalan was not at all what I had been expecting and I could not recall the last time anything had surprised me. Much less a woman. Women tended to blur together for me, in truth. Those who approached me hungered for my wealth, my power, and were willing to trade their bodies for a taste of it. And who was I to refuse these generous offers? I accepted them, I enjoyed them, and then I promptly forgot them.

I had always known that I intended to marry a woman who could give my children the only thing I could not buy for them myself: blue blood.

But until that day came, I had always been perfectly happy to revel in the demands of the common red blood that coursed freely in me. It was a heavy pulse in me even now, surrounded by the pale blue aristocrats on all sides and the sort of ancient, theatrical objects cluttering every surface that I knew were meant to trumpet the value of their owner. I was surrounded by the worst sort of wolves, yet I was thinking about sex. All thanks to the bride I had expected would be a cold, prim virgin unable to make eye contact.

I wasn't sure what to do with the surprise I felt. I wasn't sure I liked it.

I made my way to the windows that overlooked the gloomy gardens out back as the fog rolled in to cap off another miserable French day. I preferred the bright heat of Spain, the warmth of my people, and the rhythm of my native language. I nursed my drink as I watched some of Europe's wealthiest men circle each other warily as if violence might erupt at any moment, when I knew very well that was not how men like these attacked. They preferred a stealthier approach. They came at their enemies through hostile takeovers and cruel buyouts. They wielded their fortunes like the armies of lesser men.

They didn't scare me. Not one of the men in this room had created what was his with his own hands. I was the only one here with that distinction.

It meant I was the only one here who knew what it was to live without these privileges. To grow up hard and have nothing but myself to rely on.

And that meant they had a weakness, a blindness, that I did not.

I was smiling at that notion when Celeste swept into the room on the arm of the animated corpse who had made her a countess. The decrepit aristocrat she had chosen over me.

I waited for that kick that I recalled so well at the sight of her. I had called it lust, back then. Lust and fury, need and madness.

But I knew it better now. Or I knew myself. It had been a kind of covetousness, the way I lusted after the finest cars and the most luxurious residences in the best locations. I had wanted Celeste, desperately. I had imagined she would be the crown jewel of my collection.

Yet tonight, as I saw her operate the room like the shark I hadn't realized she was ten years ago—despite that flat gaze and the smile she leveraged like a weapon—that kick was missing. Was it that I was a decade older now? Perhaps I had seen too much to be turned around by a gracefully inclined neck and too many pretty lies. Or was it that I had finally tasted something sweet today and wanted more of it instead of these bitter dregs of once proud family lines?

If they are bitter dregs, what are you? a harsh voice inside me asked. *As you are here to drink deep of what little they have to offer.*

I didn't know the answer. What I did know was that this evening wearied me already. It could have been any night on any continent in any city, surrounded by the same people who were always gathered in places like this. The conversation was the same. Measuring contests, one way or another. In the dangerous neighborhoods of my youth, men had jostled for position with more outward displays of testosterone, but for all the bespoke tailoring and affectations, it was no different here. Learning that had been the key to my first million.

And still all I could think about was Imogen. That ripe mouth of hers that looked like berries and tasted far, far sweeter. And better yet, her scalding softness that had clung to my fingers as she'd clenched and shook and fallen apart.

I had tasted her from my own hand as she sat before me on that table, attempting to recover, and now it was as if I could taste nothing else.

I'd forgotten about Celeste entirely when she appeared before me, smiling knowingly as if we shared a particularly filthy secret. As if we'd last seen each other moments ago, instead of years back.

And as if that last meeting hadn't involved operatic sobs on her part, vicious threats from her father, and a young man's blustery vows of revenge from me.

In retrospect, I was embarrassed for the lot of us.

"How does it feel?" she asked in that husky voice of hers that was so at odds with all her carefully icy blond perfection. But that was her greatest weapon, after all. Hot and cold. Ice and sex. All those deliberate contradictions at once, that was Celeste.

I eyed her entirely too long for it to be polite. "Are you suddenly concerned with my feelings? I somehow doubt it."

Celeste let out that tinkling laugh of hers, as if I had said something amusing. "Don't be silly, Javier."

"I can assure you I have never been 'silly' a single moment in my life. There is little reason to imagine I might start now. Here."

I did not say, *with you.*

"You and I know how this game is played," she told me, managing to sound airy and intimate at once. "There are certain rules, are there not? And they must be followed, no matter what we think of them. I must commend you on thinking to offer for poor, sweet Imogen, the dull little dear. But it will all work beautifully now."

"I have no idea what you're talking about."

"You were wise to wait," she continued gaily, as if the harsh tone I used was encouraging. As if this was an actual conversation instead of a strange performance on her part. "For men with bloodlines as pristine as the count, there can be no stain upon his heirs. Not even a stray whisper. But I have already done my duty and given him spotless children without the faintest bit of scandal attached to their births. Why should he care what I do now?"

I stared at her. So long that the sly, stimulating smile faltered on her lips.

"You cannot imagine that you hold the slightest enticement for me, can you?" I asked with a soft menace I could see very well hit her like a blow. And she was lucky that I knew very well that no matter how disinterested the crowd around us might have seemed, everyone was watching this interaction. Because everyone knew that a decade back, I had made a fool of myself over this woman. "Is your opinion of yourself so high that you honestly believe I would so much as cross a street for you? Much less marry another woman for the dubious pleasure of becoming close to you in some way? I am interested in the Fitzalan name, Celeste. The blood of centuries of kingmakers. Not a single faithless woman I forgot the moment you made your decision ten years ago."

But this was Celeste, who had never faced a moment she couldn't turn into a game—and one in which she had an advantage. Though I was certain I saw a hint of uncertainty in her gaze, it was gone in an instant.

And then I was assaulted with that laughter of hers that had haunted me long after I had left this very house way back when. And not because I had longed to hear it again—ever—but because it was the soundtrack of my own, early humiliation. One of my very few losses.

"You do what you must, Javier," she murmured throatily at me. "Play hard to get if your pride requires it. You and I know the truth, do we not?"

And, perhaps wisely, she did not stick around to hear my answer.

But when they called us into the formal dining hall for the banquet sometime later, I made my way over to Fitzalan and curtly told him that I would not be joining him at the table.

"I beg your pardon," the man said in his stuffy way. I couldn't tell if he looked more affronted or astonished—and this could have been as much because I had approached him without express invitation as what I'd said. "Perhaps you are unaware, Dos Santos, but you are the guest of honor." In case I had failed to pick up on that little dig, that suggestion I didn't know enough to realize the dinner was supposedly for me, he inclined his head in a show of benevolence that made my jaw clench. "You are the one getting married in the morning. It is customary for you to take part."

I forced myself to smile, though it felt raw and unused. "I suspect you will all enjoy yourselves more if you can talk about me rather than to me."

And I only lifted a brow when the other man sputtered in obvious insult.

Not because it wasn't true. But because a man like Dermot Fitzalan was far more offended that anyone might dare call him out on his behavior. Especially if that "anyone" was a commoner like me.

I didn't wait for his response, which no doubt insulted him all the more. I left the crowd without any further awkward discussions, then I made my way through the great house, not sure where my feet were taking me. My thoughts were a strange jumble of Celeste, then and now. The Fitzalan family and how Imogen fit into it, so different was she from her father and sister.

And I even thought about my own family, who it had never occurred to me to invite to take part in this spectacle.

My mother had never taken to the new life I had provided for her. She viewed it all with suspicion and saved the worst of that suspicion for me—especially because of the deal we'd struck. Namely, that I would support her only if she gave up her former life and habits entirely. No opiates. No drink. Nothing but the sweet prison of my money.

"Why must you have a wife such as this?" she had demanded the last time we spoke, when I had subjected myself to my usual monthly visitation to make sure neither she nor my sisters had backslid into habits that would—sooner or later—send the wrong sort of people to my door.

I would pay for their lives as long as they kept them quiet and legal. I would not pay to get them out of the trouble I'd insisted they leave behind in their old ones.

They had all flatly refused to leave Madrid. I had only convinced them to leave the old, terrible neighborhood after a criminal rival had murdered my father—years after I had cut him out of my life because he'd refused to quit selling his poison.

It had taken longer than that for my mother and sisters to kick their own seedy habits. And none of us pretended they'd done it for any but the most mercenary reasons. They all wanted the life I could give them, not the life they'd had—especially not when they might find themselves forced to pay for my father's sins if they stayed there.

But that didn't mean they liked it. Or me.

"The Fitzalan girl is an emblem," I had told my mother, sitting stiffly in the house I kept for her and my sisters. I would not have discussed my marital plans with her at all, but had run out of other topics to discuss with these people who hated me for bettering them. "A trophy, that is all."

"With all your money you can make anything you like into a trophy. What do you care what these people think?"

My mother had a deep distrust of the upper classes. My father had trafficked in too many things to count as the local head of a much wider, much more dangerous operation—and she had always been in peril herself because of it—but she knew that world. On some level she would always trust the streets more than the fine house I had provided for her.

Just as she trusted the desperate men who ruled there more than she ever would me.

"My children will have the blood of aristocrats," I had said. "There will be no doors closed to them."

My mother had made a scornful sort of noise. "No one can see another person's blood, Javier. Unless you spill it. And the only people who worry about such things are too afraid to do such things themselves."

My sisters, by contrast, had praised the very idea of a Fitzalan bride for their only brother, because they believed that if they pretended to be kind to me, I might confuse that for true kindness and increase my generosity.

"It will be like having royalty in the family!" Noellia had cried.

"She might as well be a princess!" Mariana had agreed rapturously.

My sisters had taken to my money with avid, delirious greed. They had not disagreed with me in years. On any topic. Because they always, always wanted more. And the longer they lived lavishly at my expense, the less they wanted to find themselves tossed back into the dank pit we'd all come from.

Or more precisely: the pit from which I had clawed my way, with all of them on my back.

I had made the same bargain with all of them. I would finance their lives as long as their pursuits never embarrassed me or caused so much as a ripple in the careful life I'd built.

We had always been family in name only. My father had used us all in different ways, either as mules or distractions or accomplices. We were all tainted by the man who had made us and the lies he'd told us.

And worse still, the things we'd done back then, when we'd had no other choices.

Or what I had done to get away from the tragedy of my beginnings.

Of course I hadn't wanted them here, surrounded by so many of Europe's hereditary predators, each and every one of them desperate to find something—anything—they could use to weaken my position in any one of the markets I dominated.

I wandered the Fitzalan house for a long while. Eventually I found myself in the library, cavernous and dimly lit this night. The roof up above was a dome of glass, though rain fell upon it tonight with an insistent beat that made me almost too aware of its potential for collapse. It felt too much like foreboding, so I focused on the books instead. On the shelves that lined the walls two stories high, packed tight with volume after volume I had never read. And had likely never heard of, for that matter.

I was not an educated man. There had been no time to lose myself in books when there were worlds to be won. And yet I felt it tug at me, that insatiable thirst for knowledge that I had always carried in me. Knowledge for knowledge's sake, instead of the kind of intelligence I had learned to assemble to carry into boardrooms and stately homes like this one, so I might best whoever I encountered.

There were times I thought I would have killed for the opportunity to immerse myself in these books men like Dermot Fitzalan had grudgingly read at some or other boarding school in their youth, then promptly forgot, though they always considered themselves far more educated than the likes of me.

Men like him—men like all those who gathered around that dining table even now, no doubt trading snide stories of my barbaric, common ways—preferred to build beautiful monuments to knowledge like this library, then never use them. I didn't have to know a single thing about Dermot Fitzalan's private life to know that he never tarried here, flipping through all these books he had at his disposal simply because he wished to improve his mind. Or escape for an hour. Or for any reason at all.

Meanwhile, I still remembered the first library I had ever entered as a child. We had been rich for our neighborhood because my father ran product, but still poor in every meaningful way. There had never been any cozy nights at home, reading books or learning letters or tending to the mind in any way. Anything I knew I had been forced to pry out of the terrible schools I'd been sent to by law, often without any help from teachers or staff. And any bit of information, knowledge, or fact I'd uncovered in those sad places had been a prize to me.

The library in the primary school I had attended had been a joke. I knew that now. But what I remembered was my sense of awe and wonder when I had walked into a room of books, however paltry the selection or small the room. I hadn't understood that I could read whichever of them I chose at will. It had taken me years to trust that it wasn't another trick like the ones I knew from home. It had taken me a long time to truly believe I could take any book I liked, read it elsewhere, and return it for another without any dire consequences.

Here in this hushed, moneyed place that was palatial in comparison to the libraries in my memory, I pulled a book with a golden spine out from the shelf closest to me, measured the weight of it in my hand, then put it back.

I drifted over to one of the tables in the middle of the floor, set up with seating areas and tables for closer study. The table nearest to me was polished wood, gleaming even in the dim light, and empty save for three uneven stacks of books. I looked closer. One was a pile of novels. Another was of nonfiction, the narrative sort, in several languages. The third, the shortest, was of poetry.

"May I assist you, sir?" came a smooth, deferential voice.

I looked up to find one of the staff standing there, looking apologetic the way they always did. As if they wanted nothing more than to apologize for the grave sin of serving me. I had gotten used to service after all this time, but that didn't make me comfortable with it.

"I am enjoying the library," I said, aware that I sounded as arrogant as any of the men I had left to toast my humble roots in the banquet hall. "Does the family prefer it to remain private?"

"Not at all, sir," the man before me replied, unctuously. He straightened. "The Fitzalan collection is quite important, stretching back as it does to the first recorded history of the family in this area. The most ancient texts are protected, of course, in the glass cases you may observe near the—"

He sounded as if he was delivering a speech from a museum tour. A very long speech. I tapped my finger against the stack of books nearest me. "What are these?"

If the man was startled that I had interrupted him, he gave no sign. He merely inclined his head.

"Those are for Miss Imogen," he said. When I only stared back at him, he cleared his throat and continued. "Those are the books she wishes to take with her into her, ah, new life."

Her new life. With me.

The servant left me shortly thereafter and I told myself that it was time to go back to my rooms. There was business waiting for my attention the way there always was, and I had better things to do than linger in a library.

But I couldn't seem to move. I stared at those three stacks of books, and it was as if her taste flooded me all over again.

Imogen. Red-gold and wild. Tilting at windmills from all sides.

Because I knew without a shadow of a doubt that had I married Celeste the way I had wanted to do ten years ago, she would not have come to me with a collection of books. Just as I knew that while there was very little possibility that Celeste had spent any time in this library of her own volition growing up, it was a certainty that Imogen had.

There was no reason that should have washed through me like heat.

I picked up the first book of poetry on the stack before me and flipped it open, not surprised that it fell open to a well-worn page. My eye was drawn to a poem that someone—and I was certain I knew who—had clearly liked so much that she'd underlined the things that had struck her most.

"'For here there is no place that does not see you,'" I read, with two lines drawn beneath it in blue ink. "'You must change your life.'"

I closed the book again and left it there, that odd heat still surging in me.

And when I finally started back toward my rooms, I found that I was far more intrigued with this business arrangement of mine than I had been before I'd arrived here.

I had wanted a Fitzalan wife. And I prided myself on getting what I wanted, by any means necessary. When I had decided at a mere eight years old that I would get out of the stark war zone of my youth, I had done whatever I needed to do to make that happen. I had lied to liars, cheated the cheaters, and had built my own catapult before I rocketed myself straight out of my humble beginnings. It had required a ten-year wait to bend Dermot Fitzalan to my will the way I had done, but I had never wavered.

I had wanted the Fitzalan blood. The Fitzalan consequence

and breeding. All the aristocratic splendor that went with a connection to these people and the nobility they hoarded like treasure. I had wanted all of it.

I still did.

But I also wanted Imogen.

CHAPTER FIVE

Imogen

I DIDN'T KNOW how most weddings were meant to go.

I had no idea how they were conducted out there in the world
where people made their own choices, but mine was not exactly
the festival of emotion and tearful smiles I'd been led to expect by entirely too many bright and gleaming online wedding
sites. Or reports from my friends at the convent, whose glittering nuptials had been spread across glossy magazine inserts all
over the globe—and as such, had been far too crass and common for my father to permit me to attend.

Not that I had truly imagined it would be otherwise.

I had been presented in my father's rooms first thing, after
a long evening and another long morning—already—of what
one of my attendants had euphemistically claimed was my opportunity for *pampering*.

If this is pampering, I'd thought a bit darkly as they'd worked
on me as if I was the Christmas goose, *I'm glad this is the first
I've had of it.*

But soon enough it had been time to parade me before the
only person whose opinion mattered. I had been marched down
the hall of the family wing to my father's sitting room and pre-

sented. He had been taking his usual breakfast and had deigned to lower the corner of his newspaper, the better to glare at me as he took in my appearance.

He glared at me for a long time.

The attendants he'd ordered to handle the problem that was me had done their duty. I was buffed and shined and beaten to a glow. But the true achievement was my hair. They had straightened it, time and again. They had poured product on it. They had ironed it and brushed it and had blown it out, more than once, so ruthlessly that it still hurt. Then, not to rest on their laurels, they had painstakingly crafted the kind of sweeping, elegant chignon that my sister made look so elegant and easy.

It had taken hours. I felt...welted.

"I see I should have taken you more in hand years ago," my father said acidly, as if my transformation was somehow as upsetting as my usual appearance was to him. "Why have you roamed about in your usual state of disarray all this time if it was possible for you to look like this?"

I didn't think that was a real question. I could still feel yesterday's bruises on my arm, reminding me of the many virtues of silence, but he continued to glare at me until it occurred to me that he meant me to answer it.

"Well, sir, it took hours," I said, awkwardly, given my scalp still ached and the movement of my jaw needed to form words made it worse.

"Yet you felt the reputation and honor of your family did not merit putting in these hours at any other point in your life." My father shifted his glare to the attendant at my side, dismissing me with a curl of his lip. "See to it she does not mess herself up as she is wont to do. I want there to be not so much as a single hair out of place at the ceremony, do you understand?"

"Of course, sir," the attendant murmured, also not looking at me.

Because what I thought about the discussion did not signify. To anyone.

And that, naturally, comprised the entirety of the fatherly advice I received before my wedding.

When I was escorted back to my rooms, they were buzzing with activity. My things were being packed by one set of attendants while another set was responsible for dressing me, and no one required my input on these matters. I let them herd me into the wedding ensemble that had been chosen without my input, muttering to each other as they sewed me into the gown I knew my father had paid a fortune for, as it was nothing short of an advertisement for his power.

But then, Javier had also paid a fortune for this, I assumed. So I supposed it was best if he, too, got his money's worth in the form of a proper bride. Even I knew that what mattered on occasions like this was perception. No one in this house cared if I was happy. But they likely all cared deeply that I *look* happy. As well as elegant and effortless and *fully a Fitzalan*, the better to honor the blood in my veins.

They might whisper about the ways I was lowering myself. They might titter about *lying down with the dogs*. They would talk among themselves about the variety of ways money was neither class nor nobility and amuse themselves with their feelings of superiority every time they looked at Javier, who could buy and sell them all. A few might even tut sympathetically about the sacrifice I was making.

But if I dared show so much as a hint of trepidation, they would turn on me like the jackals they were.

When I was dressed in acres of sweeping white and draped in fine jewels that proclaimed my father's consequence and taste to all and sundry, my attendants sat me on the bench at the foot of my bed and ordered me not to move. I had been sitting there stiffly, certain I would somehow spill something on myself without actually having anything to spill, when Celeste appeared.

My father felt bridesmaids were gauche—or he was unaware and/or uninterested in the fact I'd actually made friends at school—but I supposed it didn't matter anyway, as Celeste filled all those roles for me.

I sighed a little as she came into the room, careful to maintain my painfully perfect posture, lest I inadvertently wrinkle something. Or make my hair curl. Celeste looked beautiful, as always, and she certainly didn't look as if it had taken hours upon hours and an army to achieve it. She wore a dress in another, warmer shade of white that only enhanced all her blond beauty.

"I'm supposed to be the bride, but I think everyone will be looking at you instead," I said, and smiled at her.

She smiled back. But I couldn't help thinking it took her too long.

"You've made the guests quite curious, you realize," she said, her voice so light and merry I forgot about how long it might have taken her to smile. "How mysterious, to hide away the night before your own wedding. What on earth were you doing? Engaging in some last-minute contemplation and prayer?" She shook her head at me as if I was a silly, hopeless creature she'd happened upon in the gardens and had rescued out of the goodness of her heart. "I hope you weren't continuing the same futile line of thought as yesterday."

"I was enjoying an enforced battery of spa treatments, courtesy of Father." I held up my hand so she could behold the manicure. It wasn't my first manicure, of course, but the women had done more than simply try to shape the ragged nails I had presented them. They had built me new ones, long and elegant enough to rival Celeste's. "I had no idea that so-called pampering could be so painful."

"A wedding is the last day where a girl should look like some kind of dreadful *tomboy*, Imogen," Celeste said with one of her carefree laughs that somehow landed strangely on me. I told myself it was the unnatural way I was sitting there, like some kind of wooden doll. "But don't worry. I can still see the real you in there. A little bit of makeup and pretty nails doesn't change the truth of who you are."

That should have made me smile, surely. But for some reason, instead, it raked over me as if the words had an edge.

An edge I found myself thinking about a little too much as she conferred with my attendants and determined the time had come at last to transport me to my fate. Because once I started thinking of such things, all I could see was that edginess. Celeste looked beautiful, certainly, but she was holding herself as if all her bones had gone brittle in the night.

And when she returned to my side, it again took a moment for her to summon her smile. I didn't let that fact drift away this time, and saw that no matter how she curved her lips, it did not reach her eyes.

A hollow pit seemed to yawn open in my belly.

But I didn't say a word as she motioned for me to rise to my feet and I obeyed. Because I only had one sister. And if she thought as little of me as everyone else in my life, did I really wish to know it? This was the only family I had left.

That hollow pit had teeth, I found. But I endeavored to ignore it.

"Have you seen my groom?" I asked as she linked her arm through mine and led me toward the door, her steps measured and purposeful. "I'm hoping he might have changed his mind."

I was joking, of course. And yet the look Celeste gave me then was…odd. It was as if I'd somehow offended her.

"One thing you should know about Javier, Imogen, is that he never changes his mind," she told me, no hint of her usual laughter in her voice. And no attempt at the light and airy tone I associated so strongly with her. "Never. When he is set upon something, when he has made up his mind, nothing else will do."

That settled uneasily in my gut, right there in that same hollow place, but I didn't question her on it. The brutal way she was holding herself next to me, so rigid and sharp, and the way she looked at me kept me quiet.

And besides, I could still feel the way Javier had touched me. Kissed me. Turned me utterly inside out without it seeming to affect him in the least. While I was still boneless at the very thought—though it was the next day.

I tried to conceal the shaky breath I let out then, but the sharp look Celeste threw my way told me I hadn't fooled her.

She seemed to soften a bit beside me then. Another thing I opted not to prod at. Something else I didn't want to know.

Downstairs on the main floor of the house the great ballroom had been transformed into an elegant wedding venue. My father waited for me at the doors. He swept a critical glance over me when Celeste presented me to him, then slipped inside herself.

"Let's get this over with quickly," he said gruffly, looking down his nose at me. "Before you revert to type."

And without any further conversation, and certainly no inquiries into my state of mind or feelings about this momentous occasion, he nodded to the servants to fling the doors wide. Then he led me down the center of the room.

I had dreamed about this, too. A wedding. *My* wedding. I had spent years imagining how it would feel. What I would do. How magical it would all seem, even if it was an exercise of strictest duty, because it meant the next stage of my life was about to begin.

But *magical* was not the word that came to mind today. I gazed out at the assembled throng of people my father deemed important, all those greedy-eyed men and the haughty women they had brought with them as decoration. The members of my own extended family, those cousins and relations who I wasn't sure I'd recognize out of context, who were entirely too impressed with themselves to do more than stare back at me as if I was inopportuning them by marrying in the first place.

I was tempted to pretend my mother was still alive. And here. And just out of sight, beaming with a magic all her own…

Because there was precious little magic in this room today. And maybe I was the empty-headed, disappointing creature everyone seemed to think I was, because the lack of it surprised me. I suppose I'd imagined that if I was going to dress up like this and play the part of a fairy-tale bride, everyone else might do the same.

But the way the guests all eyed me as if I was nothing more than a piece of meat laid out for their consumption, I thought we might as well have forgone this ceremony altogether, signed a few papers in the presence of an authority somewhere, and been done with it.

I was trying my best not to let any of my thoughts show on my face when my gaze slid—at last—to the center of the make-shift aisle my father had placed between the tables and the man who waited at the head of it.

And it was as if everything else simply…disappeared.

Every time I saw him I was struck anew. This time was worse than before, not least because I felt the impact of him in so many different places. My breasts felt heavy. My stomach was a knot. In between my legs, I was soft and hot at once.

And Javier could tell.

I knew he could.

He watched me approach as if he had already claimed me in every possible manner. As if this was nothing but a formality. Inevitable in every way.

Something about that hummed in me. Like a song.

I forgot about this crowd of mercenaries and snobs, none of whom I would ever have invited to anything had it been up to me. I forgot about the strange way my sister was behaving, all edges and angles when I had expected at least a modicum of sisterly support. I even forgot about my father, who gripped my arm as if he expected me to fling myself out of the nearest window.

None of that mattered. Not while Javier watched me come

to him, dressed for him, his gaze like lightning and the storm at once.

As if he had commanded me to do this thing for the simple reason it pleased him.

As if this was nothing more than an act of obedience.

I didn't know why that word somersaulted through me the way it did. Like a sweet little shiver that wore its way down into the depths of me, deep into places I hadn't known were there.

When I had never wanted to obey anyone, and no matter that I'd had no choice in the matter for most of my life. My father. The nuns. The attendants who were less servants than prison wardens. That was the trouble with the way Javier looked at me. That light in his dark eyes made me imagine the kind of obedience that I might choose to give him.

That faint curve to his hard mouth made me wonder what he might give me in return.

We reached the head of the aisle and my father swiftly handed me over to Javier, as if he dared not risk a delay.

My fate, I thought as Javier's hands wrapped around mine. *My doom.*

This monster I had to hope was truly a man, somewhere behind his harsh exterior.

A man who I knew without the slightest shred of doubt would be inside me, and no matter if he was a monster to his core, before I saw another dawn.

I hardly heard a word of the ceremony. The priest intoned this and that. We made our responses.

But nothing was real to me. It was all a kind of dream until Javier slid that heavy gold band onto my finger, as if it was an anchor.

"You may kiss the bride," the priest said severely, as if, were it left to him, he would rid the world of kissing altogether.

But I didn't care about the opinions of a priest I would never see again. Because Javier was pulling me toward him with the same easy confidence my body remembered all too well, bending his head—

And I was filled with a sudden panic.

Did he really want to do this here? What if I responded to him the way I had yesterday? Right here, where everyone could see me… Where my father could watch as I fell apart and shamed him…

I shuddered at the notion. And I saw a corner of Javier's hard, cruel mouth curl as if I'd amused him.

"Be strong, Imogen," he ordered me. "It is only a little while longer until you will leave this house and be entirely in my hands."

"That is not exactly a relaxing thought," I murmured in reply.

That curl deepened, only slightly.

And then he claimed my mouth with a sheer ruthlessness that nearly took my knees out from under me.

He gave no quarter. He made no allowance for the fact we were in public.

Javier, it was instantly clear to me, didn't care who saw me tremble in his arms.

And when he finally raised his head, there was no mistaking it.

He was smiling.

That was what stayed with me as the guests applauded anemically, and the servants swept in to begin serving the wedding breakfast. His ruthlessly male, deeply satisfied smile.

I expected Javier to leave me so he could make his rounds, talking the usual dry business men always did at these things. As far as I knew it was the point of them. But instead, he stayed beside me. So close beside me, in fact, that I could feel the heat of him.

It sank deep beneath my skin, then into my bones, as if he was that restorative bath I hadn't had last night. Though I did not have to study the man who stood with me—the man I had married, which I couldn't quite take in—to understand that he was nothing so easily comforting as a warm bath.

He was something else altogether.

"Are you very hungry?" Javier asked.

I found the question perhaps more startling than I should have. I chanced a look at him, feeling that same shivery thing wind its way through me, making my knees feel weak. Because his gaze was so direct, so dark and confronting. His nose was a harsh blade, his mouth that hard line, and I felt scraped raw.

And unable to look away.

"No," I managed to say, after taking much too long to stare at him. "I am not hungry at all."

"Then I see no reason to participate in this circus."

I didn't really process what he said, because he wrapped his arm around my back. That heavy arm of his, all roped muscle and lean, leashed power, and I…floated off somewhere. There was nothing but the wild buzz in my head, Javier's arm around me, and that shivery thing that became a flush, working its way over me until I thought that intense heat between my legs was actually visible. Everywhere.

But I came back to reality with a sharp crack when Javier steered me directly toward my father.

"Fitzalan." Javier nodded curtly, which was not the way people normally greeted my father. They tended toward obsequious displays of servility. But that was not Javier. That was not the man I'd married. "You will wish to say your goodbyes to your daughter."

My father drew himself up into the human equivalent of an exclamation point, all hauteur and offense. He gazed at Javier, then turned that same gaze on me.

I flinched. Javier did not.

"I am afraid I am not following you," my father said in the same distant, appalled voice he used when forced to have a conversation with the servants instead of merely issuing demands.

I thought that really, I should have jumped in to assure Javier that my father was not about to launch into any protracted farewells. That had I slipped off without a word he would likely have had no idea I'd gone.

But I couldn't seem to operate my mouth. I couldn't seem to form any words.

And Javier's arm was around me. It was all I could focus on.

I looked away from whatever strange, male showdown was happening between Javier and my father, and found my gaze snagged almost instantly. It was Celeste. She was sitting at one of the tables next to her husband, paying no attention to whatever conversation the count was having with a selection of other European nobles who looked as close to death by heart attack and advanced age as he did. She looked as effortlessly gracious as always, not a single glossy hair out of its place.

It was the look on her face that struck me. It was so…

Bitter, a voice inside me supplied.

And she wasn't looking at the count. Or my father. Or even me.

She was looking at Javier.

I didn't have time to process that, because Javier was moving again, striding away from my father and leaving me no choice but to hurry to keep up or be left behind. Or, more likely, dragged.

"Are we truly leaving our own wedding breakfast?"

I told myself I was breathless from the sudden sprint, that was all.

"We are."

"I didn't think that was allowed."

My breath caught when he stopped, there on the other side of the great doors that led into the ballroom. Because we were suddenly something like alone, out here in the grand foyer that my father always said had offered gracious welcome to a host of Europe's aristocrats. It was a shock after all the eyes that had been on us inside.

And it was even more of a shock because I was suddenly even more aware of how...difficult it was to be near this man.

My palms felt damp. There was that awful, betraying flush that only seemed to sizzle against my skin. There was heat in all the most embarrassing places.

And still I could only seem to manage to stare at the man who had married me as if I was mesmerized. I thought perhaps I was.

"Listen carefully, Imogen," Javier said sternly, but his tone didn't start any alarms ringing in me. There was still all that mad electricity in his gaze. And that hint of a potential curve in one corner of his mouth. "You are my wife now. Do you understand what that means?"

My heart began to pound, hard. "I think I do."

"Clearly you do not."

He reached over and smoothed his hand over the glossy surface of my chignon, grimacing slightly. No doubt because my hair had been shellacked so many times it was now more or less a fiberglass dome.

"This hair," he growled. "What have you done to it? I prefer your curls."

I blinked at that, aware that if he hadn't still been touching me, I would have assumed I was dreaming. No one liked my curls. Not even me.

Especially not me.

"My father wanted me to look the part today," I managed to say despite my confusion. "He has very specific ideas about how a proper Fitzalan heiress is meant to look."

Javier dropped his hand from my head, but it was only to take my hand. The hand where he had slid that heavy ring that I was sure I would never grow accustomed to. He looked at the ring a moment, then he looked from the ring to the place on my arm where my father had grabbed me yesterday. My attendants had done what they could to cover the marks, but he was so close now. I was sure he could see them.

His hard mouth turned grim. And his gaze when it met mine seemed to shudder through me, so intense was it.

"Your new life begins now," he told me in the same dark, gruff way. "You are a Dos Santos wife, not a Fitzalan heiress today. You need no longer concern yourself with the petty concerns of the man who raised you. It does not matter what he likes, what he wants, what he allows."

He toyed with my hand in both of his, almost idly—though I knew somehow that nothing this man did was truly idle.

"This is true of the whole of the world," Javier told me gravely. "It has nothing to do with you. There are no laws, no leaders, no men of power anywhere that you need consider any longer. You are above all of that."

"Above...?" I echoed, as caught up in his intensity as I was in the way he traced my fingers and warmed my hand between his.

"You are mine," Javier told me, that dark gaze like a new vow, hard on mine. "And that, Imogen, is the beginning and end of everything you need to know, from this moment on."

CHAPTER SIX

Javier

I COULDN'T LEAVE that old pile of self-satisfied stone fast enough.

Or its equally smug inhabitants.

We could have stayed for what would likely have been an interminable wedding breakfast, of course. I could have subjected myself to more condescension. I could have stood in that room, choosing not to let myself get offended by every sanctimonious or outright snobbish comment aimed in my direction. I could have pretended I didn't see the way Celeste watched me, as if she still somehow believed that I would waste all these years and all this time chasing after her when she had made her choice.

But I saw no point in playing those games. I already had what I wanted.

I had already won.

A Fitzalan heiress wore my ring as I had told Dermot Fitzalan one would, sooner or later. Nothing else mattered. Nothing in this old house, at any rate.

I had won.

That Dermot Fitzalan had clearly put his hands on what was mine did not surprise me. Men like Dermot wielded their power in every petty way they could. But it was a rage for another time, beating in me like a pulse.

If I gave in to it here, I feared I would raze these stone walls to rubble.

And I didn't know what to do with the notion that the woman at my side—my prize, my wife—was clearly so used to her father's behavior that she not only hadn't commented on it, she didn't look particularly cowed by it, either.

I took Imogen's hand in mine and started toward the grand entrance, ordering the servants to bring my car around as I moved. One thing men like Fitzalan always did well was train their staff to perfection, so it did not surprise me to find my car waiting when we stepped out of the house and, more, another car idling behind it with all of our bags.

I had left instructions, but even if I had not, there was no way all of Imogen's belongings could have fit into a Lamborghini Veneno. Even if they could, the point of a Lamborghini was not the hauling of baggage, as if it was some kind of sedate, suburban SUV.

I handed her into the sports car that was more a work of art than a vehicle, and then climbed into the driver's seat myself, taking pleasure in the way her wedding gown flowed all over the bucket seats and danced in the space between us. It threatened to bury us both in all those layers of finery.

I wouldn't mind if it did.

I liked the dress in the same way I liked the ring I'd put on her finger. I like signs. Portents and emblems. I liked the optics of a Fitzalan girl at my side, dressed in flowing white with my ring—*mine*—heavy on her finger. I could see faces at the windows inside and knew that those same optics weren't lost on our audience.

I had won a major victory and no matter how they looked down on me, these stuffy, inbred aristocrats knew it. In fact, I thought the snobbier they were to my face, the more aware they likely were that my money and its reach had surpassed them in every possible way.

I was a nobody from the gutters of Spain, and yet I was the one the world still bowed to. They were ghosts holding fast to a past few remembered any longer.

But I remembered. And I had done the unforgivable. I had used all my filthy money to buy my way into their hallowed little circles. I had dared to imagine myself their equal.

They would never accept me, but I didn't need acceptance.

I had what I wanted. The past in the form of the lovely aristocrat beside me, and the future we would make together with my influence.

I drove off from the Fitzalan manor house, allowing the car to growl and surge forward like the high-powered, predatory beauty it was. But as I drove it down the lane, half of my attention was on Imogen, who was leaving her childhood home behind her. It would have been normal if she'd shown a bit of trepidation. Or emotion.

Something complicated, even, to match those marks on her upper arm.

But she didn't look back.

I made it to the landing strip where my plane waited for us in record time, exhilarated by all the power and speed I had in my hands again. Especially after these dreary days locked up with ponderous old men who talked about long-gone centuries as if they'd personally lived through them.

It was Imogen I was focused on as we climbed out of the car near the plane, however, not the haunted remains of what had once been Europe's most powerful families.

"You look as if you have seen a ghost," I said as I helped her—and all the filmy layers of her wedding dress—out of the car. I tried to imagine what might upset a sheltered creature like this. "Do you miss your late mother, perhaps?"

She looked a little pale, it was true. Though I couldn't tell if that was an emotional reaction on her part after all, or if it was that damned makeup slapped all over her face, hiding those freckles I liked so much, despite myself.

When I looked closer, however, her copper eyes were sparkling.

"I miss my mother every day," she said. "But that was *fast*."

In that same demure voice she had used at our wedding ceremony. The one that made me almost wonder if the half-wild creature who had turned up in my rooms yesterday had been nothing more than a figment of my clearly oversexed imagination.

I was wondering it again when she smiled at me, big and bright enough to make me very nearly forget all the ways they had muted her for the wedding. "I think I like fast."

I felt that directly in my sex.

"I am glad to hear that. I believe I can promise you fast."

I was not only speaking of cars, but I wasn't sure she took my meaning. She reached over and ran her fingers lightly over the sensually shaped hood of the Lamborghini, then jerked them away. And her smile turned guilty.

"I'm sorry. I shouldn't have touched it."

"You can touch it whenever you like."

"Oh. Are you sure? Only, I was under the impression that most men are very picky about who they let touch."

"They are perhaps choosy about *how* they are touched," I said in a darkly amused voice I made no attempt to hide. "But if you show me a man who claims to be overly picky about where a beautiful woman places her fingers, I will show you a liar."

She curled the fingers in question into a fist, and swallowed hard enough that my gaze drifted to that neck of hers I longed to taste.

When her eyes met mine again, she seemed almost…shy. "Are we still talking about your car?"

I felt my mouth curve. I didn't want to answer that. "If you like."

"I think I may have given you the wrong impression yesterday," she said in a rush, as if it had been difficult for her to get the sentence out. "I don't know why I came to your rooms in the first place. And it certainly wasn't my intention—"

"We will have nothing but time to revisit what happened in my rooms," I told her. "Not a single detail will be overlooked, I assure you."

She looked nervous, and another man might have taken pains to put her at her ease. But I was enough of a bastard to enjoy it.

"Oh. Well. I mean, I think you might have come to a certain conclusion…"

Her voice trailed away as I took her hand again, and I liked that. I liked the way her pulse beat wildly in the crook of her neck, there where I could see it. I liked the heat of her hand in mine and the smoothness of her manicured fingers twined with my hard, calloused ones.

I wanted to be inside her more than I wanted my next breath. I wanted her beneath me, above me. I wanted her in every position I could imagine, and I was a creative man. But they had turned her into a stranger with all that makeup and alien hair.

I didn't like it at all.

"I had intended to jump straight into the sweet satisfaction of consummation," I told her as I led her toward the plane's folded-down stairs.

And I made a split-second decision as we moved. I had planned to take her to my penthouse in Barcelona. It was not the place I considered my true home, but it had seemed to me to be more domestic and private than other properties I had. But she was naive and she was mine. There were marks on her shoulder and they had rendered her unrecognizable. And I wanted things I couldn't quite name.

I followed an urge I hardly understood, and decided I would take her home instead.

"It is not a long flight to the Mediterranean, I grant you." I sounded stiff and strange. I knew it was because I had made a revolutionary decision—when no one was usually granted access to my private island but me. "Still, I thought there would be ample time to take my first taste of wedded bliss."

I could feel her tremble. It was another show of those nerves that lit me up from the inside out, like heat and triumph all at once. Because I liked a little trepidation. I was not an easy man, nor a small one. And Imogen might have indicated that she had already rid herself of her innocence, but I could tell by all these jitters that she had not gotten much experience out of the bargain, no matter who she had been with.

I shoved away the little twist of something darker and stickier than simple irritation that kicked around in me at that thought. Of Imogen spread out beneath another man's body, allowing him inside her...

She was mine. The thought of another's fingers all over her... rankled.

But I was not in the habit of showing my emotions. To anyone. Even myself, if it could be avoided.

"Do you have some objection to the marital bed?" I asked her instead as I allowed her to precede me up the stairs and into the jet. I even attempted to keep my tone...conversational.

I couldn't see her face then. But I saw the way she froze, then started again almost at once, as if she didn't want me to see her reaction any more than I wished to show her mine. I saw how hard she gripped the railing in one hand, and the way she bent her head as she wound as much of the fabric of her heavy dress around her free hand as she could.

I didn't have to see her face to watch the way she trembled. Again. Still.

"I have no objection," she said over her shoulder, in a voice that didn't sound quite like hers. As if her nerves were constricting her throat.

I waited until we had both boarded the plane. I spoke to the captain briefly about the change in flight plans, and when I made my way back into the sleek lounge area, it was to find

Imogen seated on one of the leather couches, prim and proper and still awash in all that white.

I threw myself down on the couch facing her, stretching my legs out so that they grazed hers. And then waited to see if she would jerk herself away. Because she was a girl raised to suffer through her duty no matter what, and it had occurred to me that she might very well consider the marital bed one of those duties.

I didn't care to interrogate myself about why, exactly, that idea was so unpalatable to me.

When she didn't move her legs away from mine—when instead she sighed a little bit and stayed where she was—it felt a great deal like another victory.

And the creeping flush that turned her ears faintly pink told me she knew it.

"It looks as if they spent a great deal of time making you into a mannequin today," I said after a long moment spun out into another. "This was certainly not for my benefit. Is this how you prefer to present yourself?"

She took her time raising her gaze to mine, and when our eyes met, hers were cool. I found I missed her wildness. "My father takes his reputation very seriously. You have been saddled with the disappointing Fitzalan daughter, who, I am ashamed to say, requires the aid of a battalion of attendants to look even remotely put together. I assumed you knew."

I didn't think she looked ashamed. If anything, I would have described her as faintly defiant somewhere behind all that composure.

"Remember what I told you, please. The only disappointment that need concern you now is mine. And I am not disappointed."

I saw her work to keep her face still. Polite and composed, which I knew in her world meant wiped clean of anything but that slight smile. Still, there was emotion in that copper gaze of hers that I couldn't quite read.

"My father does not share your taste, it appears. He insisted that for once in my life I represent the family appropriately." She reached up and patted that smooth helmet of a chignon they'd crafted for her. It didn't move. I doubted a blowtorch could move it. "The main point of contention, as ever, was my hair. It offends my father. He has long been under the impression that I will it to curl for the express purpose of defying him."

I studied her as the plane began to taxi for our takeoff. She looked as elegant as I could have wished. She looked pulled together and carefully curated, the jewel of any collection, even mine. I had no doubt that every man in that ballroom today who had sneeringly referred to her as the lesser of the two Fitzalan sisters had kicked himself for his lack of vision. She looked like what she was: the lovely daughter of an extraordinarily wealthy and powerful man who had been raised to be adorned in gowns and stunning pieces of jewelry. A woman who would function as decoration and an object of envy, whose pedigree was as much in the way she held herself as in the decidedly blue blood that ran in her veins.

She looked perfect, it was true.

But she did not look like Imogen.

She did not look like my Don Quixote bride, who carried windmills in her smile and an irrepressible spirit in her wild red-gold curls.

I wondered how I would have felt about the vision before me now if I hadn't seen the real Imogen yesterday. Would I have been satisfied with this version of my Fitzalan bride? Would I have accepted this smooth version of her, no edges or angles? Would I already be inside her to the hilt, marking my claim upon her tender flesh?

I couldn't answer that. But I did know this: the woman sitting before me looked entirely too much like her sister.

I wanted the Imogen who was nothing at all like Celeste.

And I opted not to look too closely at why that was.

"You say I have not disappointed you," Imogen said as the plane soared into the air, then turned south to cross France, headed toward Majorca and the Balearic Islands off the coast of Spain. "And I appreciate the sentiment. But you're looking at me as if I'm every bit the disappointment my father always told me I was."

"I'm staring at you because you do not look like yourself at all."

"Are you an expert, then?"

"I did meet you before the wedding, Imogen. Perhaps you have already forgotten."

Her ears pinkened yet again, telling me clearly that she hadn't forgotten anything that had happened yesterday. Neither had I.

"I'm not sure why you think that was an example of me looking more myself." She gave the impression of shrugging without doing so. "Perhaps it was yet another costume. The many faces of Imogen Fitzalan."

"Imogen Fitzalan Dos Santos," I corrected her, all silken threat and certainty. I considered her another moment. "Are you planning to maintain *this* costume?"

Her expression was grave. "I shouldn't think so. It took quite a long time. And several battalions of attendants, as I said."

"This I believe."

I stayed where I was, lounging there as the plane hurtled along, my arms stretched out along the back of the sofa. I did not dare move—because if I did, I was quite certain that I would stop caring all that much about what was the real Imogen and what was not. I would put my hands on her and that would be that.

I was not a man given to denying myself much of anything. So I wasn't entirely sure why I didn't go ahead and do it.

I suspected it had something to do with those marks on her arm and the fact I could not—would not—make myself yet another brutish male she would have to suffer. That was not at all what I wanted from her.

I nodded toward the rear of the jet instead.

"I have no interest in claiming a mannequin," I told her, not certain I recognized my own voice. "Your bags have been taken into one of the staterooms. I suggest you use this flight to wash away all traces of—" I let my gaze move over her hair, her face "—this."

"'This,'" she repeated. She made a sound that I thought was a laugh, though her expression was clear of any laughter when I raised a brow at her. "Which part of *this*? Do you want me to re-chip my nails? Un-exfoliate my skin?"

"Do something with your hair," I told her, aware that I felt very nearly...savage. It was need and lust mixed up with that possessiveness I didn't quite know how to handle, much less that softer thing I couldn't name. "It doesn't suit you. And I cannot see your freckles."

"That is for your benefit," she replied, quick enough that I felt the lick of it in my sex again, the reappearance of that defiant girl I had met after all. "Surely everyone knows that the sight of a stray freckle on the nose of one's carefully vetted and purchased bride might scar a man for life."

"Wash it all off," I ordered her quietly. "Or I will come back and do the washing myself, and I'm not certain you will enjoy that as much as I know I will."

There was no mistaking the bright sheen of heat in her gaze then, no matter how quickly she dropped it to her lap. For a moment, I thought I could feel flames leap and dance between us, taking up all the oxygen in the cabin.

"That won't be necessary," she said, addressing her lap. Because, no doubt, she imagined that was safer. "I may play the part of a helpless female, Javier, but I assure you I can handle a simple shower."

CHAPTER SEVEN

Javier

I WATCHED HER go in a great cloud of white—moving as quickly as I supposed a person could on an airplane without actually running—and sat where I was for a beat or two after I heard the door to the stateroom open and then shut. Emphatically.

I pulled out my mobile, scrolling through the nine or ten million things that needed my attention immediately, but set it down again without retaining anything. I could feel her, still. Her taste was in me now, and I wanted more.

I wanted so much more.

Even though I had just told her that I wasn't going to help her wash off her bridal costume unless it was necessary, there was a part of me—a huge part of me—that wanted to head back there anyway.

It had never occurred to me that the other Fitzalan daughter would get to me in this way.

I had assumed, in fact, that she would not. Rumors had always suggested that she was awkward and shy, unused to the company of men. I had expected a shy, trembling flower. I had assumed she would require patience and a steady hand and I had been prepared to give her both to get what I wanted.

"The best-bred ones are always crap where it counts," one of the braying jackasses last night had informed the whole of the room as I'd claimed my drink and cautioned myself against swinging on any of the genteel crowd. Not because it wouldn't have been entertaining, but because it would only prove their wildest speculation about my monstrous, animalistic tendencies to be true and I refused to give them such satisfaction. "They make it such a chore. Best to get a few brats on them as quickly as possible and move on to more tempting prospects."

He had not been speaking to me directly. I was not sure he had even been aware I was in the room. The man in question had been a group or two away, perfectly happy to spout such a thing next to the ratchet-faced woman I could only assume was his unhappy wife. The chore herself, in other words.

All the men in the group had laughed. None of the women had.

And I understood this was how things worked in such circles. I understood that the unpleasant submission of wife to husband was a part of what made their world go round, and they all made the best of it. Because there were lands to think of. Inheritances. Bloodlines and legacies.

Easy enough to lie back and think about the comfortable future. Easy enough to suffer a little in order to gain so much in return.

If I understood anything, it was that particular math.

But I was not one of those blue-blooded aristocratic horror shows, a fact they had taken great pains to make sure I understood this weekend. And understand I did. I understood that they would hate me forever because I could take what they wanted, I could claim it as my own, and I could laugh at the notion that it mattered how little they thought of me.

Just as I could dismiss the notion that I needed to treat the aristocratic wife I'd gone to such trouble to buy the way they would have, if she'd been theirs.

I did not need my wife to be my partner, the way I knew

some wives were to their husbands, each of them committed to the continuation of their family's influence. And I'd watched my parents sell out each other—and us—too many times to believe in love. But if there was one thing I knew I was good at, and took pride in the practicing, it was sex.

I had been certain that in this, at least, I would manage to work a bit of magic, no matter how repressed and overwhelmed my convent-trained wife appeared.

But that was before Imogen had appeared in my rooms and let me taste exactly how sweet she was. How soft, how hot.

And now I had no doubt at all that whatever else there might be between us, we would always have that deliciously wild heat and everything that came with it.

Windmills all around.

Steady, I ordered myself. There was no point rushing things now when I had waited ten years to get here.

I picked up my mobile again, and forced myself to concentrate on my business. And when I looked up from putting out fires and answering the questions only I could, hours had passed. The plane was landing.

And the woman who walked out of the back of the plane to meet me was the Imogen I remembered. The Imogen I wanted.

Gone was the wedding dress and all its gauzy, bridal splendor. In its place, the first Senora Dos Santos wore another dress like the one she'd had on yesterday when I'd first caught sight of her. Three-quarter sleeves and a hemline no one in their right mind would call provocative. Another pair of glossy, polished leather boots.

But what got my attention most was the hair. Her glorious hair, curling this way and that. I could see that it was still damp, so it looked darker than its usual red-gold, but I hardly minded. Not when I could see the curls I already thought of as mine and, even better, those freckles scattered across her nose.

"Much better," I told her.

"I'm glad you approve," she said, and though her tone was

nothing but polite, I found myself searching her face to see if I could locate the edge I was sure I had heard. She looked out the windows. "Where are we?"

"This is the Mediterranean," I said, gesturing out the window at the deep blue surrounding us. "Or more properly the edge of the Balearic Sea, somewhere between Menorca and Sardinia."

She came and sank down on that sofa across from me again. "I've seen pictures of the Mediterranean, of course. But I've never been before."

"I was given the impression you haven't been anywhere."

"My role is to operate as an ornament," Imogen said, without any particular bitterness. "Not to travel the world, collecting experiences. I've had to make do with pictures on the internet."

"I am not at all surprised that your father feared that if you left, you wouldn't return to his tender mercies."

Imogen gazed at me, a faint, sad curve to her lips. "Do you know, I never tried to leave. I'm not sure he was the one who was afraid. He might not have been much in the way of family, but he was the only one I had and I suppose that meant more to me than it should have."

I didn't know why that touched me. I hated that it did. It was one thing to enjoy the fact that we had chemistry, and all the things that could mean for the marriage ahead of us and the sort of sex I had not been looking forward to doing without.

It was another entirely to feel.

Especially when those feelings tempted me to imagine I could relate in any way to a girl who had been raised wrapped up tight in cotton wool and convent walls when I had never been protected or sheltered from anything. On the contrary, my parents had often used me to help sell their poison.

I had learned how to mistrust everything by knowing full well no one could trust me.

"I have an island," I told her coolly, determined that there be no trace of those unwelcome *feelings* in my voice. "It is not very big. But I think it will do nicely enough."

Her gaze moved from the deep blue of the water below to me, then back again, and I could see the trepidation written all over her, stamped into her skin, and yet her anxiety didn't thrill me as much as it had before.

What I could not seem to get straight in my head was why I had presented my island to her in the fashion I had. My own words seemed to hang there in the cabin as the plane lowered toward the ground. Had I truly dismissed it—called it *not very big*? The private Mediterranean island that I had long used as my primary home? It was the one place on the planet I could be sure there would be no eyes on me unless I allowed it. Unless I expressly invited it.

Which I never did.

When I had stood in that house with Imogen's father and all the stuffed shirts he called his contemporaries, there had not been a single part of me that had felt in any way inferior. The very idea was laughable. But let Imogen gaze at me, her freckles uncovered and her curls unleashed because I had demanded she reveal herself to me, and I was undermining myself.

Until this moment, I hadn't known I had such a thing in me.

To say I loathed it was an understatement.

I let that betrayal of myself simmer in me as the plane touched down. I said nothing as we disembarked, allowing Imogen to take her time down the metal stairs, making noises of pleasure as she went.

Because, of course, the island I called La Angelita was—like everything in my collection—a stunning thing of almost incomprehensible, unspoiled beauty. In every direction was the sea, flirting here, beckoning there. The island was barely ten miles across, with the ruins of an old villa of some sort on one end, and high on the cliffs at the other, my own version of a manor house.

Except mine was built to bring the island inside instead of keeping the dour northern French weather out. I had insisted on wide-open spaces, graceful patios, arches beneath red-roof tiles so that everything was airy and expansive. Notably unlike the depressing blocks of flats I'd been forced to call home as a child.

I was proud of this place and the way I'd had it built to my exact specifications. I showed it to very, very few. My own family had never merited an invitation.

It was possible, I thought as I swung into the Range Rover that had been left for my use by my staff, that I was experiencing a most uncharacteristic attack of nerves myself.

Except Javier Dos Santos, Europe's most feared monster, did not have *nerves*. I did not suffer from any kind of performance anxiety. If I had, I would likely have remained in the neighborhoods of my youth, working a dead-end job if I was lucky. Except young men in those neighborhoods were very rarely *lucky*. They usually ended up dying as my own father had, victims of their own greed and circumstances, slinging poison until it killed them one way or another.

"What a lovely spot," my wholly unaware new wife said, beaming around in all the Mediterranean sunshine as if she hadn't the slightest idea what she was doing to me. I supposed it was possible she didn't, though that suggested she was far more innocent than she had told me she was. "How often do you make it here?"

"La Angelita is my primary residence."

"You mean it's your home."

That was what I called it, but only to myself. The word *home* had too many associations I shied away from. Too many *feelings* attached. "That is what I said."

Her smile only widened at that. It made me…restless.

By the time we drove up to the house itself, sprawled there at the highest point of the island to capture the sweeping views in all directions, I was certain that I had made a terrible mistake. I should have taken her to Barcelona as planned, where I could have been far more certain there was nothing of *me* to be found. I had properties in every major city across the globe, and even more than that in tucked-away, hard-to-reach places. There was a beach in Nicaragua that I had been meaning to visit for some time, for example, to bask in the lack of crowds. There was a mysterious rain forest in Uganda, a spectacular oasis in Dubai.

I should never have brought her *here*.

Especially when I pulled up to the front of the villa and my brand-new wife turned to me, her eyes shining, as if I had given her a gift.

"This is *wonderful*. I thought I would be marched off to some dreary place like my father's house. Somewhere in the pouring rain, very grave and serious and cold, where I would have the opportunity to contemplate the occasion of my marriage in daily sober reflection in the bitter chill. This already seems much better than that."

"Far be it from me to keep you from sober reflection of any kind."

She was still smiling. "I suspect I'll enjoy all kinds of reflection a great deal more in all this *sunshine*."

"I do not know how you are used to spending your days," I heard myself say as if I was auditioning for the role previously played by her own officious father. "But the first thing you must know about your new life, Imogen, is that I am not a man of leisure. My primary occupation is not finding ways to live like a parasite off the interest of family investments without ever having to lift a finger. I work for my living. I always have and, I promise you, I always will."

I expected her to be offended at that, but instead she gazed at me with a thoughtful expression on her face. "Does that mean I am expected to work, too?"

I scowled at her. "Certainly not."

"That's a pity. I have always wanted to."

"Let me guess." My voice was too harsh. She didn't deserve it. But I noticed that she also didn't seem to react to it, particularly. It was almost as if she was so used to being badly treated that she hardly noticed it at all, and I couldn't say I liked that, either. But I didn't stop. "It has long been your heart's dearest dream to find yourself working in a factory, is it? Backbreaking hours on a factory floor, canning, perhaps? Doing boring, repetitive work, where mindless perfection is required hour after hour after hour? Or let me guess, you would prefer something in a field somewhere? Hideous physical labor among the crops, perhaps. Or there is always the oldest of all professions."

"You are mocking me, of course," she said, in such a calm voice that something I hadn't felt in a decade shifted inside of me, then shot out oily tentacles. *Shame.* I'd last felt it when I'd burned all bridges with my father and used the fire to propel me out of his world, once and for all. "Though now that you mention the oldest profession, you should probably know that the most famous Fitzalan widow of the twelfth century was rumored to have been quite the mistress of her field. I'm sure it was terribly scandalous at the time. Now it's just a story my father likes to tell."

"Even if I wished to put you to work tomorrow, what could you do?" I asked her, still unable to stop myself, and still not sure why I was angry in the first place—and her matter-of-fact talk of ancient prostitutes in her family line only made it worse. "By your own admission you have been trained to be a quiet, genteel decoration, nothing more."

She said nothing for a moment, and I was too aware that we were still sitting in the drive as if frozen there. The sun danced over her, catching those freckles and the gold in her curls. My jaw ached, I was clenching my teeth so hard.

"I am more aware than you could ever be of my own limitations," Imogen told me quietly. With a dignity that felt like a slap. "I know that there is no possibility that I will ever find myself working in a factory. But perhaps I could contribute to the welfare of those who do. There are supposed to be advantages to this much wealth and privilege. Would it be the worst thing in the world if I tried to use them for good?"

I didn't know what I would do if I stayed where I was, caged up in that Range Rover. As if I had somehow shut myself in a box and couldn't find my way out. I slammed out of the vehicle, then stormed around the front of it, my gaze hard on Imogen's.

I opened her door and took her hand as she exited, because she might know her limitations, but I had studied mine. I had determined that of all the things that might trip me up or get in my way in the world I chose to inhabit, manners would not be one of them. I knew which fork to use. How to address whoever might be standing in front of me. How to tie my own damned tie. That was what I had done with the ill-gotten money I'd stolen from my father when I'd left his particular den of iniquity. I'd learned how to look like the man I wished to become.

Then I'd become him.

I was aware that in the places people like Imogen frequented, acts of chivalry were considered the very height of manners. The difference between me and those who practiced it—because the act was what mattered, and the more public the better—was that not one of them had any respect for this woman.

And I was terribly afraid I had more than was wise.

I led my wife into my house, aware of something primitive that beat in me, forcing me to examine it with every step. I had never been possessive like this before. I hardly knew what to make of it.

"I don't suppose you have a library?" she asked me as we crossed the first atrium, where the sun and breeze brought the sea inside. I could hear the hope in her voice.

Just as I could hear how hard she had worked to strip the sound of it from her words.

It pierced me. It was as if she had taken one of the ceremonial blades that hung as decoration on my walls and thrust it straight through me. I thought of those three stacks of books on the table in her father's library. Telling me things about her I wasn't sure I wanted to know.

I didn't understand why it felt like this. As if I could see her, straight through her, and yet was somehow showing her entirely too much of me.

I was not a man who needed to be known. I was more than happy to remain a mystery. I actively courted it, in fact. And at the same time I didn't want to think of Imogen in my house the way she'd been in her father's. Hiding in out-of-the-way places like that library, steering clear of her father's ego and cruelty. And I certainly didn't care for the comparison.

"Yes," I said stiffly. "There is a library. But most of the books in it are in Spanish."

If I expected that to dim her enthusiasm, I was sadly mistaken. If anything, she brightened. "I need to work on my Spanish. I'm not quite fluent yet."

And that was too much. I had an unsolicited vision of Imogen, with her red-gold curls and those sparkling eyes, crawling over me. Naked. And whispering sex words in Spanish. *Mi pequeño molino.*

I didn't think then. My hands did the thinking for me. Before I knew what was happening, they were pulling her to me.

"There is only one word you need to know in Spanish, Imogen." I bent my head. Her lips were a temptation almost beyond imagining. Ripe and sweet, and this time I already knew how good she would taste. "*Sí.* All you need to learn is *sí.* Yes, my husband. Yes, Javier. *Yes.*"

I could feel her tremble. But it wasn't fear. I could tell that from how pliant she was, there between my hands. But if I had been in any doubt, her copper eyes glowed.

I crushed her mouth to mine, as if in a fever.

I didn't care that we were in the wide-open foyer of my house. My staff was paid handsomely for their discretion. But that was the last thought I gave the matter.

I feasted on her. Her mouth was plump and ripe and *mine*, and I had married her, and the fact I was not yet inside her was like torture.

I could feel the pulse of it in my neck. My gut. And in my sex most of all.

I lifted her up, high against my chest, then pulled her thighs around me so she could lock her ankles in the small of my back. I didn't break the kiss, carrying her with me as I moved, my arms wrapped around her to keep her from falling even as she held on to my neck.

I found the first available surface, an incidental table against the nearest wall, and propped her on the edge of it. I kept her at an angle, moving my hands down to find their way beneath that skirt with an urgency I had no desire to temper.

And still I kissed her, deeper and more wild with every stroke. I could taste the addicting heat in her. I could taste every small cry she made in the back of her throat. I could smell the shampoo and soap she had used in the shower on my plane, and they struck me as impossible aphrodisiacs.

There was no time left. I felt mad with the need to claim her. Now.

It was like a drumbeat pounding in my head, and everywhere else besides.

I hooked my fingers on the scrap of lace I found beneath her dress, and tore it off. She made a noise of surprise against my mouth, but my fingers were in the soft heat between her legs, and I felt her turn molten.

I felt clumsy and something like desperate as I fumbled with my own trousers, shoving them out of the way, and letting the hardest part of me spring free at last.

I shifted, and picked her up again, notching the head of my sex against her heated furrow. I angled my head, taking the kiss deeper, thrilling in her uninhibited response to me and those greedy little noises she couldn't seem to stop making.

I didn't understand why this woman got to me the way she did. I didn't understand the things she had made me feel. But I told myself none of that mattered, because there was this.

I gripped her bottom, positioned her perfectly, and then slammed myself home.

And everything changed.

Imogen cried out. Her body, which had been pliant and soft, stiffened.

And I knew.

She was so tight around me it was something like a dream—and I knew.

I muttered a curse and clamped down on the vicious need stampeding through me, bringing myself under control.

"You are a virgin," I bit out, vaguely surprised that I was even able to speak.

Her eyes were slick with unshed tears. Those fine, ripe lips of hers looked vulnerable. Her hands had somehow ended up in fists against my chest.

But still, she tilted up her chin and met my gaze, her curls tumbling over her shoulder as she moved. Because this was Imogen.

"Of course I'm a virgin," she said, and though her voice was scratchy, there was no mistaking the challenge in it. "I was under the impression that was what you paid for."

CHAPTER EIGHT

Imogen

IT HURT.

Oh, how it hurt.

I had meant to tell him, despite my bravado back at my father's house. But I hadn't. And then he had kissed me, sweeping me into his arms, and everything had been so thrilling, so wild—

I felt betrayed that had turned to this. To pain, though the sharpness was fading. But there was still this impossible… *stretching*.

I could feel him inside me. And that part of him, it seemed, was as mighty and powerful as the rest of him.

"You told me you were not a virgin." Javier's voice was the darkest I had ever heard it. Strained, almost. Gritty and harsh, but that seemed the least of my worries. "You made certain to tell me you had given your innocence to another."

It struck me as more than a little ridiculous that we were having a regular conversation. Like this. Both of us half-naked and parts of us *connected* in that too real, still heavy and unsettling way. I thought that all things considered, I'd very much like to cry. Though I refused to dissolve in front of him. I refused to prove that I was every bit the too-sheltered convent girl he already thought I was.

"I didn't actually *say* I'd slept with someone else," I pointed out.

We were so *close*. I wanted to shove him away from me even as he continued to hold me in the air, wrapped around his big body. And at the same time I wanted to move even closer to him, though I didn't think that was even possible.

And I had no idea why I couldn't catch my breath. I told myself it was the way he continued to stretch me from the inside out. I didn't know if it was the picturing it that made my throat go dry, or the actual sensation.

Javier's expression was far too intent. His dark eyes glittered. "This seems as good a time as any to tell you that I cannot abide lies. Of any kind. Ever. You would do well to remember that, Imogen."

I wanted to tell him what he could do with his dire warnings, but he was inside me and I was...*wide-open* in ways I could hardly process.

"I wanted you to think I had slept with someone, yes," I corrected myself, and then hissed out a little breath when he moved, there below, where I felt exposed and too soft and split open and shivery.

He didn't move much. He pulled the littlest bit out, then slid in again, and I shifted in his firm grip, irritably, to accommodate him.

He still held me up and it was odd to think about that. That he could be so strong that he could continue to hold me like this, my legs wrapped around him and all of my weight propped on his hands.

And on that other part of him, I supposed.

When I flushed a bit at that, he moved again. Still, only that very little bit. He did it once, then again. And again.

"Why would you tell me something like that?" Javier did not sound angry, exactly. His voice was too rich. Too dark. It was as if his voice was lodged inside me, too. "It was never my intention to hurt you, Imogen. And now I have. I wonder, does this fit into the story you have in your head? The barbarian commoner who took you like an animal and hurt you on your own wedding night?"

My breath was doing funny things. And he hadn't stopped that odd little rocking of his. "I don't have any stories in my head."

"I told you how I feel about lies. They say I am a brute, do they not? A monster? Did you want to make sure there could be no debate about that? Do you plan to report back that I am actually far worse than you'd imagined?"

"I don't know what you... I would never... I didn't mean for this to happen."

But I didn't know if that was true. Had I meant it? After all, I hadn't told him any different and I was the only one who knew the truth. If there was someone to blame for my discomfort, I was very much afraid it was me. I might not have had much experience—or any, come to that—but I had only met him yesterday and he'd had his hands between my legs with dizzying speed.

I had known the moment he swept me into his arms today where he was headed, hadn't I? The destination might have been fuzzier in my mind. Gauzier, perhaps. But I'd known where we were going.

Maybe he's right, a terrible voice inside me whispered. *Maybe you* wanted *the pain.*

I couldn't tell if the wave of sensation that washed through me then was heat or shame, frustration or need, and I wasn't sure I cared. I moved against him instead, making my own kind of rocking. And something was different then. Something had eased a little, deep inside me, and so I shifted again.

And that time, the wild sensations that swirled around in me were somehow a part of that feeling that stretched me. A part of it and yet something else, too. Something infinitely hotter.

Something that seemed to reflect in Javier's eyes as well.

He gripped me harder. And then he began to move. Or more to the point, he moved *me*.

He lifted me up, then settled me back down on that insanely hard part of him, and waited. When I only sighed a little, then sneaked my hands back up around his neck again, his eyes gleamed.

"I do not wish to play into your stereotypes," he murmured, lifting me and settling me again. Then again. "There are any number of ways this marriage can and may yet be terrible, *mi esposa*, but it will not be because I am a monster in this way. I will not brutalize you in bed. That is the very last thing I would ever wish to do while inside you."

He lifted me up, and put me down again, and every time he did it there was…*more*. More heat. More sensation.

More greed, stampeding through me like some kind of sudden rain shower. I wanted to dance in the storm. I angled myself closer, heedless and needy and amazed, so I could rub the tips of my breasts against the hard wall of his chest.

I did it once, not sure why I wanted to do such a thing until the mad sensation of it made me shudder. I did it again, and he laughed.

Then he picked up his pace.

And I had meant to say more. I had meant to somehow explain the decision I had made. Why I hadn't told him that I was a virgin and why that didn't count as the kind of lie I shouldn't have cared if I told him or not.

But I couldn't concentrate on anything except that glorious heat inside of me. *Him*. The thickness, the length. The way he seemed to fit me perfectly, over and over and over.

I began to feel that same crisis. I began to pant and shake. And all the while he held me as if he could do it forever, thrusting into me over and over again as if I had no purpose on this earth but this. Him. *Us*.

And when I finally broke, it washed over me like another

kind of storm, intense and endless. I sobbed out his name, tipping my head forward to bury my face against his neck.

But Javier wasn't done. He shifted me back against the table, angling me so he could hold me against him with one strong arm and brace himself against the wall with his other hand.

And when he thrust into me then, I understood he had been holding back.

This was deeper. Harder.

So wild I wasn't entirely sure I would survive. So hot and glorious I wasn't sure I wanted to survive.

I had already exploded into too many pieces to count, but something about his ferocity lit that fire in me all over again, tossing me from one great crisis straight into the arms of another.

And this time, when it hit me, I screamed.

I felt him pulse within me as he let out a deep groan I only wished was my name, and then he dropped his head to mine.

I had no idea how long we stayed there like that. Panting. Connected.

And for my part, anyway, completely changed.

But eventually, Javier pushed himself away from me. He reached down to release himself from the clutch of my body, and I didn't understand how I could feel…empty. When I had never known what it was to feel *filled* before.

I watched him, half in embarrassment and half in fascination, as he tucked himself away into his trousers again. Then he tugged me off the table and onto the floor, my dress falling down to cover me as if he'd planned that, too.

He didn't say a word. He studied my face for a moment and I regretted the sunlight that poured in from all the open spaces in this house of his, no doubt showing him things I would have hidden if I only knew how. He slid his hand to the nape of my neck, set me in front of him, and propelled me through the sprawling, open house that way.

I should have objected. I should have told him I didn't require that he march me about as if his hand was a collar.

But I was too busy concentrating on putting one foot in front of the other when I felt as if I was made out of froth and need and might shiver to pieces again at any moment. I was surprised I could walk at all. I felt giddy. Silly.

And that didn't change when Javier brought me into a huge, sprawling set of rooms I understood at a glance were his. And likely also mine, though my brain shied away from that, as I had never shared a room—or a bed—with anyone in my life. I couldn't understand how it worked. I'd seen a thousand images of couples tangled around each other, of course, but I couldn't imagine how *I* would settle like that, with arms heavy over me, or my face pressed against someone's back, or…

It was possible I was panicking.

I forced myself to breathe as Javier led me over to a set of the floor-to-ceiling windows that made up the outside walls of this room. This house. Up close, I saw they were actually sliding doors. Javier nodded toward the series of sparkling blue pools outside, each reflecting the blue of the sky above and the sea beyond, and it seemed some kind of dream to me after such a cold, gray January at my father's house. After all the cold, gray Januaries I'd endured there.

It was a gift. It fell through me like the sunlight itself, warming me from the inside.

"The top one is the hottest," he told me, and there were things in his voice I didn't understand. Dark, tangled things. Intimate things. I shuddered. "Go sit in it and soak."

"I didn't bring a bathing costume," I heard myself whisper.

His hand tightened at the nape of my neck, just the slightest bit. Just enough to assure me he felt every shivery, shuddery thing that worked its way through me. "You will not require one, *querida*."

It didn't occur to me to disobey him. He pulled open the heavy sliding door and I walked through it of my own volition.

The breeze was warm, or I was warm, and I breathed it all in, deep. I went over to the side of the first, highest pool, and busied myself unzipping boots that seemed too clunky and severe for all this Mediterranean sunlight. He had done away with my panties, another thing I couldn't quite think about directly without blushing, so I pulled off my dress, unhooked my bra, and then went to the edge of the pool. I could see the steam rising off it in the air that could only be the slightest bit cooler. I didn't question it. I eased my way in, sighing a little as the heat enveloped me.

And only as I sat there did I understand the true beauty of these pools and the careful way they had been arranged. Because as I sat, I couldn't see the other pools I knew were there, laid out on different levels here on this cliff high above the water. I could only see the sea.

I thought I had never seen anything so beautiful in person, with my own eyes. There was the sun up above, the blue sea wherever I looked, and the sweet January air that I suspected might be considered cool to those who lived in this climate year-round. But it felt like some kind of prayer to me.

And when Javier slid into the water next to me, I was tempted to imagine that prayer had been answered. I didn't look at him. I was afraid to look at him, I understood, because he was so big and *male* and I could still feel where he'd been inside of me.

And looking at all his flesh, stretched out in such an unapologetically male fashion beside me, might...change me.

We sat in the hot water overlooking the endless stretch of blue for a forever or two. The water soaked deep into my bones, or so it felt. It made me feel as boneless as he did. Maybe it was the sun, washing over the both of us and making me feel all kinds of things I never had before.

Light. Airy. As if I was made of the sunlight and the deep blue water, infused with all that glorious warmth. As if I were connected to the bright pink flowers that crawled up the stone walls of the villa, or the almond tree blossoms, or even the sweet scent of jasmine that danced on the breeze.

"Your life has been lonely, has it not?" he asked after a long while. "Is that why you pretended you weren't a virgin? To confuse the issue?"

And I should have felt ashamed, I thought—but I was too boneless and warm, suspended in all that sunlight and blue.

"Lonely compared to what?" I turned to look at him, my breath catching. And that place between my legs pulsing with fascination. And hunger. "What of your life? You had no friends or family at your own wedding. Are you lonely?"

He eyed me as if I had grown fangs there before him. "I do not get lonely."

"Well, neither do I."

"You told me you miss your mother every day."

The air went out of me at that, but I managed to smile at him anyway. "Yes, but that is no more than another part of me. A phantom limb. I miss her, but it doesn't make me lonely. It reminds me that I loved her." And that she had loved me the way my father had never managed to, but I didn't say that. "I thought you lost your father, too."

"I did." There was an arrested look on his face then. "But I do not miss *him*, Imogen. If I miss anything, it is the father he never was."

I didn't know how long we merely gazed at each other then. I only knew that somehow, I felt more naked than I had before. When Javier moved again, rising from the pool, I wasn't sure if I felt a sense of loss or relief.

"Come," he said from behind me, and I felt as glutted on sunshine as I did shaky and exposed, but I obeyed him.

It was not until I climbed from the pool that I realized that I was showing myself to him. Fully naked, as I had felt in the water. I stopped at the top of the stairs and froze, though the alarm I surely ought to have felt seemed dulled, somehow, as if the sun had taken that, too.

Or that look in his dark gaze had.

Javier had wrapped a towel around his lean hips and something about the contrast between the bright white of the fabric and his olive skin made a different kind of heat tumble through me. And his dark gaze blazed as it moved over me. I felt the heat of it in the fullness of my breasts, the flare of my hips.

He did not speak as he came toward me, then wrapped me carefully, so carefully, in a towel of my own. His expression was grave, that gaze of his intent.

And he made me shudder. Simply by tucking me into the embrace of that towel, then smoothing a few curls back from my face, with a kind of quiet heat that spiraled through me like reverence. And then again when he ushered me over to a table, saw that I was seated with a courtesy that made me ache, and only then raised a finger to beckon his servants near.

I hadn't known I was hungry until the table was covered, piled high with all sorts of delicacies I knew must be local to the region. Cheeses and olives. Marvelous salads made of wild, bright-colored produce. An aromatic chicken, steeped in spices. Almonds and various dishes. I hardly knew where to look. What to taste first.

The food seemed like a part of the sun, the sea. Javier himself. As if there was not one part of this new world I found myself in that wasn't different from the one I had left behind, down to this meal before me with all its sweet, bright colors and savory combinations instead of my father's routine meals made to cater to his vanity in his trim physique, never to tempt him in any way.

Here, with Javier, everything was a temptation.

Especially Javier himself.

He sat across from me, the acres of his bare chest as lush and inviting as the food between us, all mad temptation and sensory overload.

And this man had bought me. Married me. He had taken me from my father's house, and then he had taken me in every other meaning of the term. He had brought me out of the rain, into the light. And now it seemed I found every part of him as sensual as his hands on my body or his hard, cruel mouth and the wicked things it could do against mine. Or that impossibly hard heat of him, surging deep inside me.

He leaned back in his chair, lounging across from me, and I discovered that watching him eat was almost too much for me to bear. Those big, strong hands that I now knew in an entirely different way. Even his teeth, that I had felt graze the tender flesh of my neck. I felt goose bumps dance up and down my arms, then down my spine, and all he did was tear off a crust of bread and dip it into a saucer of olive oil.

Javier was beautiful. Rugged and demanding. He was harsh and he was beautiful and I knew, now, what it was to have him deep inside me.

And I understood that I would never be the same. That I was changed forever, and even if I didn't know quite what that meant—even if I wasn't sure how it would all play out or what it meant to be married at all, much less to a man so different from my father or my sister's husband—I knew that there was no going back to the girl I'd been on that window seat a mere day before, staring out at the rain and dreaming of a safe, sweet stable boy I had barely met.

Here, now, sharing a table with a man like Javier in all the seductive sunlight, it was clear to me exactly how I'd been fooling myself.

There were girlish dreams, and then there was this. Him.

And even as I shivered inside, the shiver turning into a molten heat there where I was still soft and needy, I was glad I knew the difference.

"Let me know when you have eaten your fill," Javier said almost idly, though there was something about his voice then.

Stirring. Intense. As if he knew full well why I couldn't quite sit still.

"Why? Do you not have enough?"

A flash of his teeth. Another man's smile, though in Javier, all I could see was its menace. As if I had insulted him.

"Do I strike you as a man who goes without, Imogen?"

"I only meant... Well, it is an island."

Javier's mouth kicked up in the corner in that way it did, so rarely. His real smile, I knew. Not that other thing he deployed as a weapon.

And this was wired to that molten heat in me, because all I could feel was the fire of it.

"I want to make sure you have your strength, *querida*," he murmured, which did not help the fire at all. If anything, it made it worse. Because I could see the same bright flame in his gaze. "As we have only just begun."

CHAPTER NINE

Imogen

"TODAY WE FLY to Italy," Javier announced one morning weeks later, without warning. "You may wish to prepare yourself for a touching reunion with your family."

He sat, as he always did, at that table out on the terrace overlooking the pools and the endlessly inviting ocean where he preferred to take his breakfast each day. The morning was bright and clear, and yet as I sat there across from him I felt as if I'd been tossed back into the shadows, cold and gray, I thought I'd left behind in France. I must have made some kind of noise, because Javier set aside one of the many international newspapers he scanned each morning and raised his dark brows at me.

"We will be attending a charity ball in Venice. It is an annual opportunity to fake empathy for the less fortunate, something at which your father excels." He studied me for a moment. "Do you have an objection to charity, Imogen? I seem to recall you mentioning you wished to make it the cornerstone of your existence."

I realized I was gaping at him and forced my mouth shut. It was ridiculous that I was reacting like this. There was no reason at all to feel that he had…broken something, somehow, by announcing that we had to leave this place. Particularly for the sort of event that I knew would thrust us both back into the world I had done such a great job of pretending no longer existed these past weeks.

A world that included my father.

I didn't want to leave. I wanted to stay like this forever. The days had rolled by, sunlight and deep blue, the sea air and the soft, sweet breeze.

It was the first holiday I had ever been on in my life.

And yes, of course, I knew it wasn't truly a holiday. Javier worked each and every day. I would have worked myself, had there been something for me to do, but every time I asked he shook his head and then told me to amuse myself as I pleased. So I swam in the pools. I braved the sea on the afternoons when the temperature edged toward hot. I took long, rambling walks down to the ruins on the far end of the island and back, basking in the sunshine and solitude that felt a great deal like freedom.

And anytime he wasn't working, Javier was with me.

Inside me.

All over me, and me all over him, until I could no longer tell the difference between this day or the next. Between his hand and mine, clenched together on the coverlet as he surged inside of me.

I learned how to kneel down and give him pleasure with my mouth. I learned how to accept his mouth between my legs in return. I learned how to explore every inch of his fascinating body with my hands, my mouth, my teeth. We ate the food that always seemed to be taken directly from the heart of all the brightness and calculated to be as pretty as the sun-drenched island around us, and then we rolled around more.

He called me adventurous. He called me *querida*.

I called him my husband, marveled that I had ever thought him a monster, and every day I wondered how any person could be expected to hold so much sensation inside. I could scarcely imagine how my one, single body could contain all these things I felt. All these joys I dared not name.

I didn't want to leave.

I didn't want to return to that cold, cruel world I had left behind without so much as a backward glance, or anything that reminded me of it. I didn't want to start what I knew would be the endless circuit of balls and events that comprised the bulk of the high-society calendar. I had been raised to make that calendar the center of my life. From events like the Met Ball in New York that made the papers to the aristocratic private house parties all over Europe that were only murmured about later, behind the right hands. I had allowed myself to forget that part of my value was appearing at these things, dressed to communicate my husband's wealth and might.

If it were up to me, these weeks on La Angelita would have been a permanent relocation. I wanted us to stay here forever, wrapped up in each other, as if everything else was the dream.

But somehow, I knew better than to say it.

Because this is not his *dream*, a foreboding sort of voice whispered in me, like a blast of cold air down my spine.

"I have always wanted to see Venice," I managed to say.

I even forced myself to smile. To meet that considering gaze of his.

"You are not so convincing."

"I am drunk on the sea air and all this sun." *And you*, I thought, but knew better than to say. Because in all these halcyon days of sex and sun and nights that never seemed to end, there had been no talk of emotion. No whisper of the things I had been raised to consider the province of other, lesser people. "I will have to sober up, that is all."

"I have business that requires my sobriety. You will have nothing to do but party, which certainly doesn't demand any teetotaling should you oppose it. Though I suppose the party itself is your business."

I felt some of the magical glow that had been growing in me

by the day stutter a bit, and I resented it. I rubbed the stuttering spot between my breasts and resented that, too.

"If parties are my business, I'm afraid you're going to be deeply disappointed. There were not many parties in the convent."

"Which is why you were sent to that finishing school to top off your chastity with dreary lessons in how to bow, and when, and to whom. You know this very well." Javier set his newspaper aside entirely then, and regarded me for a moment that dragged on so long I almost forgot there had ever been anything but the stern set to his hard mouth and the way his gaze tore into me. "If there is something you would like to tell me, Imogen, I suggest you do so. I have no patience for this passive-aggressive talking around the issue you seem to enjoy."

"There is no issue. I have nothing to tell you."

"Did you think that you would stay on this island forever? Locked away like a princess in a fairy tale? I know I have a fearsome reputation, but I do not believe I have ever tossed a woman in a tower, no matter the provocation." That curve of his mouth caused its usual answering fire in me, but today it felt like a punishment. "I do not believe I have to resort to such things to get what I want. Do you?"

He did not have to resort to anything to get what he wanted from me. I gave it to him with total, obedient surrender. And happily.

And it hadn't occurred to me until now that he wasn't as swept away as I was. That this was all…his design.

I had to swallow hard against the lump in my throat then.

"This is no fairy tale." It cost me to keep my voice light. "For one thing, Fitzalans are not princesses. We have long been adjacent to royal blood, but very rarely of it. Royals are forever being exiled, revolted against, decapitated. Fitzalans endure."

I felt as if I'd been slapped awake when I hadn't realized I'd fallen asleep. When I'd no idea how deeply or long I'd been dreaming. It had been weeks since I'd spared a thought for my father and all the ways I was likely to disappoint him. Or since I'd worried about Celeste and the way my favorite—and only—sister had looked at me on my wedding day. Or how she'd looked at Javier as we'd left the manor house.

I didn't welcome the return of these preoccupations.

Or, for that matter, the fact that it had been weeks since I had given a single thought to the state of my hair and its defiance of all accepted fashion dictates. I clipped it up or I let it curl freely, and that was all the attention I gave the curls that had so dominated my previous life. I hadn't thought about how badly I played the part of a graceful, effortless Fitzalan heiress. I hadn't thought about how different things would be now that all the snide society wives could address me directly instead of merely whispering behind their hands as I walked behind my father in my slovenly way, with the dresses that never quite fell right and the hair that never obeyed. I hadn't thought at all about the many ways I stood in my more accomplished, more beautiful sister's shadow, not for weeks, and now it was likely I would have to do it all over again.

And this time, where Javier could watch and judge the two of us side by side.

I didn't like thinking about it. My stomach rolled at the very notion. I glared down at my coffee and told myself there was nothing wrong with my blurry eyes. Nothing at all.

"We will be attending one of the most famous charity balls of the season," Javier said, his voice darker than it had been before. Darker and somehow more intense. "I was asked to donate a staggering amount of money, and my reward for this act of charity is that I am forced to attend the ball. We will all put on masks and pretend we do not recognize each other when, of course, we do. It is all very tedious. But this time, I will at least be spared the endless advances of the unmarried. And the unhappily married."

I shifted in my chair, still blinking furiously at my coffee.

I had gotten too much sun on my nose, causing even more

freckles. I knew my shoulders were in no better state. The sun had brought out more gold and red in my hair, and more curls besides. I tried to imagine myself swanning about a Venetian ballroom, surrounded by women like Celeste. Elegant, graceful women. Silky smooth, sleek women who never worried about dripping their banquet dinners down the front of their gowns, or tripping over the hems of their dresses as they strode about in their impossibly high heels.

I had been to the convent, yes. And I had spent those years in what was euphemistically called finishing school, too. My friends and I regaled ourselves with memories of the absurdities we'd suffered there almost daily in the group chats that kept us connected, shut off as we were in our very different lives. But all the schooling in the world couldn't make me over into Celeste, no matter how many hours I'd spent walking around with a heavy book on my head to improve my posture.

"You are the very definition of a silk purse made from a sow's ear," my father had snarled at my debutante ball. Right after I'd tripped and nearly upended the punch bowl and the table it had been set upon.

That had been the first and last time I had been let loose in aristocratic society, aside from my wedding.

And now this. Where I would bring shame not only upon my father, which I did so often it hardly signified, but on Javier.

This man who knew how to make me sob with joy and need. Who broke me wide-open with more pleasure than the human body should have been able to bear, and yet he did it again and again, and I not only bore it—I craved it. The man who did not want to hear the words that bubbled up in me, so I moaned them out instead in a meaningless, wordless tune.

The very thought of humiliating him the way I knew I was more than likely to do made me want to curl up into a ball. And sob for a few hours.

"Or perhaps you are only comfortable with this marriage when it is conducted in private," Javier said, snapping my attention back to him. "Out of sight. Off on an island no one can access but me. Hidden away where no one can see how far you have fallen."

I blinked at that. Because he sounded almost...hurt. "I don't... I don't want..."

But something had gone horribly wrong. Javier pushed back from the table, rising to his feet and tossing his linen serviette onto the tabletop. He glared down at me in much the same way he had once stared up at me in my father's house. With commanding, relentless fury that should have burned me alive.

And I felt exactly the same as I had then.

Frozen. Paralyzed. Intrigued despite myself.

And in no way immune from that fire.

"You are happy enough to glut yourself on my body," he growled down at me, an expression I didn't recognize on his harsh face. Again, I was tempted to believe that I'd hurt him. *Him.* "You are insatiable. No matter how much I give you, you want more. When you call out for God, I believe you think I am him. But that does not mean you wish to show the world how much you enjoy your slumming, does it?"

He could not have stunned me more if he had overturned the table into the nearest pool and sent me tumbling after it. I felt myself pale, then flush hot, as if with fever. "That's not what I meant at all. I'm not the one who will be embarrassed, Javier. But I'm almost positive you will be."

His mouth was a flat, thin line, but in his gaze I swore I could see pain. "Yes. I will be humiliated, I am sure, when the world sees that I truly married the woman I intended to. That I procured the last Fitzalan heiress. You will have to try harder, *mi reina*, if you want me to believe the stories you tell to hide your true feelings."

I found myself on my feet across from him, my heart kicking at me. I felt panicked. Something like seasick that everything had twisted around so quickly. That I had possibly wounded him, somehow. "I'm not telling you a story."

He said something in guttural Spanish that I was perfectly happy not to understand. Not completely.

"You must have heard what they call me," I continued, holding myself still so he wouldn't see all the shaking I could feel inside of me. "The disappointing Fitzalan sister. The unfortunate one. It was never a joke."

"Enough." He slashed his hand through the air, still staring at me as if I had betrayed him. "We leave in an hour. I have a phone call to make. I suggest you use the time learning how to control your face and the truths it tells whether you are aware of it or not."

He left me then. He stormed off into the villa, and I knew there'd be no point following him. When he disappeared into the wing he kept aside as his office, he did not emerge for hours, and he did not take kindly to interruptions. I had learned these things the hard way.

But today, everything felt hard. I stood where I was for a long time after he'd gone.

That does not mean you wish to show the world how much you enjoy your slumming, does it? he had demanded.

Slumming was the sort of word my father used. It felt like poison in me, leaving trails of shame and something far sharper everywhere it touched. And it touched every part of me. And, worse, corroded the sweet, hot memories of our high blue, sun-filled weeks here.

My eyes blurred all over again.

It had never crossed my mind that Javier even noticed what people like my father thought of him, much less how they might act when he was around. He hadn't seemed the least bit interested in the guests at our wedding, or the things they might have said about him. He hadn't even bothered to stay for the whole of the wedding breakfast, dismissing them all as insignificant, I'd thought.

Yet he'd thrown out that word, *slumming*, as if he was far less impervious to these slights than I imagined.

I moved out of the sun, as if that could somehow retroactively remove my freckles, and stood there in the cool shadows of our bedroom. I tried to calm my breathing. That wild beating of my heart. But I was staring at that vast bed and I was…lost.

Javier had been intense these past weeks. More than intense. He was demanding, in bed and out. Focused and ferocious, and it sent a delicious chill down my spine and deep into the softest part of me just thinking about it. He turned me inside out with such regularity that I hardly knew which was which any longer. I'd stopped trying to tell the difference.

And now we had to leave here. I had to parade all these things I felt in front of the whole of the world and, worse by far, my own family.

I squeezed my eyes shut, but that didn't help, because then all there was to do was *feel*. And sometimes I told myself that Javier must feel the things that I did. Sometimes I dreamed that he felt as torn apart, then made new, every time we touched.

I wrenched my eyes open again. In the harsh light of day, when I was out on another walk or tucked up beside the pools with one of the Spanish books I was steadily making my way through, I knew better. I had been the virgin, not him. He was a man of vast experience—as I had seen for myself when I searched for him online.

Javier could have anything he wanted. Anyone he wanted. *The only thing he ever wanted from you*, a nasty little voice inside me whispered, *was your surname*.

Because all the rest of this, I was forced to admit to myself as I stood there—staring blindly at the master bed where I had learned more things about myself than in all my years at the convent—Javier had already had a thousand times over. With women the whole world agreed were stunning beyond measure.

And one of them had been Celeste.

My knees felt wobbly, or maybe it was that my stomach had twisted so hard it threw me off balance, but I found myself sinking down onto the bench at the end of the bed.

Sometimes I told myself sweet little fantasies that Javier might feel as I did, or might someday, but if I was honest, I'd known that was unlikely. I'd pretended I didn't know it, but I did. Of course I did.

Because the only time I had seen any hint of feelings in him was just now.

Now, when we were finally stepping out into public together. Now, when he would have to parade the lesser Fitzalan sister before the world. Maybe it wasn't surprising that our first outing would be to a costume ball. I'd read entirely too many books that used masks and costumes to terrible advantage. Why should this be any different?

Because this was an arranged marriage, plain and simple.

I had spent these weeks in some kind of a delirium. A daydream. Sex and sun and the gleaming Mediterranean—who wouldn't be susceptible?

But Javier had not been in any such haze. Javier had known exactly what he was doing.

He had married me for my name. My fortune, and not because he needed money, but because he was now a part of the Fitzalan legacy.

He had married a pawn, but I had made the cardinal sin of imagining myself a wife in truth. Somehow, in all these weeks, my actual situation had not been clear to me. This was an arranged marriage, and the arrangement was not in my favor.

Javier had not promised me love. He had not promised me honor. And crucially, I realized as I sat there, feeling like the child I had never thought I was until today, he had never promised me fidelity, either.

If Javier noticed my silence—or any of those feelings I was afraid I wasn't any good at hiding, though I tried my best—he gave no sign.

He spent the flight to Venice on his mobile and seemed as uninterested in the fairy-tale city that appeared below us as we landed as he was in me. I pressed my face to the window, not caring at all if that made me look gauche. Or foolish. Or whatever word I knew my father would have used, if he had been there to see my enduring gracelessness.

But I didn't want to think about my father. Or any of the things that waited for me tonight. All the ways my foolish heart could break—I thrust them all aside.

We were delivered to a waiting boat and that was when my treacherous heart flipped over itself, as if this was a romantic journey. As if any of this was romantic.

I knew it wasn't. But Venice was.

The haughty, weathered palazzos arranged at the edge of the Grand Canal. The piers with their high sticks and the curved blue boats. The impossible light that danced on the dome of Santa Maria della Salute. Gondoliers on the waterways and pedestrians on the arched bridges.

Venice was like poetry. Arranged all around me, lyrical and giddy at once.

The private water taxi delivered us to a private island in the great lagoon.

"Another private island?" I asked, then wished I hadn't when all I received in return was that darkly arched brow of his and that dark gaze that still looked pained to me.

"I prefer my privacy," Javier replied. Eventually. "Though this is not mine. It is a hotel."

I blinked at the pink stone building that rose before me and the rounded church facade that gleamed ivory beside it. There were gold letters on the stones, spelling out the name of some or other saint. "Why are there no other people?"

Javier angled an arrogant sort of look down at me.

And I understood then. He had bought the place out. Because of course he had.

He was Javier Dos Santos. How had I managed to forget all that meant?

I felt flushed straight through as we walked across the empty courtyard, following the beaming staff up from the water and into the hotel itself. This was not like his villa, so open and modern at once. I was struck by the age of the rooms, and yet how graceful they remained, as if to encourage guests to revel in all their mystery and grandeur. And yet it was far more welcoming than my father's residences, all of which had always erred on the side of too many antiques. Cluttered together, simply because they were pieces of history that broadcast his taste in acquisitions.

Our footsteps were loud on the floors. The staff led us to a sprawling suite that encompassed the whole of the top floor, and I told myself it shouldn't feel like punishment when Javier disappeared into the designated office space. Especially since he didn't glance back.

But I summoned a smile from somewhere, because I wasn't alone.

"You have some time before you need to begin getting ready for your evening, signora," my attendant told me in deferential Italian. "Perhaps you would like some light refreshment?"

My smile hurt. "That would be lovely."

I watched as she left, wondering what I looked like to her, this woman who attended the fabulously wealthy and astronomically celebrated occupants of this suite. She must have seen a thousand marriages like mine. Did it begin here, I wondered? Was she rushing down to the kitchens to snigger about the freckled, mop-headed wife who had somehow found herself with a man like Javier Dos Santos in a hotel he'd emptied of all other guests because he preferred the quiet?

But I was making myself crazy. I knew it.

I moved across the grand salon where my attendant had left me, then out through the shutters to the balcony that ran down the length of our suite. And though the air was bracing, especially after all those weeks on the island, I made my way to the edge and leaned against the railing to watch the winter sun turn the sky a pale pink.

If Venice had been pretty in the light, it was magical at dusk. I breathed in, then let it out, and I thought I felt a kind of easing deep inside.

The city was otherworldly before me, spread out as it must have been at the feet of all the women who had stood on this balcony before me. So many lives, begun and ended right here. All those tears, all that laughter. Panic and fear. Joy and delight. Down through the ages, life after life just as it would continue on after me, and somewhere in the middle of all of it was me.

What was the point of working myself up into a state?

My problem was I kept imagining that I could make my marriage what I wanted it to be when that had never been in the cards, and I should have known that. I did know that.

The day before my wedding I had dreamed of the sweet blue eyes of a stable boy because that was some kind of escape. The day after my wedding I had been punch-drunk on the things my new husband could do to me, the things he could make my body feel, and I had lost myself in that for far too long.

The truth of the matter was that I was a Fitzalan. And no matter if I was the lesser one, I was still a Fitzalan. The women in my family had been bartered and ransomed, kidnapped and sold and held captive across the centuries.

And if my fierce old grandmother had been any indication, not a one of them had dissolved in the face of those challenges. On the contrary, Fitzalan women made the best of their situations. No matter what.

Fitzalans have a higher purpose, Grand-Mère had always said.

There wasn't much I could do about my curls or my clumsiness, but I could certainly work on my attitude. It was perhaps the only thing that was truly mine. Javier had called the party I was headed to tonight my business, and I had been silly to dismiss that.

He wasn't wrong. I had spent years in finishing school learning all the ways an aristocratic wife could use her role as an accessory to her husband to both of their advantage.

"Your greatest weapon is the fact no one expects you are anything but window dressing," Madame had always told us. "Use it wisely, ladies."

And that was why, when I was dressed in my mask and gown and was led out into the main hall to meet Javier that evening, I was ready.

I'd had them pull my hair back into another chignon, though this one did not pretend to be smooth. My curls were obvious, but I thought if they were piled on top of my head it would look more like a choice and less like the accident of birth they were. My inky-black gown had been made to Javier's exacting specifications, my attendants had assured me, clasped high on one shoulder and cascading down on an angle to caress my feet. The mask itself was gold and onyx, and I couldn't deny the little thrill it gave me to see it on my face when I looked in the mirror.

Better by far, however, was Javier's stillness when he saw me, then the gruff nod he gave me.

It told me the same thing I'd told myself while I'd stood outside in the cold and gazed at the fairy tale of Venice laid out before me in the setting sun. Javier might feel nothing for me at all. I needed to accept that. But he wanted me with at least some of the same desperation I felt in me.

It was more than I'd been raised to expect from my marriage. I told myself it would be more than enough.

Because it had to be enough.

"I am ready," I told him. When he held out his arm, I slid my hand through it. And I angled my head so I could look up at him. Then wondered if my breath would always catch like this at the sight of him, even more overwhelming than usual tonight in his dark black coat and tails. "This will be our first society event as a married couple. You must have imagined how it would go."

I could see his dark eyes behind his mask. And that mouth of his, hard and tempting, that I would know anywhere.

"I have."

"Then you must tell me exactly how you see it all in your head, so that I can be certain to do my part."

His gaze was a harsh, glittering thing. He was dressed all in black, including his mask, and yet the way he looked at me made me think I could see all the bright colors of the Mediterranean. "Your part? What is your part, do you imagine?"

"My part is whatever you prefer, of course. You can use me as a kind of weapon to aim however you like. You have no idea how indiscreet men like my father are around people they think are too far below them to matter."

His hard mouth curved slightly, though I did not mistake it for a smile. "I know exactly how they treat people like me, Imogen. And I do not need weapons to handle them. I am the weapon."

"Then it seems we have an arsenal."

When he only watched me in that same stirring and vaguely threatening way, I lifted my chin as if I was preparing myself for a fight. With him.

Even though I knew we were both aware I would never, ever win.

"And if I say all I want from you is decoration?" His voice was silk and menace. It wound around me like the ties he'd used to secure me to that bed of his, one memorable night. "Silence and submission and a pretty smile on your face? What then?"

"You bought me, Javier," I reminded him, and it wasn't until I heard the edge in my own voice that I understood there were all manner of weapons. And that I didn't need his permission to wield them. "I can be whatever you want me to be. I thought that was the point."

CHAPTER TEN

Javier

IF SHE MENTIONED the fact that I'd bought her one more time, it might send me over the edge—and I chose not to question why that was when it was true. I had. And would again. There was no reason at all to resent the way she threw it at me like some kind of challenge.

I didn't like the fact that I was so close to the edge as it was, and we hadn't even made it to the ball yet.

And it didn't help that Imogen looked good enough to eat.

Her hair was more gold than red after our time on La Angelita, even tucked back into a complicated, curling mystery she'd secured to the back of her head with some or other gleaming thing my fingers itched to remove.

She looked like every dream I'd ever had about the wife I would one day win. Or, yes, buy. She was elegant, masked in a way that showed off the aristocratic bones of her face and draped in the finest black that clung to her generous figure in ways that made me ache. She looked gracious beyond measure and far, far out of the league of a drug dealer's son who'd been raised in a gutter. She was as beautiful as she was unreachable, as befit a woman with blood so achingly blue.

Imogen was exactly the wife I wanted on my arm at this or any other society event. She would exude all that Fitzalan superiority without even trying and my dominance would continue unabated and unchallenged from all these men who fancied themselves better than the likes of me.

And she was standing here in front of me talking about what I'd paid for her, as if this union of ours was nothing but the oldest profession in action on a grand scale.

I told myself I was outraged at the insult. When wealthy men hired prostitutes, they were called escorts. And when they bought wives, it was not called a purchase, it was deemed a wise marriage. To think about my choices in any other way suggested I was still in the gutter, despite all my accomplishments.

I assured myself I was furious, but that hardly explained the heaviness in my sex.

The same heaviness that had become my obsession.

The very last thing I wanted to do was take her out of this hotel I'd emptied for my own privacy when it would have been far more entertaining to experiment with that privacy. I wanted to undress her, right here in the cavernous lobby. I wanted to worship every silken inch of her fine, soft body in the filthiest way imaginable. Starting with my mouth.

But there was work to be done. There was always work to be done. Charity balls were only merry social occasions when a man's donations were relatively minor. For me, they were necessary appearances that had to look social and offhanded when they were anything but.

That beguiling, demanding need for her scraped at me with a raw force that was nothing short of alarming, because Imogen was the first woman I'd ever met that I couldn't get enough of—but I ignored it. I had no choice but to ignore it tonight. I kept her arm linked in mine and I led her down to the boat that would take us to the ball, and if my jaw ached from clenching it, that was at least a different sort of ache from the one currently driving me mad.

"I knew it would be beautiful here," she said softly, standing at the rail as the boat cut through the waves, though the night air was cool and whipped at her curls. "But I had no idea it would be *this* beautiful. I had no idea it was possible for anything to be this beautiful."

I moved to stand next to her at the rail, my gaze on the water of the lagoon. And then the canals of Venice before us, inky and dark. Very nearly brooding, this time of year. "I keep forgetting how sheltered your life has been."

"I have been nowhere," she said simply, and I thought it was the lack of bitterness in those words that cut me the most. "I have seen nothing outside the walls of the convent or that dreary finishing school. Not in person, anyway. And it turns out that you can watch a thousand things on the internet, read as many books as you can get your hands on, and they still won't prepare you for reality."

That word bit at me. *Reality.* Because I knew that on some level, no matter her protestations, she had to be embarrassed that she'd been forced to lower herself to marry a man like me. Of course I knew it. It was one of the defining truths of my life, and it didn't matter that she hadn't said such a thing to me in so many words. I knew it all the same. And I had never felt inferior in her father's house, but it was amazing how easily I slipped into that space when it was only Imogen. When she was the one who looked at me and made me feel that odd sensation I had never felt before—that slippery, uncomfortable notion that I would never get as far away from my wretched origins as I wanted.

It rose between us like a ghost.

And it was a feeling I should have been used to. I was. Still, when it came from Imogen, it made me ache in a new way. I couldn't say I liked it.

Even so, I couldn't keep myself from reaching over to one of the curls that had already escaped. I tucked it behind her ear with a gentleness I knew made me a stranger to myself.

"You mean Venice, of course," I murmured, that stranger firmly in charge of me now. Was I...*teasing* her? Was I a man who...*teased*? I never had been before. "Or the legendary Mediterranean Sea, perhaps. Not the great many more prurient things a person could read about or watch online, if they wished."

Her gaze met mine, filled with a laughter that I shouldn't have liked so much. I couldn't figure out why I *cared* so much about this woman who came apart in my hands so easily and yet imagined she could fashion herself into some kind of weapon, mine to command.

I didn't want any part of that. The very notion made me have to fight to hold back a shudder.

I told myself it was rage.

Though I knew full well it was connected instead to a hollow place in me that recalled an eight-year-old boy who had understood he would never be as important to those who should have loved and protected him as that poison they took to deliver them into oblivion.

But I refused to think about my parents. Not here. Not now.

There was still so much of the innocent about Imogen as she gazed at me, despite all I had done to claim her for my own. "Of course I mean Venice. What else could I mean?"

"Tell me more about what, precisely, you watched from the confines of the convent. All to better aid your education."

"Documentaries, mostly." Imogen smiled. And it was worrying, I thought in some distant part of me, how much I liked to see her smile. As if I craved it. As if I was a man who had ever allowed myself to crave anything when I knew full well it was the kind of weakness people like my parents lived to exploit. "About Venice, naturally, in all its splendor. And the Mediterranean Sea, too, now that you mention it."

"They will make a documentary about anything these days," I murmured.

I traced the edge of her mask, the place where the gold and

onyx met the soft skin of her cheek. I meant to say something. I was sure I had planned it, even.

But there was something about the water. The echoes and the ancient buildings around us and the particular, peculiar magic of this submerged city, and I couldn't find the words. Or I could, but I didn't want to say them.

I didn't want to name the things that moved in me when I looked at her. Every time I looked at her.

And then we were landing at the palazzo where the ball took place, all gleaming lights and noise spilling out into the winter night, and the moment was lost.

I told myself it wasn't disappointment that crashed over me as I led Imogen toward the entrance of the charity ball and handed off our winter coats. It couldn't be anything like disappointment as I waited for us to be announced, then drew her into the thick of the crowd, because that suggested a depth of emotion I didn't feel.

Because I did not *feel*. I refused.

I had spent all these weeks on the island making certain of this. I had forced myself away from Imogen when I wanted to stay. I had remained in my office for hours though I was distracted and, worse, uninterested.

I kept pretending I could think about something other than getting back inside Imogen, and I kept proving myself wrong.

Tonight appeared to be no exception.

Once inside, I could see the business associates I had come here to meet. Masks did nothing to hide the power that certain men seemed to exude from their very pores no matter what they did to conceal their features. The ball was taking place on the ground-floor ballroom of the ancient palazzo, with mighty old pillars and chandeliers three flights up ablaze with light. There was an orchestra on a raised dais at one end, and enough gold everywhere to make the whole world gleam.

But I wasn't ready. I couldn't quite bring myself to let Imogen loose into this particular pack of wolves. And not because

I feared them, but because I was the most fearsome wolf of all and I wasn't nearly done with her. I wished that the weeks we'd spent on my island, happily isolated and removed from all this, had been twice as long.

That felt like another betrayal of the person I had always imagined myself to be, and I wasn't sure I could speak. I was as close to terrified as I'd ever been at what might come out of my mouth if I tried.

Instead, I swept my lovely wife out onto the dance floor. I held her in my arms, gazed down at those perfect lips of hers that I could taste anytime I wished, and told myself my head swam because there were too many people here. It was hot. Noisy.

But she tipped back her head and smiled at me.

And I understood that it wasn't simply that I didn't recognize myself around this woman.

She had made me a liar. A liar with far too many feelings.

Worse, I did nothing with this realization but accept it. And dance.

"I never thought…" Imogen's voice was breathy. Her eyes gleamed brighter than the blaze of lights all around us. "You are a marvelous dancer."

"You sound slightly *too* surprised."

"It's only that I would never have dared imagine you dancing. You're too…"

I felt my brow rise. "Beneath you?"

"Elemental, I was going to say."

What was it about this woman? Why did she turn me into this…sniveling creature who advertised his own weaknesses at the slightest provocation?

"I taught myself," I said. Stiffly, but I said it.

It had been part of those early years, when I'd decided to make a guttersnipe a gentleman. And there was a part of me that expected her to laugh at the notion of a monster practicing a waltz. I might have joined in. But she didn't laugh.

"I took comportment and ballroom dancing lessons. First with the governesses at home, then in the convent. And it was not until I was in finishing school that Madame told us that proper dancing was merely another form of battle."

I studied her face as it was tipped up to mine.

"Battle? I was unaware that finishing school was so... aggressive."

"We find our weapons where we can, Javier."

Her soft voice echoed in my ears long after the song ended, and I was forced to take a step back. To allow her to loop her arm through mine again. To do what I knew I must, rather than what I wanted.

And it occurred to me, with an unpleasant sort of jolt, that I couldn't recall too many instances of doing what I wanted. Rather than what I must.

I had more money than I could ever spend. It would take commitment and effort to rid myself of my wealth. It would take years. Decades.

And yet I still behaved as if I was that kid in the sewers of Madrid. I still expected that at any moment, the authorities might step in and take it all away from me. Denounce me for my father's sins and throw me back where I came from.

I knew better than anyone that we were all of us nothing but self-fulfilling prophecies. And still I allowed those same old obsessions to own me. To shape me. To determine my every move.

I felt far closer to uncertain than I was comfortable with as we drew close to a group containing a man I couldn't help but recognize. He, too, was masked—but his mask was the sort that only drew attention to him, rather than making any attempt at concealing him from view.

"Hello, Father," Imogen said from beside me.

I don't know what I expected. I had seen and loathed those marks this man had left on my wife's skin. I had watched what passed for Fitzalan father/daughter interactions before. Most notably at our wedding, when for all the paternal emotion on display Dermot could have been handing me a large block of granite.

That stoniness was in evidence again tonight.

"It is such a pity that you could not take a little more care with your appearance on a night like this," the old man said, his voice bitter. Cruel. It took me a moment to realize he was speaking to Imogen. "It is your first introduction to society as part of a married couple. Surely you could have done something with your hair."

Imogen only smiled. "I did do something with my hair."

Fitzalan gazed at her with distaste. Then shifted his cold glare to me, as if he expected an apology. Certainly not as if he was giving me one. "I am afraid that no amount of correction has ever worked with this level of defiance. If I were you, I might consider a firmer hand."

Beside me, I felt Imogen stiffen, even though her expression did not change at all. It put me in mind of the sort of weapons she had mentioned. But more than that, Fitzalan dared to speak to me of a *firmer hand*?

I wanted to rip Dermot Fitzalan asunder, here where all the circling wolves could watch. And tear into him themselves when I left him in pieces.

But that was not how men like this fought. Well did I know it. I made a mental note to hit Fitzalan back hard, where he lived.

In his wallet.

And in the meantime, I would force myself to stand here and speak to him as if he did not deserve a taste of his own medicine. My fingers itched to leave their own dark marks on his skin to see how he liked it.

Somehow, though Fitzalan did not deserve it, I kept the true monster in me at bay.

"You are not me," I said coolly to this father who cared so little for his own daughter that he would send her to a marital bed with marks from his own hand. This pompous man who likely had done it on purpose, because it was the next best thing to actually branding Imogen as if she was truly property. "I believe this simple truth fills us both with gratitude, does it not?"

But I didn't hear his response. Imogen excused herself with that same serene smile and her head held high. And instead of attending to the conversation with this man I had cultivated for a decade or more and now had every intention of ruining—instead of taking pleasure in deceiving him or decimating him in turn, one or the other, as long as I came out the winner—I watched her go.

I couldn't seem to stop myself. I couldn't seem to force myself to pay attention to Fitzalan or the men standing with him. I was aware they were talking around me—possibly at me—but I didn't care the way I should have.

The way I always had in the past.

I watched Imogen instead. I watched the light reflect off her glorious curls from those dizzying chandeliers. I watched the easy, unselfconscious way she navigated through the crowd, aware she had no sense of her own grace.

As if I wanted to chase after her like some kind of puppy. Like the kind of soft, malleable creature I had never been.

Like a man besotted, though I knew that was impossible.

And worse, as if what I felt when she walked away from me was grief.

CHAPTER ELEVEN

Imogen

I LOCKED MYSELF in a bathroom stall in the elegant ladies' powder room, perching there on top of the cold porcelain lid and making no attempt to use it.

And then stayed there, where no one could see me.

Or stare at me. Or talk about me where I could hear the unkind note in their voices, yet none of the words, as a group of society women I knew I ought to have recognized had done as I'd found my way here.

Or make disparaging remarks about my hair. My dress. Whatever it was they found lacking in me.

It isn't that you're lacking something, a voice inside of me whispered. It reminded me of the low, husky way Javier spoke to me in the middle of the night when we were wrapped tight around each other in bed, fitted together like puzzle pieces in a way I hadn't been able to visualize before our wedding. And now craved the way I did everything else that involved touching him. *It's that you have the misfortune of being related to your sister while not actually being her.*

That had the ring of an unpleasant truth. And part of me wanted to stay where I was for the rest of the night, the pride and ferocity of the Fitzalan women be damned, because I was tired of all the comparisons. Especially when I was always coming out on the wrong side of them.

I wanted to stay hidden here, but I knew I couldn't. I had to gather myself together. I had to smile sweetly, serenely, while people compared me to my perfect sister. I had to pretend I was oblivious to the way people looked at me and the things they said to me or about me.

But I couldn't seem to make myself move.

That was when I heard the doors open, letting in a burst of sound of the ball outside. And more than that, a merry, tinkling laugh that I had known my whole life.

Celeste.

I surged to my feet, reaching over to throw back the lock and launch myself out of the stall and at my sister. She would know what to do. She always knew what to do. She had somehow gotten that gene while I had gotten...madly curling, obstinately red hair.

But I froze there, my hand on the lock.

Because I could hear what she was saying and I suddenly wished I was anywhere in the world but here.

"Did you see her lumbering furiously across the floor?" Celeste was asking her companions, all of whom tittered in response. "Storming off with that look on her face in the middle of the ballroom. As if she was planning to break out in some kind of brawl at any moment!"

I had no reason to be standing there, I told myself sternly. No reason at all not to reveal myself. But I still didn't move.

"Your sister does seem a bit *overwhelmed* by things, doesn't she?" asked another woman, in a syrupy sweet voice that I knew I could identify. If I wanted to identify it.

I didn't.

"Imogen is my half sister, thank you very much," Celeste said with a sniff. "I don't know what my father was thinking, messing about with that common trollop."

"I was under the impression Imogen's mother was a duchess or something," someone else murmured, managing to sound apologetic, as if they weren't sure about correcting Celeste even when they were right.

I squeezed my eyes shut. I could feel my hands curled into fists, but I didn't know who or what I wanted to hit. Or even how to hit. My stomach was a terrible knot and there was something too heavy to be simple pain at my temples. I might have thought I was sick, but I knew it wasn't as simple as that.

"Oh, she was the daughter of someone. The Viscount Something, I think. Who can keep track of all those endless British titles?"

That was Celeste speaking. Celeste, who I had always loved. Celeste, who I had trusted.

Celeste, who very clearly hated me.

There was something about that terrible notion that spurred me into action at last.

I shoved open the door and stood there, aware that my chest was heaving as if I'd been running. There was a wall of mirrors in front of me, which allowed me to see exactly how pale I'd become.

It also allowed me to lock gazes with my sister.

Half sister, I reminded myself bitterly.

If Celeste was surprised to see me, she didn't show it. She was dressed like a column of gold tonight, a color that drew attention to her sheer perfection. Her blond hair was elegantly styled in a sweeping updo that I only dared to dream about. She was tall and long and lean. She was the sort of woman who belonged on the covers of a thousand magazines, smiling mysteriously.

Though she didn't smile at me.

"Lurking about in bathrooms now?" she asked, and I couldn't tell if she had always looked at me that way. Or if, after those bright weeks with Javier, I could see all kinds of things in the shadows that I had never seen before.

It was amazing what a difference it made to be wanted.

Loved, something in me whispered, though I didn't dare call it that.

All I knew was that I'd never felt anything like it before. And that meant that this had always been bubbling in my sister. The way she was looking at me. That awful tone I'd heard in her voice. None of it was new. It couldn't be. And that meant...

"My mother, Lady Hillary to you, was the daughter of a duke," I said quietly, not wanting to accept what all this meant. "As I think you know."

"If you say so," Celeste said dismissively, and then made it worse by rolling her eyes for the benefit of her group of minions.

There was no more pretending. It didn't matter if Celeste had always been like this or if this was something new. She wasn't making any attempt to hide it.

"Are you just going to stand there, Imogen?" Celeste asked after a moment. That was when I realized I still hadn't moved.

"When I first heard you walk in, I thought I might come in for a hug," I said drily. "That seems to be off the table."

Her friends tittered again, but not with her, this time. It was likely childish that I felt that as a victory.

Celeste certainly didn't like it. Her perfect features flushed, and when she turned back to face me, it was as if I had never seen her before. Temper made her face twist.

And for the first time in as long as I could remember, she didn't look beautiful to me at all. I knew what beauty was now. I knew what warmth was. And I couldn't help thinking that I deserved better than spite in a bathroom stall, no matter who it came from.

"Eavesdroppers never hear anything good about themselves, or did you not learn that in all your years locked away in that convent?" Celeste let out one of those laughs. "You certainly didn't seem to learn anything else."

I thought about that look on her face the day of my wedding. I studied the look she wore now. And I remembered what it had been like ten years ago. Her dramatic sobs, loud enough to be heard all over the house, but more important, the fact she hadn't run outside to prevent Javier from leaving. Very much as if it was a performance designed to hasten her own wedding and her own exit from my father's house.

Maybe everything about Celeste was a performance.

But I played my hunch anyway. "Jealousy doesn't become you, Celeste."

This time, that peal of laughter she let out had fangs. I could feel it sink into me and leave marks. Yet I refused to react. Not even when she stepped closer to me, a mottled sort of red sweeping down over her neck to her chest.

"You foolish, absurd child," she said, her voice scathing and pitying at once. "Don't you understand what Javier is doing? He's using you."

I would die before I showed her how that landed on me like one of the walls around us, hard stone crushing me into dust. I stared back at her, lifting my chin, and it occurred to me in some dim part of my mind that I had been preparing for this for years. Hadn't I?

Because my feelings were hurt. There was no getting around that. But I couldn't say I was surprised.

"Yes, Celeste, he is. In much the same way your count used you to fill his coffers and provide him with heirs. Some might call this sort of thing mercenary, but in our family we have always called it marriage."

Something rolled through her. I could see it, ugly and sharp, all over her face.

"You mistake my meaning." Behind Celeste, her group of tittering friends had gone silent. The better to listen so that they might repeat it to the crowd outside, I knew. "The count married me for all the reasons you name, of course. That is simply practical. *Realistic*. But look in the mirror, Imogen. You know what I look like. Do you ever look at yourself?"

"My husband has yet to turn to stone, if that's what you mean."

But my heart beat too hard. Too wild. As if it already knew what she would say.

Celeste leaned closer so there could be no mistake at all.

"Javier could have had anyone's daughter. He is wealthy enough that even royals would have considered him in these progressive times. But he chose you. Have you never asked why?"

I wanted to say something that would hurt her, I realized. But before I could pull myself together enough to imagine what that might be, she kept going.

"He chose the ugly, embarrassing Fitzalan daughter when he is a known connoisseur of only the most beautiful women in Europe."

If she saw the way I sucked in a breath at that, she ignored it. Or worse, liked it.

"Don't you see?" Celeste's voice only grew colder the longer she spoke. Colder. Harder. "He is Javier Dos Santos. He possesses wealth greater than kings. He can do what no other man can, Imogen. He can flaunt an ugly duckling and pretend she is a swan. He can make even the disappointing Fitzalan heiress into a style icon if he so desires. He can do whatever he likes."

I made a sound, but it wasn't a sentence, and in any case, Celeste ignored me.

"Are you truly as simple as you act?" she demanded, pulling herself up to her full height. She shook her head at me, haughty and something like amazed at my naïveté. "It's a *game*, Imogen. Nothing but a game."

For a moment, I heard nothing else. I was aware that Celeste's friends were whispering among themselves. The water was running in one of the sinks. Someone opened the door and I heard the music again. But the only thing I was truly aware of was the scornful way Celeste had said that last bit.

Nothing but a game.

She smiled then, but this time I could see the pity in her gaze. And worse, what I thought was triumph.

"I am sure you find this cruel," she said with great dignity. "But in time, when you have resigned yourself to the reality of your position, I think you'll realize that I was only trying to be kind."

I knew, beyond any shred of doubt, that she was lying.

Or performing, anyway.

And then it didn't matter, because Celeste had always been better at both than me. She swept around, gathering up her skirts and her friends, and left me there to stew in what she'd told me.

And for some reason, I didn't break down when the door shut behind her. Instead, I thought of what it had been like to step off that plane on Javier's island after a lifetime, it seemed, of gray and gloom. I thought of the light. The blue.

I thought of the heat and fire I had found in Javier's arms. Again and again and again.

I took a deep breath, blew it out, and understood deep into my bones that I would rather steal a few weeks of fantasy with Javier whenever he had a mind to indulge himself than subject myself to all of Celeste's chilly, practical "reality."

I would rather be filled with almost too much sunlight to bear. I would rather have wild curls and freckles all over my shoulders. I would rather earn the contempt with which these people treated me than slink around trying to please them and only find myself in the same place.

And there was something about that that felt like liberation.

Because the glory of never fitting in, I realized in a sudden rush, was that I was never *going* to fit in.

And there was no one left to punish me for it.

No governesses. No nuns. My father had no more power over me. He had sold that right. And Celeste…didn't matter. I knew that Javier was determined and relentless enough to have chosen the Fitzalan daughter he wanted no matter what my father might have said about it. And he'd chosen me.

He could have had anyone, as Celeste had said. And he'd still chosen me.

Because he had, he was the only one who mattered.

I knew it was possible—even likely—that Celeste was right and Javier was playing some game. But I wasn't sure it mattered.

I was in love with him either way.

I didn't know a lot about love. Or anything about it, really. Grand-Mère had always banged on about *higher purposes* and *duty*, but *love* had never been a part of the Fitzalan experience. I had assumed that Celeste and I had loved each other the way sisters did, but it turned out I was wrong about that, too. And it was possible there was a part of me that would mourn the loss of a sister it turned out I never quite had and the family that might as well have been carved from the same stone as my father's manor, but I couldn't process that here. Not now.

Because I was in love with my husband.

I was *in love* with him.

And I knew that of the sins women in society marriages like mine could commit, this was perhaps the worst.

Just as I knew that the man who touched me so softly and held me so closely, who made me cry and sob and shake around him, would not want to hear that I loved him.

That didn't change the fact that I did.

And I might have been afraid of the things he made me feel. They overwhelmed me. They were sticky and dark, too much and too wild to contain. I could hardly believe they were real. Or that he was.

I was afraid that he would tell me it was only sex and I was unnecessarily complicating a simple business transaction. I was afraid that he would banish me, send me off to one of his other properties where he could keep me under lock and key and my feelings couldn't inconvenience him. I was afraid that he would laugh at me.

I was terribly afraid that Javier would never look at me again the way he had this morning, when he'd been deep inside of me and I'd thought I might die. That I had died. That I wanted to die. I was afraid I would never feel any of that again.

But I wasn't afraid of him.

And I had spent a lifetime locking myself up before anyone could come and do it for me. I had tried to minimize myself. Hide myself. Stuff myself in a box and be something I wasn't. No matter how many times I'd sneaked off down the servants' stairs, I'd always come back and tried to be what was expected of me.

I wasn't going to do it anymore.

I stepped up to the wide counter, ignoring the sinks before me and keeping my eyes on the bank of mirrors. I peeled the mask off my face and tossed it aside.

Then I reached up, tugged the clip from my hair, and threw it on the counter as well.

I shook my head, using my fingers to help pull out all the pins. I tugged and I pulled, and I tore down the hairstyle I'd considered a compromise. There would be no more compromises.

My hair fell around me, red and gold and curling wildly.

And it wasn't fear that moved in me then, I knew. It wasn't reality according to Celeste.

It was that power I hadn't been able to access, cringing in a bathroom stall.

It was that long, tough line of women who had come before me and survived, one after the next.

It was what had happened in those weeks with Javier. On that beautiful island, the place where I had learned that surrender was not weakness. That it could be a glorious strength.

I had fallen in love with my husband, and that changed everything.

Me most of all.

I didn't think it through. I didn't worry or prepare. I wheeled around, ignored the other women in the powder room who looked my way, and pushed my way back out into the ball.

I was tired of hiding.

Finally, I was tired of it.

I kept my head high, moving through the crowd as if I was made of silk. I paid no attention to the commotion I caused. I kept my eyes on my husband, finding him easily in the crush and then heading straight for him.

Javier, who I had considered a monster.

If he was a monster, I thought now, then so was I. If what it meant was that all these people, these circling wolves, considered us too different from them to matter. But I thought the truth of the matter was that this ball was filled with the real monsters, gorgons fashioned from snobbery and toxic self-regard, bitterness and centuries of living only to get richer.

I kept my gaze trained on Javier. The one man here who didn't belong. He was too…real. Even with a mask on, the truth of who he was seemed to fill the whole of the palazzo. As if everyone else—as if Venice itself—was little more than a ghost.

"You changed your hair," he said in that dark, stirring way of his when I made it to his side. It was the kind of voice that made me wish we were naked together, sprawled out in our bed, where none of this mattered. As if he heard that same note in his voice, he stood straighter. "I didn't realize this was the sort of party that called for different costumes."

"Imogen can always be trusted to do the most embarrassing thing possible," my father sneered from beside him.

I hadn't even seen him there. Because I was free of him, I realized. And it felt like an afternoon of La Angelita sunlight, here in the middle of a cold winter's night.

"My wife's hair—and indeed, my wife herself—cannot be embarrassing, Fitzalan," Javier bit out, with the kind of violence that usually never made it into ballrooms such as this. My father stiffened. My husband's dark eyes blazed. "She is *my wife*. That makes her, by definition, perfect in every way."

"Javier." I liked saying his name. I more than liked it. I waited for him to drag that thrillingly vicious glare away from my father. When it landed on me, it was no softer, but I liked that, too. "I love you."

I saw the way he froze. I heard the astonished laughter from my father and the terribly genteel men around him, none of whom would ever use that word. Or allow it to be used in their presence—especially not in public.

But I had decided not to hide. Not from anyone. Not ever again.

"I love you," I said again, so there could be no mistake. "And I've had enough of this nonsense tonight, I think."

I turned around like some kind of queen. I held my head high as I started across the floor.

And only breathed again when Javier walked beside me, taking my arm in his.

I told myself that come what may—and there was a storm in those brooding dark eyes of his that already felt like thunder inside me, a reckoning I wasn't sure I wanted to face—I would never regret falling in love with my husband.

CHAPTER TWELVE

Javier

I FOLLOWED HER.

I had no choice.

Imogen had made a scene when she'd dropped her little bombshell, and if I let her walk away, they would say I had already lost control of my brand-new marriage. They would smugly agree with each other that it was only to be expected. *Blood will out*, they would assure themselves.

But if I truly didn't wish to lie to myself, I didn't much care what they said.

I cared more that the bomb she'd dropped was still going off inside me.

Again and again and again.

I did not allow myself to think about my hand on her arm. I ignored my body's automatic response to her scent. Or her firm, smooth skin beneath my palm that made me want to touch her everywhere.

I did not feel. I could not feel.

And no matter that I had already felt too much today already, when she had made it so clear she, too, was as ashamed of me as I was.

You do not wish to feel, something in me whispered harshly. It was the truth. And I had built my life on truth, had I not? No matter the cost?

"Javier—" Imogen began when we stepped outside.

The music inside the ballroom played on, bright against the dark. Light from those chandeliers inside the palazzo blazed, dancing over the stones. But the temperature had dropped significantly, on the water and inside me, and our coats seemed little protection against the cold.

And my wife thought better of whatever it was she had been about to say.

I did not speak when I summoned our transportation and climbed on board. Or when I pried the mask from my face and sent it spinning into the water with a flare of temper I couldn't conceal. We floated back down the Grand Canal, but this time I did not marvel at the palazzos that lined our way. I did not congratulate myself on my climb from grimy flats in Spain to famous canals in Italy's most magical city the way I usually did.

Instead, I stood apart from Imogen and cautioned myself.

I needed to remain calm. Contained.

There had always been a monster in me, but it wasn't the one her father and his pack of wolves imagined.

Whatever this was—this need people had to hurl emotions around like currency, though I had thought better of Imogen—I had never understood it. I had always stood apart from it, gladly.

She had told me she loved me and it beat in me like a terrible drum, dark and dangerous, slippery and seductive.

And I wanted no part of it.

We made it all the way across the lagoon, then docked at our hotel, and I still had not uttered a single syllable.

There were lights around the hotel's courtyard, making it look festive though it remained empty of any guests but the two of us, just as I had wanted it. I waved away the waiting hotel staff and accepted the blast of the January wind—slicing into me as it rushed from the water of the lagoon—as a gift. It would keep me focused.

It would remind me who I was.

"Do not ever do that again," I told her harshly when we had both climbed out of the boat. "It is not up to you to determine when we leave a place. Particularly not if I have business."

"You could have stayed if you wished. I didn't ask you to come with me, I merely said I was done."

She was different. Or she was herself, again—the creature I had beheld what seemed like a lifetime ago now in her father's house in France. She did not avert her eyes as I scowled at her. If there was any meekness in her at all, any hints of that uncertain innocence that had driven me mad on the island, it was gone.

Tonight Imogen was electrifying. Her curls cascaded around her shoulders like fire. Her eyes gleamed in the dark, inviting and powerful at once. She reminded me of an ancient goddess who might have risen straight from the sea in a place like this, gold-tipped and mesmerizing.

I wanted nothing more than to worship her. But that was what I had spent these last weeks doing, and what had I gained?

Protestations of *love*, of all things.

I was more likely to believe her a deity than I was to imagine her *in love*.

I started for the hotel and she was right behind me, hurrying as if she had any chance at all of catching me if I didn't allow it.

"Will you chase me all the way up to our rooms?" I asked her from between the teeth I couldn't seem to keep from clenching when I made it to the stately double doors that discreetly opened at our approach.

"Only if you make me chase you. When I was under the impression that the great and glorious Javier Dos Santos has never run from a fight in the whole of his life."

She was a few feet behind me, looking serious and challenging as she closed the last of the distance between us. She didn't look as if she'd exerted herself unduly running across the courtyard, despite the shoes she wore. Not my Don Quixote bride, who was perfectly happy to tilt at any windmill in sight.

Even if the windmill was me.

I strode inside, not sure what I was meant to do with the temper and din roaring inside of me. Not sure I could keep it locked away as I should, and equally sure I didn't want to let any of it out.

I told myself I didn't know what it was, that howling thing knotting loud and grim within me, but I did.

And I didn't want to feel any of this.

I didn't want to feel at all.

Imogen stayed with me as I made my way across the lobby and I cursed myself for having bought out the whole of the hotel, ensuring that this torturous walk took place in strained silence. I could hear Imogen's shoes against the marble floors. I could hear my own.

And I could hear my heart in my chest, as loud as the roaring sea.

We got into the elevator together and stood on opposite sides as if sizing each other up.

I didn't know what she saw, but I wasn't at all pleased to find she looked no less like a goddess in close quarters.

"What happened to you?" I asked her, too many things I didn't wish to address there in my voice.

"I was born a Fitzalan. Then I got married. Not much of interest happened in between."

What did it say about me that I was tempted to laugh at that?

But I already knew what it said. This had gone on too long, this wildfire situation I should have extinguished the first time I'd seen her in her father's heap of stone and history. I should never have brought her to La Angelita and, once I knew how it would burn between us, I should never have allowed us to stay as long as we had.

The responsibility was mine. I accepted it.

So there was no reason at all that I should have let my head tilt to one side as I beheld her there on the other side of the elevator, dressed in that sweep of deep black, the bright red-gold of her hair a striking counterpoint to the wall of gilt and flourish behind her.

"I think you know that I mean tonight. What happened at that ball?"

She didn't smile this time. And somehow that only drew my attention to her mouth and those berry-stained lips I had tasted time and time again. Yet I could never seem to get my fill.

"My sister suggested I face reality." I couldn't read that gleam in her copper gaze. "I declined."

I hadn't spared a thought for Celeste, I realized now. She would have been there, of course. Annual charity balls like this one were exactly the sort of places Celeste liked to shine. But if she had been there tonight, I had missed it entirely. What was a bit of shine when my wife was like the sun?

I was appalled at the train of my own thought.

"Your sister is the last person on earth I would expect to comment on reality," I said, perhaps more witheringly than necessary. "Given that her own is so dire and uninspiring."

The elevator stopped at our floor, opening directly into our paneled foyer. This time it was Imogen who moved first, sweeping through to the grand salon that made up the bulk of the sprawling hotel suite's public rooms and was even more ecstatically decorated than the hotel lobby, all statuary and operatic sconces.

She moved into the center of the room, leaving me to trail her as she had me down below. I stopped short when I realized that was what I was doing, following her about like some kind of...pet.

And when she turned back to face me, she still didn't look the least bit sorry for what she had done.

"You could have married her. You didn't. Why?"

It took me a moment to stop seething at the notion that I

could be the pet in any scenario. And another to comprehend her meaning. When I did, I scowled.

"I believe we already covered this subject in some detail the night before our wedding. If the reality Celeste wished to discuss with you had something to do with me, you should already know she is in no way an expert on that subject."

"Javier. Did she love you?"

The way she asked that question suggested she knew something I didn't. And worse, I didn't get the sense that simple jealousy was motivating the question.

I could have handled jealousy, but I didn't know what *this* was.

"Your sister and I hardly knew each other." It was hard to speak when my jaw was clenched so tight and my hands wanted so badly to curl into fists. "And as time goes on I consider that a great blessing. You must know Celeste better than anyone, Imogen. Do you believe her capable of loving anything?"

She didn't tremble. Not exactly—and yet something moved over her lovely face. "No. I don't."

"But you must step away from all this talk of love," I cautioned her. Though my voice was little more than a growl. "It has no place in an arrangement like ours. It has no place in the kind of lives we lead."

It had no place this close to *me*, I thought, but did not say.

"I'm sorry you feel that way," my blithely disobedient wife replied, without looking the least bit apologetic as she said it. "But it doesn't change the fact that I'm in love with you, Javier."

That torment inside me knotted harder, deeper, and only grew more grim.

"Love is the opiate of the weak," I threw at her. "A gesture toward oblivion, nothing more. It is only sex dressed up to look pretty."

"You are the most powerful man I have ever met. And yet you let my father send you away ten years ago, which tells me you must have wanted to go. Then you came back and took the only daughter available. Not even the one you'd come for the first time."

I didn't know where she was going with this. I only knew I didn't like it. "You were a virgin, Imogen. I understand why this is difficult for you. Virgins are so easily confused."

"You didn't even know she was there tonight, did you?"

That took me by surprise. Another unpleasant sensation only she seemed capable of producing in me.

"No." I knew I shouldn't have said it when Imogen smiled as if I'd made some kind of confession. "Why do you continue to talk about your sister?"

"They whisper when they think I can't hear, but I do," my wife said in a soft, quiet way that only a fool would mistake for weakness. And I might have been acting the fool tonight, but I wasn't one. "They think you only married me to get to her. I assume she thinks so, too."

"I don't want her." I didn't mean to say that, either, but it was as if that furious growl came out of me of its own volition. "She got what she wanted and so did I. There are no second chances where I am concerned, Imogen. You are either the best or I am bored."

I didn't understand the way she looked at me then. Almost as if I was causing her pain. But she was still smiling, though it was the kind of smile I could feel like a blow.

"I don't care why you married me," she said after a moment. "I don't care if it was purely mercenary or if it was a means to an end like they all think. It doesn't matter to me. What matters to me is what's happened since."

My heart was beating in that strange way again, that insistent and terrible drum. I recognized it. It reminded me of when I was a child, hiding from my parents' demons in filthy hovels, surrounded by too many desperate people.

I shook the memory off. But the fury in me only grew.

"Once again, Imogen, you are confusing sex and passion

for something else. But that something else does not exist. It cannot exist."

Her eyes gleamed and I didn't want to understand what I saw there. It made me perilously close to unsteady.

"I love you, Javier," Imogen said. She kept saying it. "I don't think it's something you can order away."

"You might think you do," I gritted out, my voice like gravel. All of me like gravel, come to that. I felt as if I was turning to stone the longer I stood here. "But I know that you do not."

"Don't I?"

"It is a lie, damn you. Love is a weakness. It is a fairy story people tell themselves to excuse the worst excesses of their behavior. Our marriage is based on something far better than *love*."

"Money?" Imogen supplied, and I found that defiance of hers grating tonight. "The fickle support of selfish old men?"

"Neither one of us walked into this marriage with any unrealistic expectations. That is more than any fool who imagines himself in love can say."

"But I want more than easily met expectations," Imogen argued, that gleam in her gaze intensifying. "I want everything, Javier. What's the point otherwise?"

I knew that there were counterarguments I could make. Or better still, I could walk away and end this conversation altogether. I didn't understand why I did neither of those things. Or why I only stood there as if I was rooted to the hotel floor, staring at this wife of mine as if I didn't know her at all.

When I would have said I knew everything there was to know about her. From the poems she read to the sounds she made in the back of her throat when the pleasure I gave her was too much to bear.

"I told you I cannot abide lies," I said, as if from a great distance. "Love *is* lies, Imogen. And I will never build my life on lies again."

She made a noise that could as easily have been a sob as a

sigh. She swayed slightly on her feet, and I had to order myself to stay where I was.

My protection was earned, I thought gravely, not given out like candy or sold like street heroin. But it was better when I saw she wasn't toppling over where she stood, felled by the force of her inconvenient emotions. She was squaring her shoulders the way fighters did.

"Show me the lie," she said.

At first I didn't understand what she meant. But as I watched, she reached up and undid the clasp at her shoulder that held her dress on her body. And then, I could only stare in a mixture of astonishment and pure, mad lust as that beautifully inky dress slid down her lush body like a caress and pooled at her feet.

I stood as if I was merely another statue in this salon full of lesser Renaissance offerings. Imogen's copper eyes glowed with more than a mere invitation. I saw in their depths a knowledge I refused to accept.

"I was raised by criminals," I heard myself say as if the words were torn from me. "They trafficked in lies and poison, down in the dirt and the gutters. And love was just another drug they sold, a high that wore off before morning."

I watched as she took that in, waiting for the censure. The revulsion. I watched emotion move across her face like a storm, but she didn't recoil as I expected her to. Instead, she gazed at me with a kind of understanding that I wanted to deny with every breath in my body.

"We can play any game you like, Javier," my wildfire wife told me as if she was the one with years and years of experience. As if I had been the virgin on our wedding day, locked away in a stone house for most of my life, and therefore needed her patience now. "We can start with an easy one, shall we? When I lie, I will stop."

"Imogen."

It was an order, but she didn't heed it.

And I didn't know if I would survive this. I didn't know if

I could. I wasn't sure what was worse—if she obeyed me, put her clothes back on, and stopped confusing me with the sight of all that glorious flesh...

Or if she didn't.

As I watched, she unwrapped the particular feminine hardware that held her plump breasts aloft. She reached down and hooked her fingers into the lace that spanned her hips. And I nearly swallowed my tongue as she rolled her panties down the long, shapely legs that I loved to drape over my shoulders as I drove into her. I watched as she kicked the panties aside. And then, still holding my gaze, she kicked off her shoes.

And then my wife stood there before me like the goddess I must have known she was from the very first moment I laid eyes on her on that balcony.

All of those red-gold curls tumbled over her, calling attention to the jut of her nipples and, farther down, that sweet thatch between her thighs in the same bright color.

"Is this a lie?" she asked, all challenge and defiance as she started toward me.

My mouth was too dry. My pulse was a living thing, storming through me and pooling in my sex.

She crossed the floor and stood before me. I could smell the soap she used in her bath and, beneath that, the warmth of her skin. And further still, the sweet, delirious perfume of her arousal.

I could feel my hands at my sides, fisting and then releasing. Over and over. But I didn't reach for her.

"Or perhaps this is a lie," she murmured, her voice hoarse and almost too hot to bear.

But then she put her hands on me, and taught me new ways to burn.

Especially when she ran her fingers over my abdomen, then down farther still, so she could feel the proof of my desire herself.

"What do you want?" I demanded.

CAITLIN CREWS 465

I sounded like a man condemned.

"You," she replied, much too easily. "I only want you, Javier. I love—"

But I'd finally had enough.

I heard the noise that came out of me then, like some kind of roar. It came from such a deep place inside of me that I didn't know how to name it.

I didn't try.

I pulled her into my arms, crushing my mouth to hers.

There was no finesse. If I was an animal—if I was the monster they'd always said I was—this was where I proved it. I lifted her from the floor, hauling her into my arms. Then I carried her over to the nearest antique chaise and laid her out upon it. My own sacrifice, once an innocent and now my tormentor.

I followed her down, too far gone to concentrate on anything but my own greed and the way she grabbed my coat as if I was taking too long. And the way her hips rose to meet mine long before I had finished wrestling with my trousers.

There was no time. No playing. There was only this.

There was only the slick, deep slide into all her molten heat.

There was only Imogen.

"Is this a lie?" she whispered in my ear as I lost myself in the rhythm. The deep, sweet thrust in, then the ache of the retreat.

I didn't believe in love. I wanted this to be a lie. That was the only world I knew.

But it was hard to remember what I knew with Imogen beneath me, holding me as tightly and as fiercely as I held her. It was hard to remember my own name as she met me, spurring me on, wrapping her legs around my hips and arching against me to take me deeper.

And the first time she exploded, I kept going. On and on, until she was sobbing out my name the way I liked it.

Only when she convulsed around me a second time did I follow.

But it still wasn't enough.

When I could breathe a little again, I rose. I stripped off what remained of my evening clothes, and swept my still-shuddering wife up into my arms again. I carried her through the sprawling suite, not letting go of her when I reached the bedroom.

I threw her onto the bed and went down with her, and then, finally, I took back control.

Over and over.

I had her in every way I could imagine.

I tasted her, everywhere. I made her sob, then scream.

I took her into the shower and rinsed us both, then started all over again while the steam rose in clouds around us and the hot water spilled over us both.

I took her and I worshipped her. I imprinted myself on her.

And if there was a lie in any of the things we did, I couldn't find it.

There was pink at the windows when Imogen finally slept, smudges beneath her eyes as she sprawled where I'd left her after the last round. I sat on the side of the bed and forced myself to look away from all of that lush sweetness.

It took some doing.

She would not stop talking of love. She'd kept it up all night, charging that same windmill again and again.

Over and over and over.

And I had spent the whole of my adult life telling myself only the truth. Or trying. I could do no less now.

I was a man, not the monster they imagined I was. Or I believed I was. And no windmill, either. And if there was any creature on this earth who could make me believe in things I knew to be lies, it was this one.

And I could not have that.

I could not bear it.

That was how I, who had never run from anything, found myself out in the Venice dawn.

Running like hell from a woman with red-gold curls, an impossibly sweet smile that cut into me every time I saw it, a defiance that I wanted to taste, not crush—and no sense at all of how she had destroyed me.

CHAPTER THIRTEEN

Imogen

FITZALANS ENDURED.

That was what I told myself when I woke up that morning in Venice and found myself alone.

And without him there to insist on those truths he seemed to hate so much, I lied.

I told myself that he had gone out, that was all. Perhaps to conduct some business. Perhaps to exercise the way he liked to do in the early morning back on the island. I made up all kinds of excuses, but I knew. Deep down, I knew.

He was gone.

His staff arrived at noon.

I didn't put up a fuss. I didn't even ask any questions. I let them collect the bags and lead me out of the empty hotel. I didn't look back.

Nor did I ask where I was headed once they bundled me onto a plane. Not Javier's plane, I noted. Or at least not the one I had been on before. I stared out the window as we soared over Italy and I wondered where he was. Where he had gone to.

And when—or if—he might return.

I didn't know if I was relieved or hurt when we landed back

at La Angelita. I held my breath as the car pulled up in front of the villa, telling myself a thousand different and desperate stories about how he'd needed to rush back here, that was all. I would walk inside, past that table in the foyer that still made me blush every time I saw it, and he would be here to greet me with that tiny curve in the corner of his hard mouth…

But he wasn't there.

For the first week, I jumped at every noise. Every time I heard a door open. Every time the wind picked up. Every time a window rattled. I jumped and I expected to see him standing there.

But Javier did not return.

It was sometime into the third week that I found myself sitting in his library, surrounded by books that failed to soothe me for the first time in my life. I was rereading one of my favorite novels, but even that didn't help. I felt thick and headachy and on the verge of tears, all at the same time, and it got worse every day.

I told myself it was a broken heart, that was all. But identifying what was wrong with me didn't help. It didn't fix it. It didn't bring my husband back.

I sat in that library, I thought about the grand sweep of history that had led down through the storied history of the Fitzalan family to me. Here. Alone.

I found myself thinking about my sister and the life she led. How much worse would I feel if I had been married, claimed in such an intimate fashion, and then abandoned…by my sister's husband? By the pursed-mouthed count who never smiled or one of the many indistinguishable men of father's acquaintance just like him?

Despite the way the memories of the ball still smarted, I felt the stirrings of something like sympathy for her. Celeste hadn't had much choice in the matter of her marriage, either. What must it be like for her, shackled to the count until he died, with her unhappiness expected on all sides—and held to be wholly unimportant?

The truth was, I was lucky. I loved Javier. More, I couldn't help believing that he loved me, too, though he might not know it.

If marriage was forever, and I knew full well that this one was—that the kinds of marriages people like me had were always permanent, because they were based on all those distressingly practical things Celeste had mentioned and Javier had echoed—then it didn't matter how long Javier stayed away.

I didn't have to hunt him down. I had already said my piece in Venice.

All I had to do was wait.

The days rolled by, as blue and bright as ever. I found that I was less interested in being on holiday, and started to amuse myself in different ways now that there was no one here to tell me any different.

"I do not think that Senor Dos Santos would like you in his office," the worried butler fussed at me when he found me behind my husband's imposing steel desk, helping myself to Javier's computer and telephone.

"Would he not?"

"The senor is deeply concerned with his privacy, Senora. He does not like anyone in this space when he is not at home."

I beamed at the butler. "Then it is a great shame that he is not here to tell me so himself."

I busied myself as I saw fit. I couldn't put myself to work the way others might, it was true. But I could do my part, so that was what I did.

And if Javier had a problem with the way I was spending his money on what I held to be worthy charities, well. That was his problem. If he wanted to make it *my* problem, he would have to come back to this island and face me.

I filled my days with all that glorious Mediterranean sunshine. I walked through the budding olive groves, looking for signs of spring. I sat in the pools outside the bedroom when dark fell so I could gaze up at the stars and do my best to name them. I walked the length of the unspoiled beaches on all sides of the island, letting all that crisp sea air wash over me, into me.

I spoke to the ocean when no one was around to hear me. And I always felt it answered me in the relentless way the waves beat against the shore.

It told me stories of endurance, deep and blue and forever.

It was a full month since the ball in Venice when I woke as I always did. I stretched out in the vast bed where I lay alone at night and tortured myself with memories of those lost, beautiful weeks when I'd first come here. When I'd given Javier my virginity and my heart and he'd given me light. I blinked at the sunshine as it poured in through the windows.

And then, instead of rolling to my feet and perhaps going for a morning swim, I was seized with the sudden certainty that I was about to be sick.

Horribly sick.

I barely made it across the room and into the bathroom in time.

It was only when I had finished casting out my misery and was sitting there on the tiled floor with a cold washcloth against my face that it occurred to me my evening meal of the night before might not have been to blame.

I wore nothing but one of Javier's shirts that I had liberated from his closet so I could pretend he still held me. And I told myself it was close enough to him actually being here as I sat there on the floor, my back against the wall, and spread my hands out over my belly in a kind of half wonder, half awe.

I hadn't cried since that morning in Venice. Not since I had finally accepted the fact that Javier had left me, and had taken myself into the shower because I knew that there was no way he would simply abandon me to my own devices. Not after what he'd paid for me. I knew that his staff would turn up, sooner or later. I needed to be dressed and ready.

But first I had stood beneath the hot spray in that Venetian hotel, loved him, and cried.

These tears were different. There was still that same despair a month later, but it didn't quite take hold of me. Because beneath it was searing, irrepressible joy.

I knew that in my world babies were seen as insurance, not people. Heirs and spares and collateral damage. Too many children and the inheritance was diluted. Too few and tragedy could send all that wealth and history spinning off to someone else's unworthy hands.

But here, now, on the bathroom floor in a villa that was the only place I had ever been truly happy, I forgot all that. I pushed it aside.

"I don't care what they say," I whispered, a fierce promise to the new life inside of me. "I will always love you. You will always know it."

And when I was done, I climbed to my feet and washed my face until there was no trace of tears. Then I called for my attendant and told her what I wanted.

Two hours later, I received a delivery from the nearest chemist's, somewhere on the Spanish mainland. Fifteen minutes after that, I confirmed the fact that I was, in fact, having Javier's child. My child.

Our baby.

And when night fell on that very same day, the sun making its idle way toward the horizon while it painted the sky golds and pinks, I heard the same sort of noise I always heard. And as I always did, I looked up from my favorite chair in Javier's library, expecting to hear the wind or see one of the servants hurrying past.

But this time, he was there.

Right there in front of me after all these weeks.

And he looked murderous.

CHAPTER FOURTEEN

Javier

SHE WAS MAGNIFICENT.

The truth of that slammed into me like a hammer, one hit and then the next, and I had to fight to breathe through it.

Imogen sat with her feet folded up beneath her in an armchair and a thick book open in her lap. I had been standing in the doorway to the library for some time before she noticed me, so enthralled was she with her reading.

It was like torture. She worried her lower lip between her thumb and forefinger. Her skin was flushed from the sun and from the walks the staff had told me she took daily.

And because she was carrying my child.

My child.

She lifted her gaze and instantly made me wonder if she'd known I was there all along.

"Hello, Javier," she said, as if I had happened out for an hour or two. "I wasn't expecting you."

"Were you not?"

I didn't wait for her to answer. I hardly knew what moved in me then. Fury, certainly. Something like panic. And that same dark current of need and longing that had chased me all over the planet and had never let me escape.

She had haunted me everywhere.

And it was worse, somehow, now that we were in the same room.

"I gave up expecting you in the first week," she said, and what struck me was the tone she used. So matter-of-fact. Not as if she was trying to slap at me at all. Which, of course, made it sting all the more. "How long will you stay, do you think?"

"I am told you have news to share with me, Imogen. Perhaps you should start with that."

"News?"

She looked flustered. But I didn't quite believe it.

"Surely you cannot have imagined that you could ask my staff for a pregnancy test without my knowing of it." I stepped farther into the room, expecting her to shrink back against her chair. But she only gazed at me, those copper eyes of hers wiser than before. Or perhaps it was only that I noticed it more now. Now that I knew how completely she could take me apart. And had. "There's nothing you have done in this house that I have not been made aware of within the hour."

She lifted her chin to that challenging angle that I had imagined a thousand times. And that I had wanted to touch a thousand more.

"If you have complaints about the way I choose to donate to the charities of my choice, I'm always happy to sit down with you and discuss it."

"Is this how our marriage works? Is this how any marriage works, do you imagine?"

"If it doesn't, that would also require that you sit down with me. Face-to-face. And have an actual conversation." She lifted one shoulder, then let it drop with an ease I didn't believe. Or didn't *want* to believe, because nothing in me was easy. "It is so hard, I find, to conduct a marriage all on one's own."

I found myself circling her chair, much as I had circled this island again and again since I'd left her in Venice. I had flown all over the world, dropping in on my various business concerns wherever I went. But I always returned to Spain. And I always had to fight myself to keep from coming straight back to this island.

To Imogen.

"That depends, I think, on what marriage it is you think we are having." I was filled with that same dark fury I hadn't been able to shake in all these weeks—the fury I had begun to suspect wasn't fury at all, but feelings. "I bought you for a very specific purpose. I never hid my intentions. You are the one who changed the rules. You are the one who made everything—"

"Real?" she supplied.

"You don't know what real is," I hurled at her, and I could hear that I was spinning out of control. That quickly. That completely. But I couldn't stop it. "You have no idea what it is to grow up the way I did."

"No, I don't."

I was so taken aback by her agreement that I froze. Then watched as she rose to her feet, the light, summery dress she wore flowing around her. I was struck by the expanse of her legs and her bare feet with toes tipped pink. I couldn't have looked away from her if my life depended on it.

She had become no less of a goddess in the time I'd been away, and it was worse now. Because I knew she carried my child. I couldn't see it, not yet, but I knew.

It made her more beautiful. It made everything more beautiful, and I didn't know how to handle it. Beauty. Love. Imogen.

This is what I knew: I wasn't built for happiness.

"I don't know the precise details of how you grew up, or every last thing your childhood did to you. I know the bare bones. I know what little you told me when you thought you could use your past as a weapon. And I'm never going to know more than that unless you tell me. Just as there are things you don't know about me that you never will unless you're here to ask. But it doesn't matter, because our marriage will last for-ever. That's the benefit of a business arrangement." She waved an airy hand that I didn't believe and wanted, badly, to take hold of with my own. Yet I refrained. "We have all the time in the world to tell each other everything, one detail at a time."

Yet it was the phrase *business arrangement* that I couldn't get past, not this light talk of *details* when I had already shared more with her than anyone else in this life I'd scraped together by force of my own will. *Business arrangement* was in no way an incorrect way to describe our marriage, and yet it scraped over me, then deep inside me, as if it was hollowing me out.

"Why am I not surprised that a few weeks of solitude and the threat of motherhood are all it takes?" I shook my head. "No more talk of love."

And it was not until my own, bitter words hung there in the quiet of the library between us that I realized how much I'd been depending on hearing more of those protestations she'd thrown my way in Venice.

Or how certain I'd been that she'd meant all those words of love I'd refused to accept.

Imogen's eyes blazed copper fire. "You have everything you want, Javier. The Fitzalan heiress of your dreams. A child on the way to secure your legacy. And right when I was tempted to get ideas about my station, you put me in my place. Mention the word *love* and that's a quick way to get a month of solitary confinement." She wrinkled up her nose. "I can't complain. I've spent a lot of time in far worse prisons than this."

"La Angelita is hardly a prison."

"I love you, you fool." But she sounded something like de-spairing. "It isn't going to go away just because you do."

"You didn't come after me."

I heard the harsh, guttural voice. And it took me a long, hard kick from my own heart to realize it was mine.

"Javier…" she whispered, one hand dropping to cradle that belly where my child already grew.

And something in me…broke.

"You have ruined me," I told her, as if I was accusing her of some dark crime. "You took my home. You took my heart when I did not think it existed to be taken. And you left me with nothing. You talk of prison? I have spent these past weeks flying from country to country, looking at every last part of my collection…and none of it matters. None of it is *you*. The whole world is a prison without you in it."

Her lips parted as if she was having trouble believing what she was hearing. "You can have any woman you choose."

"I chose you!" I thundered. "Don't you understand? All I ever wanted was to *collect*. To win. You don't have to feel anything to do these things, you just have to have the money. And I always had the money. That is why, whatever the thing is, I have the best of it. But then you stormed out of a bathroom in Venice ranting about love and nothing has been the same since."

"Because I love you," she said again, in that same *absolutely certain* way she had in Italy.

Those words had chased me around the world. And back to her side again.

"I don't know what that is," I told her, the emotion in my own voice nearly taking me to the floor. "But I do know that a collection is not a life. And I want to live. I want to know my own child. I want to raise him. Not the way my parents raised me, feral and grasping and out of their minds. And not the way your father raised you, shut up behind one set of walls or another. I want to *live*, Imogen. And I think that must be love because I cannot come up with any other name for it."

That had come out like another accusation, but she only whispered my name. And it sounded like a prayer.

Maybe that was why I found myself on my knees before her after all, my hands on that sweet belly of hers that I had tasted and touched, and now held the start of our very own family. The future. All the hopes and dreams I'd told myself I was far too jaded to allow.

"I cannot live with lies," I told her, tipping my head back so I could look up at all those curls. And her shining eyes. Her lips like berries, trembling now. "But I do not know how to feel."

"But you do." She held my face between her hands and made me new, that easily. "You call it sex. You dismiss it. But it isn't just sex, Javier. It never was."

"How would you know this? You have never had anyone but me."

"Because I know."

And again, she struck me as a creature far wiser than her years. Far more powerful than the sheltered girl she had been.

I understood then.

She was all those things and more. She was everything I needed.

I had bought a bride, but she had given me life.

"I think I looked up to that balcony and lost myself," I told her, fierce and sure.

"I married a monster," she whispered in return, her face split wide by that smile of hers that made the floor seem to tilt beneath me, "but it turned out, he was actually the very best of men. And better yet, mine."

"Yours," I agreed. "Forever."

She sank down before me, wrapping her arms around my neck, and something inside me eased.

"Forever," Imogen said solemnly. "And you can leave me alone if you must, Javier. I am quite happy with my own company—"

"I have wandered the world alone and without you for quite long enough. I do not plan to do it again."

"I love you," she whispered.

There was a truth in me then. I had been denying it for a long time. And I couldn't pretend that it didn't unnerve me, but the truth of it haunted me all the same.

It had chased me all over the world. It had never let me go.

Just as she wouldn't, I knew. Marriages like ours were built to last.

And ours was far better than most.

"I love you, too, Imogen," I said in a rush.

But when she smiled, brighter than the Mediterranean sky outside, I said it again.

And found it got easier every time.

"I love you," I said as I fit my mouth to hers in wonder.

"I love you," I told her as I smoothed my hands over the belly where our child grew, and pressed my lips to her navel.

And then I showed her what it was to love her, inch by beautiful inch, all across that beautiful body of hers.

I loved her and I'd missed her and I showed her all the ways that I would never, ever leave her again, right there on the floor of the library.

And when she was shaking and laughing and curled up against me, her face buried in my neck as she tried to catch her breath, I understood at last.

The Dos Santos marriage was a love match, not merely good business, and it would confound them all. It would add to our legend. It would make me more powerful and it would make Imogen an icon, and none of that would matter half so much as this. Us.

The way we touched each other. The children we would raise together. The life that we would live, hand in hand and side by side, forever.

This was love. It had always been love. This passion was our church, these glorious shatterings were our vows.

And we would say them, every day and in every language we knew, for the rest of our lives.

* * * * *

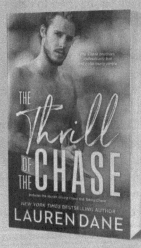
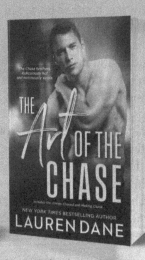